THE SANDMAN

MATTHEW F. WINN

To
Sharon
Read with the
lights on!

Bay City
4/12/04

This book is dedicated to Tom and Chris Lackey for their unwavering love and support over my lifetime. The best brother and sister anyone could ever hope for. And to Little Laura Lackey who brought hope, love and laughter to us all.

CHAPTER ONE

Timothy Duggan stared up into the haunting blue eyes of the blonde straddling him. Her long hair cascaded down past her shoulders in flowing golden strands that gently blanketed her supple breasts. Her nipples excitedly forced their way through her straw colored locks to wink enticingly at the man responsible for their host's arousal.

Beads of sweat formed on his lover's upper lip as her face contorted in pleasure. Her cat-like fingers dug into his chest and the couple's passion rose to feverish heights. They matched each others rhythmic ebbing, flowing together as one. Her eyes were closed tightly and her head was tilted back so far that she could feel her hair tickling her buttocks while she moved slowly up and down like a well-oiled piston. Timothy ran his hand gently up and down the small of her back while tracing tiny circles around her belly button with his fingertips. She arched her back under his caress. He had found her magic spot, and his as well.

In one swift motion Timothy Duggan thrust his knife, a long, slender double-edged Arkansas toothpick, into the small of the woman's back. Grabbing the front of the blade as it exited her navel, he forced the knife blade upwards and jerked it violently to the side, destroying several major organs and severing her spine in one lightning quick motion. In the blink of an eye her world had changed. Her eyes darted wildly about the room as confusion and pain wracked her psyche. Her body convulsed wildly as the realization of her imminent death set in and the struggle for life began. A deluge of her blood spilled out of her wounds and onto Timothy's naked, writhing body. He was too lost in the throes of ecstasy to notice she was silent; gone.

"Christ!" Tim shot up in bed, covered in sweat.

"What's the matter, honey? Another bad dream?" His wife asked groggily and reached over to pat him lovingly on his stomach.

"Yeah," he whispered faintly. Dragging himself out of bed, he made a beeline for the bathroom.

He paused near the toilet, afraid of what he might find. *It was only a dream, Tim, get a grip on yourself.* He reached into his boxers and immediately his fears were confirmed. Drawing his moist hand to his nose he breathed in apprehensively. Sex. He smelled like fresh sex. And something else as well. Being a doctor he was all too familiar with the malignant smell; blood. Wet sex and blood. He withdrew his hand as if his pants were on fire, forgetting all about his need for morning business.

Tim's mind replayed the hauntingly vivid dream over and over again as he let the hot water rain down onto his naked form. He prayed that the shower would save him the awkward embarrassment of even attempting to explain this to his wife. He loved Elsa so, and she him, but just how much Tim wasn't sure. Enough to believe this madness? Did she love him enough to listen to his stories of killing young women in his dreams without getting angry or leaving him for being completely insane? And would she stand by him once she discovered that he was waking up covered in evidence of this brutality? His heart raced with fear. He felt as if his mind were slipping away from him like water raging over a falls.

As he sat on the edge of the bed drying himself with a towel, he watched his wife climb out of bed. She smiled at him as she did each morning and headed to take her turn at the bathroom. He almost burst into tears at the sight of her radiant blue eyes. She had a way of melting him with those eyes. And the last thing he wanted to do right then was to reveal his deepest, darkest secrets to her.

Tim studied his wife's naked form as it flowed across the room. Her waist length blonde hair formed to her figure. It shimmered like sheer golden corn silk in the summer sun. Her shoulders sloped gently and her athletic arms hung loosely at her sides. She was almost a dead ringer for the girl in last night's dream. The only differences were that his Elsa was prettier, and still very much alive. A tear formed in the corner of Tim's eye as he blinked the crude thought away. It was an image with no apparent emanation. Granted, he had always found his wife attractive, sexy and alluring, but not with such lecherous overtones. He fought with his urges, trying desperately not to become aroused at his wife's nakedness. He was too afraid to kindle those feelings, terrified of what his dreams might symbolize.

"I love you," he voiced quietly, poking his head partially through the bathroom door. Her scent was inescapable in the steamy cubicle. Elsa didn't wear perfume very often. She bathed with an imported French soap that left the luxurious scent of Lily of the Valley lingering on her skin for most of the day. Tim generally lusted after the gentle fragrance on her skin, but not this morning.

"What?" She asked over the din of the shower. She hadn't heard him. Morose, he turned and walked away. Wiping his eyes he started for downstairs, where in the kitchen a nutty, alluring aroma announced that the automatic timer on the coffee pot had done its job correctly yet another day.

———

"Rene', this is Tim. Do you have a slot you can fit me in today?"

"Tim? You're not a patient, you don't need an appointment. My last patient is at four, how about we meet at Harry's for a couple of beers, say around four thirty," he replied, sensing something awkward in Tim's voice. Having known the man for most of his life he had a certain Spidey-sense when it came to Tim's problems.

"I'd really like to talk to you sooner, if it's no trouble, and privately, in your office if it's possible. I don't want to put you out or anything," Tim almost pleaded. Rene' was his best friend in the world and he knew that he could confide in him about anything. However, he needed his medical expertise now, not just his friendship and listening ear.

"Sure, sure pal. I can eat my lunch while we talk. I could squeeze you in at noon, that is if you don't mind listening to me chomp away at a salad."

"No, I wouldn't mind that at all. Connie, huh?"

"Yes, another one of her damned diets. I don't know why I always have to eat like crap every time she puts on a couple of pounds."

"Thanks, you're a lifesaver," Tim chuckled and hung up the phone. He left his hand on the receiver for a few moments longer, wanting to savor the sense of security his conversation with his friend had provided him.

Tim and Rene' had been friends for as long as Tim could remember. They were inseparable all the way through high school and even into college. They had helped each other get through the rigors of medical school, where they each ultimately chose separate paths to follow. They were a unique pair of individuals. Although they thought a lot alike they were still diverse enough to keep from getting bored with each other. Mutual friends and family constantly gibed them about their marriage to one another, including their wives. Ever so often Tim could sense a little jealousy from Elsa, especially times like now, when he didn't dare confide in her, but he felt comfortable enough around Rene' to share his fears. He decided it was best not to even mention to her that he was going to meet with his Rene'.

The drive to Rene's office was a blur. His mind was drudging through his limited memory of the quagmire that had become his sleep world. He eased into a parking spot and thanked God that he hadn't hit anything while he mindlessly drove across town.

"Hi, Tim," Rene's receptionist greeted warmly.

"Good morning, Vicky," he smiled painfully back, his mind still awash with the gory details from his nightmare. A distressing recollection shuddered through him as something in Vicky's smile reminded him of the woman in his latest nightmare. The recollection brought the disturbing images vividly back to life.

"Rene's waiting for you," she buzzed the intercom to let the doctor know he had company.

"Hey, what's going on pal," Rene' stood from his desk and took a posture that demanded a hug. "Have a seat," he offered after their embrace.

Tim sat down and stared at his feet awkwardly. He still couldn't shake the brutal images from his monstrous nightmare. "I just don't know where to begin, Rene'," he finally spoke.

"From the beginning is as good a place as any, I suspect," he said, donning his therapist's cap.

"I don't really remember the beginning."

"What's going on, you don't look so good? Are you and Elsa having troubles?"

"No. No, nothing like that," he paused. "It's worse than that actually. I wish it were something as simple as declining marital bliss. Besides, we've already been through the 'you're a bastard' phase, remember?" He did his best to smile.

"I'm starting to worry about you. I've never seen you so tongue-tied before. Usually nobody can get you to shut up," Rene' laughed, his laughter dying out quickly when he realized that Tim didn't laugh with him.

"I'm having bad dreams, Rene'. Really bad dreams. I think I might be going insane," Tim finally blurted out. It was painfully obvious to Rene' that the man was teetering on the brink of tears.

"That's not so bad, we all have nightmares once in a while. And I highly doubt you are suddenly losing your mind," Rene's spoke slowly, giving himself time to chose his words carefully. He could tell that his best friend was perched precariously close to the edge of something terrible.

"No, it's not like that. These are so real. So vivid. And I'm afraid they are getting worse."

"Dreams about what?"

"Murder," Tim replied without even attempting to soften the blow.

Rene' was speechless for a wrinkle in time.

"Yours or someone else's?"

"They are always about me murdering someone, usually a woman. Brutally murdering them. I'm not talking about a simple 'gunshot to the head because I am pissed off at you' kind of murder, but the 'I get my jollies off by killing you' kind of murders."

The room fell into an eerie silence on the heels of Tim's revelation. Rene' was shell-shocked by his best friend's confession and was momentarily caught at a loss for words. And Tim, hearing the words spoken aloud for the very first time was equally as stunned. Suddenly, he became acutely aware of the grave predicament he was facing. They listened to each other's breathing for a few agonizing minutes, allowing the bombshell to fully detonate.

"Wow. Okay. But, Tim, you have to realize, these are merely dreams. I can understand them giving you the willies, but you haven't really murdered anyone, have you?" He tried to speak in a playful tone while making sure to make eye contact with Tim.

"I don't know. I don't think so," his voice trailed off and he laid his head in his hands.

"What do you mean you don't know?"

"I'm starting to have my suspicions. There's been some evidence."

"What kind of evidence?"

"When I woke up this morning I was wet, you know, down there."

"I guess I am missing your point, Tim," Rene' looked both concerned and confused.

"I was wet from sex. I smelled it. But it wasn't just sex. There was blood too."

Once again the room filled with an uncomfortable silence. Both men stared into each other's eyes, brooding over the weight of Tim's shocking disclosure. They both sensed a sudden urge to cry.

"What about Elsa, could she have . . . "

"No, I don't think so. Even if she had, it's not her time. It wouldn't explain the blood."

"Have you said anything to anyone else about this?"

"Not even Elsa," he replied, shaking his head.

"Good, keep it that way, at least until we can talk some more. I really believe you are reacting to stress and these nightmares are nothing more than your mind playing tricks on you."

"Let's hope so, but I don't mind admitting that I'm a little scared."

"I can imagine so."

"It gets worse, Rene'"

"What do you mean?" He asked, truly fearing the answer.

"I am losing control over my sleep. I mean, I have been falling asleep without warning. And I've only explained a small portion of my new dream world to you."

"It sounds like you might be experiencing narcolepsy? But that's not my field of expertise. I'm sorry to say that I am not too well versed in the affliction."

"I don't know very much about it either, that's one of the reasons I wanted to talk to you. I thought you might know someone."

"Well, there is this guy I went to post-graduate school who's now working down in St. Augustine at a clinic for sleep disorders. He sent me some literature about it after we met at some alumni thing a while back. I guess in case I ever got a patient I needed to refer."

"It probably wouldn't hurt to talk to him. I need to do something. I'm really starting to get freaked out about this. Especially after this morning."

"I'll give Dan Hughes a call this afternoon between patients and set up an appointment for you."

"I'd really appreciate that, Rene'."

"Are you going back to the hospital?"

"No, I called in sick. I'll be at home if you want to call later."

"Try to relax, Tim, we'll get to the bottom of this," Rene' offered a comforting word as he watched his best friend walk out of his office with his head hanging lower than he had ever seen it before. Even Tim's marital problems hadn't left him looking so haggard and mentally taxed.

Tim desperately needed some rest, but was too afraid to lie down. The last thing he wanted to do was to dream.

———————

"Hey, Cracker, you need anything today?" An aging man asked while pushing a cart load of well-read books down the long corridor. The man they called Cracker spooked him so badly that he wanted as little to do with the man as possible. But this was his job. It earned him extra time on the floor, so it was worth it.

"No, True, I'm still reading the same one," the lanky inmate called from his solitary cell. "But I sure could use someone to talk to."

"Man, I wish I could help you out, but my ass is busy today. Everybody wants something up here today," he replied, pushing his cartload of books.

The inmate used to be imposing once upon a time, in another life. But now the erosive effects of time and degenerative arthritis left him hunkered into a permanent stoop. His gnarled hands barely worked anymore and there was hardly a day that went by when he wasn't besieged with pain. There were plenty of days when he felt like giving up, but then his thoughts would turn to his Regina. His lovely, lovely Regina. True let the memory of his granddaughter's face invade his mind. With a renewed energy he made his way down the row to Cracker's cell.

"Awe, c'mon, True, I know you don't like me, but I also know that I'm the last stop on your rounds. What are you afraid of. I can't possibly get at you from in here. Not saying that I wouldn't try," he guffawed, his face twisted with an impish grin. The prison corridor echoed in a cacophony of his devious laughter.

"Forget you, you crazy bastard," the old man pivoted back around.

"C'mon, I'll give you three squares of smokes just to talk. Just to talk, man. I'm going crazy in here. I haven't talked to anyone since you were up here last."

"I must be nuts," the old man mumbled and wheeled the cart back around. "You was always crazy," he responded.

"Thanks for noticing."

"If you didn't always act like such a damned fool maybe you'd get more visitors."

True slowly ambled to the man's cell, making certain to catch the eye of at least one of the two guards on the floor. He wanted to be sure they knew he was going to Cracker's cell and to be on the look-out for any trouble. He stopped the battleship gray cart full of books and magazines in front of the cell, putting it between him and Cracker as a buffer. He wanted to make damn sure he kept his distance from the notorious inmate. The headlines played like a rolling marquee in True's mind. *Another mutilated female found. Sixteen deaths attributed to the Sandman.* True figured the press gave him that name for lack of a better one. It probably grew out of the streets as a warning from mothers to their little girls. He seemed to only strike at night under the comforting cover of darkness. And once the press had given him the name, Cracker had played it out to the hilt. He began pouring little handfuls of sand into his victim's hollowed out eye sockets as a calling card.

"So what's on your mind, Cracker?" He asked, averting his eyes from the convict's.

"I just wondered, do you believe in magic?"

"Some of it I guess, but mostly it's all mirrors and hand tricks."

"No, I'm talking about real magic, True. The kind of magic that makes things happen for no apparent reason. The kind that works from the hidden powers of your mind."

"No, I don't believe in all that mumbo jumbo stuff. Things just happen in this world, people can't make them happen."

"You don't believe in voodoo?" Cracker sounded genuinely surprised.

"What? You think every black man in this world believes in voodoo?" He made eye contact, trying to get his point across. True's eyes gave Cracker the willies and the old man knew it. The once dark, piercing orbs, now victims of cataracts and old age, were a hazy shade of milky blue, not unlike the eyes of a fish that had been dead on the river bank for quite some time.

"All of them that are from the bayou's of Louisiana, anyway," he said innocently. True realized from the tone of his voice that the poor bastard really didn't have a clue.

"Not all of them, Cracker," he responded, emphasizing the inmate's moniker.

"But you do believe in destiny, don't you True?" Cracker asked, his eyes narrowing into tiny slits, giving his face an even more ominous appearance. His time on the row had thinned him out and his hollowed cheeks accentuated his high cheekbones.

"Yes. I believe our lives were already mapped out for us the day we was born."

"So, you're saying that I was born to be a killer and you a thief?"

"No, nothing like that. The map is there, but it's up to us to follow the right paths. You and I, we just chose the wrong roads to follow is all."

"What if my destiny is to be a magician?"

"You're not talking about being a magician, Cracker. You're talking about witchcraft; black magic."

"Aren't they one in the same? Magic and witchcraft, I mean?" His voice was taunting and sarcastic.

"No, not hardly. Now you're just talking crazy."

"Don't you think that some of the great magicians, like Houdini and Blackstone, sold their souls for the sake of their craft?"

"No, I don't believe that shit for a minute. Now, I got to go. I've got things that need to get done."

"Wait, wait. I need your help with something, True," Cracker took an obsequious tone.

"What," he shot back, tired of the con's insane babbling.

"I think I've found a secret, a trick, here in this book you got for me," he commented, pointing at the book lying on his bunk.

The book had an antiquated appearance and was ominously foreboding. Its title shouted out in red raised leather lettering, Insomnium Obitus, across the exact center of the volume. True had had no clue what the title meant when he had first seen it, but it looked as though it would be strange enough to satisfy Cracker's insane lust for the macabre. True had accidentally found the volume while looking for a book about dreams for the bothersome man. It had been buried in a box of tomes in a storage closet in the back of the library. The books were slated to be destroyed so True figured no one would miss the odd looking book. He was certain that the oddity would placate Cracker, at least for the time being and he hoped that it might keep the demented inmate off his back for a while.

"I'd love to try it out."

"Man, you're not doing no freaky stuff on me," True commented, putting some more distance between himself Cracker.

Laughing, he said, "Nothing like that, True. I don't even need your help."

"Then what do you need from me?"

"All I have to know is if it works. You tell me if you dream about something strange tonight when you go to sleep. Come up here and tell me about it in the morning."

"You're crazy," he turned and started back down the corridor.

True's limp was a little more pronounced and he knew it must be raining. The limp was a gift from the good ol' boy sheriff that had arrested him after the accident. Of course he waited until they were well enough away from the scene to teach True his lesson.

"I can make you see things, True," Cracker taunted.

The old con waved a dismissing hand and nodded at the guard to let him know he was finished on the tier.

"I can make you do things too, True. You just wait. You'll see," he laughed almost hysterically as he watched True hurrying as fast as he could to get away from him. True didn't believe a word of what Cracker was spouting, but he just couldn't shake the queasy feeling he felt the rest of the day. That night, True lie in bed for hours, unable to get to sleep. He cursed himself for letting the lunatic burrow into his brain.

CHAPTER TWO

"Mr. Duggan?"

"Yes," Tim looked up from the magazine he was reading.

"Dr. Hughes will see you now," the receptionist announced and pointed the way to a small consultation office in the homey clinic. The interior of the place resembled a woodsy lodge, complete with a fireplace at one end of the room. Paintings of peaceful forest scenes and majestic animals in their natural habitat adorned the cozily paneled walls. Gentle flamenco music chimed through hidden speakers. Although the music seemed somewhat out of place, it was still quite soothing. It was better than some new age sounds of nature thing playing, which would have made the whole setting seem even more contrived than it already did. Tim felt more at ease than he had in quite some time.

"Good morning, Mr. Duggan, have a seat please," Dan Hughes said, offering a big, meaty hand. "Doctor Meade has told me a little bit about your circumstances, but I'd like to hear the details straight from you."

"You can call me Tim," he said, easing down into an oversized leather chair that mimicked gastrointestinal troubles whenever he moved.

"Okay, Tim, I'm Dan. So, can you tell me a little about yourself to get us started. How old, are you married, that kind of stuff."

"I'm thirty-two years old and have been married for eight years but we have no children yet. Elsa and I were waiting until we were both done with school and settled into our lives before adding the turmoil of a child into the mix," he explained when he saw the look that Dr. Hughes had given him. It was the same look that Elsa's mother gave them every time they were together. Eight years of marriage with no children was a crime in the eyes of some people.

"What do you do for a living?" The doctor asked, taking careful notes.

"I'm a pediatrician, I do urgent care work at Memorial Hospital."

"That has to be pretty stressful at times."

"It can be, but I've learned to cope with the battles I know that I can't win, and make damn sure I win the ones I know I can."

"What do you do for relaxation? How do you deal with the stress of your job?"

"Elsa, and I try to get in at least a couple of rounds of golf a week and I go to the gym almost every day for at least an hour."

The doctor paused to take catch up on his note taking. "What does your wife do? For work, I mean."

"She works with mentally and physically challenged youths, trying to ease them into mainstream society."

"Sounds pretty challenging," he jotted on a legal pad without looking up.

"It is, but it's very rewarding for her as well. She loves her job. What are all these questions for? I thought I was here about my sleep problems," Tim queried, starting to get agitated with the line of questioning. He wanted answers, not clinical brouhaha.

"To be honest with you, I am trying to rule out stress as a cause for your sleep abnormalities."

"I understand that doctor, but truthfully, the only stress I have in my life right now is this sleep disorder I'm experiencing."

"Fair enough. Let's move on. Give me some clinical history of this problem. Explain to me exactly what is going on with you to cause this stress?"

"It started out as bad dreams, but they were so real I felt like I was awake the entire time. But now it seems like I wake up and I don't even remember falling asleep."

"Do you drink much?"

Tim looked at the doctor like it was a ridiculous question and felt his anger rising out of control. He was ready to unleash a barrage of insults on Dr. Hughes and then he remembered some of the questions he asked of parents when they brought their injured children into the emergency room. As harsh and uncaring as they were, they were routine, and some were even required by law.

"My drinking is minimal. A few beers on Sunday watching the game is about it."

"Good. So, tell me how frequent are these sleep episodes?"

"It started out just once or twice about a month ago, but now, it happens at least once a day. At first the dreams were nothing more than me walking around, exploring, watching people. They were a little disturbing because they felt so real, but nothing screamed at me as being abnormal about them. I just thought I was having a bout with bad dreams."

"And now?"

"Now they have progressively grown in intensity little by little. They've manifested themselves into something very disturbing to say the least," Tim vaguely explained.

"How do you feel when you wake up?"

"Disoriented to say the least. Almost like I am coming back from somewhere else, not just a dream state. And I am never well rested when I wake up."

"Would you ever say that you were paralyzed, or couldn't move upon waking?"

"Not really, but I'm not too coherent for the first couple of minutes. So I guess the answer to that would be yes, but mentally, not physically."

"What are these dreams typically about, Tim?"

"Murder," he blurted without giving himself the opportunity to think about his answer first.

The doctor stopped writing and looked up from his notes. "Your own murder?"

"No, I am the murderer. Brutal, vicious killings. These dreams are so real I can almost smell the blood and hear the victim's screams," Tim quickly decided it best to withhold the particulars of finding physical evidence on himself. He wasn't sure how far he could trust this doctor.

"Sounds like you might be suffering from hypnagogic hallucinations."

"What are those, in English please?"

"They are dream-like hallucinations brought on by chronic fatigue and narcoleptic episodes."

"Hallucinations? But it seems so real."

"In essence, they are real, or at least to your subconscious they are. These hallucinations can become so vivid that one can actually hear sounds and smell things that are associated with the hallucination. They can be so strong that they have been known to cause temporary paralysis," Dr. Hughes explained.

"And what about my suddenly being tired all the time?"

"What you have been describing are some classic symptoms of narcolepsy, but without the proper tests I can't be too certain."

"Why all of the sudden? I've been feeling great up until recently."

"Sometimes the symptoms are very subtle at first. A lot of times the symptoms are overlooked, being attributed to the rigors of the hormonal roller coaster known as puberty."

"But I didn't feel like this during puberty, in fact I was extremely active in high school."

"Like I said, the symptoms can sometimes be very subtle. Furthermore, maybe this isn't even narcolepsy all. I'd like to schedule you for a nocturnal polysomnogram and a multiple sleep latency test," the doctor advised.

He kept the fact that he also suspected the possibility that his patient might be suffering from fugue episodes a secret for the time being. He felt that there was no need for the undue stress that a premature diagnosis of that nature might cause. Mainly because he would have to reveal to his patient that if fugue states were indeed the case, then Timothy Duggan was truly doing these things and not just dreaming as he supposed.

"Whatever you just said," he chuckled. "Okay, I'm game for anything. I would do anything to rid myself of these nightmares."

"We'll do our best, Tim. I will have my receptionist call you with an appointment. We're quite busy here but I will make certain she schedules you for the very first opening."

"Thank you. I really appreciate this Dr. Hughes," Tim rose to his feet.

"Just relax, Mr. Duggan, we'll figure this thing out soon enough," he expertly masked the concern in his voice, a trick he had mastered after years of dealing with deeply troubled souls.

"It can't be soon enough for me.," Tim replied, walking out of the doctors office. The elevator ride down to the first floor was long and agonizing. His brain was cycling through the events of the past few weeks, causing him to relive his nightmares in broad daylight. He couldn't help but think he was losing his mind. He had to fight back his tears as his thoughts turned to Elsa. He should have been aroused that morning, out of control with desire at the sight of her flawless naked form. Yet, all he could do was tremble with fear. Tim couldn't begin to fathom what was happening to him.

Tim drove south along A1A until he came to a town named Marineland. In dire need of some quiet time to mull things over, he parked and began walking through the park. As he passed by the attractions and sights, they became only fleeting images in his mind. Tim must have wandered around for an hour before finding himself at the Dolphin Encounter exhibit. Tears streamed down his cheeks as he recalled the day he and Elsa had shared in the tanks with the dolphins together. It was an adventure that had been well worth price. It's not very often in life a person can have an experience that will forever forge itself into their brain as a distinct moment in their existence.

Elsa's smile came rushing back at him like snow at a speeding car's windshield; beautiful and mesmerizing. Tim lost track of time while reminiscing about better days. A security guard brought him back to reality and let him know that the park would be closing in five minutes. He sighed and nodded, walking aimlessly back toward his car. The world was a lonely place for Tim Duggan at that moment, but that wasn't the worst of it. He knew it was about to get even lonelier.

Two cold eyes scrutinized the investigation from the safety of a child's tree fort several blocks away from the crime scene. The spectator couldn't quite see everything that was going on, but he had seen enough to know the police hadn't found all of her yet. From his vantage point the onlooker could savor the flavor of his work without fear of being caught. He would be able to see anyone coming long before they would ever see him escaping into the shadows.

The eyes counted each time the emergency personnel exited the house with yet another department regulation evidence bag. So far they had brought out less than half of her, if his count were correct. The big pieces were yet to come. He chuckled to himself, remembering the exhilaration he felt as he carefully hid her pieces. He was no stranger to this game, in fact, he considered himself a professional. Jacksonville's finest had better get a little more creative if they planned to find all of the bitch! He laughed under his breath, catching sight of a man in a blue blazer hunkered down behind a bush, inspecting the remnants of his last meal. All the players were there, forensics, the coroner and of course, Jacksonville's two dumbest detective's.

"Poor kid, this must be his first one," Detective Premoe commented, nodding his head in the direction of the young uniformed officer regurgitating in a spirea bush next to the house. The once pristine dainty, white flowered bush now looked like an artist's favorite smock.

"Hell, Blain, I'm pretty close to joining him," Detective Todd Freeman responded sympathetically. His normally tanned face was pale and ghostly.

The darkened house flashed brilliantly with explosions from camera flash assaulting the once peaceful domicile. The dispiriting documentation of a shattered life in progress. The two detectives impatiently waited outside for their turn at the gruesome spectacle.

"Damn, how much longer are they going to take," Premoe grunted, flicking his cigarette into the street, the cherry bursting into a miniature fireworks display and drawing an admonishing glance from his partner.

Another parade of waxen faced men exited the victim's home carrying several small containers. Freeman shook his head in disgust.

"How are you boys doing tonight?" The crass, young medical examiner greeted.

"Not too good as you can see, Swaggart," Premoe didn't bother to conceal his contempt for the man.

"Are you finished?" Freeman asked.

"As far as the house is concerned. It's going to take a hell of a lot longer with the remains. I've got a jigsaw puzzle to put back together."

"Paul, just give us the skinny before we walk in there, please."

"Sure thing, Blain. I hope you guys skipped dinner. I can't tell you how many pieces of her we brought out already, I quit counting. He hacked her up pretty bad. Charlie is in there waiting for you guys, but be careful, it's messy in there. Especially the kitchen."

"Is that where he killed her?"

"Yes and no," the medical examiner replied with a chuckle.

"What does that mean?"

"You'll see when you get in there", he turned and walked to his car, leaving the horror behind him, secure in the knowledge that it would soon follow him.

The wicked sentinel continued his vigil of the crime scene, regretting only that he could not able to see the detective's faces when they first set eyes upon the repugnance inside the house. He so desperately wanted to smell their fear and taste their anger as it seeped from their every pore. The stage was set, it was time for their performance.

The metallic smell of fresh blood hung heavily in the air. The odor of death mingled with that of forensic chemicals creating an aroma found nowhere else on earth but at a murder scene. Both detectives glanced pensively at each other before walking through the threshold and into the living room to begin their investigation.

"Walk us through , Charlie," Premoe directed the forensic team leader.

"Follow me. He started back here in the bedroom," the trio walked through the blood stained house. Detective Freeman grimaced, noticing a set of crimson hand prints streaking down the wall from the corner of the room. It was obvious that the victim had tried in vain to hang onto the door jamb before being dragged down the hall.

Stepping through the threshold of the bedroom they were confronted by a blood soaked bed. The bedroom showed signs of a bitter struggle. Bloody hand prints were smeared on the edges of various pieces of furniture. There were several stains in the carpeting where the victim and her killer had struggled. The forensics investigator squared himself to the detectives and prepared for his gruesome monologue.

Charlie Fitzpatrick was a short, dumpy, unkempt fellow who would look more at place out in some back alley rummaging through dumpters than in a police department. His short, uneven brown hair was waging a never ending war with his comb, a battle in which the comb was losing. Charlie could have easily dressed up in a brown burlap sack, cracked open a bottle of vino and joined Robin Hood's merry men. But in stark contrast to his looks, he was a genius at analyzing a crime scene. Freeman was certain that Charlie's appearance had more to do with maintaining his sanity than it did with laziness.

"They had sex first, consensual, no rape at this point as far as we can tell from the preliminary evidence. We haven't quite determined at what point she was hit in the head, if it was during the act or immediately after. However, it looks as if he wasn't careful enough, he left this behind," he said, holding up a paper evidence bag with a used condom in it.

"Where did you find that?"

"Under the bed. It probably got kicked around during their struggle and he couldn't find it," Charlie offered.

"By the looks of things she put up quite a struggle," Freeman observed.

"I don't think he wanted to kill her right away," Charlie started. "He wanted her alive for what else he had planned. They struggled here for a very short time before he hit her again, dazing her this time. Then he dragged her down the hallway to the kitchen," the forensics expert pointed to each location around the room like a morbid tour guide as he explained the crime scene to the detectives.

The investigators followed a set of drag marks in the carpeting leading from the bedroom, through the living room and into the kitchen. The trail was sparsely splattered with blood and clearly accentuated by the streaks of bloody hand prints on the carpet that stretched up along the lower edge of the wall and baseboards.

"Doesn't look like she was hurt too badly at this point," Premoe noticed.

"Not at all. It was a simple head wound requiring a dozen stitches or so. No fatal blow had been struck at this point."

The detectives entered the kitchen and were immediately taken aback by the amount of blood smeared across the stark white tile and linoleum surfaces. Freeman just made a gargled sound and quickly regained his composure.

"This is where he cut her up," Charlie reported, pointing to a portable butcher block set on wheels. There was a knife rack built into one of the sides of the culinary oasis. Several of the knives were missing from their slots. Freeman noticed them scattered across the countertops, a bloody meat cleaver lay on the top of the maple block. Premoe had to control his own gag reflex when he noticed claw marks and broken bits of brightly polished fingernail embedded in the sides of the wooden block. He felt it best to keep that information to himself for the time being, certain that little tidbit of information would send Freeman scampering out to paint the spirea with the rookie cop.

"What's this on the floor?" Blain asked, scuffing his feet through a substance on the floor.

"My first guess would be that it is sand. I'll know more once I get a sample back to the lab and analyze it."

"Sand? Why sand?" Freeman asked.

"We found some sand in the eyes of the victim."

Both detectives looked apprehensively at each other.

"You guys get the same feeling, huh?"

They both nodded.

"It doesn't look like he cared about cleaning up after himself," Freeman observed, swiveling his head around while gazing upon the soiled contents of the room. He wanted to change the subject for the time being. He didn't have the energy to think about the possibilities that were running through his mind..

"No, he sure didn't. Are you ready for this, we found pieces of her flesh in the garbage disposal."

"So, he wanted to dispose of the body and ran out of time. That's not as unusual as I would like it to be," Premoe said.

"No, that's not the case here. The pieces we found were too small, in fact, we believe they were her breasts. And I think he made her watch."

"Are you telling us that this maniac cut off her breasts and made her watch him grind them up?"

"Unless you guys have a better explanation for this," Charlie pointed to a telephone cord dangling from a ceiling fan in the kitchen. The phone cord had a large tuft of hair tied to one end," he pointed to the remnants of the victim dangling from the ceiling.

"He elevated her head so she could watch him?" Freeman shuddered.

"That's not the worst of it. I'd have to speculate that she lived through most of the dismemberment. He took his time with her. It was as if he wasn't too concerned about being caught."

"How about prints?"

"No visible prints, and it's very unlikely that we'll find any latent prints either. The killer wore surgical gloves," Charlie explained with a sigh.

"Can't we take prints from the inside?" Premoe asked?

"No, there was not enough of them left. We found them in the garbage disposal. There were just enough scraps left for us to ID them as surgical gloves," Charlie explained.

"Damn, he knows what he's doing."

"Oh, very much so. Like I said, he is very methodical and uses time to his advantage. I think you guys have a real winner on your hands here. He left some incidental traces of DNA evidence, but nothing that would be useful, at least not until we have a suspect."

"This looks like it might be similar to the Orange Park murder, what do you think so far, Todd?" Premoe asked aloud, more for his own benefit than anything else.

"There seems to be a lot of uncanny similarities. Let's just pray it's the same guy, Blain. I'd hate to have two guys like this working our town."

"They are very similar in nature, that's for certain," Charlie added. "One more thing."

"What's that, Charlie," Premoe asked gingerly, having had his fill of information for the moment.

"We found semen on the floor where he stood while dismembering her."

"He got his rocks off while killing this poor girl?"

"But then why the rubber?" Freeman interjected.

"I won't have a clue as to how to answer that until serology gets finished with their report. But that's the way it looks for now. I'll have more detailed information for you by the first of next week, once I get this stuff analyzed and I get more info from Paul. On the bright side, he did leave us some DNA evidence."

"If it's his DNA. Do your best, Charlie, I know it's a tough order. You know where to reach us," Freeman commented, nodding toward the door suddenly in desperate need of fresh air.

From his shielded vista, the watcher examined the expressions on each of the detective's faces as they exited the house. Scrutinizing their emotions he slipped into a euphoric, highly erotic state. With his eyes closed tightly he drifted off, allowing his lecherous mood to waft over him. He was almost there. He had found a new freedom, a new way to search for the ever-elusive nirvana. Contented, he laid down and let the night birds sing him to sleep.

——— — —

Tim awoke to the sounds of sparrows singing their praises of winged flight to each other. A baneful ray of sunshine cut into his eyes like a laser. Groggily he rolled over and was immediately gripped with fear. His eyes bolted open and quickly focused on his surroundings. The careworn wooden slats of a child's tree house screamed back at him. He bulldozed his hand into his pants, withdrawing a wet, bloody appendage. His heart began to race and his mind was overcast with clouds of confusion. He had no recollection of the night before, nor of how he came to be where he was. The last thing that Tim could tangibly remember was driving through Ponte Vedra Beach on his way back home. And then there was nothingness. A blackness to his memories.

Panic gripped his consciousness and Tim scooted across the floor of the tree house like a whipped puppy until he reached a corner. He pulled his knees tightly to his chest and began to weep. Uncontrollable, gut wrenching sobs.

——— — —

"You seem awful active this morning, Cracker," True called down the corridor in response to the sounds of the con's morning exercise ritual echoing from his steel and concrete cubicle.

"Nothing special, True, I'm feeling mighty good today," he replied, letting loose a guttural growl as an after thought. Blood raced through his veins with a new found fire. He might be trapped on death row, but he had found a way to live again. But still, something nagged at him. He needed to know if his dreams were real, if he were truly escaping his cell at night.

"Come here, True, I need to talk."

"I'm busy right now, Cracker," he looked into the eyes of the inmate on the other side of the cage door. The inmate completely understood and began slowly scanning through the cart of books. He had overheard their conversations ever since being transferred up to the row six months earlier from isolation. He was quite aware of the fact that True was deathly afraid of the man, and in essence, that scared him as well. He might be on death row, and he certainly was a killer himself, but the man known as Cracker could turn the devil's blood to ice water. Something just wasn't right about the man. Carl Lettimore was relieved that they were kept in their cells and weren't allowed to mingle, at least this way he could sleep a little more comfortably at night. He would just as soon Cracker not even know he was there.

"How about a western, do you have any of those, True?" Carl Lettimore asked, shooting a glance back to the trustee, letting him know that he understood and would help him out as best he could.

"I've got one of them by Louis L'Amour. I hear his books are pretty good."

"Let me see the cover."

"Damn it, True, I need to talk to you," Cracker cranked his voice up a notch.

"I told you I was busy right now. I'll get there when I can," True responded with a shudder.

"No, this one don't look so good. Got any of them action series ones?" Carl asked, trying to delay the inevitable.

"Yeah, I got a couple of Mack Bolen's and one about a guy called Casca or something like that."

"What's the Casca one about?"

"Damn you, True, don't make me get into your head!" He spat vehemently.

"True, you better get down there, no sense riling him too much. Just make it quick, do your business and get off the floor," Carl advised, taking the Casca book from the trustee's weathered hand.

True tediously wheeled his way down the corridor, dreading his inevitable rendezvous with the deranged man. He knew he should talk to the warden and let him know he hated dealing with the bastard, but he was no snitch. Besides, how much harm could the maniac really do sitting behind his steel fence? Once more True made certain to catch the eye of the guards on the floor. For what little good it did, at least it gave him some peace of mind.

"What's so important, Cracker," he tried to assert himself as to have at least some control over the situation.

"Did you feel it last night?"

"Feel what?"

"The magic."

"What magic are you talking about?"

"Me, I came to visit you last night in your sleep."

"Man, you're crazy, you ain't been out of this cell in three years 'cept for your hour out in the yard and your twice a week shower, and last night wasn't one of them times," he knew what Cracker was talking about, he just didn't want him to know.

"You didn't have any bad dreams last night?"

"Nope, slept like a little babe," he lied.

"Are you sure? Didn't you find the note I left for you on your table?"

"Nothing there but a blank notepad," he hoped his facade wasn't too transparent.

The truth of the matter was that he had indeed suffered through a chilling nightmare the previous night. True dreamt he was writing bad things about what he wanted to do to the warden's family. When he awoke that morning he was scared beyond comparison. Cracker had somehow gotten into his head and had forced him write some very bad things. He was afraid the psychopath could make him do things too, if he wanted.

"You lying bastard!" Cracker jumped off his bunk and rushed across his cell, grabbing the bars right in front of True. The muscles in his arms flexed as he grabbed the bars, showing the cuts he had developed by exercising in his cell. He was much stronger than he had been before his incarceration and he was eager to use the new found strength for his pleasure. He heard the lies rolling off True's lips, but he had his answer, he knew that the old convict was lying. He could taste the fear. He could read it in the man's eyes.

"There's no need to call me names. Get your own damned books from now on," True commented, turning away, trying to conceal the shudders careening through him.

"I'm sorry, True, don't go. Hey, you never told me, why do they call you True?"

He tried to change the topic of conversation, desperately needing someone to talk to. Even though his nightly excursions were becoming easier to pull off, he still screamed for human interaction.

"None of your damned business."

"Come on, don't be pissed at me, I'm sorry," he pleaded fallaciously. *You little bastard! I got into your head didn't I? Fuck with me, go ahead, see where it gets you!*

"You got to calm down, man. If I tell you something, you can bet it's the truth. That's why they call me True. "So tell me somethin', why do people call you Cracker?"

"It's kind of a funny story. Some bully back in grade school gave me the nickname for the first time, it has kind of stuck with me ever since. The little bastard got his jollies by ridiculing me because of my name, you know Graham, Cracker. He would say it over and over again, punching me each time for emphasis until it was all I ever heard. Graham Cracker, Graham Cracker. And the teacher knew, but she never made him stop. My best guess was that the teacher never did anything to stop him because my mother had a reputation around town and I think she whored around with my teacher's old man so it was her little pay back. Made me bear the brunt of my mother's sins so to speak. Dumb bitch never realized that I hated my mother worse than she did. Well this kid teased me day after day after day, until I had finally had enough. One day on the playground he was really going at it. He was sitting on the monkey bars hitting me in the head with stones he kept pulling from his pocket. Well, I waited until he had his hands deep in his pocket digging around for another stone when I jumped up and grabbed his leg and pulled him down through the monkey bars. He must have hit his head pretty good because he was pretty dazed. I got on top of him and pulled a nutcracker out of my back pocket. I went to work on his fingers, crushing the bones one by one. I would have got them all too, had that bitch teacher not gotten in the way. But I got her back, got her back and then some," a fire raged in his eyes as he regaled his story.

True watched the man's eyes and knew that he had lost himself in the retelling. It was painfully obvious that he enjoyed being a sadist.

"So the name Cracker stuck with you your whole life from grade school?"

"I continued to earn the name as I got older, and chose the paths I chose. I worked collections for a connected guy once. I kind of got the reputation for liking the way bones sounded when they broke. I used to piss him off by being a little bit too convincing when I collected on a late payment. He starting losing bettors and borrowers, they were too afraid of dealing with me, too scared of what I might do if they were to miss a payment. So he fired me.

"Are you trying to tell me a wise guy fired you for being too tough?" True's voice smacked of skepticism.

"Exactly, sounds strange I know. That's what I tried to tell him. He wouldn't listen to reason though, just called me a psycho son of a bitch. He was my first. Broke my cherry, so to speak."

"Your first?" True asked, sure he knew the answer already.

"Murder. I had to teach people not to fuck with me, didn't I? You don't fuck with Graham Cracker, got it," suddenly his demeanor took a turn. "I know that you are lying to me, True. I saw your cell through your eyes last night. I saw myself writing those things about the warden's family last night with your shriveled black hands. A little note about how you are going to teach his little daughter all about sex if you ever got out of here. You better start being nicer to me, a lot nicer. What if I were to make sure the right people found those notes. How would the warden treat you then? Would you still be his little bitch boy?"

True's blood froze in his veins. This bastard had his number. Cracker had never lost control of the situation. For the first time in his life, True was terrified.

"I've got to go, Cracker. I've got more rounds to make."

"Don't lie, True. Be honest, I can forgive you for being afraid of me, I kind of like that. But I won't forgive you if you lie to me."

"Okay, I admit it, you scare the shit out of me. Now I got to go," True revealed, turning away with his cart of books and hustling toward the large steel door at the end of the tier.

"Just remember, True, if you piss me off, I'll make sure you hurt, hurt real bad," he called after the fleeing man.

Once True was off the row Cracker burst into laughter. Not only was he actually able to transcend the ethereal plane of existence and live vicariously through others, he had succeeded in scaring the shit out of a man he thought was unshakable. He quivered as an uncontrollable wave of ecstasy rushed through him. He was free to kill again.

Cracker still didn't quite understand the mechanics of his transference. After several attempts to worm his way into the souls of others he had given up and settled for his current host, who for some strange reason, was very easy to link up with. He shrugged it off as something he would never understand, and really didn't need to.

It did, however, bother Cracker that he couldn't figure out why with True it had been very difficult and had taken so much out of him. After his mental attack on the inmate he had suffered through the rest of the night with a terrible migraine. And the whole time he was with True he could feel him fighting, struggling to break free from the trespass.

Nevertheless, none of that mattered, because this other's eyes he had been living behind was proving easier and easier to impregnate with practice. Although he was grateful for this willing host, he was still bothered by the particular aspects. He would have loved to be able to get into anyone's mind at any time. And while this would do for now, he had to learn how to control this beast. He had plenty of uses for a monster such as this.

CHAPTER THREE

S calding water from the shower cascaded over Timothy
Duggan's body. An array of cleansers lay at the bottom of the
bathtub. He was presently working on his flesh with an S.O.S.
scouring pad, trying desperately to remove the memory of the
woman's mutilated form. The foreign blood had long since mixed
with his own and flowed down the drain into the city's underground
river. But the memories remained behind to plague his every waking
thought.

Tim climbed out of the shower only after the water had finally
turned icy cold. He stared at himself in the mirror, tilting his head like
a dog does when they hear or see something completely unfamiliar.
His puffy eyes, reddened by crying and the lack of restful sleep stared
back at him. He didn't even know who he was anymore. How could it
all be just a dream?

"Tim," Elsa called from downstairs.

"What is it?" He responded almost too weakly for her to hear.
He knew he had better get his act together or his wife would easily
surmise that something was terribly wrong with him. And the last
thing he wanted to do was to try and explain all this to her, at least not
until he knew the truth for himself.

"Rene' is on the phone."

"Thanks, I'll be right there."

He thanked God it wasn't anything that he would have to discuss with her. He wasn't sure how long he could keep up his mas-
querade of normalcy, but he speculated it wouldn't be for very long.
He put on a long, thick bathrobe hoping to conceal his tender, cerise
skin from his loving wife.

"Hello, Rene'," he said, taking the phone from his wife and
kissing her lightly on the cheek, followed by a forced smile.

"How are you doing, buddy?"

"Honestly? You don't want to know."

"I heard back from Dan today. He seems to believe that you are
indeed experiencing symptoms cognizant of narcolepsy, but I'm sure
he told you that. Have you had any more bad dreams?"

"He mentioned something about needing to do some tests before
he can diagnose my problem as narcolepsy. And yes, I've had another
nightmare and this one really took the cake."

"Want to talk about it? I could make some time," Rene asked
warmly.

"No, not yet anyway. I'm still trying to get it out of my head.

Maybe once the initial shock of this wears off I will feel comfortable enough that we can talk about it."

"Whatever is best for you, buddy."

"Did Dr. Hughes happen to mention to you when I would be able to have these tests done?"

"No, he didn't mention anything at all about when they would be able to get you in. But I suspect it won't be too long."

"I sure hope you're right. I can't take much more of this, Rene'. Especially since my dreams are getting worse. They are getting much more vivid and," Tim cut himself off before divulging any more information.

"And what, Tim?" Rene's voice was thick with concern.

"Not right now, okay? Please, don't push me on this one."

"Backing off, sorry."

"Thanks, I mean it. I will tell you when the time comes. But right now, I'm scared as hell," his voice cracked.

Rene' felt tears welling up in his own eyes and his throat constricted to the point he could barely speak. He could tell by the tone of Tim's voice that his friend was not doing too well. Something was going on in his head, something catastrophically wrong. Rene' felt so helpless, he had seen Tim through the toughest of times just as Tim had helped him. Never, in their nearly thirty year friendship had his best friend clammed up on him.

"Are you going to be all right?" Rene' asked.

"Yeah, I think so, it's just going to take some time. And some damn good drugs," he forced a bogus laugh.

"Now that, I can help you with. You know us psychiatrists, we've got all the good drugs," Rene' returned his own canned laughter. Both men laughed, yet struggled to contain a wealth of tears.

"I'll talk to you later, Rene'."

"Promise?"

"Yeah, yeah, I'll call you at home. Don't you fret none over me, ya hear," he emoted his best Scarlett O'Hara impression which was at best, borderline illegal.

"You do that, and get some rest, doctor's orders."

"No rest for the wicked," he hung up the phone before their conversation turned any mushier. He thanked the heavens for a friend like Rene'. He knew if he were going to get through these dire straits, it wouldn't be without Rene's help, guidance and understanding.

Tim stood in the breakfast nook holding onto the phone receiver as it securely rested in its cradle. He wanted to call Rene' back. He needed to open up to him and tell him everything he was holding inside, if for no other reason than to hear how crazy it all sounded for himself and dismiss the entire mess as nothing more than nightmares. And he would do that too, if it weren't for the blood. He couldn't explain the blood to himself, let alone Rene'. He was certain that Rene' had justified his earlier recanting of finding himself smelling of sex and small traces of blood as nothing more than his having sex with Elsa while she was menstruating. Maybe that's all it was. Maybe he was so fatigued that he didn't remember. Nevertheless, nothing, not one damn thing was going to explain away the morning's event of finding himself in that tree house, smeared with drying blood. Nor could it account for the tiny scraps of human flesh he had dug out from under his fingernails. Again, he had to fight back his tears.

"What did Rene' want, honey," Elsa called from the other room.

"Just setting up a racquetball game," he lied.

"I thought he gave that up after his knee injury?"

"Me too. He must be healed up and feeling better. You know how cocky he gets," he allowed his voice to lower a notch as he walked into the living room where his wife sat watching the midday news.

"It's Saturday, hun, would you like to do something tonight? Maybe we could catch dinner and a movie?" He asked, trying to be normal, more for his sake than hers.

"Shhh, watch this," she pointed to the TV screen and pressed the volume key on the remote.

Tim concentrated on the little green indicator bars creeping from left to right across the bottom of the screen. Anything to shield himself from the familiar face staring back at him from the screen. She had beautiful eyes. But he remembered them as being much sadder. As the volume began to roar in his ears, he could no longer hide from the inevitable.

"Last night a woman's body was found in a house in the Riverview Terrace subdivision. The police were sketchy with the details, but sources close to us report that the scene was quite bizarre and very gruesome. It has also been suggested that this grisly murder may be related to the Orange Park homicide. The police report there are no suspects as yet in this case. This marks the third brutal homicide in as many weeks. Sheila Carver reporting for News Watch Eleven," the newswoman reported.

"Kyle Turney reporting live from city hall. The city council has once again made slashing budget cuts to the police and fire departments which has caused quite a few ill feelings," his voice trailed off as Elsa pushed the mute button on the remote control.

Tim vehemently despised Sheila Carver at that moment. What right did she have to intrude upon his sanity? He felt his wife's hand gently overlapping his, and suddenly as it appeared, his loathing vanished, replaced with pure, unadulterated fear.

"That's scary stuff. That's not very far away from here," she shuddered visibly. "And don't you think she looks a lot like me?"

"It's quite a ways away from here. And no, she doesn't look a thing like you," Tim replied nervously, knowing that the Riverview Terrace subdivision was less than a mile away from their house. This he knew, because he had crept through the neighborhoods to get back home that morning.

"Still, too damned close for my comfort," she stood up from the couch, turning the TV off in the process.

It's closer than you think dear.

"Why are you still in your robe? It's beautiful outside," she taunted, playfully tugging at the sash holding his robe together.

"Hey now, be careful, you might let the monster out," Tim pulled back away from her. He could still feel the sting from the morning's shower and new he must still be beet red all over.

"And what if I wanted to see the big, scary monster this fine day?"

"How much money do you have?"

"What's that supposed to mean?"

"I mean, this monster doesn't work for free you know," he playfully turned his back on her. As desperately as he tried not to be aroused, he felt himself stiffening at her mischievous frolicking. He wasn't so sure he was ready to be that close to Elsa right now. He was afraid of what it might do to him. Afraid it might bring back memories of his haunting nightmares.

"Maybe not, but I got some nice toys he can play with," she teased, lifted her shirt and bra in one quick motion, exposing her ample breasts to him.

"Damn it, Elsa, not now," he blurted uncontrollably. He saw the pain and confusion immediately distort her face.

"Fuck you, asshole," she replied, pulling her shirt back down over her breasts. "Why are you being such a prick," she stormed out of the room stunned and hurt.

Tim knew immediately how badly he had screwed up. The strongest language that had ever come out of Elsa's mouth was an occasional damn, or maybe a hell, but never before had she used that word in his presence.

"I'm sorry, it's just that I have a terrible headache," he called weakly behind her, his voice trailing off into nothingness. As much as he had hated Sheila Carver earlier, he detested himself even more right then.

Elsa might be pissed. And she might hate him. But at least she would be alive.

———————

The two men waited outside the county building, Blain Premoe to finish his cigarette and Todd Freeman to chew him out about it every time he took a drag.

"I told you I was trying, now give it a rest," Premoe chided his partner.

"I thought you were an athlete?"

"Was an athlete, now I'm just an ordinary bum with a bad leg and a pack a day habit."

"It's going to kill you someday, you know?"

"I'm going to kill you someday," he flicked the half-smoked butt into a molded pea stone ashtray full of white sand. The black flecks across its surface made it look as though someone had put an overabundance of pepper on a diner plate full of leftover mashed potatoes. Premoe held the door open for his partner.

"No sense putting this off any longer, Todd."

"I hate this shit, always have. The morgue is no place for a detective."

"Yeah, but Paul won't come to us, no matter how much we pay him. Besides it's much better being a visitor than a guest."

"I guess you're right about that," Freeman replied as the elevator doors slid open to reveal the basement morgue.

"I hope he's not his usual self."

"Amen. I'm not in the mood to put up with his mouth today."

The smell of death instantly assaulted their noses, however faint it was. All the air fresheners and deodorizers in the world could never conceal the fact that dead people whiled away the hours down there. Freeman gagged slightly on the tangy scent of formaldehyde.

"You okay, partner," Blain laughed.

"Shut up!" He shot an evil scowl back, only causing Premoe to laugh harder.

"Good afternoon, gentlemen," Paul Swaggart greeted, looking up from a stainless steel table scattered with human remains. He was a slight man with a slight appearance who had an ego that far surpassed its relevance. His wispy blonde hair was long and he kept it in a pony tail with several rubber bands in incremental stages. Swaggart would have looked perfectly at home on the back of a Harley-Davidson, but Premoe was certain the man didn't have the balls to ride anything more dangerous than a Vespa. And although he still had the aroma of the morning's shower lingering on him, his hair looked dirty.

Paul Swaggart was a man that had led two different lives. As a convict, he used the benefits of the prison system to learn a skill and then as an ex-con he used the aid of the taxpayers to put himself through school. Premoe wouldn't have had a problem with the man going straight and coming over to the right side, if he would have left his punk attitude behind. Unfortunately the man had brought it with him into Premoe's world.

Premoe greeted the man with a cordial grunt.

"We got your message, what have you got?" Freeman inquired.

"What I don't have is a whole body. We didn't find her left hand," the medical examiner responded while humming the old childhood song about which bone was connected to another.

"I thought they were finished at the house?"

"They are. Everything that was there was brought back here. What I am telling you is that the hand was never there."

The partners exchanged familiar glances, logging this tidbit of information into their analytical minds.

"Besides the missing hand, what else can you tell us?" Premoe asked laconically. He never liked Paul Swaggart. He had always considered him a big pain in the ass as the man never seemed to be able to give a straight answer to anything.

"It's pretty much your cut and dry mutilation here fellas. Nothing really spectacular, from my end of it anyway."

"Just give us the particulars, will you?" Freeman blurted, starting to like the man even less than Premoe did.

"Female. Caucasian. Roughly around twenty five years old. Hard to tell, but she was approximately 5 foot 6, one hundred and ten pounds, give or take a few pounds," he laughed at his own morbid joke.

"One more crack like that, and you're going to lose a few pounds. Christ man, she was a human being with a family and people who loved her, even if you don't give a shit about her, show her the respect she's due. Now, save the rhetoric for someone else and do your fucking job," Premoe slammed his hands down on top of a stainless steel table causing a deafening sound to reverberate throughout the examination room. He had finally had enough of the little man.

"Simmer down, big guy, just trying to lighten things up around here," Swaggart said coolly without as much as batting an eye. If the detectives even slightly intimidated Swaggart, he didn't show it in the least.

"Get on with it," Freeman added, his knuckles turning white as he balled his fists tightly to his side. Premoe was right, one more crack and the punk was going to get it.

"The killer was pretty clean with his cuts, not so much that he knew what he was doing, but he has a steady hand. Pretty smooth lines. I think he started with her legs first, there are a few random slashes, as if the victim were thrashing as he cut. But the cuts are shallow which leads me to believe that he pulled up when slicing. He was inflicting as much pain as he could before he killed her."

"So, she was alive when he cut her up?"

"Squirming like a worm for quite a bit of it I would say. She probably bled out within twenty minutes or so, hopefully sooner. If you want my opinion, I think it's the same guy who did Lucy Chapman in Orange Park and the other girl, I forget her name, from Woodland Hills. Same kind of cuts and definitely the same brutality, and of course the sand and missing hand," Paul observed.

"Prick!" Premoe blurted and quickly exited the room before unleashing his anger on the crass examiner.

"Thanks Paul, and watch your mouth around him or he's liable to bury you one of these days."

Paul Swaggart grinned back and slid his headphones back over his ears and pushed play on his portable Compact Disc player. Alice Cooper's "I Love the Dead" roared in his ears. He watched the two getting onto the elevator and couldn't resist one last comment.

"Oh, and fellas, if and when you catch this guy, tell him I said thanks for the overtime. It'll come in handy at Christmas time," he beamed widely, knowing his remark would get Premoe's blood boiling. Sure, he would hear about it later from his boss, but it was well worth it. Premoe was a college jock prick and Paul Swaggart had absolutely no use for that type.

"I'm going to kill that son of a bitch," Premoe said, pushing the button on the elevator's panel for the basement and drawing his service revolver.

"Come on, don't let the little fiend get to you. Working down there must get to a person after a while. It's probably just his way of dealing with it so he doesn't go nuts," Freeman tried to calm his partner down while making a mental note to find out where the uncouth bastard liked to have drinks and kick his ass some dark and stormy night.

Premoe grunted in disheveled agreement.

"I wonder if forensics has anything for us yet?"

Again, Premoe grunted, he was lost in thought.

"What's on your mind? Besides Swaggart back there I mean."

"Several things. The sand, the fact that each of these girls were tortured and mutilated, and the missing hands of course."

"Hit you the same way, huh?"

"We put him away more than five years ago. He's on death row damn it," Premoe used his partner as a sounding board.

"Copycat, maybe?"

"Possibly. I hate thinking about having to investigate this one all over again. What if we got the wrong guy?"

"We caught him in the act. We found Graham at the scene, with the victim's blood all over him, remember?"

"Yeah, I remember, but we never recovered the hands and that is something I still think about it to this day. And now, in light of all of this new evidence, this case is giving me the willies. What if there were two killers and the other one just laid low until the heat was off?"

"That's definitely a possibility as well," Freeman agreed.

"Damn it!" Premoe exclaimed, shoving open the doors to the outside world, a world that now harbored a maniac on the prowl.

The two men pondered what little evidence they had as they drove to the forensics lab on the other end of town. Jacksonville is two separate cities, one on the west banks of the St. Johns River and another on the east leading to the Atlantic Coast. The river cuts a swath through most of northern Florida with branches and tributaries leading as far south as Daytona. A city of nearly two million, including the beaches, Jacksonville is as diverse as any large city, if not more so. And being a widely diverse city meant she had her share of problems, Premoe and Freeman were interested in only one of them.

He breathed in deeply of the woman lying there so peaceful and serene. He was not quite able to place her scent, yet it was so tantalizingly familiar. He was sure he had partaken of that cologne somewhere before.

He preferred rousing his women out of a deep sleep. It allowed him time to savor their terror as it crept into their veins with their consciousness. The moment right before they let loose their first shriek of panic afforded him a few seconds of pleasurable inspection before he had to smash them in their mouths to shut them up. He wasn't completely convinced that he should be ignoring the dangers of not gagging his women, but it was a necessary evil, if he were going to be able to enjoy listening to them begging and pleading for their lives. It was the only way for him to be able to listen to their harmonious voices ringing in his ears.

Her chest rose and fell softly as she breathed, completely un-aware of his presence. She moved ever so slightly, causing the blan-kets to fall away from her, exposing her delicate skin. She was sleep-ing topless. He felt a rush of blood flow surge through his loins, im-mediately exciting him.

He glided around to her side of the bed and carefully slid a chair into place. This one was so beautiful that he wanted to be able to sa-vor every moment he spent with her, up until her last.

Comfort was not an option with the large flashlight jutting out of his back pocket. He hated carrying the damn thing, but it was very necessary. It was an indispensable tool of the trade.

Gently he blew across the short distance between them, creating a genial breeze to flow across her bare breasts. He squirmed in the chair as her nipples hardened against his breath, tantalizing him be-yond his known boundaries. He could barely wait until he was able to suckle the buxom blonde as she begged him for her life. Her skin drew taught and became covered in gooseflesh as his breath blew across her naked form. He was engorged with blood and throbbing. His head swooned with sheer delight. He could wait no longer.

Standing, he moved closer to her, putting his nose directly be-tween her cleavage and breathed deeply of her scent; Lily of the Val-ley. He placed the scent. His eyes rolled back in his head as he rev-eled in the moment.

Lightly he brushed his lips against her, sticking his tongue out so only the tip traced across her skin. It was time for sleeping beauty to wake up. He reached into his back pocket and pulled out the large metal flashlight. He laid the flashlight on the bed and slowly, quietly took off his clothes.

Standing naked in front of her face he raised the flashlight high above his head. He took a few practice swings to get the perfect angle of attack. He didn't want to kill her, not yet anyway. Just a glancing blow to daze her. With the flashlight high above his head he reached out with the other hand and cupped her breast, certain this would awaken the fair maiden. He was already dangerously close to his first orgasm, having over-indulged in his fantasy. Her eyes opened just as his arm came crashing down.

Tim caught his arm in mid-swing and was able to angle the blow away so that it landed on Elsa's pillow next to her head. He would never know why he was there, nor would he know what had saved his wife's life.

"Jesus, Tim, are you trying to kill me!" Elsa screamed in the darkness.

Tim stood there, unable to answer, his chest constricting so tightly he thought he was having a heart attack.

"What are you doing?" She demanded, quickly standing to confront him.

"I, I don't know. I was up watching a movie and I fell asleep," he stammered while quickly fabricating an alibi which was shaky at best.

"When I woke up the lights were out, must have blown a breaker or something. I came up here to get this," he explained holding out the flashlight for her inspection. He fought desperately against his nausea, wanting to run away. He knew he had to face her then and now, or she would never trust him again. Nevertheless, he wondered if he could ever trust himself again.

"So, you tried to hit me with a flashlight while copping a feel?"

"No, nothing like that. I saw you sleeping there and you looked so beautiful I guess I got caught up in the moment. When I finally decided to go down the basement, I tripped over my pants and fell onto the bed. That's when you woke up," he prayed she was buying his story because he sure the hell wasn't but he needed away from there, and fast. He needed to go someplace and completely break down.

"You were going down the basement naked, Tim?" Her tone had lessened a little but she was still bitterly confused.

"I was going to crawl into bed with you first, to make up for earlier today. But then I thought better of it. I thought you might still be pissed at me. I love you so much, Elsa," he could no longer hold back the tears and his voice broke into small sobs.

"Oh, baby, come here," she reached out and pulled him to her. He was terrified of this closeness, but he needed her now more than he ever had in his life. Maybe he could confide in her. Maybe. He fell asleep in her arms, spent, and completely drained of emotion.

Elsa couldn't contain her own tears. While her husband slept, spent, in her arms, she wept. Suddenly her picture perfect life was no longer looking so bright.

CHAPTER FOUR

"Graham! Graham!" The guard's voice resounded against the concrete walls. He was unable to roust the sleeping convict by yelling.

"Here, let me try," Premoe commented, throwing a Styrofoam cup filled with lukewarm coffee through the bars. The lid flew off the cup when it landed on Cracker and the liquid saturated the slumbering inmate.

"You can't do that," the guard admonished.

"I just did."

"Take it easy, Blain," Freeman said, gently nudging the bear of a man.

"What the fuck!" Cracker screamed, bolting up from his cot. His mind was still foggy from the night's dream. He was still lost within the throes of his passion.

"Wake up call, compliments of the Jacksonville Police Department," Premoe commented, unable to contain the snide remark, which in turn drew a bruising jolt to the ribs from his partner.

"Who the fuck are you!" Cracker spewed out. He sat up in bed, quite aware of his throbbing organ concealed beneath his blanket.

"I'm hurt, Graham, you don't remember us?"

"Is that you, Premoe? Only you could smell that bad," he taunted from the darkness.

"Can we get his light on?" Freeman asked the guard.

"Yes, sir," he disappeared to a switch panel at the far end of the corridor, not wanting any part of the lawsuit that would surely be filed by lunchtime.

"We want to ask you a few questions," Premoe said as warmly as he could muster, which was still ice cold.

"You want some lessons?"

"Don't get cute, one asshole already riled him up today, another one might make him do something I'll regret," Freeman warned.

"Why should I care?"

"We think there's a copy cat working your MO."

"Let me say it again, why should I care?"

"We don't care if you show any concern, just answer some damn questions," the big man barked.

"Not without my lawyer, and a warrant."

"Fine, have it your way. Officer, I would like Mr. Graham down in the interrogation room in an hour. I want him deloused and I would like you to make certain he gets a full body cavity search. Never can trust a guy like this, if you know what I mean," Premoe solicited the guard who had returned from turning on the lights.

"Yes, sir, I can make it take longer than an hour if you'd like," the corrections officer replied, shooting a look at Cracker that actually made the stone faced convict cringe. He knew that the guards didn't like him, and hour alone with them might prove to be quite an uncomfortable experience.

"Okay, Premoe, I get your point. What do you want to know, but make it fast, I got a dream I want to get back to," Cracker's mind was working overtime, trying to find some way to turn this chain of events into something that would benefit him.

"Did you have an accomplice?" Freeman asked.

He paused, knowing the answer, but thinking he might want them to consider he might be lying, "no, sorry to disappoint you boys. I did it all on my own," he paused for effect, turned his eyes to the ceiling and then back to the detectives. "Or did I?"

"Why did you do it?"

"Because I felt like it."

"Who knew about you taking the left hands of the victims?"

"Everybody. The newspapers loved my story, remember?" He gloated.

"Yeah, I remember, but I also recall that we misinformed them about which hand was actually missing in every case," Premoe said smugly.

"So, who did you tell?" Freeman asked again, seeing the surprised look on the convict's face.

"I didn't tell anyone. I worked alone on every bitch! You think I'm the kind of guy who likes to share my women?"

"Why does this copy cat know to take only the left hands?"

"I couldn't tell you that, I don't know."

"And you never had an accomplice?" Premoe asked, a look of disbelief washing over his face. The longer he talked to this maniac the more he was starting to believe he and Freeman's new theory about these crimes be the work of a duet.

"I said no, didn't I," he made certain to look away from the detectives for two reasons. One, he wanted them to believe he was lying and two, he didn't want them to see how much he was enjoying them believing he was lying to them. This new development was definitely going to work to his advantage. He was definitely going to have to do some more reading once they left him alone. This was no longer a game. It had grown from something he merely used to occupy his time and get him a few cheap thrills into something far more consequential. This was going to buy him his freedom. He felt a sudden, albeit brief, tinge of pity for the poor bastard who was going to have to pay for his crimes. He almost broke out into laughter when he thought about Florida not getting to sing him his eternal lullaby.

"Listen here you little bastard, there's a copy cat out there that knows things only you would know now quit lying to us," Premoe started getting ugly.

"As I recall from my trial, there are a few more than just me that know all the gory details, including you two," he insinuated. "Besides, if you recall, during my trial I professed my innocence to the very end. I didn't do the things you two, and the state of Florida, have accused me of. Now, that's my story and I'm sticking to it. You two bungling idiots arrested and convicted the wrong man. Now, I am done with you two, you bore me," Cracker laid back down on his cot with his back to them. He snickered lightly to himself. He could almost see Premoe's face twisting into grotesque shapes and changing multiple shades of red while contemplating his options, one of which was to kill the scrawny bastard. Cracker hoped the large bull of a detective would come into his cell and try something. He would quickly find out that although Cracker was only five foot eight and weighed no more than a hundred and thirty pounds, not only was he deceptively strong, but he knew pressure points and techniques to put the big man down; forever.

"Come on, Blain, we're through with this clown anyway," Freeman tugged at his fuming partner's elbow.

"Why did you do it?" He blurted.

"Do what?" Cracker responded without looking up.

"Take the hands?" Cracker slipped into a moment of silent reverie.

I took their hands because it was the same dirty hand my mother always jacked off her clients with. And the same hand the bitch had the audacity to slap me with, cook my food with and even the occasional tender caress came from that very same fucking hand.

"I don't recall ever admitting to taking the hands. In fact, I do believe that I adamantly denied it, as well as any involvement with those poor girls' deaths," he let a smug grin smear across his face.

Premoe slammed his hands against the bars and hissed, "You're lucky, damned lucky."

"Why? You're are more than welcome to join me anytime, detective. I haven't had a good piece of tail in a long time," he sneered, rolling to one side and looking into Premoe's eyes. Something deep inside him wanted a confrontation with the big bastard, show him who the real man was. Slow bleed him all over his cell. Cracker smiled. If everything worked out, as it had a way of doing for him, he might just get a shot at the bear.

"Fuck you! I can't wait until 'Old Sparky' gets his turn at you, you miserable son of a bitch."

"You know, detective, that's the first thing you've said all day that I agree with, my mother truly is a bitch. But I hate to disappoint you, by the time my appeals and motions are exhausted, you'll be an old man. Much too old to get to watch me fry," he taunted further. He almost let it slip that he had some tricks up his sleeve, but thought better of it. Premoe might be an asshole, but he was a damned good detective and he wouldn't let anything get by him.

"Come on, Blain, he's not worth it."

"Let's go detectives," the guard directed them toward the exit door. The last thing he need was to be trapped up here on a Saturday night with Cracker in one of his moods.

"Hey, Rodgers, leave the light on will you please, I have some reading to do," Cracker called out as the steel door echoed shut. "And detectives, please answer me one question before you leave," he called after them.

They both spun around on their heels and turned their attention to the imprudent inmate.

"Have you found sand at any of the scenes? If I remember correctly, the killer left sand in the eyes of his victims."

Premoe and Freeman didn't respond, they knew the man had made a point. As they left the floor both men looked as though they had just guzzled a glassful of sour milk.

"I know mother, but he's been acting very strange lately," Elsa said, her face twisted with confusion.

"But you can't possibly think that Tim was trying to murder you," her mother replied, her voice wrought with consternation.

"What other explanation could there be?"

"I really think you're overreacting. You and Tim just need to get away for a little while. Why don't you two think about a vacation?"

Elsa sighed deeply and said. "Maybe you're right. Tim's been under a lot of stress lately, especially since losing those last two at the hospital."

"Of course he has, it can't be easy for a doctor to lose a patient and it must be horrible when the patient is just a child."

"I just don't know, mother, things don't feel quite right between us right now."

"Honey, just give him some time."

"I guess I owe him at least that much. Look, here he comes, I have to let you go. I love you," she said, hanging up the phone.

"Who was that?' Tim asked weakly.

"Mom, she was just checking up on us," Elsa smiled weakly.

Tim chuckled and asked, "Are you through with the phone?"

"Yes," she said, handing him the cordless handset.

Tim took the phone and disappeared into a different part of the house. Elsa didn't like the fact that he was being secretive. She knew there was something wrong with him, it showed in his eyes. They no longer sparkled like a curious child's the way she was used to seeing them. Tim's exuberance for life seemed to be slipping away from him. Elsa wondered if something had happened at work, something that was weighing heavily on his heart. Suddenly she felt herself getting angry with him. Never once in their marriage had her husband failed to share anything with her. And no matter how sinister this demon was, he had no right shutting her out.

"May I please speak with Dr. Hughes," Tim pleaded.

"I told you, sir, he's not in today," the answering service receptionist tried to explain pleasantly, yet firm enough for him to get the point.

"You don't understand, miss, I need to speak with him, right now. Is there any way for me to get in touch with him? His home number, a pager, cell phone, anything? It's a matter of life or death."

"Dr. Hughes left explicit instructions that he was not to be disturbed today, for any reason," she replied curtly yet polite.

"Please, at the very least can you page him and leave an urgent message that Timothy Duggan needs to talk with him," he was downright begging now.

"It's his daughter's wedding day, sir. He asked not to be disturbed and I intend to follow those instructions to the letter," the woman tried to remain as cordial as possible under the circumstances.

"Thanks for nothing," Tim rudely disconnected the call. He would apologize to her later. But for now, he needed to talk with Doctor Hughes. He needed those tests done, he needed some drugs, something to make the nightmares stop.

Tim left the secluded comfort of the den and walked out to the kitchen where he grabbed a phone book out of the drawer near the phone and began scanning through the residential section. He was cursing the fact that his doctor wasn't an immigrant with a distinctive name from Pakistan, India or some other far away place. Hughes, there had to be more than two hundred of them in the Jacksonville phone book.

Tim surely wasn't looking forward to his Sunday afternoon ritual of watching football with Rene'. Although he desperately needed his friend's company, he didn't think he could be in the same room with him for very long.

He smelled the faint scent of Lily of the Valley and knew Elsa had come into the room with him. Quickly he shut the phone book and slid it back into the drawer.

"What are you looking for, honey?" She cooed, bending to kiss his neck. He felt her warm skin against his and fought against the tremble building up deep inside of him. He could not go on with this charade very much longer. He was about to explode, spewing forth his deepest, darkest secrets. He was starting to think like a killer trying to hide his identity. Guilt raged through his veins.

"A new sports bar for Rene' and I to watch the Jags play. It's a blacked out game today and we're getting kind of tired of Harry's. The food sucks and the beer is warm," he lied, something he was getting very good at.

"But isn't Harry is your friend?"

"Yes, but warm beer is still warm beer, Elsa," he faked a smile. "What big plans do you have for the day?" He asked, grateful she hadn't even as much as mentioned the previous night's incident, although he could read the puzzlement still looming in her eyes. She still hadn't completely digested the whole affair.

"I thought mom and I could do some shopping, Christmas is just around the corner."

"Way around the corner, football season just started," he laughed and it felt good. It was a therapeutic laugh, genuine, and from the heart. Immediately pangs stung at him like the flames of a fire lapping against his skin. His deep love for his wife terrified him. He wanted to tell her to run, escape his menacing nightmares and his new persona. Again, he had to fight back the tears.

"Got any money?" Elsa played, sticking her hand out to him palm up.

"Sorry, tapped out this week."

"Okay, credit it is."

"I canceled the cards," he played along.

"I got new ones."

"I'll call and report them stolen."

"I'll seduce the store clerks and get what I want for free then," she smiled triumphantly at him. She knew she had scored a coup.

"Okay, okay you win. But hey, if you can save me some money by letting your mom seduce the store clerks, then by all means, feel free."

She scowled.

"Sorry, that was out of line."

"Yes it was, but maybe she does need to get laid. It's been five years since her and dad divorced and I don't think she's had a date since."

"Give her some time, I know if anything were to ever happen to us, I would never date again," he held back his tears.

"Awe, even though that's such a sweet thing to say, don't ever talk like that. Til death do us part, remember?"

"Yes, I remember."

"Good, don't you forget it either, mister," she scolded.

"I promise," he replied weakly.

"Well, mom's already on her way over, I better hop into the shower."

"And I had better call Rene' and let him know the change of plans," Tim said, still attempting to cover his tracks.

He reached for the phone, having no intention of calling his friend. They would just meet at Harry's as they had every Sunday afternoon for most of their lives. He hoped Rene' wouldn't be too prying this Sunday afternoon.

The crowded bar erupted into a frenzy of cheering as a Jacksonville defensive back ran an interception in for a score. Tim wanted to cheer more whole-heartedly, but the emotion just wasn't there. In the face of his monstrous predicament, football seemed so trivial. He reached across the table and clinked schooner glasses together with Rene' and cracked a shit-eating "we scored" smile for his friend's sake, but he really felt nothing. He was numb from the inside out.

The waitress sat two more schooners of Molson Ice on the table and collected a healthy tip from Rene'. Judging by his lecherous grin, she had earned ever penny. Tim chuckled, Rene' never could help himself around the cute, large-breasted waitresses in tight shirts. God forbid they ever take a trip to Hooters, Rene' would wind up behind bars. Harry's was overflowing with rabid Jag fans as usual. They were playing the Denver Broncos, a game every Jaguar fan looked forward to. The crowd erupted into a flurry of boos as the refs blew yet another call.

Although the Jacksonville Jaguars were a relatively new team they leapt into the NFL like gangbusters. The Broncos and the Jaguars had a history dating back to the 1996 playoffs when Jacksonville came from behind to defeat the Broncos. Ultimately the loss robbed the Broncos of a possible three-peat of super bowl victories. This created a heated rivalry between the two teams and their fans.

"So what's on your mind, pal?" Rene' commented, bringing Tim out of his trance.

"Nothing much, thinking about the game is all," Tim misrepresented himself once more. He could feel his mind starting to drift. He was starting to feel really tired, and suddenly very nervous.

"Have you heard from Dan?"

"Nothing. And I was really kind of hoping for something, anything."

"His office will probably call tomorrow."

"I'm sure they will."

Their attention turned back to the large screen TV with life-size images of the players running around on screen. The quarterback was dropping back into the pocket, eventually letting loose a long fly pattern pass that fell incomplete to the disapproval of the bar crowd. Several of them were screaming for a yellow flag to be thrown, but it was obvious even before the replay that the receiver simply dropped the ball. After the replay another round of disparaging remarks echoed throughout the bar, this time most of them were directed at the receiver and his hefty salary, a salary the fans felt was unearned at the moment. The waitress made eye contact on her latest pass by, Rene' ordered another round, complete with shots of tequila.

The alcohol was already starting to affect Tim's judgment and he had to wonder just how dangerously close he was playing it. He knew he should have shunned drinking, at least until he had seen this ordeal through. A warm feeling spread throughout his consciousness and suddenly he didn't care about much of anything, except for the football game. The raw brutality of the sport began to work on Tim's primal instincts. The bone crushing blocks, the barbaric tackling and the masticating taunts set him on the edge of his seat. It was as if he were experiencing football for the first time. His muscles tensed and flexed as he mimicked the movements of the players on the screen.

"Here you go, gentlemen. Seven dollars, please," the comely brunette said, sliding her tray of drinks down onto the table and setting their Molson's in front of them.

43

"Thanks, sweetie," Rene' flirted, slipping her a ten. "Keep the change."

"Hey, keep your hands to yourself," she turned and swept Tim's hand away from her butt and walked angrily away from the table.

"I'm sorry," he jolted back to reality.

"I didn't know you had it in you, buddy," Rene' laughed, wishing deep inside he had guts enough to grab her enticing behind.

"It must be the alcohol," Tim tried desperately to dismiss the fiasco.

"Yeah, the alcohol and her prime rump."

"Damn it, Rene', I mean it, it was the alcohol and nothing more," he got up and stormed to the restroom, avoiding the icy stare of the violated waitress.

Tim stayed in the bathroom for ten minutes, splashing water on his face. He felt terribly guilty about spouting off at Rene' and even more guilty for grabbing the waitress. And worse yet, he couldn't even recall consciously reaching for her "prime rump." By the time he figured out what was wrong with him, Tim would be alone in the world, having alienated his family and friends. Tears streaming down his face, Tim slipped out the back door of the bar. He would make up an excuse to tell Rene' later, but for now he needed the serenity of being alone.

———————

Cracker had forgotten how much fun football was to watch. The raw savagery of it fed the monster living within him. He would have to make certain he visited Harry's the following Sunday as well, with his host of course.

Cracker was getting much better with his transference into the other's mind. He could see things much more clearly. He even thought he could taste the beer as it flowed, cold, down his host's throat. And that waitress, he wanted to do her right there in the bar. If he didn't already have bigger plans, he would have. She would have paid for her insolence with her hand. His seething anger began to rage deep within his soul. He needed another release soon. It was almost time to prowl through the other's eyes. But for now, he had some more reading to do. Cracker allowed his anger to subside before opening his sacred tome. Reverently, he traced his fingers around the raised lettering.

The volume was covered with a thick leather binding and the title had been stamped into the hide. The letters seemed to jump from the cover, springing to life whenever he touched it. The pages were a thick parchment that appeared to have seen a multitude of years pass by on this earth and possibly another. Cracker embraced the inanimate object as if it were a product of his loins. He had truly developed an undying affection for the book.

CHAPTER FIVE

"Number four, doctor," the trauma nurse yelled after Tim as he crashed through a set of double doors and dashed down the polished tile corridor. A rainbow of striped colors reflected off the highly polished tile. Yellow branched off toward radiology. Green led the entire length of the building down to the Outpatient Care Facility. At one time it was the mental ward of the hospital, but now during lean years and emergence of health maintenance organizations, inpatient mental care was almost a thing of the past. There wasn't enough money for anyone to be able to enjoy the luxury of insanity anymore. Tim's eyes focused on the next branch of tape. The red lined corridor led straight to the Trauma Care Unit. He hated Monday's.

Tim's Monday morning had commenced with an explosion of cataclysmic episodes. He had slept late so he was late leaving the house and on the way to the hospital he was forced to wait while a police officer issued him a ticket which led to even more delays. And now, the minute he walked through the door he was informed that there was a child in the trauma unit who required his immediate attention.

"What have we got?" He asked, bursting through the doors of the trauma unit into a world of controlled chaos.

"Auto accident. Two year old girl. Deep laceration on her upper arm. Mild abrasions to her forehead. Possible concussion," the trauma nurse rattled off robotically.

Tim's eyes began growing heavy from the assault of the stark fluorescent lighting. They felt like there were buckets of sand poured into his eyelids. Desperately he searched for an excuse to escape that room, to escape the familiar feeling beginning to wash over him. He felt himself slipping into a zone he was quickly learning to despise. A zone where he no longer had any control over his own life.

Pure enjoyment coursed through Cracker's veins at the sight of fresh blood. It wasn't as satisfying as when he was the one doing the bloodletting, but the sheer intensity of the child's pain gave him inexplicable pleasures. Cracker struggled to get a grip on the doctor's mind. He was fighting the intrusion, but the madman was winning the battle.

The injured toddler cried.

He held a deep sense of respect for the little child, squirming and struggling for its life beneath his tightening grasp. He felt the power of playing God coursing through his every fiber. Gently wrenching the damaged appendage, he applied just enough pressure to cause the toddler intense pain, yet not enough to alert the nurses as to the cause of the toddler's discomfort. Second by precious second he increased his grip while keeping everyone occupied with the head trauma. No one in the emergency room noticed the whitening of the baby's arm under his grasp, in fact, the more the poor child struggled the more they helped the monster to hold her down. Cracker quickly relinquished his control over the man, spilling Tim back into the real world. It was time to start setting the stage for his great escape and the best way to do that was to make the doctor look as bad as possible.

Tim's head was foggy and he wasn't quite sure of what was going on. He quickly babbled some medical mumbo jumbo at them to cover himself while trying to regain his grip on reality. He didn't want to be squeezing this child's arm; but yet, he seemed to relish every moment of the toddler's pain. Tim's mind struggled for control. He felt a wave of euphoric bliss rush over him.

"Doctor," the nurse said, hoping to get his attention away from whatever it was he was thinking about.

Squeezing ever harder he started to wish he could get his hands up around the throat of the screaming little demon. He needed the release that only a death could bring.

"Doctor," she barked louder once she realized he wasn't paying attention to her, or anything else in the room for that matter.

Tim fought with his inner self, he knew what he was doing was terribly wrong, yet he gladly continued.

"Doctor," the nurse started crossing the room toward him.

Quit fighting me, let me in doctor, let me take total control of you. Give me your mind doctor, it is inevitable.

Tim squeezed the child even harder yet.

"Doctor!" The nurse jerked his hand free from the baby's arm. "She's out, she's not struggling anymore, you can let her go now," the nurse gave him such a look that guilt surged through him like thick sludge.

The guilt ate at him so badly that he became nauseated. Tim

quickly excused himself with a glance and bolted from the room.

Confusion reigned over all emotion. Had he really been hurting that child, or just dreaming it? Suddenly, Tim had a desperate fear of going insane. He was losing his mind. He swore he had heard voices in his head. He staggered through the stark white hallways to the doctor's lounge. There he retreated into an empty bathroom, locking the door behind himself. He went into a stall and sank to the floor next to the commode, put his head between his knees and cried.

———————

Cracker had now come to the realization that his host, his benefactor, was a doctor. The vivid images of the emergency room raced through his ever alert mind. It was pure adrenaline. The screaming. The pain. The chaos. The blood!

"I've got you, now, doc!" Cracker said aloud, beaming from ear to ear. It was the widest, purest smile he had been able to muster for more than five years. Suddenly, his six by nine foot cell didn't seem so claustrophobic. Normally, Cracker despised the intrusive sunlight that glared into the row from the windows across from the cell block. It wasn't the brightness of the light, nor the warmth, but the nagging fact that he had no control over whether he was going to see it or not. The guards controlled the sunlight, and in essence, what remained of his paltry life. But not any longer, the magical phenomena of the book had given him back his life.

He had truly begun to master the use of the book. He could come and go as he pleased and do anything he wanted to anyone. He didn't know why it only worked this well with the doctor, but at this point he didn't care. Now, a part of him desperately yearned to get even with True for his pompous attitude. He wanted to make the old bastard pay for not liking him.

Cracker caressed his blessed book. He traced his fingers across the raised lettering on the cover as if her were teasing an expectant lover. Opening the book, he raised the parchment pages to his nose and breathed deeply, partaking in the very essence of the magic held within its pages.

Not even the slightest trace of remorse entered his mind when he decided that ultimately the doctor was going to have to trade places with him. It was time to set the wheels of this machine in motion. He smiled smugly.

"Hey, Benedict," he called to the guard on the floor.

"What do you want, Cracker?"

"I need to use the phone."

"It's too late for that today. You know that kind of request has to go through the warden's office at least twenty-four hours in advance."

"Can't blame a guy for trying. Can you please put the request in for me for tomorrow then?" He talked sugary sweet to the guard who only nodded his affirmation of the request.

Cracker knew he was going to have to keep his fiery emotions in check until he could manipulate things to his advantage. He was going to have to be pleasant to some people whom he deeply resented, but they were essential pawns in his game. He was going to need all the resources he could muster to pull this one off even if it meant kissing some ass.

Tim felt the chill of the bathroom tile seeping through his every pore. He stood up and tried to straighten himself up. He washed his face in the sink, hoping to wipe away the haggard look. It didn't help much. His eyes were growing darker and more sullen with each passing episode. Tim shuddered at the reflection staring back at him. It wasn't his own. Those weren't his eyes. Even the color of his irises were fading. They were no longer the vibrant blue he had carried with him for most of his life. No, these were no longer the lady killers that had won Elsa's heart. These were cold, steely eyes that seemed to calculate his every move.

He wandered down the lonely corridor to the elevator. Once inside the car he pressed the button for the upper floor, the administration floor, and tried to maintain the contents of his stomach as the elevator car bolted upward. Tim's life was slipping rapidly out of control. His sanity was caught in the elliptical grip of a whirlpool, spinning and twisting him until he could no longer see things from a level headed perspective. Everything was warped. In one week's time everything he had considered normal about his life had ceased to exist.

Apprehensive, he stood in front of the large wooden door. He stared at a golden name plate with the words, Emelina Rivera, Chief Administrator carved into its glimmering face. He wasn't sure if this was going to be the right move for him, but it certainly would be the right one for his patients. He was relieved that Emmy maintained an open door policy, at least this way he didn't have to go through her receptionist where eventually word of this meeting would become the latest gossip in every nurse's station throughout the hospital. He knocked, lightly at first, then harder when she didn't reply the first time.

"Come in," her voice chimed from inside the office.

Emmy was an extremely attractive woman and sometimes Tim found himself uneasy being alone around her. He knew that this was going to be one of those times.

"Good morning, Emmy," he averted his eyes from her dark brown stare, not wanting her to be able to see his guilt.

"Well, what do I owe this pleasure to, Tim?" She commented, pointing to a chair for him to sit in. Her thick red lips pulled gently back as she offered Tim her best smile.

Her long brown hair perfectly framed her cherubic face. Her haunting brown eyes stared back at him compassionately, like little dollops of chocolate, letting him know that she was truly interested in what he had to say.

"I need to talk to you about something."

"You sound pretty serious," she sympathized. She turned in her chair to get more comfortable, unaware of what her silky, bare legs were doing to the entity living within Tim's eyes.

"It is pretty serious," he responded, trying to fabricate a good story on the fly while ignoring her long, sleek legs dangling from her chair.

He knew the story was going to have to hold enough truth to it so that Emmy wouldn't be able to see through his deceit. They had known each other for a long time and had worked very close during their tenure at the hospital, eventually becoming good friends as well. Tim knew that he would never get away with deceiving Emmy very long.

"What's going on, Tim?" She folded her hands on top of her desk and gave him her undivided attention. Her fingernails were the same crimson color as her lipstick. Tim flinched at an image of thick, oozing blood worming its way into his thoughts.

"I need to take a leave of absence, right away," he said with a shaky voice.

"Why, is there something wrong between you and Elsa?" Emelina asked, truly concerned.

She had become as good a friend to Elsa as she was to Tim over the years. She began to stroke her long brown hair instinctively, a habit that Tim had always found enjoyable. It showed a youthful side to her. But this morning it wasn't striking him as a playful habit, it was alluring and enticing.

"No, nothing like that at all. I'm having a medical problem right now and I don't think I should be placing my patients in any jeopardy. At least not until I can get a proper diagnosis and find a treatment for it," he tried to explain. For a moment he wondered if he could trust her enough to explain his problem in detail with her.

Hey Doc, you ever hit that fine stuff?

"What's wrong? Nothing serious I hope," Emmy voiced her concern.

She was noticing something was a bit peculiar about Tim's demeanor, but she couldn't quite put a finger on what it was that was different. She sighed and her breasts heaved enticingly. They weren't large breasts, the kind a man notices from blocks away, but they were more than ample. Her petite waistline made them appear much larger than they actually were. And the clothes that Emmy wore seemed to accentuate all of her positives.

Tim fought desperately to stave off the illicit thoughts prancing around in his head. He couldn't understand why he was suddenly becoming so aroused by his boss's appearance. But everything about her seemed to be working on his manhood.

"I think I am suffering from narcolepsy. It is pretty serious right now, I haven't slept well for weeks. I am waiting for a clinic to schedule me for some tests to find out exactly what is wrong with me. They gave me some literature to read over and it looks like it is treatable. But until then, It's that I just don't feel like I can benefit my patients like this."

"Narcolepsy? Are you sure of this, Tim?" She asked, her face contorted into disbelief.

"No, I'm not certain. I will know more about my condition after I have had these tests run and we see the results."

"I have to admit that this comes as quite a shock. I wish there was another way, Tim. I really can't afford to lose you right now," she said, twisting a strand of hair around her index finger.

Tim felt himself beginning to swell. "Can you afford a lawsuit?" Tim said, starting to panic.

He knew he needed to end this conversation before he lost all control. He wanted nothing more than to be out of there, fast. He wasn't sure what was going on or what he was capable of, but he was not liking the odds.

Quit fighting it Doc, you know she would be good.

"I guess you're right," she smiled weakly and reached her free hand across the desk and affectionately covered Tim's.

He smiled back at her weakly and tried to concentrate on anything except her tender caress and libidinous presence. He was certain she was going to notice his growing interest in her if not his lecherous stares.

"No, I don't suppose that would do us any good. What if I was to arrange something for you up here, in administration, just for the time being? I'd like to keep your knowledge and expertise around here, even if I can't have you on the front lines," She said.

He wanted to draw his hand back away from her, but he didn't want to offend her. Her warmth licked at his skin like flames from hell. He felt his desire growing with her radiance.

"That might be an option once I've had these tests done and find out exactly what it is I am up against."

"Good, then that settles it. You take the rest of the week off, do whatever it is you need to do and call me on Friday to set up some kind of work schedule. I am not going to lose you without a fight, Tim," she looked at him with those eyes and immediately he felt himself stirring.

"Okay, you win," he chuckled lightly.

Tim gave up without a fight, he knew better than to argue with her once she had made up her mind. Besides, he felt he was extremely close to losing control of himself and then where would they be. Would he wake up with Emmy's blood all over him? Tim quickly rose to his feet and strode to the door, he was trying to give himself one last chance to work up the courage to confide in his longtime friend.

"Friday, don't forget," Emmy reminded sternly.

"I know, Friday. I am going to leave right from here and drive down to St. Augustine where the clinic is," he announced optimistically.

"Let's just hope they can help you as quickly as possible. Good luck, Tim. And don't forget," She said.

Come on, Doc, let's give her a whirl. A test drive so to speak. Just look at the way she looks at you, she wants you bad.

"I know, Friday," Tim responded, cutting her off and stepping nervously out into the hallway.

The elevator ride down wasn't nearly as traumatic as it had been coming up. The voice in his head seemed to relinquish its grip on him once they were out of the administrator's office. Tim was grateful that Emmy didn't try to pry too much out of him. Yet, part of him was saddened by the fact he wasn't able to talk this problem out.

Tim lost himself in the rolling scenery as he drove down highway A1A toward St. Augustine. He watched the waves gently lapping the coastline out of his left window. St. Augustine's claim to fame was that it was the oldest city in the United States. Ponce De Leon had landed there in fifteen thirteen during his infamous quest for the fountain of youth. According to the history books, Ponce saw the coast of Florida for the first time on Easter Sunday. Ironically, retiree's now flock to the country's southernmost peninsula, maybe Ponce had found what he was looking for after all.

St. Augustine had been a French, as well as a Spanish, stronghold during the golden age of pirates. Many of the stone forts and embattlements still dot the historic coast. Tim and Elsa ventured down to St. Augustine quite regularly. It wasn't very far from Jacksonville, but located far enough away to retain its small town flair.

Many shipwrecks lie in the waters off St. Augustine. Tim reminisced about the times he and Elsa had gone scuba diving to look for long lost treasures. Most of the shipwrecks had been picked clean by bandits and thieves over the years, the main culprits being the numerous preservation societies and the federal government itself. But the possibilities of treasures still existed, making the dives quite exhilarating. His thoughts of Elsa bettered his mood. He loved her more than life itself. He would see this thing through, if only because of her.

A billboard for Ripley's Believe It Or Not museum came into view. Tim wondered if he should take a detour and go sell them his story for millions of dollars.

Tim pulled into a parking spot in front of the modest clinic which looked more like a residence than a doctor's office. The drive had been enlivening to say the least. His mood seemed to brighten once he pulled into the clinic's parking lot. He casually walked up the walkway to the front door. His mind was an endless jumble of unanswered questions, the biggest of which was whether or not this doctor was going to be able to put an end to his nightmares.

"Hello, I'm Tim Duggan, is Dr. Hughes in?"

"Yes he is, he has been trying to get in touch with you. Have a seat, I will let him know that you are here," the receptionist replied.

From her cold tone, Tim quickly ascertained that she must have been the receptionist that he had berated on the telephone. He sat down in the lobby and closed his eyes in exasperation.

CHAPTER SIX

"What do you make of that conversation we had with Graham?" Freeman asked, already knowing his partner's answer.

"He's guilty as hell and we all know it, including him," Premoe rubbed his hand across his square jaw. He felt the stubble and realized that he couldn't remember when the last time he shaved was. It couldn't have been more than three or four days, but definitely more than a couple. He had only worn a beard once in his lifetime and it itched him so badly that he had shaved it off within the week. Premoe entertained the thought of making it a personal resolution not to shave until this case was resolved. He could never begin to imagine the pain the victims or their families had endured, but as long as the killer was still loose on the streets, he didn't feel he had the right to be comfortable.

"He did make some valid points, what if this isn't a copy cat?"

"Are you saying that you believe this maniac?"

"No, not entirely. But I don't want to rule out the possibility that we put the wrong guy in jail and the killer is still walking the streets," Freeman responded.

He took a hard look at Premoe and wondered if he looked as badly as his partner did. This case was wearing on the both them and it was just beginning from the looks of it. He couldn't help but notice how sad Premoe's eyes had become. He recalled when they had first met and he looked into those big brown orbs for the first time and likened the man to a big overgrown puppy. He seemed playful and full of life, but that was a lot of years and a lot of corpses ago.

"We didn't do anything, a jury put him away just like he deserves. He's a psychopath and you know it."

"You are such a cynic. Just entertain me for a minute. I mean, some of the things he says are hard to overlook. Why would a copy cat have waited over five years to become active again?"

"I won't know the answer to that one until we catch him. But what does make sense is that the killings stopped immediately after putting Graham behind bars."

"I'll give you that one, Blain. But why have the killings started up again now? And we know that Graham isn't committing these murders, he's on death row."

"I still like the accomplice theory. An accomplice would have waited out the heat."

"But would someone insane enough to commit these murders be able to go this long without killing anyone else? Not to mention the fact that there are too many similarities, things we never let the press in on, for this to be a mere coincidence or a copy cat."

"Maybe he didn't kill here. Maybe he moved out of state for a while. The bottom line is that we caught Graham red handed. You were there, don't you remember?"

"Yes, I remember, but I am having a hard time discounting his accusations that we got the wrong man. Remember, we have run Graham's MO through NCIC more times than I care to remember and we have never had a hit since he has been in prison. I just want to be damned sure about this one, Blain."

"Okay, if he isn't the true killer, then explain to me why he was covered in that young girl's blood? And let's not forget the overwhelming amount of DNA evidence at the scene. Including his semen," he argued while shooting a fiery stare into his partner's deep blue eyes.

Eyes that had always seemed so calculating and analytical, even on the day when they were partnered up together nine years earlier. Premoe had sized him up from the moment they had been introduced to one another in the captain's office. He had been a junior detective for a couple of years and was ready to move on. When Freeman lost his partner to cancer Premoe moved up to fill the gap. It was a little rough for the both of them at first, Freeman had resented the intrusion and made things a lot harder on Premoe than they had to be. But eventually the big man wore down Freeman's wall and the marriage was complete. The fact that Premoe lived by his gut and Freeman by the evidence is what made them such good partners, .

"I've been going over Graham's testimony. He claimed that he was so drunk that he passed out. He claimed to have been at the bar, and even admitted that he might have picked the woman up there and brought her home. But he has no real recollection of the events of the night. He only admitted that when he woke up he was in her bedroom covered in her blood, and that is when we walked in on him."

"I remember his testimony word for word, but it was all bullshit. We didn't just happen to find him, we were tracking him, hunting him, and for damned good reason I might add," Premoe grunted.

"The toxicology report backed up his statements," he said, looking up from the court transcript and raising an eyebrow.

He knew Premoe hated it when he did that, it made the big man start thinking on his own, rather than go with his initial reaction. And the one thing that Blain had learned to trust more than anything else was his gut instincts.

"There were sixteen girls, remember? We had plenty of reasons to suspect Graham. Damn it, Todd, what would you like to do, tell the judge to set him free and we'll start investigating the whole damn thing over again," he finally lost his temper.

Premoe's massive neck swelled like a buck during the rutting season and several thick veins pulsated at the skin's surface.

"There's no need to get all pissed off, Blain, I am just trying to point out that there are other circumstances we need to be looking at. I don't think we should count out the fact that Graham may not have been lying," he tried not to laugh.

It wasn't so much that he enjoyed irritating his partner, but he wanted him to learn to think things through, as well as react. Something he had failed to teach him so far in their seven years together. Sometimes Freeman wondered if he might be creating a monster.

"Truthfully, what do you think, Todd?" He asked, letting his temper abate enough so that he could look at things a little more rationally.

He knew that his partner was baiting him, and he also knew that he should probably analyze things a little more closely, but his instincts had yet to fail him and it was a hard habit to break. Besides, he wasn't about to give the man the satisfaction of knowing he had won the battle.

"Honestly? I think he's guilty as hell myself. I just don't want to make any mistakes that might get someone else killed. I think we need to get our ducks in a row, and quick. If I can see the holes in this case, you can bet your ass a judge certainly will."

"I see your point. Where do we go from here?"

"I think we need to start asking a lot of questions. We need to find a link between Graham and someone he was very familiar with during that period. All the evidence points to the fact he is a loner, but there had to be some people that knew him better than we think. Time to start rereading all these case files," he commented, sliding a box of file folders to Premoe.

"I'm starting to get a headache," he grunted and pulled a handful of files out of the box.

Cracker shuffled down the long corridor. The shackles on his legs allowed him just enough room to take baby steps and the sounds they made as they rattled against the tile floor were more than nerve wracking. Nevertheless, he sported a grin that let the world know that he had them by the balls. The only souls present were himself and the two gargantuan guards escorting him to a room to meet with his attorney.

Although the shackles were digging into his ankles, Cracker shuffled along at the fastest pace he could muster. It felt good to be able to use his muscles. Except for the pacing in his cell and the hour a day he was allowed to go out into the exercise square, this was the most he had been able to use his legs in a long time. Besides, he was excited about the bombshell he was about to drop on his attorney.

Cracker hated the man, absolutely despised him. He was a scrawny, chicken shit of a human being who wasn't smart enough to spell IQ let alone have one of any significance. Cracker wasn't certain who his lawyer had been scared of the most, his own client or the prosecuting attorney. He may never have been sent to death row had his attorney shown any backbone during the course of the trial. He had never once objected to any line of questioning the prosecutor threw at them, nor did he visit with Cracker as much as he felt he should have. Cracker felt that the little weasel could have helped him come up with one hell of a story, instead, he just sat quietly listening to the accusations the prosecution made. Nevertheless, he was the only attorney Graham could afford; free. American justice at its best.

Cracker peered through the wire mesh in the small one-foot square window in the door. Patterson was already fidgeting. His greasy black hair was combed to the side in a failing effort to hide a growing bald spot. Sitting in a plastic chair normally intended for use for someone's backyard barbecue, he inspected his fingers, nervously awaiting the arrival of his psychotic client. Cracker felt the best thing about court appointed attorneys was that they had to serve the defendant, no matter what. Cracker knew the man would love to just wash his hands of the entire affair, but he couldn't. And Patterson was fully aware of the fact that Cracker knew that Patterson couldn't just walk away. As long as he continued to appeal his case, Patterson was locked into the deal. Cracker experienced a certain perverse enjoyment knowing that his own attorney wanted to see him dead.

"Mr. Graham," Simon Patterson coolly acknowledged his client, pushing his black rimmed glasses back up on his nose.

"You look tired, Mr. Patterson," he taunted.

"I am tired, Mr. Graham. My office gave me the message that you have some information about your appeal," he remained cold.

Simon Patterson wanted nothing to do with the man sitting across from him, but he was scared. Scared of losing his job. Scared of ruining his reputation, and more importantly, scared to death of the inmate himself.

"Yes, I do. While you have been on the outside, working so diligently on my behalf, I got a lucky break," he began sarcastically.

"I have more than one client, Mr. Graham."

"I know how hard you work, Mr. Patterson, please, don't take that as an insult. I watched your diligent efforts all throughout my trial," he sneered.

"Can you get to the point, please, I have another meeting in an hour on the other side of town," he looked into the man's eyes for the first time that meeting and saw what he had always seen in the man.

Graham's eyes seemed to be able to peer right through to his soul, learning even his innermost secrets. Patterson had been threatened by clients before, it was nothing new and it was nothing catastrophic. Normally he didn't believe them, nor did he ever let them get to him. They were behind bars what the hell could they do to him? And this client had threatened him before too, during the trial, but Simon had believed him. It was written in his eyes. Patterson was certain that Graham would, and could do anything he set his mind to.

"Please, contain your enthusiasm," Cracker changed his tone of voice and expression to one of pure contempt.

He deliberately slowed his speech and stared deeply into the counselor's eyes in an effort to intimidate him. Cracker was pleased to see that his browbeating was working.

Simon Patterson began putting file folders back into his briefcase and rose to his feet, "I'm not going to play your sick games with you, if you have something to tell me, then by all means tell me. But I am not going to sit here and listen to you berate me or threaten me in any way. You do not intimidate or frighten me, Mr. Graham," he said, fighting with his nerves to keep his hands from shaking.

"Please, sit down, Mr. Patterson, I am very sorry. Prison has a way of making a prick out of a person."

As I recall, you were always pretty much of a prick!

"What is this great revelation you would like to share with me?" He asked, sitting back down and trying to contain his trembling to his insides.

"Do you read the papers?" Graham asked, rapidly leaning forward and slamming his hands down onto the stainless steel table in front of him.

He found it almost impossible to contain his grin at the sight of Patterson leaping out of his skin. He humorously wondered if the man would need to change his shorts before meeting with his next client.

"I try to find the time, but no, not very often," he replied, trying to ignore the inmate's intimidation tactics.

"Have you read about the latest string of murders they believe to be the work of a deranged serial killer?"

"I have caught some information briefly over the evening news, and my car radio, stuff like that. But I have to admit, I don't know very much about the case. How is this relevant to your case?"

"Didn't it strike you as odd that the killer is using my alleged MO?"

"What do you mean? I wasn't aware of this," he said, perking up in the face of a challenge.

"The bodies of the victims. So far the bodies have all been missing their left hands. And they have all had sand in their eyes," he gloated.

"And what do the police think?"

"They came here questioning me about an accomplice theory they had. I told them that because of my appeals I didn't want to talk about the old cases. But they kept pressing the issue and when I tried to lawyer up they threatened me with brutality if I didn't cooperate," he softened his tone to illicit some sympathy from his attorney.

Cracker could read the man like a book. Cracker knew that Patterson was an extreme liberal and was certain that any mention of police wrong doing or brutality would set the man's stomach on fire.

"That's very interesting. You specifically told them you didn't want to answer question without talking to your attorney first?"

"Yes, sir. And they threatened to delouse me and violate my person, if you get my meaning," he glanced behind him to indicate that his anal virginity had been threatened.

Cracker was playing the victim to the hilt, something he truly despised, but it was totally necessary. He knew he was going to have to be playing the sycophantic role of the poor misunderstood victim for a while.

"Do you know who they were?" Patterson began to fume. If there was one thing he hated worse than defending guilty clients, it was overzealous cops. Maybe this Graham character was right, maybe he hadn't worked hard enough during the trial. It was quite possible he had counted this guy out before he should have.

"Yes, sir. It was Detective Freeman and the big dumb one, Premoe."

"And they threatened you?"

"Yes, sir. The big ugly one even threw a cup of coffee on me while I was sleeping. They know that I am innocent, they just don't want to admit their mistake."

"I don't want you to get too worked up over this new development. Just because there is someone committing murders you may have been accused of, there is still the hurdle of the DNA evidence at the scene. It's is going to be hard to get a judge to overlook that, and even harder yet to get it past a jury. Do you know how many more murders have been committed?"

"I think three or four so far," he knew exactly how many.

A quick recall of events brought a familiar stirring to life. He shifted in his chair for comfort's sake.

"That maybe just enough to at least push for a retrial. It may sound morbid, but the best thing that can happen for you is that this killer continues his indiscretions until he finally gets caught. That will be the ultimate coup, if he gets caught committing murders you were accused of," Patterson had become quite animated as he lost himself in thought.

Cracker just smiled back at his lawyer. He wanted to tell him that there was nothing to worry about. He would make certain there were more murders. But just how many would be enough.

"Let me get out of here and get to my other meeting. As soon as I am back to my office I will start making a few phone calls. And don't you worry about any more late night visits from these detectives. I will have a conversation with my boss, who will have a nice long talk with the Chief of Detectives, who in turn will have a conversation with his people. I will be contacting you as soon as I have something new to pass along," Simon Patterson said.

He felt revitalized. It was as if suddenly his life had a purpose, that he truly could make a difference. He was ready to fight for the first time in a very long time.

"Thank you, Mr. Patterson, I look forward to hearing from you again," Cracker tried to remain as cordial as possible.

He had the schmuck eating up his every word, no use spoiling that over a few snide comments. Still, help or no help, Patterson was on the top of his shit list, right along with Freeman, Premoe and True. The pieces of the puzzle began formulating themselves in his brain. Cracker knew that within a few days he would be able to work out all of the details and concoct a precise plan of attack. Pay back time was coming soon.

———

"Good morning, Mr. Duggan, please come in and have a seat," Dr. Hughes greeted.

"Let me start by apologizing for being so short with everyone on the phone, but I am going through hell."

"I understand completely. It's a nerve wracking condition to have to deal with. Did you have a chance to read through the literature I sent home with you?" He asked.

Tim found himself to be at ease around the man. His eyes seemed to exude compassion. The thick lenses in his glasses made his eyes look larger than they actually were, like the wide eyes of a curious child. And although they were approximately the same age, Tim felt himself looking at the man as a fatherly figure. He was as big as a grizzly, yet he was very soft spoken and seemed to wear a perpetual smile.

"Yes, but I'm not sure how much of it I retained, my mind has been a million miles away," he smiled.

"Have you steered clear of caffeine today?"

"Yes, but it was tough, especially with the morning I've been having," Tim chuckled.

"I will be explaining this test to you as we go along. You do understand that you'll be here for most of the day don't you?" He asked, putting his large hand on Tim's shoulder and guiding him into the room where the testing would take place.

"From what I gathered, yes. Whatever it takes, doctor."

"Then let's get started. Take off your shirt for me please."

Tim did as he was instructed and sat quietly while the doctor and his assistant placed electrical leads at various points on his body. A few circular patched had to be shaved on his chest which bothered him a little, but he knew eventually it would grow back. Although, it would earn him more than a few strange glances at the gym, if he ever got back to the gym again.

"Okay, you can put your shirt back on and find a magazine or book to read, unless you brought something of your own with you."

"No, these will be fine," Tim commented, scanning over the spines of periodicals and books lined neatly on a solid oak bookshelf.

Once he was alone, Tim began to inspect the room he was in. It was small, but not so much so as to feel confining. The wood paneling on the walls was a deep walnut color which allowed the subtle mood lighting in the room to be more effective. In opposite diagonal corners were two potted plants. Real ones, not fakes like one would find in most doctor's offices. A thick-leafed, quite healthy looking rubber tree sat in one corner while a fern with full, wide fronds occupied the other. Their deep green coloring was soothing to the eye.

Tim smiled, half expecting a man in a pointed helmet and German uniform to part the fronds and comment about how interesting Tim's day was becoming. In the center of the room was a large, very comfortable looking recliner. Its black leather covering seemed to lend a perfect accent to the room. Almost instantly, Tim felt at ease.

Tim spent the first few minutes of his visit admiring the bookshelf. It was solid white oak with gold trim accents along the shelf edges. Ornate designs adorned either side of the bookshelf , highlighted with even more gold accents. The bookshelf stood on pedestal legs, lavishly carved into the likeness of atlas holding up the bookshelf. His muscles rippled in the beautiful wood grain. Tim made a mental note to ask Dr. Hughes where he had acquired such a fantastic piece of furniture. Hopefully it was something he could purchase for his home. Elsa would absolutely love it.

Tim pulled out a copy of Popular Mechanics and sat down in the chair which he immediately found to be remarkably comfortable. He spent another five minutes admiring this piece of furniture, although it wasn't ornately decorated, it was the most comfortable chair he had ever had the pleasure of sitting in. It seemed to envelop him as he fell into it.

"Mr. Duggan, there is a control panel under the arm of that chair if you'd like to recline, vibrate or a number of other functions," an assistant's voice rang out from a hidden speaker in the room.

In his earlier observation of the room he had failed to notice the video camera deftly concealed in a planter filled with blue lobelia hanging in a corner. The chromed blue camera lens was barely detectable intermingled with the delicate flowers. Tim smiled for the camera and turned his attention to the arm of the chair. With a slight amount of investigative skills he was able to find a semi-hidden latch that when opened reveled the chair's hidden secrets. He touched the button controlling the soft-vibrate function. Immediately the chair sprung to life. Tiny rollers began to caress his back and thighs. For a moment, Tim thought he might never leave this place. He adjusted the chair's temperature to a balmy seventy eight degrees and sank further into the depths of nirvana. For the final touch, Tim turned up the volume button and waited to be caressed by sound. Speakers in the back, arms and seat of the chair began echoing forth sounds of a tidal pool lapping gently against a rocky shoreline. Ever so often a distant gull would make its presence known. Tim felt as through he were traipsing through the Elysian fields themselves. He was more relaxed than he had been in a very long time.

And then the fear set in. The fear of falling asleep. The inescapable dread of his neoteric dream world. The lights began to dim slowly as the sweet scent of ambergris filled the room. Tim felt his final waking thought slip away from him. His world went dark. And for the half an hour he lay sleeping, it remained dark. There were no dreams to haunt his sleep.

Suddenly the room was illuminated with a wash of soft lights. Tim's eyes bolted open. He was exactly where he last remembered being. There were no vivid images of naked, dead women. There was no recollection of disparaging screams. And most importantly, there was no blood.

A sigh of relief rushed past his lips as he took his first waking breath. Maybe they were really only bad dreams. He smiled groggily for the camera. He had to admit to himself, that even if for only a short time, the nap was quite refreshing.

"Okay, Mr. Duggan. You'll be awake now until lunch time and then we will monitor another nap."

"How did I do?"

"This isn't a pass or fail test, Mr. Duggan," the voice replied, obviously unaware of the playful tone interlaced within Tim's question.

Tim smiled for the camera once more and returned to reading his magazine. After an hour and a half of magazines, Tim was starting to get quite bored with the testing process. And then he remembered the alternative and gladly returned from the bookshelf with another magazine. Sports Illustrated this time.

Lunch time came and another sleep sequence was behind him without incident. He was beginning to worry about what kind of results the doctor might be getting from the tests. He didn't think he could stand the disappointment of an inconclusive test. And he certainly didn't want to leave the clinic, only to dream a malicious dream that evening when he was at home.

The anxiety built up in Tim until he couldn't stand much more. He continued to glance down at his watch, hoping the day would just get over with. He was angry with the doctor for not sharing any information with him between sleep periods. He should have told him something; anything. The lights began to dim once more and Tim felt his anger slowly ebbing away. The more he thought about it, the more ridiculous he knew his thinking was. Doctor Hughes would tell him everything when the testing process was completed.

The sounds coming from the chair had changed from that of the ocean to a peaceful song of nocturnal creatures. An owl's eternal question pealed through the darkness, followed by the gentle howl of a lupine conversationalist. Tim gently swayed to the pseudo moonlight concerto. Once more he slipped into the total darkness of

MATTHEW F. WINN

his dreams.

Alertly, his eyes darted open. This place the host had taken him was unfamiliar. The sounds were annoyingly mellifluous. He wanted nothing more than immediate escape. He craved the outside world, not another prison. He conducted a quick surveillance of the room, spying a door in the corner. He went for his freedom.

"Doctor Hughes," the lab assistant called into an intercom.

"What is it?"

"I think you better come here and watch this."

Dan Hughes left the comfortable confines of his office and walked down the hallway to the observation room. His first glance through the window set him on edge a little. Images of Tim Duggan's recounted dreams flashed through his mind. He felt a sliver of fear rush through him.

"Mr. Duggan," he called into the room's intercom.

There was no response.

"Is the door locked?" He asked the technician.

"Yes, doctor, it is secured with the magna-lock. There's no way he can get it open."

"Well, then I guess we just sit back and observe. Make sure the video tape is rolling, I want to catch everything that he does in that room."

Cracker tried the door, but found it securely locked. He felt something very uncomfortable under his shirt. Running his hands under the doctor's shirt, he located the monitoring leads and ripped them loose from his borrowed anatomy.

"That did it for data collection. Make certain the camera is catching all of this, we won't have anything else."

"Yes, doctor," the technician replied, checking an array of knobs and buttons on a control panel.

He stood in the center of the room. They, whoever they were, had stolen his freedom. His anger seethed. How dare they intrude upon his sacred kingdom. He tried to deduce where he was from his surroundings.

"Where have you taken me, doc?" Cracker's fury was rapidly gaining in intensity.

As he spun slowly in circles trying to absorb every nuance of the room, he spied the camera in the hanging planter. He grabbed the chair and shoved it across the room until it was directly beneath the planter. He then climbed up and ripped the wires loose from the back of the monitoring device.

"Let's see how they like that!" He barked, flinging the remnants of the camera to the carpeting.

Sounds of chaos echoed from the sleep chamber. He tore the bookshelf from the wall and threw all its contents about the room. His anger was out of control. They would pay. Suddenly he smiled, a brilliant thought played in his head. This episode would play right into his hands. It was time to show just how crazy this host was.

"Let me the fuck out of here!" He screamed, not knowing whether or not anyone could hear him.

"What do we do now, doctor?" The technician asked.

"I don't really know, I've never come across this problem. I guess we can try to get him under control by sedating him."

"Did you hear me? I said I want out of here, now. Open the fucking door!" He found it hard not to laugh.

"You had better call security and get them down to the test chamber as soon as possible."

"Yes, Dr. Hughes," the technician answered, turning to the phone immediately, his face a ghostly pale. He had never seen anything like this before in all his years at the clinic.

Two security officers met Dan Hughes in the reception area of the clinic. The doctor stopped long enough to prepare an injection of Thorazine he hoped would do the trick. The doctor and his modest security team walked down the carpeted hallway to the testing room. There the three of them stood apprehensively outside the door, trying to gather their nerve before confronting the crazed patient.

"I'm going to kill the first son of a bitch who tries to lay a hand on me," Cracker yelled from inside the room.

He had seen their shadows cross the threshold in front of the door. It was only a brief alteration in the lighting, but enough to alert him to their presence. He was a predator after all, he was quite tuned to observing his prey.

He would fight them, but not too valiantly, just enough to get his point across. He had too many plans for his host, he didn't need the man getting hurt now.

The two security guards stood at either side of the door and waited diligently as Dr. Hughes swiped his access card through a card reader attached to the magna-lock door. A resounding click split the nervous silence.

Nothing happened.

Unexpectedly the door burst open, catching the two guards off balance. The guard to his left turned his back toward the opening door out of reflex. Cracker pounced on the guard and sank his teeth into the nape of the man's neck. His veins flooded with adrenaline. He was ecstatic from the thrill of the battle. The guard thrashed around wildly on the floor, trying to dislodge him from his neck. He waited for the tell-tale prick of the hypodermic needle before relaxing his grasp on the hapless guard. He felt himself drifting back to his world, leaving Timothy Duggan to face a completely foreign world all on his own.

CHAPTER SEVEN

"Premoe," he spoke into the phone as he lifted it from the cradle.

The detective and his partner had been putting in a lot of overtime and they were both damn near exhausted. Freeman looked up from his paperwork, preparing to eavesdrop on the conversation if it were appropriate.

"Blain, Charlie here. I've got some disturbing news for you."

"Nothing too bad I hope. I don't think I can take any more bad news."

"It's interesting, let's just put it that way. But I don't think you're going to like it," the forensic expert stated.

"Just give it to me straight, I'm a big boy," Premoe snorted.

"I've got the results of the DNA testing back this morning from the first two homicides and it doesn't look good. I compared the results with the evidence we collected from Graham's case files like you asked. I hate to tell you this. Even though they are not an exact match, they are similar enough to be able to easily raise doubts in a jury's mind if there is a retrial. I've already put a rush on the rest of the evidence we've sent to the lab."

"You've got to be shitting me. So there may be some truth to Graham's story?"

"I'm not saying there is any truth to it, but what I am saying is that this killer is someone with a DNA pattern frighteningly similar to his."

"Meaning what?" Premoe asked, gaining Freeman's undivided attention at this point.

"Meaning, that if Graham is really innocent and there is another killer, then whoever they are they are more than likely related to Graham in some way or another. And the fact that Graham was convicted on evidence that will now be in question is going to mean that all of the evidence will be scrutinized a lot more closely."

"What if there were two killers? Graham and someone else."

"That is always a possibility as well, but they would still be related to one another. Listen, Blain, I am not saying that Graham is innocent, nor am I saying we made a mistake with the DNA evidence in the first place. The odds against this sort of thing are astronomical. However, I am saying that with this latest wrinkle in the DNA evidence, any two-bit attorney will be able to raise reasonable doubt in a jury's mind, let alone a trial judge's," Charlie explained.

"Damn, this is definitely not what I wanted to hear this morning. Thanks, Charlie. Keep me posted would you please?"

"Not a problem, Blain, wish I had better news."

"Thanks, again, Charlie," he said, hanging up the phone. "Let's go, Todd," he said, grabbing the case files and heading for the door with Freeman in tow.

"What's up, Blain?"

"We've got problems."

"What is it?"

"To make a long story short, there's a glitch in the DNA evidence."

"What?"

"The DNA evidence from Graham's murders matches the DNA found on the latest victims. It's not an exact match, but according to Charlie, close enough to raise more than a few doubts."

"Don't tell me that," Freeman's face twisted into an ugly scowl.

The duo walked briskly down the corridor to the Chief of Detectives office. Neither of them relished having to share this new information with their boss. There were several possibilities for this DNA evidence match, however, not a one of them would be good news.

"Frank, we need to talk," Premoe commented, knocking and opening the door at the same time.

"I'm busy Premoe. What is it?" Frank Walker inquired.

He had been the Chief of Detectives for nearly five years, earning his promotion from his impeccable work on the Sandman case. He had been the lead detective in that case, with Freeman and Premoe offering their invaluable assistance. Frank, Blain and Todd had become quite close during the grueling investigation. He held a soft, warm spot in his heart for the both of them. That would soon change.

"I've got some really bad news to pass along."

"Can you make it quick? I've got a briefing for a press conference about these murders in less than an hour. Damn, I hate the press," he shook his head, and I've got a feeling you're going to make me hate them more.

"It's about the case, sir," Premoe offered, showing every bit of respect he felt the man deserved.

"Christ, what now?" He slammed a legal pad full of notes onto his desk top. He glared at the detectives with his dark eyes.

"Thought you'd feel that way," he started. "I just got a call from Charlie. We didn't bother you with our conversation yesterday with Rueben Graham. It was a little disturbing, but nothing we felt we needed to talk to you about," he explained, making sure he included Freeman in the picture.

"Go on," Frank sighed and brushed his hand over his short cropped hair.

The tight dark curls were sprinkled with a modest amount of gray which heightened the man's distinguished appearance. He had been on the job nearly thirty years and had all the worry lines to prove it. And he was getting damned sick and tired of surprises.

"We went out to Starke to question Graham with our copy cat theory. We were hoping the arrogant bastard might give us something we could use. When we asked him if he had worked with an accomplice, he just smugly maintained his innocence in the entire affair. He still claims he was just in the wrong place at the wrong time," Premoe illustrated.

"Get to the point, please, Blain."

"Just thought you might like some background."

"I don't have time for that," Frank replied, digging through desk drawer for a stray Rolaids.

"Like I said, we just got a call from Charlie, he says that the DNA evidence in these recent murder cases is very similar to the evidence collected in the Graham case. He says that this wrinkle doesn't completely exonerate Graham, but it does raise enough doubt that he will more than likely be granted a retrial."

"Damn it! I didn't need to hear this right now. And that sounds like a hell of a lot more than a wrinkle. What are your theories?" Frank's face distorted into a scowl as he turned to face Detective Freeman.

"We don't really have any yet, we just got wind of this. But Charlie says there are two distinct possibilities and I tend to agree with him."

"Let me hear them."

"First, Graham is truly innocent and the real killer, who is probably related to Graham in some way, just laid low until the heat cooled. Secondly, that Graham had an accomplice who was related to him and is now killing all by himself now that Graham is in prison."

"I don't like either of them. They both suggest that we screwed up this investigation in the first place," Frank observed.

"There is a third possibility," Freeman interjected.

"Yes?" Frank asked.

"That this copy cat killer could quite possibly be a distant relative of Graham's and this is all just one big coincidence. I truly believe that Graham was the killer five years ago and that he was rightfully convicted. However, I also believe that this new killer is only a copy cat, nothing more. But I also fear whoever it is, has some inside information, this person seems to know way too much about the first investigation to be a coincidence. There are things being done that were never leaked to the press."

"I don't like your theories either, Todd, you make it sound as though Graham is somehow communicating with the killer from death row," Frank said.

"Although that is highly unlikely, I think we had better keep all of our options open right now."

"I didn't say you weren't right, I just said I don't like it. I don't like any of this," Frank commented.

"Sorry about the bad news, but I thought you'd like to know," Premoe said.

"Thanks, Blain, and you too Todd. Sorry if I sound like a prick, but now I have got to come up with something else to feed to the sharks."

"Maybe we can come up with something to get us out of hot water," Premoe offered, meandering toward the door with Freeman right behind him. "I need a damn cigarette," he looked over his shoulder at his scowling partner.

———————

"How did you like that book?" True asked the inmate.

"It was pretty interesting, got any more?" Carl Lettimore asked.

"I think I've got one here on the cart, there are a few more making their way around the block, I'll get them for you as soon as I can," True explained.

He felt a lot of compassion for the men condemned to death row. In fact, so much so that years earlier he had approached the warden with the idea of his being allowed up on the tier to deliver books to those who had been condemned to die. He had convinced the man that it would be good public relations. True had convinced him that it would prove invaluable in his quest to help quiet the anti-death penalty squalor that cropped up before every execution.

And granted, in all essence of the word, True himself had been sentenced to die in this hole as well, but at least he didn't have the black cloud of "Old Sparky" hanging over his head. Over the years he had made enough jailhouse friends to protect him from the few enemies he'd had the misfortune of making, so getting shanked wasn't too much of a concern, ensuring him that he would live to a ripe old age within the confines of Starke. He had tried to keep pretty much to himself and treat everyone with the same respect as he felt he deserved to be treated with. So far, that philosophy had kept him alive and celibate. Now, as for Cracker, that man was just pure evil. There was no respect due him, other than the respect one gives out of fear. True didn't have much longer to have to worry about him. He had heard they were warming "Old Sparky" up for the lunatic.

"True," he sang out the convict's name. "We need to talk."

"In a minute, Cracker. In a minute," he finished under his breath.

"Why don't you just tell the warden the man harasses you? You know he would take care of it," Lettimore questioned.

"Just not like that, Carl. I like to handle my own problems my own self. Besides, the way McIntyre handles things, he would probably just refuse to let me come up here anymore."

"I hear you, True. But damn, that man's got a screw loose or two."

"More than one."

"True, remember what I told you," Cracker's voice mocked.

A cold chill ran through him. The last time he felt that kind of chill was when he realized he had accidentally killed a man during a robbery getaway. True hadn't meant the man any harm, he had just simply run across the street at the wrong time. He hadn't seen the man, he was too busy looking behind him as he sped through the streets. True never forgot the look on the man's wife and child's faces. And when he had looked into those cold, gray eyes and realized that the man's soul was gone, he felt a chill, like God had given up on him. It was this very same chill he got whenever he was around Cracker.

True's lawyer had saved his life by convincing him to plea bargain and save himself a trip to the chair. True knew better now. He probably wouldn't have done more than twenty years if his lawyer would have played it right. But even True himself felt he deserved to be locked away for what he had done. There was no repaying that man's family for the damage he caused. So True suffered out his years in prison, hoping to at least get back into God's good graces in the end.

"True, written any notes to the warden lately?" Cracker's voice was loud and threatening.

"You better get down there, True. And remember what I told

you about the warden, he would see things were right," Lettimore said as True reluctantly turned to his cart load of books.

"You just stay out of this, Carl, don't want me in your head do you?" Cracker taunted.

Lettimore chose to remain quiet, no sense getting the man all pissed off, at least not until True was gone, then maybe he'd mess the crazy man's mind. He knew that was a lie, he didn't need the man chewing in his ear until dying time. Carl Lettimore knew that it was just best to leave things alone.

"Morning, Cracker," True greeted inhospitably.

"You better be nice to me, True, I'll be getting out of here soon. I'll remember you if you treat me nice, but I'll remember you even more if you keep shitting on me. I might get into your head again, make you teach the warden a lesson. Or maybe I'll just do it the old fashioned way, put some money in some con's account to shiv you and leave you bleeding in the shower. That's if I feel nice, if I don't feel nice, I might pay to have you made into someone's prize bitch."

"Fuck you, Cracker," he had finally had enough of the man's bullshit.

"Fuck me? Oh no, fuck you, True. I already don't like you, don't make me want to get even with you," he threatened.

"Listen here you little Mary, how are you going to fuck with me, huh?" He spat. "You are on your way to see 'Old Sparky' soon. You planning' on paying me a visit from the grave?"

"I told you, I'm getting out of here. There ain't gonna be no trip to the chair scheduled for this boy any longer."

"What are you talking about, you crazy bastard," True retorted, finally at the point where he no longer cared whether or not he offended Cracker.

"I found my angle. You just wait, you'll see. But first I'm going to make your life a living hell," he intimidated.

"You can't touch me and you know it. Try to get into my head, you haven't been able to have you? The other night was just luck. You put things into my head and made me dream, but no more. You can't get in here unless I let you, and I ain't letting you," True said, thumping his forehead with a thick, crooked finger.

"I haven't even tried getting into your head, True, I've been busy with someone else's."

"Like I said, fuck you, you do whatever it is you think you have to do. I am going to have a talk with the warden and get you off my back one way or the other."

"Are you threatening me, True?"

"What does it sound like to you?

"It sounds like I have to teach you lesson."

"Goodbye, Cracker, give 'Old Sparky' my regards," he grinned his best shit-eater and walked toward the door.

True left the floor with a warm glow, even though Cracker continued to hurl obscenities at him long after he had left the man's cell. He wished he had enough courage left to stare the man in his eyes and watched his hatred eat him up alive. But he had used all his courage up confronting the man. True prayed that getting into his head thing was all just a fluke. Something deep within him told him this battle was not over yet. Cracker wasn't one to give up. He made a note to throw away all his paper and pencils as soon as he got back to his cell. He would have to do without them for a while, at least until the crazy convict cooled down. There was no sense tempting fate.

———————

"So what happened, Dan?"

"I don't really know, Rene'. The test was going fine. If anything it was proving him not to be narcoleptic. He would fall asleep, but there were no REM patterns to detect, meaning he wasn't out very deep. Just a normal, every day nap."

"So you had to sedate him?"

"On the last leg of the test he just went berserk. We were able to collect some data before he ripped the leads off, but not very much. We did get enough to tell me that he is suffering from something well beyond my scope of knowledge. Quite frankly, I think it's more along your lines of expertise," Dr. Hughes explained.

"What are you saying?"

"It was like he was a completely different person. This wasn't the same man who calmly went to sleep. No, this was a crazy man. I'm thinking there might be more than one of him living inside that head of his."

Rene' paused to ponder the possibility before speaking. "MPD? But I would have noticed the signs long ago. He's my best friend for Christ's sake."

"He wasn't in REM sleep, Rene'. He was wide awake. He wasn't hallucinating. He saw us, he knew we were real. Like I said, he was a completely different person. So to answer your question, yes, I think it he is suffering from Multiple Personality Disorder. There is always the possibility that these episodes are fugue states, but his personality seemed to change. It wasn't like the same person going mad and not realizing it, it was like Duggan turned into a completely different person. It was as if this second entity knew exactly what he was doing. You're the expert in this field, I'm not," Dr. Hughes explained.

"Thanks, Dan, sorry if I, we, caused you any problems."

"Christ, Rene', he chewed up one of my security people. Duggan damn near killed the poor man," he explained, shaking his head in confusion. "He seemed so normal."

"He is normal, Dan."

"No, what I witnessed was not a normal human being. He was an animal. Here, see it for yourself," Dr. Hughes said, handing Rene' a copy of the video surveillance tape.

"Where is he?"

"Room 414. It's locked, so you'll have to get with security and the head resident on staff for that floor."

"Thanks again for meeting me here, Dan."

Dan Hughes turned his back and walked away with only a gesture of dismissal with his hand. He was glad to be getting rid of this patient and getting back to his customarily quiet practice.

Rene' spent the next hour and a half wading through the hospital red tape of getting in to see his best friend. He wished that Doctor Hughes would have let him handle things himself rather than admitting Tim to the psychiatric ward. After getting the run around for half an hour, he finally used his credentials to get past the hard-nosed charge nurse, introducing himself as Tim's doctor instead of his friend.

Before going to see Tim, Rene' secured the use of a video player and television in the doctor's lounge. Once he was alone, he locked the door and popped the cassette into the player. He was flattened by the episode he witnessed. He couldn't believe how Tim was acting. The person on the tape may have looked and sounded like his best friend, but Rene' still found it nearly impossible to accept the fact that it was Tim. The sheer barbarism and brutality of his acts shocked Rene'. He had been worried about Tim's unique condition before, but now, after viewing the tape he was petrified.

Rene' called Elsa at home, but there was no answer. He waited as long as he felt that he could, but then decided that it was best to get the reunion started without her.

"How are you feeling, buddy?" Rene's voice blared in his throbbing head.

"Okay, I think. Where am I?" Tim said, shielding his eyes from an onslaught of bright lights.

"You're in St. Luke's."

"What? Why am I in the hospital?" He tried sitting up, but was restrained. He struggled for a few seconds, but quickly deemed it useless and opted to save his energy.

"Take it easy, Tim, you've had a rough day," Rene' tried to calm his friend.

"What is going on, Rene'? The last thing I remember is falling asleep at the clinic," He explained.

He felt a need to rub his jaws, the muscles hurt terribly. He had a vague familiarity with the strange taste permeating his mouth.

"You don't remember anything?"

"No, nothing. How did I get here?"

"Dan tells me that you went berserk and fought with him and the security guards. He claims you tore up his office and attacked them when they tried to calm you down. They sedated you and had you brought over here. He called me at the office and I rushed right over. You're certain you don't remember a thing about the struggle, not even a dream?"

"No, I wish I could give you my side of the story, but I am blank right now. What in the hell is going on with me, Rene'?"

"Maybe the sedatives clouded your recollection," Rene' commented, more to himself than to Tim. He was trying to fit the pieces of his friend's shattered life back together.

Tim started to tremble and tears flowed from his eyes.

"Take it easy, Tim. We'll get to the bottom of this, I promise."

"What if there is no bottom? What if I really snapped and there's no bringing my sanity back?"

"Quit talking like that. Let me get back to my office and do a little research," he said, not wanting to unleash Dan's theory of multiple personalities on his shaken friend just yet.

"Elsa?"

"I tried to call her but no one was home."

"I don't want her to find out about this," Tim pleaded.

"What is she going to think when you don't come home?"

"Get me out of here and then we don't have to cross that bridge."

"I'm not sure I can do that, Tim."

"Pull some strings, whatever it takes. I'll go nuts in here," he laughed nervously at the irony.

"I'll see what I can do, but don't hold your breath," Rene' explained.

"Thank you," Tim sighed, and laid his head back onto his pillow. The combination of drugs and his anxiety were mixing together into a nighty-night cocktail too strong to fight. Within moments he was out like a light.

Rene' glanced back at his slumbering friend. Sadness welled

up so deeply inside him he thought he would choke. He wasn't sure what was going on in Tim's mind, but he did know he had to pull out every stop to get his friend back home where he belonged, even if it wasn't the smartest thing for him to do.

CHAPTER EIGHT

T he only visible light in the cell block was that of a single overhead fluorescent light hanging from chains near the door of the block . The only purpose for the light was to give the guards a little glow to play cards by. Cracker flattened and smoothed out an old piece of tin foil and used it to catch a glare from the dim lighting and direct it onto the book's pages.

"Knock, knock, True, let me in," he whispered through the darkness.

He wasn't sure what he was going to do to the man. But he had a festering, insatiable desire to hurt the insufferable bastard before his lawyer freed him from his hell hole. He wanted the old man to squirm and suffer, and he wanted to be able to enjoy it firsthand. Cracker knew it wasn't going to be easy, True's mind was harder than a steel trap to get in to, and even harder to stay there. The invasion also gave him a monstrous headache when he was finished as well. He wasn't looking forward to that migraine, but it would be well worth if he could make the man pay for his insolence.

He started reading the incantations from the book, allowing his mind to drift in time and space. The foreign words relaxed him as they rolled off his tongue. Before he knew it he was wandering through an ethereal plane of existence, wandering right for True's mind.

"Your honor, you just can't do that right now," the District Attorney, Ben Cooper, pleaded.

"Not only can I do that right now, I am going to do it right now. I've made my decision and that's final," the judge replied, trying to ignore the smirking Simon Patterson on the other side of the district attorney.

The judge spurned this ruling, and hated having to make it, but he also wanted to win his bid for re-election. The death penalty issue was a very volatile one and he wanted no part of anything even remotely scandalous.

Patterson hated the up and coming district attorney with a passion. He was a pretty boy from a rich blood line who never had to work at anything a day in his life, not manually anyway. His ambitions far exceeded his skills and he only succeeded in politics because of his looks, money and his family's power. Simon Patterson was truly enjoying putting the screws to him.

"On what grounds?" The district attorney blurted.

"Are you questioning my judgment? My authority?" The judge half rose out of his seat doubling the amount of room he occupied in the chambers. He was a large man, a very intimidating man, and a man who was accustomed to getting his own way.

"Sir, it is an election year for me as well. I need something to tell my constituents just like you do yours," Ben Cooper shrunk back into a defensive posture when he realized that this judge was not going to even as much as crinkle on the issue. "Fight the wars you know you can win," his father's words echoed in his head.

"Keep quiet, Patterson," the judge ordered, stopping the man with his mouth half open. "Listen, Ben, I have gone over this case file thoroughly and I truly believe that without the DNA evidence against Mr. Graham he would have never been convicted. Everything else in the case was circumstantial, based upon the DNA evidence. His story of being in a drunken stupor holds water if it wasn't his DNA at the scene."

"No one ever said his DNA wasn't at the scene," Ben argued.

"Okay, I'll concede on that issue, however, there may have been other DNA evidence on scene that was overlooked because the police believed they already had their man and ignored this other, suspect DNA. None of it may hold water once we get it back into court and you may get another concrete conviction at that time, but that is for a jury to decide. But as for now, I have to release Rueben Graham pending a retrial. It wouldn't be that hard of a decision if someone weren't murdering young girls across the city. And yes, I do want to be re-elected so all of this does have a bearing."

"Please, reconsider before making your decision. At least give us a chance to investigate this further."

"I am giving you a chance, but it will be without Rueben Graham on death row. I'm sorry, Ben, but in light of everything, I have to grant a retrial."

"Isn't there anything we can do to make sure Mr. Graham doesn't flee?"

"I don't want any kind of surveillance that would infringe upon his rights," the judge answered for the sake of the man's attorney, who was preparing to object to his client's supervision even before it was an issue.

"Okay, what about the tether program? He will only be monitored passively, meaning the tether will only alert us if it is tampered with or if he leaves a certain predetermined radius around his home."

"Patterson?" The judge looked his way.

Stammering, surprised that he was even being asked for his opinion he said. "No objections. Just as long as there is no active surveillance on my client. Also, I would also like it stated for the record that my client feels that Detectives Premoe and Freeman have been harassing him. I don't believe they should be allowed contact with him once he is released."

"I'll look into it, Patterson. Okay, then it is done. Mr. Graham will be released just as soon as the paperwork gets pushed through. Mr. Patterson, accompany him down to the police department in Jacksonville so that he may be fitted with the tether immediately upon his release. Furthermore, advise your client that if he is even late for as much as one court proceeding, I will have him held without bail for the duration of this fiasco. Do you understand?" The judge ordered.

"Yes, sir."

"Make sure your client understands this as well. You both know the way out," the judge made it painfully clear the discussion was over and all further points were mute.

His head throbbed with a vicious headache. Secretly he prayed that Rueben Graham truly was innocent, because in his heart he knew that if the man were truly the killer he thought he was, he would most assuredly kill again, and the voters would, without a doubt, remember who put a killer back on the streets. And if for some chance the voters did forget, the press would certainly remind them come election time.

His eyes were blurry from sleep and not yet being accustomed to the blanketing darkness. Sitting on the edge of his bunk for a few minutes, he tried to get his bearings straight. The shadows were dancing seductively on the walls, something he never got to see up on the row.

He had only been in True's mind for a few moments, but he already felt the man struggling against his intrusion. His head was already starting to throb from an oncoming migraine. He knew he had to be quick.

Quietly he leaned over the sleeping cell mate. He raised his arm and took deliberate aim. There was no time to be able to enjoy this kill, he just had to be thorough. His brain started to ache terribly. He could feel True grappling with his mind, trying to oust this intruder. The cell mate stirred, waking ever so slightly, but enough to make out the shadow standing above him. Quickly, Cracker changed his plans and staggered toward the toilet. He heard the man roll over and go back to sleep as he tried to force urine out of a empty bladder into a stainless steel commode. The odor of stale urine teased his nose, a sensation he found both odd and pleasing at the same time. Experiencing someone else's senses was something he hadn't really concentrated on yet. The throbbing in his brain grew worse and he could feel his grip on the man starting to loosen.

Fervently he began digging through the True's meager belongings. He opened a well worn cookie canister and found the treasure he was after. The shiv to cut True's heart out with.

He pawed quickly through a bundle letters, looking for that all important one. He had overheard True mention his granddaughter to Lettimore once or twice up on the row. That would be his key to hurting True. He ripped open the envelopes, scanning the first few lines of each letter until he found what he was looking for.

"Grampa, I hope you are doing fine. I wish you'd let us try and help you more. Nathan and I are doing much better financially now that we are both out of college and working steady." Blah, blah, blah, he continued reading. "I've got some great news, you're going to be a great grampa." He read a few more lines that ended with "I love you, Grampa." He had found what he was looking for.

Cracker's eyes were ready to burst and his head throbbed terribly. True was fighting vehemently against the intrusion. He knew he only had a few moments left before he was evicted from the man's subconscious. He scanned the envelope quickly and memorized the address.

"I'm going to pay your little baby a visit, True," he was able to echo into the man's mind before he was kicked out of his playroom.

"What's the matter, True?" His cell mate questioned.

"The bastard got to me, he got to me good," the old man sobbed, the canister of letters strewn about the cell floor.

"Who are you talking about? Are you just having a bad dream?"

"I wish I was. That son of a bitch, Cracker, he got into my head just like I said he would."

"That's crazy talk, True."

"My little Regina, she going to die, and it's all my fault," he

80

curled up into the fetal position on his cot and sobbed uncontrollably until fatigue forced him to sleep.

True's cell mate shed a silent tear for the man he had grown to love over the years. He also shed a tear for Regina.

CHAPTER NINE

"Ben Cooper is not too happy with you guys right now," Frank chewed lightly on Premoe and Freeman. "Understandably so."

"As you might know, this is an election year, and something like this won't go over too well with the voters. Half of them want to abolish the death penalty for just this very reason. And the other half want murderers killed immediately so they never get the chance to be back on the streets again. This kind of incident has a tendency of riling up both sides."

"We understand," Freeman continued to placate his boss, knowing the man just needed a few minutes to vent.

Premoe simply did the smartest thing he could by keeping his mouth shut.

"When the press gets wind of this they will have a field day."

"We know."

"Cooper is pissed as hell at us. He can't understand how we could make a mistake like this. I tried to explain to him that we might not have even made a mistake at all. But he didn't want to hear a word I had to say. He just kept saying fix it. Fix it! What in the hell is that supposed to mean?" Frank paced the room as he ranted.

A thick bead of sweat formed on his upper lip. With a quick swipe of his hand he wiped it from his mouth.

"I'm sure he is pissed."

"Would you knock that off, unless you really want to piss me off?"

Premoe jabbed Freeman in the ribs with an "I told you so" look smeared across his face. Freeman just smiled weakly back at him. He hated losing bets to the big, dumb jock, but it was all in fun.

"Are you two girls finished?" Frank fumed, realizing they were just patronizing him for the sake of their own amusement.

"Yes, sir, sorry, sir," Premoe couldn't help himself.

"Would you like to wait outside?" He pointed toward the door to his office.

"Easy Frank, we're only joking around," Freeman intervened.

"Joking around? We might very well have a maniac on the loose and have sent the wrong man to death row, or a serial killer might be on the streets again and now we have two of them out there to contend with. And you two sorry asses want to joke around. Can you even begin to imagine what the press is going to have to say about all of this? Well I sure as hell do," he ranted without giving either of them the opportunity to respond.

"Okay, we get your point, we're just under a lot of pressure right now."

"And I'm not? How many calls have you gotten from the DA's office. From the Mayor's office? And I am almost positive you won't be getting that call from the Governor's office that I expect sometime this afternoon. I should have never told that prick Cooper about any of this until we had more answers. I should have remembered he's a politician all the way. Give me some good news, damn it," Frank quit spouting and turned his attention back to his subordinates.

"I wish we could, Chief, but we haven't gotten anything new yet."

"And to be quite honest, we don't even know where to start," Premoe added.

"I don't care where you start, just get started."

They both stared back at him wordlessly.

"Listen, I know you guys don't have any evidence to work with, but there has got to be something.

"The best we can hope for right now is that this guy slips up. We need him to give us some kind of lead. I wish we could tell you that we have a few suspects, but the only suspect we have is behind bars."

"I don't expect miracles from you guys, but please, try to get me something that will keep the press and the suits off my ass."

"Should we approach this as if Graham is really innocent?" Premoe asked.

"It would probably give us the best results if you were to conduct your investigation from the beginning, as if Graham had never even been caught and convicted in the first place. Treat this as an fresh homicide case and see if that gets us any where."

"We understand. Sorry about all the bad publicity," Freeman commented.

"Hey, I had a hand in this thing too. I just pray we didn't screw up," Frank responded.

"Me too. But if there is one thing I am sure of, it's that Graham is a killer."

"I'm sure he is too, Blain," Frank agreed, "We just have to prove it, again."

The telephone rang, tearing Frank away from their conversation. Freeman and Premoe quickly left Frank alone to deal with the press and the brass, they wanted no part of that circus. Out in the hall, they just looked at each other. Both men knew they were in an impossible situation. They were caught between what was truly right and what lawyers perceived to be right.

"How are you feeling today?"

"I'm doing better, Rene'. Thanks a million for getting me out of there," Tim said.

"It wasn't easy. You'll have to be on your best behavior," he laughed, trying to ease the tension. Rene' sensed Tim was still very troubled by the latest events of his maelstrom laden life.

"I need to see that security guard and tell him I'm sorry."

"That wouldn't be a very good idea," Rene' said.

Tim noticed the sullen, distant expression on his friend's face and almost broke into tears. He was afraid he was alienating Rene' and driving him away.

"I know, but I feel so guilty. How could I have done that Rene'?"

His friend responded silently by putting an arm around his shoulder and pulling him close to his chest. Rene' felt Tim's tears seeping through his shirt and onto his chest. He felt like crying himself, but knew that would only upset Tim further. He was frustrated that he didn't have any answers, a situation he had rarely found himself in.

A light rain fell from the gray sky. The outside world looked and felt just like Tim's inside world. Gray, gloomy and lifeless. He stared into the sky, watching the raindrops falling erratically through the atmosphere. They were careening throughout their existence, just as Tim was tumbling through his. Thunderheads rolled ominously in the distance, warning the denizens of earth that a torrent was soon to come. Tim hoped it wouldn't hold the same for his internal strife.

"You've got to help me, Rene'," he blurted.

"I'll do the best I can," he paused. "But I don't think it would be a good idea for me to be your therapist. I'm just too close to you to be objective."

"I don't think I could open up to anyone else."

"You might have to, Tim. This is starting to get really serious. I want to apologize to you now for ever doubting you, that was very wrong of me. I think I would have taken things a bit more serious had you not been such a good friend. That is why I don't think I can be unbiased enough for your needs."

"You think there is something very seriously wrong with me, don't you?"

"I think the possibility is very high, yes," he replied quickly, not giving himself the opportunity to lie to Tim.

"What do you think could be wrong? Is it narcolepsy?"

"After talking with Dan Hughes while you were in the hospital, I found that your tests were very inconclusive. But he doesn't feel that you are suffering from narcolepsy."

Tim stared at Rene' for several minutes, trying to read the beleaguered expression on his confidant's face. It was sometimes hard to take the man seriously while looking into his vibrant green eyes which were highlighted by his even more vibrant red hair. He had the look of a pudgy Opie Taylor right down to the backwater American innocence. He couldn't read anything in Rene's eyes except heartache and sorrow, the comic relief just wasn't there. The silence was extremely awkward for the both of them. Never in their lives had they not been able to talk to one another.

"Then what?" Tim finally broke the silence.

"How much do you know about MPD?"

"Multiple Personality Disorder?" He asked, clearly confused by the question.

"Yes," Rene' replied weakly.

"Not much. That's your area of expertise isn't it?"

"I wouldn't say area of expertise exactly. But, yes, I have found occasion to research MPD in the past."

"What are you trying to tell me, Rene'? That I have a multiple who is committing these crimes? That in actuality, I am committing these crimes?" Tim paused and sighed deeply before asking, "Are you trying to say that all of this might be real?"

"Tim, I really can't say for certain. I mean, you exhibit a lot of the classic textbook symptoms, but the background just isn't there. Or at least what I know about your background. And I might say, Multiple Personality Disorder is extremely rare. In fact, there are certain circles who theorize that it doesn't even exist at all. There have been several dissertations that claim it is a just disorder created by psychotherapists themselves."

"What do you mean you don't know? This is not a time to be cryptic, Rene'," his tone had turned very hostile.

"I will have to consult my medical journals and speak with a few other colleagues in order to give you a more concrete, cohesive answer, Tim. Right now I don't have that kind knowledge on the tip of my brain."

"And you're saying you don't want to help me."

"I'm not saying that at all. I will go back to my office and try to find a colleague who I am familiar with and who also has extensive knowledge in this field. I have a few people in mind. Who knows, we may find out that MPD is not your problem either. There is another rare condition you may be suffering from as well."

"What would that be?" He sighed.

"Disassociative fugue states."

"Again, I've heard of them, but I have to admit my knowledge is lacking."

"I'm afraid I have to admit that I don't know nearly enough about fugue states either. Like I said before, both multiple personality disorders and fugue states are extremely rare conditions and not a general topic of study. But the good news is that I am sure I can find something in the journals, or locate someone who does know more about these things."

They walked through the parking lot together, yet apart. Tim had put some distance between them by choosing an alternating row of cars to walk between. Rene' glanced between his feet and his friend, wracking his brain as to how to help him. Tim stood at the passenger door of Rene's Corvette Stingray, wordlessly waiting for the door to be unlocked.

Rene' fired up the engine and listened to it purr before putting the car in gear and slowly driving out of the hospital parking lot. Rainbows danced off the rain slicked blacktop in ever widening pools of waterlogged oil. The low profile Stingray groaned as Rene' eased it over the multitude of speed bumps. The low slung car would bottom out if he hit them at much more than a mile an hour.

"If it's not narcolepsy or bad dreams, fugue states or even Multiple Personality Disorder, what could be my problem?" Tim asked bluntly.

"You are also exhibiting some classic signs of schizophrenia, I'm afraid."

"So, now I'm crazy too?"

"I didn't say that, Tim. Quit being so damned defensive. I am only pointing out the possibilities. You have to admit, you've been acting very strangely over the last several weeks."

"I think I've told you that already."

"Well, in my defense, you've never told me the whole story."

"You already think I have lost my mind, if you knew the whole truth you'd have me locked up forever."

"You are being very unfair."

"I'm scared, Rene'," he fought back the urge to cry. "I'm scared that you are right, and that I really am crazy."

No longer in the mood for conversation, Tim turned his gaze to the rain drops gliding across the side window of the moving car. Rene' glanced over at him, realizing immediately that their conversation was over, at least for the time being. The worst part of the whole ordeal was that Rene' didn't have a clue where to start.

When they pulled up in front of Tim's house, he just got out of the car and walked up to his front door. Rene' followed him halfway up the walk, stopping only when Tim shut the door behind him. Rene' felt it best not to push the issue at the present time. He could best help Tim by going back to his office and trying to find out just what the hell was going on. He stood there for several minutes before turning and walking back to his car.

"Rene'," he heard Elsa's soft voice call out to him just as he fired up the engine. Shutting it back off he got out of his car and met her on the porch. They stepped into the vestibule where Elsa just gave Rene' a worrisome look.

"I don't know, Elsa," he responded, not needing to hear the question.

"Can't you do anything?"

"I'm going to do the best I can. I need to get him to talk to someone other than me though. This is much too difficult for me, I'm too close to him to be of any good right now."

"Do what you can, please. I had better get inside and see if I can do anything for him."

"If he goes to sleep, watch him," Rene' commented, holding his hand up to his ear as if cradling a telephone receiver, gesturing for Elsa to call him if there was a problem.

Crickets chirped their moonlight sonata, their arias eerily resounding through the darkness. He crept through the quiet house. It was oddly familiar, even though it was completely uncharted territory for his ethereal being. The night blanketed him in an ebon shroud as he passed quietly from room to room looking for a way out of the house. It always seemed to prove much easier getting into the man's mind than it did finding an exit from his house.

Cracker froze in his tracks, the blonde was sleeping in a chair by the door. He caught the whisper scent of her delicate fragrance drifting across the unlit room. Obviously she was keeping a vigil, albeit, not a very diligent one. He stood with his eyes closed, breathing in her lustful aroma. He felt himself stir and quickly fought to regain his senses. "Not now," he told himself, there was plenty of time for her later. As for now, there was a much more special prize in his sights.

Ah, the sweetness of revenge!

He turned around and went to the rear of the house where he quietly crawled out of a window and silently gained his freedom. His host was being very congenial this evening, not even trying to contest his invasion. He was pleased to find that the man had fallen asleep in his clothes. He didn't have to take the chance of waking him while getting dressed for the outside world. And it certainly wouldn't be good to be traipsing around in the dark half-naked, at least not until after he had accomplished his mission. Cracker's mood forced a smile to crease Tim's face.

The night air was chilly and smelled of fresh earth. He squished nightcrawlers beneath his feet as he walked barefoot down the damp sidewalk. He made certain he didn't cause enough damage to kill them, only enough to make them wriggle wildly with incomprehensible pain.

Cracker stopped at the first phone booth he saw and turned to the section in the middle containing maps of the city. He spent several minutes thumbing through his memories and those of his host until he located the mental file he was searching for. The address to paradise. Regina Chamberlain's address.

"I hope you're up to entertaining unexpected company," he commented aloud with a chuckle and tore the page from the phone book.

Although the streets were of Regina's neighborhood were unfamiliar to his host, they were second nature to him. He had spent a lot of time across the river in the seedier neighborhoods when he was a struggling teen. And even more time once he had gone to work for the sharks.

He walked down the sidewalk passing well-known streets named after states and long dead presidents. His date's neighborhood was peacefully located on the fringe of decadence. If he were to travel three blocks further he would be in the heart of the city's drug and red light district. He thought he just might pay that neighborhood a visit once he had finished his work here.

Regina Chamberlain's house was a very modest ranch style home. He was pleased to find it was only one level. It meant there was less square footage and diminished hiding places for the precious granddaughter to escape his wrath. There was only one car in the driveway, indicating the odds of her being alone were greater.

He crept along the rear of the house, hidden from the street by forsythia bushes that had yet to be trimmed back for the season. Their yellow buds and heavy fragrance tickled his nose as he slid between them and the wall of the house. He peered through darkened windows searching for the cherubic face of his angel of mercy. She was going to free him from his bonds of prison, if only for a few moments. In the first bedroom he saw an empty crib. *She must not have had the baby yet.* He felt a trace of guilt for having to murder an innocent unborn child, but it quickly passed. Regret was for the weak, besides, the ends far outweighed the means.

He heard gentle snoring as he neared the next window in succession. A man lay quietly sleeping next to his princess. The man had twisted himself out from underneath the bed covers, exposing his muscular form. Cracker flexed muscles that didn't belong to him, praying that they would serve him well when the time came. This would be his first true physical challenge since learning his little magic trick. All of the others had been women with whom he'd had the luxury of wooing with his charm, money and good supply of alcohol before making his true intentions known. They had only been able to fight with him enough to excite him, not pose a threat. This man was going to have to be dealt with cautiously and expeditiously. He was suddenly grateful that his host had kept his body in good physical condition.

Cracker breathed in the quiet night air. There was no breeze to speak of and the night was deathly quiet, making his stealthy approach to the house a necessity. Cracker fought to contain his enthusiasm and exhilaration before it consumed him and caused him to act out rashly. He allowed himself to calm down before committing himself to his mission.

Cautiously he peered through the crack in the bottom of the slightly opened bedroom window. The head of the bed was against the wall directly beneath the open window. He carefully slid the window open little by little until it was open all the way. Then he gingerly sliced through the screen with a razor sharp knife he had procured from his host's kitchen and set the material on the ground behind him. He went back to the side of the house and retrieved a garbage can he had seen earlier and set it upside down underneath the window. He stood on the trashcan until he had perfect balance, then he slid quietly onto the window ledge.

In one quick motion he leapt from the ledge and landed centered on the man's chest. He sliced through the rousing man's carotid artery before he even had a chance to open his eyes. Regina Chamberlain shot up in bed, her mind awash with confusion. Instinctively he smashed the hilt of his knife into the gaping mouth of his precious and she fell backward onto the pillow while her husband clutched at his severed artery. Blood sprayed like a fountain, covering him with the man's life's fluid. He relished the sticky warmth as it seeped into his pores. He moved quickly to the woman and scrutinized her glazed over eyes. He punched her in the forehead one more time to make certain she would stay out until he was finished with her husband.

He straddled the dying man and thrust his knife deeply into his abdomen. Using every ounce of the doctor's strength he twisted and churned the blade until it was buried to the hilt. The handle of the knife became so slick with the man's blood that he nearly lost his grip on it several times. Once the man had begun convulsing in the midst of his impending death throes, Cracker found it more difficult to control his thrashing. The doctor's body just wasn't strong enough for this kind of work. In an effort to quiet the struggling man once and for all, he reached up and grabbed the headboard with one hand for leverage and used his knife wielding hand to shred the man's internal organs. He looked down into the man's tear streaked face and saw his eyes beginning to pale into the cold look of death and smiled. He was becoming far too good at what he did. The man died having never made a sound other than guttural pleas which were mostly just air escaping his lips.

He dragged the pretty young woman across the room and set her limp body down in a bentwood rocking chair in the corner of the room. With the skill and knowledge of having done this for so many years he knew exactly how much time he had before the precious one awakened. He retreated for the kitchen and rummaged around in the drawers until he found the perfect tool he was looking for. Pulling a roll of duct tape from the drawer he scampered back to the bedroom and began tightly securing her arms to the curled wooden arms of the chair. Finished with her arms he did the same with her legs, fastening her ankles to the rocker skids. Finally, he wrapped the roll of tape around her head once, ensuring there would be no screams passing her lips, at least not until he was ready for them.

Patiently he began cutting away at her nightgown, little by little, exposing fragments of flesh at an exhilarating pace. Her chocolate skin enticed him with each inch he revealed. He went back into the kitchen and brought a dining room chair and set it directly in front of her. He cut two more small pieces of duct tape and pressed them firmly down over her eyelids.

He desperately wanted to torture her. He wanted True to know just how much she had suffered because of his disrespect. He knew the man would somehow learn all the gory details from behind bars. He also knew the man would agonize over it for the rest of his days, especially in the new light of Cracker's inevitable release. There would be no chance for retribution on True's part.

He disrobed and sat down in front of the woman, sedulously awaiting her first stirrings. The wound on her forehead was already bruised and lumped up where he had hit her with the knife. He lapped at a trickle of blood escaping the inch long gash. The salty taste began to arouse him. His patience was wearing thin.

In need of some release, he took the roll of duct tape and made several passes around each of her bare breasts. He cinched it tight enough to cut off the circulation, darkening her already milk chocolate skin and forcing her unexcited nipples to harden and lactate. She was going to get the rare privilege of enjoying his sexual prowess. True would learn of that too. He would learn of her multiple violations before death finally claimed her. He leaned forward and began to suckle her.

She tasted too sweet for his liking so he cut a small slit just below her nipple, allowing her blood to mix with her motherly fluids. *Just right, said baby bear!* She began to stir. Gently at first, then she began to thrash violently at the unknown.

"Good morning, precious," he whispered in her ear, his hot breath repulsing her.

An indiscernible mumble forced its way through the layers of tape.

"Be nice to your lover, dear."

He stood and rubbed himself against her bloody breast, coating his manhood with her fluids. "Don't flinch my dear, I'm not going to hurt you. In fact, I am going to pleasure you beyond anything you've ever experienced."

She began sobbing and pleading and although inaudible, the meanings of her words were clear.

"Would you like to see your new lover, honey?" he asked, ripping the duct tape away from one of her tear stained eyes. He used the piece of tape to tape her eyelid open. He wanted her to be able to see him every moment.

She tried in vain to blink away the tears that were forming a pool in her lower lid. She glanced over at the bed and didn't see her husband. At first she felt relief, he must be in the bathroom and would be coming to save her any moment. But then she saw the enormous, ugly stain on the sheets and she knew. Tears leaked out from under the tape.

He began massaging her breasts with one hand and himself with the other, losing himself in the heat of his passion. He stared into her open eye, she was loving every minute of it.

"You want it all don't you," he hissed, glancing down at the engorged organ in his hand.

She contained her sobbing as best she could. She knew her life was rapidly coming to an end, so rather than give this maniac the satisfaction of pleading for her life, she just quietly prayed to her savior.

"You've quit crying I see, you must be starting to enjoy this," he commented lecherously.

His taunting nauseated her, but she held back her convulsions and fear long enough to formulate a plan. She had been shown the light, she knew how to save herself. This pervert was just vain enough to make it work. She struggled to talk.

"You want to say something my love?"

She mumbled louder, trying to get him to take the tape off her mouth. She tried to look at him as seductively as she could with one tear laden eye.

"Not going to scream are you?"

She shook her head no.

"Are you sure, any tricks and your baby dies," he said, digging the knife blade deep into the taut flesh of her exposed stomach.

Her heart froze. Regina felt a wave of guilt rush through her, she hadn't thought of her baby up until this madman mentioned her unborn daughter. She let the guilt pass knowing it wasn't her being selfish, but only her survival instincts. She knew this was her only chance, her baby's only chance. She had to do whatever it took to gain her freedom, no matter how repulsive. She was going to have to placate this beast while searching for a way out of her predicament.

She shook her head in earnest, trying to get him to believe her. Trying to get the repugnant beast to trust her. Trust her just enough.

"Okay, but remember, you scream, you bleed," he stabbed the knife into her about half an inch deep, causing her to recoil in pain.

Regina saw the look of pleasure wash over him at her expense and she had to force herself not to cower. He started to unravel the tape from around her head, not caring that it was ripping out handfuls of her hair by the roots. She fought the tears brought on by the pain while continuing to coach herself. She needed to keep it together just long enough. She only had one shot, and then that might not even work.

"There honey, do you have something to say to me?" the monster asked.

She didn't dare speak. Her tone or the words might not be convincing enough with fear in her voice. Instead, she just seductively ran her tongue across her lips. She tried not to tremble as she put on a sexy air for this demon.

"So, you little bitch, you like what you see, huh?" he said, again gesturing toward his manhood.

She just made a affirmative moan with her voice and ran her tongue against her lips one more time. She wiggled her wrist, as if she were reaching for him, wanting him in her hands.

"I don't think so sweetie, you haven't shown me that I can trust you yet. You have to give me something," he leaned forward and kissed her nipples.

She arched her back against his touch, wanting to regurgitate, but desperately fighting the urge. He kissed her breast again, becoming very aroused at her willingness. He had never had a woman respond to him like this. He had always had to take them by force. And then they never seemed to like it. This little vixen was enjoying every bit of his love. It was confusing, but highly erotic. Again, she teased him with her tongue.

He took her cue and put his mouth to hers. He felt her tongue immediately begin exploring the inside of his mouth. He had always wondered what a passionate kiss felt like. He could only imagine what it felt like to have a woman exploring him to that extent. He had only experienced that kind of passion from watching movies, but never for himself first hand. No one had ever kissed him like his princess was doing. He was certainly going to have to thank True for this enlightening experience. She moaned slightly and released a puff of her hot breath into his mouth.

It took everything Regina had within herself to keep from vomiting into the man's mouth. She closed her eyes and pretended she was kissing her husband. It wasn't very convincing, but it was the best she could do under the circumstances. She pulled away from his mouth and rubbed her head lovingly against his bare chest. She tried moving her head lower, trying to implant her suggestion in his head.

"I'll bet your man never kissed you like that before. Just wait until I show you what else I can do. You'll forget all about that worthless piece of shit as soon as I am inside of you," he said, nodding his head toward the floor near the bed.

He moved out of the way so that Regina was able to see her husband's paling body lying in a pool of blood on the carpet. His blank stare was focused on a spot on the ceiling. His burnt umber skin tone had already faded into a sickish gray the color of old dishwater. Regina almost burst into tears at the sight. Only her instinctive will to survive helped her to hold herself together.

"No, he didn't. And he never let me, you know," she squeaked, seductively running her tongue around her lips once more. She prayed he didn't pick up on the tremors of disgust in her voice.

"What? You want me to put it there for you?" He asked, bewildered, but more inflamed than he had ever been in his life.

Cracker couldn't believe how real everything felt to him. Although he was miles away, even planes of existence away, he could feel her soft, tender touch as though it was his body experiencing her and not the good doctor's.

She struggled with her wrist once more, praying he would take the bait.

"Promise you'll be good?" he asked, thrusting his hips into her face.

She gave a gentle kiss.

"Okay, that's a good girl," he said, reaching down and slicing through the duct tape that was holding her right wrist. He almost took her hand as his trophy right then and there he was so fervently enraptured in the moment. He needed her blood, but this would definitely suffice for the time being.

Gently she caressed him with her hand, still fighting back her tears and the compelling urge to vomit. She stared him in the eye, trying to give him her most lustful stare. She knew she had to be quick, but not too quick. She took him into her mouth.

He leaned his head back and moaned. His whole body went stiff from his excitement.

She carefully glanced down, the knife was dangling loosely in his hand. She knew it was almost time to act. She could sense that her time was running out.

He had never felt such a rush of emotion. He could really love this girl. Maybe True wouldn't mind him as a son-in-law.

In one swift, well planned motion she grabbed the knife and threw it across the room, then gripped him tightly at the base and bit down as hard as she could. He screamed and tried to pull away. She bit down even harder. She could taste his blood in her mouth and she bit even harder yet.

Frantically Cracker began pummeling her face. First with the right hand, then the left until she finally released him. He fell backwards in a complete daze. She was out cold. It was then that he realized escape would be so much easier. Cracker released his mental grasp on the doctor and returned safely to his life. Now all he had to do was wait; wait for freedom to come knocking.

Tim writhed in pain on the floor, his eyes shut tight. He couldn't understand the sudden flash of pain wracking his entire body. He rocked back and forth as he lay prone on the floor with both hands gripping his groin. He opened his eyes and realized he was no longer in his own home. It had happened again.

Stumbling to his feet in a panic he tripped over the man's body and fell crashing into the night stand and ultimately back to the floor. He quickly scrambled back to his knees. His groin burned with inexplicable agony. His eyes jetted tears of anguish as he struggled to comprehend his predicament.

Once more he made it to his feet and opened his eyes. Regina had completely regained consciousness and began bouncing in her chair in an effort to free herself. Tim became almost hysterical, heaving sobs of perplexity.

"Who are you? Where am I?" His voice was wrought with confusion.

"Fuck you," she screamed through her busted face, spraying his face with a layer of foaming blood spittle.

"Please, what is happening?" He pleaded honestly.

She began screaming rape, and for the police as loudly as she could, as if her life depended upon it.

Tim ran, staggering through the house, trying to move as quickly as he could in his damaged condition. He ran, and he cried. He busted through the front door and out into the street, naked, hurt and completely lost

———————

Cracker bolted upright in his cot and scurried into a corner with his back against the cold, concrete wall. He drove his hands to his groin and clutched at his damaged, tender flesh. With his heart and mind racing in unison, Cracker slowly rose to his feet. As the fog of transference lifted he gained enough courage to pull down his boxers and assess the damage. His organ was red and throbbing and too painful to touch. He moved to his stainless steel commode and forced himself to urinate.

"Christ!" He screamed out and punched his fist into the wall over his head.

His penis burned with an unquenchable flame. Being damaged was something that he had never counted upon. In fact, he had never even given thought to the possibility. The more he learned about the sacred book, the more he knew he needed to learn.

CHAPTER TEN

S irens blared in the distance setting every neighborhood dog's nerves on edge causing them all to howl and bark at the annoying sounds. Tim knew they were all searching for him. Naked and in pain he stumbled through the back alleys while trying to remain hidden within the shadows. His brain hurt as he tried to grasp what was going on. Finding it useless, he abandoned all hope of figuring this one out.

The unmistakable sound of a helicopter's rotor beat the air in rhythm with Tim's heartbeat. He couldn't see the green and red blinking beacons yet, but he knew they were rapidly closing in on his location. He was certain that he didn't have very much time before they found him. Blood flowed down his legs as he ran. The open wounds from the woman's bite throbbed with his racing pulse.

Tim dove for the cover of a hedgerow, obscuring himself from the luminous eye suddenly scanning the neighborhood lawns from the night sky. As soon as the beam passed, he leapt to his feet and continued his beleaguered escape, staying within the shadows of the houses. He prayed they didn't have a forward looking infrared camera on the chopper. He could hide from a spotlight momentarily, but if they had infrared he was in trouble.

The second he made it to his feet the chopper turned. He realized that they indeed did have infrared and had spotted him. He envisioned every pursuing patrol car in the city changing directions to converge upon his present location. He needed to buy himself precious seconds to escape. If he knew what neighborhood he was in he might have had a chance. But he was completely lost. Seeing the helicopter bearing down on him, Tim felt like just giving up. He was prepared to lie down in the street and wait for the patrol cars to show up.

"He's gone," the officer monitoring the infrared commented.

"What do you mean he's gone?" Another voice crackled over the radio.

"He disappeared from screen in the vicinity of Barcelona."

"Did he go into a residence?"

"Negative, he was in a yard when he disappeared."

"FLIR malfunctioning?"

"Yes, sir, I've got a jammed up system. When are we going to get some equipment that works?"

Tim trembled from the safety of a hedgerow as the chopper passed over top of him. Tense and apprehensive, Tim rose to his feet. For some reason they hadn't seen him. His mind flashed visions of being gunned down in the street the moment he was no longer prone. But the bullets never came. He watched the helicopter's shadow moving erratically several blocks to his north. Tim took to flight once more.

He turned his head in an effort to get a bead on the helicopter. They were still heading in his last direction. He had lost them temporarily. He was grateful for whatever force had saved him thus far. It was one time in his life when he didn't curse people for minding their own business and not wanting to get involved.

He caught his breath and tried to get a new bearing. It was then that he caught sight of what he hoped would prove to be his saving grace. The St. Johns River's black surface glimmered in the distance. Estimating he was only a few hundred yards away Tim bolted for the water's edge.

Once he was safely in the river and saw the chopper was at least ten blocks away from his location, a new fear set in. Alligators. The river was home to many alligators. He prayed his luck would hold out, at least long enough to formulate himself a new plan.

He eased down the river, pulling himself along the bottom with his hands. He stayed close enough to the water's edge, using the shadows and foliage to help hide him during his escape. He noticed he was coming to a better neighborhood. The houses were further apart and nicer looking. His luck was about to change for the worse. These people would report an intruder without hesitation. One saving grace was that these people kept their dogs indoors so the alligators didn't eat them for midnight snacks which meant there was no barking, at least not outside.

Tim edged himself along, inch by miserable inch, the roar of the chopper and the dancing lights never getting very far away from him. He knew sooner or later they would discover his escape route and then they would have him pinned down with no hope of escape. There would be no eluding the police once they found him in the river.

Tim hunkered in the shadows and watched carefully as a man

loaded his car with a couple of suitcases and started the engine to warm it up. The man went back into his house, leaving the car running unattended in the garage. It was the break he was looking for. Tim bolted across the yard, praying with every step. Exhaust fumes threatened to choke him as he quietly climbed into the car. He would only have a precious few minutes before the owner would call the police and they would put two and two together. He threw the car in reverse and backed out of the open garage as quickly as he dared. The owner was still busy inside and never saw the intruder stealing his car.

Tim made it several blocks away from the house before he felt it was safe enough to turn on the lights and cautiously drive away. He was quite aware of how many cops were in the area and the last thing he wanted to do was attract attention by driving erratically.

Tim stuck to the streets that lined the river knowing that he might have to ditch the car at a moment's notice. He spied a roadside park along the riverbank and quietly eased the car onto the gravel turn around. Tim stood at the rear of the car with the trunk open shivering from both fear and the cold that had eaten its way through to his bones. His teeth chattered while he dug frantically through the suitcases the man so thoughtfully left for him. Tim found some clothes that would do in his current pinch and threw them on. He grabbed a few more clean shirts to use as bandages and rags and crept down to the river bank. He soaked a T-shirt in the river and used it to clean off what blood was left after his daring escape. He used the remaining shirt as a bandage and buffer against the rough jeans he wore. He was glad they were a little big on him, allowing a little room between his throbbing organ and the scabrous material.

Tim's heart raced as he crossed the Buchman Bridge. He prayed the car hadn't been reported stolen yet. All he needed was enough time to get across the bridge, from there he knew he could find his way home on foot.

Once he was in familiar territory, Tim left the car parked in a nice quiet neighborhood and walked through the subdivision until he was near the water's edge. He knew all he had to do was keep the river to right and sooner or later he would find his own neighborhood. He was relieved to be dressed again, with clothes on he was able to make much better time, a naked man draws quite a bit more attention than he could afford at the time.

Only after he was more than a mile away did Tim begin to relax and ease himself back into society. He walked along the desolate sidewalk, crying, praying and wondering what in the hell went wrong with his life. Soon, it dawned on him that going home wasn't an option at this point. He turned and headed north. He had to get out of the city, at least for the time being.

"Why in the hell are they dragging us out of bed for this one?" Premoe slurred through a mouthful of voodoo coffee. Freeman had gotten to his house faster than his coffeepot had time to finish brewing so Blain just slid his mug beneath flowing stream of heavily caffeinated mud.

"I don't have a clue, Blain. I just got the call and was told to pick you up," he responded curtly.

"Didn't you even bother to ask?"

"Don't get short with me, I've had just as much sleep as you've had, if not less. If you want me to be cranky too, just let me know."

"No, that's okay, I've seen you're bitchy side and it's not very pretty," Premoe laughed, mainly because it was his only option.

They pulled up in front of the address Freeman had been given by the night dispatcher. It was an all too familiar scene. A horde of police personnel filtered in and out of the residence. Premoe saw a familiar face and headed toward it.

"Hey, Charlie, what's going on here? Aren't there any other detectives that could have caught this one?"

"Orders from the Chief, Blain."

"Any reason why?"

"It's already your case. I think this was your guy, The return of the Sandman, as the press has taken a liking to calling him. Oh, and by the way, if you haven't read the papers yet this morning, you need to," Charlie explained.

"Same as the Orange Park and Riverview Terrace?"

"There are some similarities, but the details are still a little too sketchy right now to make an accurate determination. I called you guys here because I thought you'd want to interview the victim."

"She's still alive? I saw a body bag roll out," Freeman offered his observation.

"That was her husband."

"How bad of shape is she in, can she talk?"

"All things considered, she is in pretty good shape. However, she is pregnant guys so take it easy on her."

"What makes you think this was our guy? I mean this neighborhood doesn't exactly feel like him."

"And to confuse things even further, the victim is African-American."

The two detectives looked inquisitively at the forensic detective, "But our guy likes white women, and in upscale neighborhoods. Are you sure about this?" Freeman asked.

"The cuts on the husband were quick, clean and precise. The killer's actions weren't calm and calculated as we have come to expect. However, I looked over the female victim and I noticed wounds on her wrists that could have been an attempt to sever her hand. The wound was clearly visible, but not deep enough to do much damage. Nevertheless, I have to believe that the intent had been there. You can probably get more from her. Oh, I also found a small baggie of sand on the floor," Charlie reported, his face its usual mottled red color of someone who complete perplexed and frustrated.

"What can we expect in there?" Freeman asked, nodding toward the house.

"It's a little messy, but nothing like the last two. He ran out of time on this one. Oh, and guys," they both turned back around. "She hurt him this time."

A grin spread across Premoe's face as the pair spun back around and walked briskly for the house.

Charlie was right, the place was pretty tame compared to the last few scenes they had worked. The young woman was lying on a gurney and being attended to by several paramedics. She looked dazed, but not completely out of it.

"Can we talk to her?"

"Okay, but only for a few minutes until we are ready to roll," a fatherly looking paramedic replied, eyeing both detectives with a glance of warning to be gentle with his patient.

"Fair enough. Miss, I'm Detective Freeman and this is my partner, Detective Premoe. We'd like to ask you a few questions."

Regina just made a hollow sound of acknowledgment.

"Did you get a good look at the man who did this to you?"

She nodded her head gently.

"We were told that you hurt him somehow?" Freeman gave her an inquisitive look. "Do you know how badly?"

"I bit him. Hard enough to draw blood," she replied weakly.

"Where did you bite him?" Premoe interjected.

She just glanced over at Blain's crotch in a gesturing manner.

The two detectives glanced back at each other with a puzzled look.

"You mean you bit him," Freeman paused, "there," he glanced down and indicated his crotch.

She nodded.

Premoe found it impossible to contain his laughter. "I'm sorry for being rude, but it serves the bastard right. So, you think you hurt him pretty badly?"

She nodded again. "Like I said, I drew blood. And I don't feel you're being rude, detective. You're absolutely right, the bastard deserved it, and anything else he gets," she explained through labored breathing. "Do me and the rest of the world a favor, don't arrest him, kill the bastard," she called out from the back of the ambulance.

"We're ready to roll, detectives," the paramedic commented, taking control of the gurney.

"Yeah, sure. I think we can get whatever else we need from her at the hospital."

"We will be up to talk to you more once you are feeling better. We're going to have to ask you some tougher questions and get a description," Premoe said sympathetically.

Again, she just nodded her head.

The paramedic began wheeling the stretcher toward the front door.

"Detectives," she squeaked and beckoned them back to her.

"Yes, ma'am," Freeman said, moving quickly to her side.

"He acted very strangely once I hurt him."

"How do you mean?"

"Like he didn't know what was going on. He acted like he woke up from a trance or something."

"Do you think he might have been just confused, like someone who is suffering from dementia?"

"No, I don't think so. It didn't seem like that at all. There was something in his eyes. He looked lost. It was as if he seemed truly surprised to find himself in my house," she spoke weakly, yet, with an unmistakable fire in her voice.

"Are you certain it wasn't just because you had hurt him? He's definitely not used to that."

"Maybe. I'm a little confused right now."

"Detective, we're ready to go now," a young paramedic announced with a look of urgency.

"Yeah, sure, get her to the hospital. I'd like to talk to you when you're feeling better though."

"Anything you need from me, just ask. I want you to make this bastard pay for what he's done," she couldn't hold her tears of sorrow and frustration back any longer.

The paramedic took her tears as his cue to get her the hell away from that house before she totally broke down.

"We will nail the bastard, sweetheart," Premoe hissed through his teeth.

The detectives watched somberly as the paramedics loaded Regina Chamberlain into the ambulance and drove away.

"Hey, Charlie," Premoe called out as he caught sight of the corpulent man scampering back into the house.

The detectives and crime scene investigator began walking toward each other. Charlie gave them an inquisitive look as they came together.

"What can I do for you, Blain?"

"I just wanted to stress how important this evidence is. We want this guy off the streets as soon as possible."

"I know the routine fellas, I've already sent a batch of prints to the lab. There will be a print technician working on them within the hour. He has your pager numbers and you'll know something even before I do," Charlie reassured.

"Thanks, Charlie, you're the best," Premoe said with a wink.

"Don't go getting sweet on me, Blain. I want this guy as bad as you do," he replied and walked away, putting an end to their conversation.

"I don't think he was joking, Todd."

"About what?"

"My getting sweet on him. I'm hurt," he laughed.

"Don't take it personally, Blain. I'm sure he says that to all the detectives."

"Let's get some lunch and wait on that call from the lab."

"Sounds like a good plan to me, I think it's going to be a long day," Freeman said and got into the car. They were relieved to have finally caught a break in the case, but were saddened at what cost it had come.

Rene closed the cover of his cell phone and set it down on the bar. He checked his watch and took a long drink from a schooner of ice cold Michelob. The peanuts were stale, but they cut his hunger as he waited for the kitchen to open for lunch. He knew it was too early to be sitting in a bar, but there wasn't much else to do but wait. Tim was supposed to have called him an hour ago. He was starting to worry about his friend's mental health. Things were getting too weird and the more he investigated the case the worse it became.

"Hey, buddy, care if I turn on the news?" the barkeep called out, bringing Rene' out of his trance.

"No, go right ahead. But I hate to tell you, you probably aren't going to hear any good news."

"You got that right. But I like to keep score between the Palestinians and the Israelis once in a while," he laughed at his morbid humor.

"Hell I can't keep score between the Jags and the Dolphins let alone that crap," Rene' spouted.

If the man was going to insist on conversing at least he could converse about a lighter topic than world peace, or the total lack of it. In an effort to discourage the man from talking Rene' ordered another beer and a roll of quarters and then moved down to the end of the bar where he forcibly lost himself in a video poker game.

The bar echoed with the chirping of the video game with its annoying fanfare whenever Rene' won a hand and even more annoying intestinal sounds it used to taunt a losing hand. The bartender had lost himself in the back somewhere, emerging ever so often with a case or two of beer to stock the cooler with. Unfortunately the man had disappeared with the remote control to the television, leaving Rene' at its mercy.

The newscaster's voices droned on in his head about trivial nonsense. Some warring faction in some global corner, some northern Florida county celebrating a tricentennial or other community event with parades and the whole nine yards, a local high school sports team makes good at the state championships, and of course a weatherman who thought himself quite the humorist. Rene' prayed for the bartender to return and at least put on ESPN or something. Hell, even an aerobics show, paid advertisement or religious offering would outdo the midday news. Then it happened, the midday news managed to rock his world. Rene' involuntarily looked up to the screen the moment he heard the shrill bleats warning everyone something of grave importance was about to be disclosed.

"This just in," the man read from papers in his hand rather than the TelePrompTer. "We have it on reliable sources that the Jacksonville Police Department has identified the killer known as "The Sandman" who was allegedly responsible for the murders in Orange Park as well as the most recent homicide in Riverview Terrace. Our sources indicate that Timothy Duggan, a local physician, was named as the man responsible for a murder last night across the river in Jacksonville Heights and that he is also wanted for questioning in connection with the Orange Park and Riverview Terrace murders. Our sources also indicate that the police are obtaining warrants and expect to be making an arrest later today."

"Wow, that's some story, Brad," the female co-anchor echoed gravely for the sake of the viewers.

"It sure is, Amanda. Let's hope they catch the alleged killer and get him off the streets as quickly as possible."

"I know I won't be able to sleep very well at night until Timothy Duggan is safely locked away," her voice stressed when she said Tim's name while her smile volleyed for the camera's attention more like a talk show host rather than the newscaster with a sense of integrity she pretended to be.

The newscasters bantered back and forth with even less poignant drivel than they had started their program with. Words that were wasted on Rene'. His grip on his glass loosened and his beer fell to the floor with a crash. Wide-eyed and agape, he stared at Tim's picture plastered on the TV screen while listening to the callous man spreading lies about his friend. He was thrust into a world of confusion and despair. Rene' threw a ten on the bar and bolted for the door. He prayed to God that Elsa had not been watching the news. Maybe he could get to her, or Tim, before this thing got too far out of control.

CHAPTER ELEVEN

"What the fuck was that all about?" Premoe screamed, sending his chair flying against the wall as he stood up from his desk. He stared down at the radio on his desk as if Satan himself had just proclaimed his own innocence.

"How in the hell did the press get wind of this?" Freeman squawked. The pair glanced accusingly around the squad room.

The two detectives stormed out of the squad room and down the hall toward Frank's office. They knew it would be more advantageous for them to attack their boss with the news rather than waiting for him to call them.

"Hey, Premoe, Walker is looking for you two," Carter, a junior detective, advised.

"Shit! Thanks," they replied in unison.

"Get in here," the Chief yelled from his office after hearing Premoe's voice.

"I don't how it got leaked," Freeman defended them immediately.

"You still banging that cute little cub reporter, Blain?" Frank bellowed.

"No, Frank, and she hasn't been a cub reporter for ten years, not to mention the fact that I haven't even talked to her in eight. Besides even if I was, I wouldn't have had the time to get laid, let alone tell her anything."

"Never mind, who really gives a shit about who, or how this damned thing got leaked to the press. Is it true? Or should I expect a call from some high priced lawyer threatening to sue the city into bankruptcy?"

"Most of the information that we have leads to this guy, including a positive ID from a photo lineup. We interviewed the victim again first thing this morning after Charlie was able to get a positive match on the fingerprints found at the scene. There was nothing on the perp in any of our files, but Charlie got a hit after running them through NCIC," Freeman glanced down and flipped through a file folder.

"The prints came back as belonging to a Timothy Duggan. He spent four years in the Air Force and carried and top secret clearance so his prints were on file. We tracked him down through the computer and was able to get a photo of him from his medical school yearbook. We included that photo in a six-pack and took it over to the hospital with us. Regina Chamberlain was able to identify Dr. Duggan immediately and without any doubt. She says she's is one hundred percent positive he is the same man who terrorized her. The look in her eye told me she knew what she was talking about. Not only is she is certain that Timothy Duggan is the man who attacked her she's willing to swear to it in open court."

"What about any other physical evidence?"

"Enough to convict and get the death penalty. Duggan's prints were all over the place. We recovered the murder weapon, fingerprint match there too. Also, the prints lifted from the deceased's body were Duggan's as well."

"Sounds like a nice, neat, tidy case to me."

"A little too neat if you ask me," Premoe spouted.

"What is that supposed to mean? Since when did you have a problem with catching killers and locking them away?"

"I have to agree with Blain on this one, Frank. It just doesn't feel right. Frank, listen, all of the evidence points directly at Duggan in this case. However, in the Orange Park, Riverview Terrace and Hunter's Ridge cases the crime scenes were clean, anesthetically clean. Why did he mess up so badly this time? I could understand the mistake of letting the woman get the upper hand on him, but not the lack of gloves. If we had found a pair at the scene that would be different, but his prints were everywhere. He never wore gloves from the time he started snooping around the house looking for a way in. It just doesn't fit," Freeman explained.

"It was as if he wanted to leave evidence this time, Frank," Premoe added.

"A cry for help maybe?"

"That's a possibility, but why all of the sudden?"

"You've got a point," Frank sighed.

"I guess we won't have those answers until we can interview him and listen to his side of the story."

"We're having the blood found at the scene typed and the DNA evidence processed as we speak. However, don't expect any miracles, there was a lot of blood, and Charlie's team is going to have decipher the puzzle before they can put it together."

"I'm certain we don't have any DNA samples from the doctor yet."

"No. We were waiting for Judge Fairbanks to sign the warrants before making any arrests. I'm sure Duggan's in hiding now anyway, but the element of surprise would have been nice."

"I'll try and keep the sharks off you two for a while so you can bring this guy in without any trouble. I'd hate to see this get any uglier than it already is."

"We really think there is something wrong with this whole thing. The pieces just don't fit. I have spent all morning talking with people about this Duggan, and he's nothing but a stand-up guy all the way around. Granted, we still have a lot of background digging to do, but on the surface this guy is clean."

"I trust your instincts, Todd, but when have you ever heard a serial killer's family say he was a fucking nut case and they knew it was only a matter of time before he was going to slice and dice people?"

"Point well taken. But this just doesn't feel right."

"Then investigate it that way. Don't rule out anything yet."

"What about Graham?" Premoe interjected.

"It looks as though he'll be released Monday barring a miracle. Looks like this miracle worked in his favor."

"Shit! None of this is any good, Frank."

"I know, Blain, I know. See what else you can get on this Duggan guy before you go after him. I don't want any media circus on this. If this guy gets weirded out and offs himself, Graham will definitely beat a re-trial. Get my drift?"

"Thanks for taking the pressure off," Premoe sighed.

"Yeah, kid gloves, we promise," Freeman interjected.

"I just want you guys to realize what you are up against. Bottom line is, this Duggan guy is connected to all of this in some way, some how. Either he is a copy cat, or he was working with Graham all along. Or for some freakish reason he was in the wrong place at the wrong time, naked, with his pecker in some girls mouth," the Chief started to raise his voice a little, realizing how absurd it sounded to presume this guy innocence in light of the overwhelming amount of evidence against him. Nevertheless, he knew deep down that Freeman and Premoe were good detectives with good instincts.

"We know how it sounds, and this guy Duggan probably did kill the husband and assault the woman, but it just doesn't feel right."

"Get out of here and find out some more about this guy. And try to bring him in alive, he has some answers I am dying to hear."

The two detectives left the office without another word, knowing there was nothing more to say about the matter.

"And don't come back here until it does feel right." He yelled after them.

"Shit!" Premoe grunted customarily.

The sun beat down in unmerciful beams, cutting a swath through the peaceful world of slumber Tim was harboring in. Blue jays screeched their warnings from high atop the crooked pine and cypress trees. The forest blossomed with sounds that once soothed his ears and calmed his nerves, but now they just served as reminders of life; a life that was in total disarray.

He spat out the old taste of forest floor and swamp air. His body shivered uncontrollably, both from the cold and the sheer realization that last night had definitely not been a dream. His groin throbbed with the dull yet sometimes shooting pain of a toothache until it began gnawing its way into his brain. This pain cemented the fact that the previous night's events were as real as the brutal sun was this morning. And he was also frighteningly aware of the monumental gap in his memory, the gap between leaving his house and waking with his manhood ripped to shreds.

He wiped his hair away from his tear-encrusted eyes, the strands having stuck firmly to his eyelids during his sleep. The once golden blonde mane was now filthy brown, coated with mud and living organisms from the river water. His hair was so squalid that it actually hurt, adding to his many discomforts.

He leaned with his back against a gnarled cypress and stared up into the sky. The foliage obscured all but a meager portion of the day, but from what Tim could see of it, it was beautiful. There wasn't a cloud in the sky, just an azure patch of atmosphere. He had a fleeting thought of Elsa and he began to cry. He thought back to his last month's nightmare filled repose and had to wonder if they had all been real as well. Was he actually living his nightmares? Was he truly a murderer of helpless women? And some not so helpless? His mind replayed images of the previous night's enlightenment, finding himself coated with the blood of yet another victim. He recalled the smell of death all too vividly. Tim quickly crawled to his knees and began vomiting with a force that left his stomach more twisted than the trees.

"Oh, God," he cried, rolling over onto his back and staring into the sky.

He undid his stolen trousers and inspected himself gingerly. He had lacerations close to an inch deep completely around the entire circumference of his penis, almost severing it completely off. There were several abrasions where the skin had been ripped away as well. Being a doctor, he knew he was in bad shape. The wound was still bleeding and he knew he needed immediate attention especially after being soaked in the bacteria laden river water. He shuddered at the thought of tiny micro-organisms feasting away on his wounded genitalia.

Suddenly the forest echoed with his maniacal laughter as the gravity of his situation finally sank in. It wasn't as if he could just waltz into the emergency room and get treatment. "I'm sure the police aren't looking for too many men with their manhood bitten almost off," he thought aloud to himself. He was no longer trapped in a dream world he couldn't understand. Suddenly and violently he had been wrenched awake and thrust into the awaiting arms of a depraved reality.

"Elsa, my sweet, sweet Elsa, how am I ever going to explain this one to you?" He asked the trees before curling up into the fetal position and succumbing to another fierce bout of dry heaves and unstoppable tears.

Rene' sat in his car outside Tim's house. He had rehearsed his opening lines over and over again, nevertheless, he knew that anything he said was not going to sound right. He had one line if Elsa was ignorant of the recent news release, and another in case she was already a basket case. His mind was cluttered with the disconcerting account he had heard on the midday news. The constant purr of the engine was somewhat comforting, at least with the motor running he still had a chance to run. Yet, he knew that running away wasn't an option. If anything, he had to be strong for himself, if not a granite boulder for Elsa. He turned the motor off and choked back a last minute tear.

Rene' never remembered Tim's walkway to his front door being so long. Nor had he ever stopped to admire the landscaping as he was doing at that moment, anything to delay this dreaded encounter.

Perfectly groomed buddleia bushes lined the walkway in admirable symmetry. Their spikes of deep blue and pink flowers attracted butterflies year round. Rene' appreciated the contrast of colors vibrantly exploding from several fruit trees adeptly planted far enough away from the house to prevent structural damage and yet provide a comfortable blanket of shade from the afternoon sun. Knowing what a perfectionist that Tim was, Rene' was certain that each tree's placement had been measured and precisely calculated before being planted in the perfect spot in the yard. He breathed in deeply, catching the slightest scent of orange blossoms surfing in the gentle breeze.

Below a large bay window in the front of the house was a sea of blue rug juniper with several clusters of blue-green festuca grass bursting forth from the sea green carpet. There were different colored clusters of astilbe sporadically thrown in for contrast. Several large conch shells, and others he didn't know the names of, were strategically placed amongst the greenery. Until that very moment, Rene' had never noticed how much the landscape resembled tidal pool. He had taken all of Tim and Elsa's hard work for granted in the past. Sure, he had always found it to be pleasing to the eye, but he never realized just how artistically groomed the lawn was.

"No putting this off any longer," he prodded himself.

Rene's self-fabricated serenity was suddenly interrupted as the front door burst open and Elsa emerged. Immediately he knew that he didn't need to worry about breaking the news to her any longer. She stood on the porch, her chest heaving with each struggled breath. Tears streamed down her once elegant face. Long black traces of her anguish stained her delicate cheeks where her mascara had mingled with her tears. Rene' almost burst into tears himself the moment he saw her. If Tim were innocent, how dare the media do this to her. And if he were guilty, how dare he do this to her. He cursed under his breath and quickened his pace toward Elsa.

Rene' took Elsa into his arms and held her tightly. He gently pat her on her back and stroked her head as her warm tears tickled the crook of his neck. He picked an ornamental gargoyle sitting on the porch to focus on. He thought of the beast's folded wings. He thought about the stones set into its face for eyes and how they glowed and twinkled when the sun hit them just right. He studied the smiling face with protruding fangs, wondering if the expression were a grimace, a pleasant, welcoming smile, or an evil grin just before another victim fell prey. He thought of everything, so he could truly think of nothing. He tried to put everything out of his mind. Anything to keep from joining Elsa in her gut wrenching sobs.

Elsa gripped him as one would a life preserver, knowing that if she let him go she would drown in a sea of her own tears. Rene' could feel her seemingly arrhythmic heartbeat against his chest, beating a pulse of torment against his sternum. Tears leaked out against his blockade and streamed down his face in ribbons of despair. Finally, after what seemed an eternity, Elsa broke their recuperative embrace.

"Would you like some coffee?" She asked stoically.

"Sure, that sounds really good right now," he replied through the tightness in his throat.

The two of them went into the quiet house. Rene' sat pensively in the breakfast nook, watching Elsa making the coffee. He counted the scoops she used and recalled the many times Tim would quickly sneak another scoop into the filter basket when she wasn't looking. She always knew what he was up to, but it was one of their cute little games. She always added one less scoop to make up for Tim's over-kill, which made for a perfect pot of coffee every time.

Quickly the air was filled with maple-sweet aroma of High-lander Grogg coffee beans brewing. He watched the black steaming stream flowing magically into the carafe below. He had a million and one things to say to her, but no words with which to say them.

"Have you seen him? Has he talked to you?" She broke the silence.

"Do you mean recently?"

"I mean at any time."

"I haven't talked to him since this news report, if that's what you mean."

"I think he was going to kill me the other night," she revealed, watching Rene's mouth drop open in bewilderment.

"What are you talking about?"

"I woke up with him standing naked over me, a flashlight buried in the pillow next to my head. He acted strange, like he didn't know what he was doing. What has he told you?"

"Tim never mentioned anything about that to me."

"Don't play with me right now, Rene'. I hate him right now, don't make me angry with you too. Screw patient, doctor confidentiality, I need the truth. Just tell me what the hell is going on," she started to cry again.

"He said he was having bad dreams, that's all," he said, fighting against the lump in his own throat.

"I know all about his nightmares."

"No, it was more than that. He said he was waking up delirious, with strange circumstances."

"Meaning?"

"He told me he had found blood on himself one morning, and claimed he smelled of sex. I thought maybe you two," he looked at her sheepishly, not wanting the conversation to take this route.

"Well, we haven't for quite some time. He hasn't wanted any-thing to do with me," Rene' knew exactly what she meant without her needing to give him any specifics.

The room fell into an uncomfortable silence. She wearily brought Rene' a cup of coffee and sat down across from him at the breakfast table. Rene' admired the delicate artwork surrounding the edges of the maple topped table. Delicate blue flowers dotted the vine carved into the top of the table, swirling and winding its way around the edge and down each leg. He used to love the little table built for two because of its intimacy, but now he cursed it for the same reason. Her eyes were unrecognizable, swollen and red from crying. This wasn't the same woman he had grown to adore over the years, this was just her hollow shell.

She laughed, startling Rene' "And to think, I was terrified he was having an affair. There's a Jerry Springer episode for you, my husband the serial killer," she said, erupting into another wave of hysterical sobbing.

"Wait a minute here, we're both being assholes about this, Elsa. We're as bad as the press. We've already tried and convicted Tim and neither of us have even talked with him yet."

"Did you listen to the report? It all fits, his strange behavior, everything."

"I know it doesn't look good, but at the very least, we need to give him the benefit of the doubt," his voice raised a notch, more irritated with himself than Elsa.

"But they said his fingerprints were everywhere. They said that one of the victims survived and identified him."

"You know how the press is though, they release these things long before they've had a chance to fully investigate them. Later, they will print a retraction on the back page and hope damage control can keep the lawsuit from hurting too much. Tim is innocent, Elsa, I just know that he is. He's just not a killer," he argued, trying to get himself to believe his own words.

"You didn't see the look in his eyes, Rene'. I was truly afraid that night. He made up some lame excuse and I acted like I believed him, but I didn't. I just know that he was going to hurt me. I could see it in his eyes. It was like he was someone else, someone who hated me."

"I think he has Multiple Personality Disorder," he blurted without looking up from his cup of coffee. He was hearing his own diagnosis for the first time and didn't like what he was hearing.

"Why haven't you said anything to me? How long have you felt like this?"

"For about one minute, that's why I haven't told you. I hadn't even told myself yet. I mean, I toyed with the notion, but I wasn't convinced, that is until now."

"So what now?"

"I suggest we get him a good lawyer. A damned good lawyer. And I better try to find him before the police do. I think it will go better for him if we can get him to turn himself into the police, he will look like he has nothing to hide that way. The main thing we have to remember is that he is going to need all the support we can give him, no matter what."

"I know, it's all such a shock to me. I guess I'm just mad, hurt and scared."

"No matter what, Elsa, even if he's guilty we have to stick by him."

She sat across from Rene' staring deeply into his eyes, trying to read his inner most thoughts. His eyes were greased with choked back tears.

"Do you think I am being a bitch?"

He paused before answering, "Why do you ask that?"

"Because, I know it sounds to you like I am being quick to condemn my own husband. I do love him, Rene', with all my heart. But the fact still remains, something about him has changed. He's a completely different person than he was even a month ago."

"No, no he's not. He's still the same man you fell in love with. I can't promise you everything will be all right, but I can say that I am going to get to the bottom of this, but I am going to need a lot of support from you. And Tim is going to need you as well. Just think about how bizarre this must all be to him. What I mean to say is that if we are sitting here questioning his sanity, then my God, he must truly be going mad."

"I just don't know what to do, Rene'."

The telephone rang, startling the both of them, making them aware of just how much on edge they were. They both stared at it. It rang again.

"Do you want me to get that?"

"Would you please. I'm already sick and tired of talking to reporters, they just won't take no for an answer," she replied.

Rene' made it to the phone on the fifth ring. "Hello?"

The other end of the line was silent.

"Hello?

He could hear breathing, but no one spoke.

"Hello, is there anyone there? If you don't say something I'm going to hang up," he threatened.

"No, wait, don't hang up, please," the caller pleaded.

"Tim?"

Elsa perked an ear to the conversation, scooting her chair closer.

"I really fucked up this time, huh, buddy?"

"I don't know. Did you?"

"No, I don't think so. But I really can't remember," he cried.

"Where are you?"

"I'm hurt, pretty badly, Rene'. I think I need a doctor."

"Where are you? I'll come and get you right now."

"I don't know, really. Somewhere near the Georgia border I think."

"Are you near A1A?"

"I think so. Somewhere between Fernandina Beach and the border," he said. There was a long, uncomfortable silence, "I didn't do it Rene', I just couldn't have done it," his crying worsened.

"Take it easy, buddy, I believe you. Now, try and figure out where you are."

"There was so much blood, it was everywhere."

"So, you were there?"

"Yes, but for the life of me I don't remember how I got there or why I was even there. I don't remember anything except waking up next to a dead man with a woman screaming. I ran. I've been running ever since, but I just can't seem to get far enough away from it all."

"Keep yourself together, Tim. I, we'll, come and get you," he nodded to Elsa and handed the phone to her.

"Hi, honey, where are you?"

"I didn't do it, Elsa, I just couldn't have done it," he slid down the wall of the phone booth until the phone jerked from his hand. He could still hear Elsa's sweet voice calling to him from the receiver hanging down near his face. He tried to talk but the fiery lump in his throat constricted every time he tried to spit out a word.

"Tim? Tim?"

"I'm here," he whispered up at the receiver.

"I can barely hear him, Rene," she started to cry again.

Tim regained his composure and slid back to his feet. "Don't cry, honey, everything will be all right, I promise."

"Where are you, Tim?"

"You just hang on there, and we'll be there as soon as we can," Rene' talked over Elsa.

"Okay, please hurry, I need you," he burst into wracking sobs that tore at her heart. And then the line went dead.

"Let's go," she looked up at Rene' and headed for the door.

The two of them climbed into his Stingray and sped away from the neatly manicured home. The sense of urgency overwhelmed Elsa. She knew by the sound of her husband's voice that he truly needed

her. All of her fears and anger subsided. Tim
needed her and that was all that mattered to her right then.

Rene' sped through the upper class community en route to the
highway. He jumped on interstate ninety-five and headed north toward Fernandina Beach. The town was a picturesque little hamlet
seated on the coast just north of Jacksonville. It was quite a small
town and most exciting activities didn't go unnoticed. Rene' was worried over the possibility of Tim being spotted in a town where the
locals hadn't many things better to do than to watch the tourists. He
was certain Tim would be quickly recognized in a place like that.

CHAPTER TWELVE

"That's not too tight I hope," the police officer commented, twisting the tether tightly against Cracker's leg. The man, quite accustomed to pain and discomfort, never even so much as flinched, robbing the deputy of his pleasure.

Although pain shot through him like a rocket. His groin was still very tender and his organ was frighteningly red and swollen. Nevertheless, he only smiled at the sadistic son of a bitch. "No, it feels fine," he commented, not wanting to give the man the satisfaction of thinking he had caused him any discomfort.

"Good, I wouldn't want to hurt you," he stated, fighting the urge to break the convict's leg.

He knew damned well they were setting a guilty man free. The level of comfort the tether was supposed to provide the politicians in charge didn't do much to ease the officer's anxiety. He knew how easy it was to circumvent the electronic ankle bracelet. It was really just a device to let the judge sleep better at night. If the man decided to ignore the court order, he could be out on the street doing his business any time he wished. By the time the police were to locate him, the damage would have already been done.

"Is this necessary?" he asked while glowering at his attorney. He wanted nothing more than to take the tether and shove it straight up Patterson's ass. He was supposed to be a free man, not a free man on a leash.

"Yes, Mr. Graham, it is totally necessary. It was the only way I could get you released from prison during your retrial," Patterson lied.

The truth of the matter was that he had only agreed to the prosecution's demand for the tether because it would help Simon Patterson sleep better at night. In fact, without it, he was certain he wouldn't have been able to sleep at all knowing that his client, the monster, was loose in his city. And although Simon Patterson would bitterly defend his client in a fight to prove his innocence, he still had no desire to become the Sandman's next victim.

"Seems to me that this goes against my constitutional rights."

"So do income taxes, but we all pay them," he officer droned.

"Well, one would think a good attorney would . . . "

"Listen, I was able to get you a retrial, I got you released from prison, what more could you possibly expect from me?" Patterson asked.

"Easy counselor, I'm just jerking your chain," he burst into laughter, making sure to add a swift kick into the deputy's chin during the distraction. He smiled at the officer, knowing damn well that he couldn't retaliate as the attack was extremely subtle and went unnoticed by everyone in the room except the two of them. The officer glared up at Cracker and touched his now tender, bloodied lip.

"You will be under house arrest, only being allowed to travel to and from the places on this list," Ben Cooper handed a manila folder to Simon Patterson. "Any additional instructions are in here."

"I don't understand how they can do this to a free man," Cracker spoke to his attorney.

"It's like this Mr. Graham," the state's attorney interrupted. "You are still under indictment for murder. None of the charges against you have been dropped. You should consider yourself extremely lucky to be getting even this sliver of freedom. Normally bail is not granted in capital cases, and especially not PR, but the judge was in a generous mood yesterday. Too generous if you ask my opinion," Ben Cooper commented.

"Well, no one asked for your opinion," Cracker spat back.

"Thank you for the lesson in procedure, counselor, but I am quite capable of informing my client about his rights," Patterson tried to take control. "Don't worry, Mr. Graham, their case is paper thin and they know it. I'll have the charges dropped by the end of the week," he explained through flushed cheeks. "Are we finished here?" Patterson turned to the district attorney.

"Yes, we are finished, you are free to go. But I strongly suggest you go over the conditions of your client's release with him very carefully. I'd hate to see him make a mistake due to an error in judgment on his council's part," the district attorney intoned sarcastically and left the interrogation room.

"And Ben, keep your goons, Premoe and Freeman on a leash," Patterson chimed sarcastically as the district attorney walked away. Ben Cooper responded with no more than a dismissing wave of his hand. Even so, Simon Patterson's ego inflated with the moral victory.

Cracker looked into the eyes of the attending officer, sending a chill through the man's veins. "You're free to go, Mr. Graham," the officer commented as he held the door open. At that moment he wanted nothing more than to be rid of the vile creature. God forbid the beast remembers his name and opts for pay back. The officer shuddered.

Cracker took notice of the officer's reaction and knew immediately what it was. Fear. He could always smell the fear oozing from a person's pores. He smiled and blew the man a kiss as he and his attorney walked through the open door.

Once they were safely out into the daylight, Cracker burst into maniacal laughter. He was free at last. Patterson cringed at the thought.

"Hey, Blain, did you read this?" Freeman tossed his partner the early edition of the Jacksonville Times-Union.

Premoe bent over his desk trying to absorb the headlines. His shoulders suddenly sunk inward, the posture of a beaten man.

"So they actually let the little bastard go free."

"Yes they did. And you two are ordered to stay away from him," Frank's voice boomed from around the corner.

"I thought the judge agreed to surveillance."

"Passive surveillance only, Blain. He's on a monitored tether. No contact whatsoever from this department or from either of you two, do you understand me?"

"No, I don't understand," Premoe argued.

"Then do you hear me?"

"Yeah, I hear you."

"Todd?"

"Yeah, yeah, I hear you, Frank. But I think this is a big mistake. We all know he's a killer."

"Frankly, I tend to agree with you, but unfortunately I'm not the one in charge of this mess. You two just keep working on this thing, but stay away from Graham. Any word on Duggan's whereabouts?"

"No leads yet, but I'm certain he will turn up eventually. We have a team watching his house, but there hasn't been any movement all day."

"His wife could have left before we were able to get the men in place though, so she could be with him right now."

"Perfect," Frank spouted.

"Not a problem, we'll just get him when they finally come home."

"If they come home. What about his bank accounts?"

"We have electronic surveillance set up on his phone, credit cards and bank accounts. If Duggan or his wife try to access their accounts or get money from an automated source, we'll know about it."

"Let's just hope he doesn't keep a lot of cash on hand."

"But Frank, the more Blain and I go over this guy's life with a fine tooth comb, the less any of this makes sense. He has lived here all his life, save for the couple of years he went off to college and the time he spent serving his country. Why all of the sudden? What would cause a normal everyday guy to snap and go on a killing spree?"

"The best advice I can give you two is to keep an open mind about this thing. Maybe we ought to look into getting some help from the feds," Frank offered.

The two detectives shot him a wounded look.

"I don't mean for you to let the feds take over your investigation, just use some of their expertise. See if you can get them to send a profiler down our way."

"Come on, Frank, you know how they are. You open the door and next thing you know, they're wanting to take over," Premoe argued.

"Damn it, Blain. I don't have time for this shit. Just get them on the phone and see what they can do for us."

"I guess you're right, Frank, but the feds?" Freeman just kind of smiled at Premoe.

"What is up with you two girls now?"

"We called them over an hour ago. They're sending all of our info to one of their best profilers from Jacksonville branch office ASAP. She will be getting back with us as soon as possible."

"Hopefully they can shed some light on this situation. I have a tendency to agree with Todd on this one though, Frank. Duggan ain't our guy, it just doesn't fit."

"See what the profiler has to say. In the meantime, try and catch this guy before he kills himself, or some vigilante squad beats him to death. The air about this thing stinks."

"Sure thing, Frank. Thanks for the support," Freeman said, trying not to sound sarcastic.

The detectives made their way back to their desks and waited for their FBI contact to fax them her reply to Duggan's profile. Frank had generously assigned them two junior detectives to help wade trough the mountain of old case files.

"How's Phillip getting along in school?" Premoe asked.

"He's doing better now. I had to threaten to take away his sports privileges if he couldn't maintain his grades."

"I'll bet he came around to your way of thinking in a hurry. Well, at least the boy doesn't spend his life in front of a television or playing video games."

"That's true. He thought his mother was going to bail him out this time, but Brenda finally backed me up on something."

"How are things going there?"

"She's still staying at her mother's, but we've been trying to reconcile things."

"I certainly hope you two work things out."

"Yeah, me too. So, how's Nikki doing?" Todd asked warily.

"Don't have a clue partner," suddenly the man's face fell into a sullen droop.

"Still gone?"

"Yeah, she's just like her mother, God rest her soul."

Freeman laughed lightly and replied, "Rochelle was quite the stubborn one, wasn't she?"

They both laughed and then the room fell silent.

"At least I know where she is this time. She calls once a week and leaves a message on my machine letting me know she's all right."

"That's something anyway."

"Damn, Todd, I don't think I could handle the day I don't get any messages from her," he fought back bitter tears.

"Maybe you should try talking to her again?"

"Maybe," his voice trailed off.

Blain loved his teenage daughter with passion, but he refused to cave in to her every whim. And his partner was right, she was a spitting image of her mother, both in appearance and personality. She had the same fiery red hair and piercing green eyes. She had the same zest for life and seemingly endless creativity and passion. And she also had the same mile wide stubborn streak.

The fax machine groaned and creaked to life, bringing both men's focus on the machine. The paper slowly began to spit out of the machine while both detectives anticipated the results. Freeman tore it off and began reading. Immediately a smile spread across his face.

"According to Agent Rivers, she read through the file we sent her and she feels that Timothy Duggan doesn't fit the profile of our killer in any way, shape or form. Of course, she goes on to cover her ass by saying that if we failed to send her all the pertinent information on the case, then there could be a chance that her analysis could be wrong. But the bottom line is that in her opinion Duggan did not kill those women. Not now, not ever."

"We better get that down to Frank and let him have a look at it."

———————

"I hear you're the man I need to talk to," True said, staring into the dark eyes of the man sitting across from him.

The giant just stared back and continued eating. True was certain one would be able to find solace in the enormous man's shadow on a blazing hot day. His massive arms were so muscular that he couldn't even reach his mouth with his fork and had to bend slightly to reach the utensil in order to eat. His thick neck made it impossible for True to tell whether or not the man was swallowing. It appeared he was just shoveling his food into his mouth where it miraculously disappeared. True found it hard not to stare at the man. Scars lined his embattled face, turning his battered and abused flesh into a living testament to his story of a bitterly fought life. True found himself wondering if the man ever smiled, if he ever found anything worth smiling about.

"I need something taken care of," he paused, fighting back the tears of anger and loss. "On the outside, I mean."

"I know what you mean," the sequoia broke his silence.

"Are you the man I need to talk to?" He said abruptly, knowing the dam was about to burst. He felt a warm trickle sliding out past his eyelids.

"Don't do that," his deep voice warned. It was a voice that would be quite fitting segueing into a Barry White or a Luther Vandross tune.

"Don't do what?"

"Try to read me. I heard about your skills at reading people. That's why they call you True, isn't it? Because you always seem to know when a man is lying and when he ain't?"

"Yes, that's how I got my name. Sometimes it's hard knowing you're being lied to, but I like to know just the same," True's lip quivered as he struggled with his emotions.

"And don't do that either," the behemoth ordered.

"What?"

"Cry. You cry, they'll make you pay for it," he nodded his head toward a group of white prisoners. True knew they were Aryan Brotherhood members. He also knew what the leviathan meant.

"I need you to . . ."

"I know what you need. News travels fast around here. I deeply regret your loss. And I understand your pain," True looked into the man's eyes and knew he was being heartfelt and honest with his feelings.

"I don't have much, and I'll have even less now that Gina's husband is gone," he choked.

"Don't need nothing from you. This one's on me. I already made some calls. I was just waiting for you to make up your mind. And I see that you have."

"Thank you."

"No need for that. It'll be my pleasure. Least I could for you. I only wish I could be out there so I could do it myself. You want him to hurt bad? I mean, really bad?" He asked between bites of something that resembled tuna casserole.

True looked at the man inquisitively.

"I could do his wife, mother, daughter, first. Send him a message. Let him know what was coming."

"No, I couldn't bear the weight of innocent blood. No, just make him disappear. But let him know why. And yeah, make it hurt."

"You got it old man. And keep your head high around those pricks. Find a quiet place to grieve, someplace private."

True just nodded his head and left the man in peace to finish his lunch. He got into the chow line, even though he knew he couldn't eat. He figured his meal could be used to repay the favors. He had one of the big man's crew take him over the dessert. He knew he wasn't expected to, but he also knew it was the right thing to do. He would be paying the big man back for the rest of his life, even though that wasn't part of the agreement. True knew that the favors would eventually have to get repaid.

True finished picking through his lunch, guzzled down the remnants of a piss warm glass of milk and went up to the nearest guard he could find.

"I need to speak with the warden, please."

"He's a busy man, True."

"I'm sure he is, but this is important."

"Everything is important," the guard said with a smirk, suddenly putting two and two together. He had read about a young black woman having been murdered in the morning paper and had heard other officers in the squad room mentioning that it was some con's granddaughter. No one had mentioned True's name so he was unaware of the con's loss, until he read it in the old man's eyes. It was just True's dumb luck that he chose the most heartless bastard on the floor to ask a favor of.

"What do you need to see the warden about?"

"It's personal."

"Now what would you have to say to the warden that you can't say to me," he replied coldly.

"I'd rather not say," True responded, eyeing a two inch square patch of gauze on the man's forearm.

"He probably already knows all about your granddaughter," the man let a lecherous grin ooze across his face.

True felt his anger raise a notch.

The guard leaned closer to True and half whispered, "I hear she squealed just like a little piglet. I bet she love that white meat. Probably left her begging for more."

True recoiled from the officer's words, unsure of how to respond. He glanced around the crowded room and felt his head begin to swim. Three clean scalped men were laughing and smiling at the guard. The guard smiled back at them.

"The way I hear it, she really enjoyed it," he incited the inmate further.

True's rage exploded. In one quick motion he slammed his tray into the face of the guard and followed him down the ground. He began to pummel the officer with both fists, ignoring the whistles and shouts from other officers rushing to the scene. He grunted as a boot from one of the Aryans met with his aging ribcage. He felt the brittle bone snap. True saw the man's forearm as he tore into the bandage hoping to inflict pain into an existing wound. A tattoo appeared from beneath the false skin. A tattoo declaring the man's loyalty to the Aryan Nation.

He continued to beat the officer as best he could until he felt the crushing weight of the big man coming down on top of him. True glanced over his shoulder to see two cold, dark eyes staring directly into his. He felt the big man grunt and spasm in the wake of several baton blows, but he never blinked and he never cried out. The big man protected the old con until the guards had finally worn out their anger and decided a more hospitable approach was in order. As the big man was pulled to his feet he smiled at True. It was then that True understood the benefits of his actions. He would be sent to isolation for his retaliation against the guard. He could grieve in isolation. He could cry in isolation.

CHAPTER THIRTEEN

R ene' veered his Corvette Stingray into the parking lot of the
small roadside park and headed for the rear of the maintenance building. He and Elsa scanned the shadows for any
signs of movement, hoping to spot Tim as quickly as possible. Her
heart pounded against her sternum so hard she was certain Rene'
could hear her heartbeat in the cramped quarters of the car.

The park was pretty busy for that time of day. Rene' hoped that
no one would have noticed his fugitive friend, whose face was now
being plastered on every TV screen in the state, if not the whole
country.

Tim crouched down in a thick tangle of underbrush leading to a
wooded lot behind a maintenance building. He had seen Rene's car
pull up and was anxious to see him and Elsa, but not too anxious. He
didn't need a degree in psychology to know that he was suffering
from acute paranoia. Everyone looked like a cop, and even the slightest glance in his direction set his nerves afire. He could hear the gentle purr of Rene's motor, even over the din of laughing children. He
really loved that car. He felt a knot twist in his stomach, it might be
the last ride he ever got to take in it.

"Should we get out and look for him?" Rene' asked.

"No, he said to wait in the back by the maintenance shack with
the motor running," Elsa replied.

Rene' watched a teen cursed with atrocious acne stumble away
from a nearby concession stand with an arm load of junk food and
shook his head. A blonde sauntered passed with the facial expressions
and attitude of a super model but the definitive air of a trailer park
bimbo. He shook his head even harder. Across from him another
woman was greased into a pair of spandex pants that made the
woman thighs look like world record sized bratwurst. Rene' knew
they had to get out of there before he broke into hysterical laughter
and Elsa began thinking of him as a monster. Then he saw the bushes
move. He patted Elsa on the forearm and directed her attention to the

stirring hedgerow.

Tim's haggard face appeared from out of nowhere behind a tangle of congested vines and hedges. Elsa gasped. The creature that emerged looked nothing like the man she married. Nothing like the man she had kissed goodbye just yesterday morning.

"My God, Rene', look at him."

Tim was hunkered down at the edge of a green trash gondola accented with stains of indeterminate origin and organisms. The fugitive was wildly eyeing the parking lot. Rene' stepped out of the car slowly and went to the trunk to pop it open. He glanced over the trunk lid in time to see Tim lurch from the shadows and make a mad dash for the car. He knew that there wouldn't be any time for a warm reunion. He saw Elsa's face peering at him from inside Rene's car and his heart ached immediately. She looked at him like he was a stranger; a monster.

Everything seemed to be moving in slow motion. Rene' felt like it was taking Tim forever to make it the hundred feet to the car. Once Tim was to the rear of the car, he looked down at the compartment and had to shake his head. If it weren't for bad luck, he'd have no luck at all. Even with the spare tire and jack sitting in Tim's garage, the amount of room in the trunk of the sports car was infinitesimal and it took several tries before they were able to get it closed with Tim inside. As soon as Rene' heard the unmistakable click of the trunk latch, he raced around to the driver's side of the car.

Rene' jumped inside and threw the car into gear and began to speed away from the crowded park, his tires spitting gravel and throwing a plume of dust in the air. Elsa reached over and gripped his arm, wordlessly suggesting that he take it easy and Rene' knew that she was right. It wouldn't do them any good to be pulled over for speeding or careless driving at this point. As hard as it was, Rene' eased the car down to an inconspicuous speed and tried to relax.

Suddenly Rene' felt a stab of guilt, "Tim's going to have to stay in the trunk until we get to where we are going. This is only a two-seater and there's not enough room to squeeze him in up front without attracting to much unwanted attention."

"You okay back there," Elsa yelled behind her seat.

A muffled sound came back from the trunk. Neither of them understood what Tim had said, but the sounds coming from the trunk reassured them that he was still alive at least.

"By the way, where are we going?" Elsa asked.

"I didn't give it much thought really. I just assumed we would just head back to your house."

"Do you think that's wise? I don't have much experience in the fugitive felon business, but I'm quite certain the police will be watching our house by now," Elsa forced a smile.

"You've got a point there. But then where do we go?"

"As soon as we reach the city limits go ahead and drop me off near a bus stop or somewhere that I can get a cab easily. I'll go back home alone, it might throw the police off a little. You take Tim somewhere else and I'll meet up with you later somehow. The police may not be watching you yet, but just in case, you probably shouldn't go to your place either," Elsa explained, her mind trying to work like that of a renegade.

"Maybe the office is safe," Rene' thought aloud.

"Maybe, but be careful."

The rest of the trip was quiet and uneventful. Both Rene' and Elsa were silently planning their next moves. Neither of them were a criminal mastermind and prayed that the plans they had come up with would at least get them through the rest of the day.

"Over there," Elsa pointed to a small diner with a bus stop right outside. "I'll go in and have a bite to eat while waiting for the next bus."

"Okay," Rene' said nervously.

"You had better not call the house, either, there's a good possibility that they will have it bugged."

"Aren't you being a little paranoid," he chuckled uneasily.

"No, I don't think so. The police believe that Tim is a serial killer, Rene', I'm certain they are going to be pulling out all of the stops to catch him. I'm really afraid they are going to kill him, Rene'," tears began to well up in her eyes.

"Okay, no calls. And don't worry about a thing, I won't let anything happen Tim," Rene' said, edging away from the curb.

Elsa waved and disappeared into the diner. Rene' cruised along the boulevard, his mind moving faster than his car.

"Don't worry, buddy, we'll get you out of there as soon as possible," he called to the trunk.

A weak, muffled reply drifted back up to the front seat. Rene' wiped tears away from his eyes as the seriousness of the situation again took a fierce hold of his emotions. He headed for his office and prayed that it wouldn't be under surveillance. He was so preoccupied with the situation that he never noticed the car that had been following them for the past several miles.

"Are you sure that's him?" The driver asked over the seat to a man in the back seat.

"The car matches. Same make, model and color."

"Fool, how many red and white '57 Stingray's you think are driving around this town," the passenger rebuked.

"What about the plate?"

"It's a hit," the man replied, pulling a pair of binoculars away from his face.

"Did you see the man?"

"No. He's not in the car. Some bitch got out and walked into the diner."

"He's not the driver?"

"No, doesn't look like the guy in the papers," he replied, holding up the front page of the early edition.

"There he goes," the passenger advised.

"Follow the car or stay with the ho?" The driver asked.

"The car's a match, fuck the bitch. Go after the car, maybe he'll take us to the dead man."

The Lexus pulled away from the curb, its three passenger intently eyeing the Corvette Stingray in front of them. They maintained a comfortable cushion behind the target car, a practice they had honed during many missions over the years. They were the masters of payback, that's why they had been given the job. Normally they fetched a high price, but this one was going to be a freebie. The man should have never messed with an innocent sister like he did. He had deservedly earned their worse wrath.

The darkness was enveloping. The quiet purr of the motor created an uncanny tranquility.

Hey, doc, no need to worry. I haven't left you yet.

"Who the hell are you? Leave me alone," Tim cried out in the darkness.

"What? I can't hear you buddy," Rene' answered.

Now, doc, just relax. I just wanted to thank you for freeing me from prison.

Tim's body trembled violently. It wasn't the first time he had felt the presence while awake, but now it was stronger than ever. Tim wondered if this was how it all started for that guy in New York. Voices in his head. He laughed aloud, at least he wasn't listening to a talking dog. At least he wasn't *that* crazy. He laughed again, then he started to cry.

It's a lot to absorb isn't it doc? Well, you can rest assured, I am almost through needing you. But you have to admit, you must be at least a little curious as to what comes next? Where's that pretty little wife of yours, I'd like to pay her another visit.

"No," he screamed in the darkness. "Get out of my fucking head," he punched the trunk lid of the Corvette as best he could given the cramped quarters. Tim felt a sudden release of pressure. The ominous weight of the other's presence was gone.

"Mr. Graham, Mr. Graham, would you please pay attention," Simon Patterson insisted, bringing his client out of his self-induced trance.

"What is it, Patterson," Cracker said with disgust.

He hated being interrupted during his altered state. He had to learn if there was a way to coexist on both planes at once. Only the book could help him do that, and it was back at the prison. He cursed the bastards for not letting him take it with him. No one had given a shit about the damned thing until he wanted it, and then all of the sudden it became state property and was not allowed to be removed from the prison.

"Do you understand all of these rules and the importance of adhering to them all."

"Of course I do, Simon. I know more than anyone else what my freedom means to me. You needn't worry your pretty little head over me, I'll be a good boy, at least until this whole thing is behind me," he laughed aloud at his insinuation.

"We're finished here, would you like me to have a car take you somewhere?"

"I'd rather walk."

"You can't walk. Haven't you heard a single word I've said? You are not allowed to just go roaming around as you please. You have to rigidly adhere to the instructions the court laid out in the conditions of your release."

"In that case, yes, you can get a car to take me to my mother's place. I guess I will have to stay with her, at least until you can find me another place," he smiled.

"I don't have the time to find you a place to live," Patterson protested.

"Well, then I will just have to wander around looking for a place on my own, I hope the judge won't mind."

"You're really a pain in the . . ."

"Careful. Simon, you wouldn't want to piss me off now, would you?" A glazed look spread over his reddish green eyes.

Simon Patterson tried to stave off the shudders he felt coming on before speaking. "What is your mother's address?" He asked, rifling through his client's file.

"It's over the bridge, on the east end of town. I'll tell the driver where to go," he smiled. "It might be kind of nice to see the old bitch again."

Chapter Fourteen

Rene' pulled his car into a parking garage located several blocks away from his downtown office. Tim was cramping up in the trunk and the g-forces thrust upon him from rounding the countless turns up to the roof were sending needles of excruciating pain shooting through him. Rene' could hear his friend's grunts and groans coming from the rear of the vehicle and tried to be as gentle as he could. Nevertheless, he couldn't fight the sense of urgency he had been feeling ever since he and Elsa had picked Tim up in Fernandina Beach.

As soon as the open sky greeted him at the top of the ramp, Rene' scanned the rooftop of the parking garage for the most secluded spot. He backed the sleek Corvette into a parking spot that was bordered by two larger vehicles. A jet black Ford Expedition blocked their view from the entrance ramp and a dark blue Chevy Tahoe blocked them from the exit side of the ramp. Although they had a perfect vantage point, they were still quite secluded. The parking spot was close enough to the exit ramp that they could be heading down before being noticed by a car coming up, just as long as they moved fast and had plenty of forewarning.

Rene' hurried back to the trunk and popped the latch. Tim immediately sprung out of the trunk. He reminded Rene' of a vampire in an old horror flick, shielding his eyes from the glaring assault of the sun. Several minutes passed before Tim's eyes were able to adjust to the brightness. His clothes were filthy, wrinkled and smelled worse than Tim looked. Rene' helped him to steady him while they both tried to make him more presentable to John Q. Public.

"Thank you, for everything" he mouthed weakly, stretching and rubbing his sore muscles.

"Are you able to move yet?"

"Yeah, I think so."

"We had better make sure we weren't followed first before we head for my office," Rene' said, walking over to the edge of the roof and peering over. He and Tim scanned the street below, searching for anything out of the ordinary.

Tim laughed faintly. "Do we even know what we are doing? What are we looking for?"

"I don't know," Rene' chuckled. "Something you might see on television or in the movies I guess. Like a telephone repairman working on a cable line or something. We should probably be looking for any suspicious vehicle that is trying to be inconspicuous."

Tim gave him a confused look and they both erupted into laughter as if they were doing nothing more than spending the day together people watching. For a few moments at least, they were able to escape the enormity of Tim's troubles.

"I guess it looks clear to me. How about you, Sherlock?" Tim laughed.

"I think the rudimentary problem of big brother's covert surveillance has been thwarted by our exercising far superior skills than that of our adversaries," Rene's spouted in his worst British accent, which was his best.

"I'll take that as a yes."

"No, you should take that as a how the hell should I know, I'm a shrink for Christ's sake, not a detective."

Again, the two men allowed a brief period of laughter to grant them a respite from their adversities. They tried their best to look nonchalant as they entered the stairwell to the parking ramp and descended to the street below. Once outside they casually walked the six blocks to Rene's office, never once giving thought to the gold Lexus parked two blocks away.

Rene' entered the office building's small lobby alone, leaving Tim outside and vulnerable on the sidewalk. Rene' spent as little time with his secretary as possible.

"Vicki, can I please have the files on Kathy Morgan and Jason Westinghouse, please," he asked, knowing that his request would keep her busy in the other room for several minutes.

"Okay," she replied.

"Just put the folders on my door. It's almost quitting time. As soon as you get the files for me, go ahead and take off for the day. I don't have any patients this afternoon and I need to catch up on some reading," he said.

"No problem," she replied with a smile. She was suspicious of her boss's strange behavior, but she needed a little time to herself and wasn't about to argue.

While Vicki was busy with the petty task of locating patient files, Rene' slipped Tim passed her desk unnoticed. Immediately Tim trotted off down the long corridor until he reached the back of the building where Rene's office was located. Rene' had specifically located his office in the rear of the building when he had purchased it for the simple fact that it had an emergency fire exit. He had a gripping fear of being burned alive and the exit offered him a little comfort cushion. Tim quickly disappeared into Rene's office using a key that had been given to him years before during a tumultuous point in his marriage. The office had afforded Tim a welcome retreat when things had gotten rough at home.

Tim sat down and tried to relax while he waited for Rene'. The combination of the silence and being alone brought his mind sharply back to reality. He missed his wife dearly and was dying to call her but he was certain that their phone would be tapped by the police by now. Contemplating his situation, Tim began to realize he was quickly running out of options. Just as he felt he was about to drown in a river of despair the door opened and Rene' came walking through with a smile.

"Vicki is sure that I am up to something. Probably thinks I am having an affair and was sneaking a strange woman in. Little does she know, Connie's the strangest woman I know," he laughed.

"Maybe we need Vicki on our side, sounds like she'd make a better detective than either of us," Tim forced a smile. "I can't help but notice that your office looks smaller. Did you move into a smaller one?"

"No, just had some remodeling done. I think the darker paneling just makes the room seem smaller," Rene' explained.

The room fell into an awkward silence. Both men stared into each other's eyes, looking for some kind of confirmation that this really wasn't a dream.

"I think I had better take a look at that wound of yours. I don't have much in the way of medical supplies but I do have a first aid kit in the bathroom," Rene' stood up and crossed the room. He pushed on a section of the paneled wall which popped open to reveal a hidden bathroom.

"I thought I remembered separate rooms in here and not just one big office."

"Ah, yes, somewhere hidden amongst these gracious lines is my home away from home. My sanctuary from the dementia of the outside world. Even Vicki can't find me in here."

"And Connie," Tim smiled.

"Are you crazy? Not a clue, buddy. I've hidden out here a couple of times. Nothing so exciting as a tryst with a big-busted waitress from Harry's, but it was just as therapeutic nonetheless. Mainly because Connie wanted to kill me," he laughed. "Now let me see that wound," he returned with the first aid kit.

"All right, you asked for it," Tim responded, gingerly loosening his pants and dropping them around his ankles. He took a little longer to gather the courage to unwrap the shirt he had used as a bandage. He knew the blood had dried by the way the fabric was clinging to the scabbed over bite marks. Tim winced in pain as he tore the shirt loose. Trickles of blood immediately began to flow. The wound from Regina's teeth had festered and become infected. The skin around the affected area was ruby red and swollen. Tim's penis looked like someone had taken and bite out of an undercooked hamburger and spit the semi-masticated meat back onto their plate.

"Damn!" Rene' recoiled. "Sorry, didn't mean to be rude or scare you, but I'd be lying if I said it looked pretty. It looks like it might even be infected."

"I told you it was bad."

"I'm sorry to have to say this, but I think this is going to hurt, a lot."

"I know it is. It already does."

"Would you like to sit down?"

"Better access to the whole package if I stand isn't there?"

"Yes."

"Then I better stand."

Rene' went to work, tenderly cleaning up the nearly dismembered member. He put a waste can beneath Tim's crotch and poured hydrogen peroxide over the wound. The peroxide bubbled and foamed as it loosened the caked and dried blood. Stinging needles of pain shot through Tim as the solution found its way to tender, raw flesh.

"I think you should have gotten stitches," Rene' observed.

"Yeah, I think you're right, but it's kind of hard to find a discreet hospital when you're fleeing the police," Tim tried to smile. The more pain he felt from his wound the more memories about that night were resurrected. Memories he was trying desperately to forget.

"Ancient Chinese proverb say, not wise to be smart ass to man who can make you cry like a little girl."

"Funny. I just hope the damn thing still works," he drew back in pain from the alcohol Rene' had failed to warn him was coming as he poured it over the open wounds.

"Sorry, thought it might be a little easier without any warning," Rene' half-heartedly smiled, yet quite aware of the pain Tim must be going through. He shuddered as he allowed his mind to absorb the trauma in detail.

"I don't mean to be grossing you out, Rene'," Tim said.
"I know how bad this has to hurt."
"Not too bad anymore. Everything's getting kind of numb."

Rene' finished cleaning Tim's wounds and then dressed the embattled organ with a thin gauze veil topped with antibiotic ointment. He then added a layer of cotton balls around the circumference for protection, followed by yet another wrapping of gauze. Tim glanced down at the finished product and snickered.

"Damn, if we head to Harry's now, I'm sure I can get at least one of those waitresses to come back here with me. Just look at the size of this thing."

Both men shared a brief moment of laughter at Tim's expense. Tim pulled up his pants and eased himself back down into the over sized leather chair and relaxed as best as he could. He watched as Rene' busied himself by putting away all of the medical supplies into the handy carrying case and put the first aid kit back into the hidden bathroom. Tim was amazed at how good Rene's office looked after the remodeling.

"I assume this would be as good a time as any to get started," Rene' broke the silence.

"What are you planning?"

"I thought I might try to hypnotize you. It might help us to figure out what the hell is going on if we have a window into your subconscious."

"In layman's terms, to find out whether or not I am lying," Tim sighed.

"Bluntly, yes."

"Do you think I am guilty?"

"Do you?"

"Yes," he began to break down. "I can see no other explanation for this mess. You saw the wounds on my penis, how else can we rationalize them unless I was there. And if I was there, then I must have murdered that man and tortured that woman," he began to feel torrential tears fighting their way to the surface.

"I didn't ask you to justify, rationalize nor explain the situation to me. I asked you simply, do you think you are guilty?"

Tim thought for several minutes before answering. "No, at least not intentionally. I mean, I know I didn't intentionally and with malice of forethought, get out of bed, leave the house and travel across town to murder someone I don't even know."

"Exactly, but subconsciously you may have."

"The evidence suggests that. Are you trying to get at something specific?"

"Tim, I'm afraid you might have multiple personality disorder. I'm not really a believer in that school of thought, but you do exhibit a lot of the classic symptoms."

"Christ, Rene'. Would it be possible for me to not know what was going on?"

"Not only possible, but quite likely."

"And you think hypnotism will prove this theory of yours?" Tim asked, trying to fight back his anger.

"Or disprove it," he replied.

"That's a little disconcerting either way. On one hand, we learn that I have a psychopathic killer locked away somewhere in my brain and now he has the key to get out. And on the other hand we're back to square one without a clue to this mystery."

"We have to start somewhere, Tim, it might as well be here."

"I didn't realize you were skilled at hypnotism."

"I played around with it during college, more out of amusement than anything else. I think it was even before I had decided upon becoming a shrink," Rene' offered, pulling a tape recorder out of a drawer and set it on top of his desk.

"What's that for?"

"In case I miss anything, and if you want to listen to it when we're through."

"I'll wait until your reaction to all of this before I make that decision."

Tim sat back in the large leather chair and allowed Rene' to guide him through his own nightmares. Neither of them were sure if the hypnotism would work, nor if it would shed any new light on the situation if it did. Tim conceded to the fact that he had to go back to the places in his mind he was desperately trying to escape. All of the answers were trapped within the darkness of his nightmares.

———

"Zimmerman just called in. Duggan's wife came home about half an hour ago, alone. He said there hasn't been any movement in the house all day and no phone calls," Freeman said to Premoe as he hung up the phone.

"Nothing from the hospital either. I just got off the phone from talking with his supervisor, she says he took an indefinite leave of absence on Monday. But she also claims the news reports are wrong, that it couldn't possibly be the same Tim Duggan we're looking for. And for some damned reason I believe her."

"I know the feeling partner."

"So what's next?" Premoe asked.

"He's not at home and he's not at work. What about this friend of his, Dr. Rene' Meade," Freeman said, glancing through his copy of the file.

"I called there once this morning, the secretary said he wasn't in."

"Maybe we should just pay him a visit. Never can tell when a secretary might be mistaken."

"I guess it couldn't hurt," Premoe said, reaching for his jacket.

The brown suede jacket was a little too heavy for the time of year, but Blain loved the coat. It had been his grandfather's favorite too. He had saved the coat from being shipped to the Salvation Army after his grandfather had passed away. Wearing it kind of made him feel like the old man was still with him where ever he went. And maybe he was. Premoe's own guardian angel, if for nothing more than an emotional savior.

"Not wearing your vest again I see," Freeman observed.

"Makes me look fat."

"You are fat."

"Fat enough to kick your ass."

"Not in a gunfight, I'm wearing my armor."

"Yeah, well I shoot for the head."

"That's because you can't shoot with your head," Freeman laughed.

"Hey, that's hitting below the belt," he joined the laughter. Premoe made certain he tagged his partner with a bruise leaving shot to the arm as they were walking out to the street.

"You see," Freeman said, rubbing his now tender arm, "this is why I piss in your coffee every morning."

"Well, you are equipped with your own stir stick," he grunted and looked at his partner's crotch.

"Just shut the fuck up and drive," he said as the two burst into laughter before putting on their somber faces for the task at hand. Their mutually warped sense of humor was the only thing that allowed them to maintain their sanity in light of the horrors they faced each and every day of their lives.

———————

Vicki Reynolds looked into the coal black eyes of the enormous man standing over her. She had not seen nor heard the trio come into the office. They crept up on her like jungle cats, pouncing when her back was turned.

136

"Listen close, bitch. I want to know where the doctor went?" Jamaal Coleman, or JC as his friends and enemies alike called him, barked. JC was quite aware of what his six foot three two hundred and fifty pound stature was doing to the terrified white woman staring back at him. And he loved the feeling.

"Which one? There's more than one doctor in this building," she whimpered. She knew they must have been talking about her boss. She prayed that Rene' would hear the commotion and call the police. Vicki tried to avert her eyes from the man towering over her. She didn't want to give him even the slightest idea that she would be able to identify him even though all three of them wore black ski masks.

"How do I lock the door?" Another one asked.

"Key. The key hanging over there," she pointed to a peg board with keys hanging from brass hooks. The key to the front door dangled obviously from an attached wooden fob with the words FRONT DOOR etched into its face. The intruder quickly snatched the key off the hook and locked the front door to the small building.

"The damned doctor that just came in here, don't make me hurt you, bitch," JC hissed through his teeth, spraying her face with his spittle. His chest was pumped up with adrenaline and he flexed just to show her he meant business. The man wore a tight, sleeveless black tee shirt that accentuated his massive chest and bulging biceps.

Vicki trembled with fear. She felt the warming spread of urine seeping down her legs onto the carpet. Her trembling had passed the point where it was controllable. Convinced that she was going to be killed, she began to pray and beg for her life.

"Listen," the third man, Luther Meeks, broke in. "If you just shut the fuck up and tell us what we want to know you'll get out of this without as much as a bruise," he said calmly. Luther wasn't nearly as large as JC was, but something about his soft spoken demeanor scared Vicki even more.

The stunned woman just trembled and stared back in disbelief. Her monumental decision of either cream cheese or boysenberry preserves on her bagel that morning seemed like a lifetime behind her.

"Let me put a cap in this bitch's ass, she'll talk then," the last of them, Little Man, said, pulling a glock out of his waistband.

He had earned the name Little Man when he was just a boy and began running with a crew on the streets. He learned to talk tough at an early age and learned how to be tough even earlier than that. He killed his first man when he was only twelve and became intoxicated with the power. Doling out pain had become an addiction that he didn't want to break. And even though he himself was quite a large man, Six foot and more than two hundred pounds, he kept the name

MATTHEW F. WINN

Little Man and wore the moniker like a badge of courage.

"You know the drill," Luther put a hand on Little Man's weapon and eased it down.

"This your family?" JC asked, holding up a picture of the secretary, a man and three young children.

The tears in her eyes nodded for her. Luther knew he had found some leverage.

"Cute kids. I'm sure if we look hard enough around here we could come up with an address."

"Suite 400, end of the hall," she blurted through a veil of tears.

"Good girl. Now you need to say some prayers."

The woman started sobbing.

"Let me finish. You need to say some prayers for an old black man, he's the only thing that kept you alive today."

Luther rolled Vicki over gently and began taping her up with a roll of duct tape. He hog-tied her with the gray tape and finished her off by wrapping a length of tape around her head and across her mouth. He checked to make sure she was able to breathe through her nose before setting her back down on the carpeting.

"Make sure she can breath all right," JC said.

"I did, she's fine. Now let's go get that son of a bitch and teach him a thing about disrespecting our peoples."

The three masked men started down the passageway toward suite 400.

CHAPTER FIFTEEN

R ene' stopped his therapeutic interrogation of Tim to listen at the door. Vicki had buzzed him on the intercom even though he had left her explicit instructions that he was not to be disturbed. It wasn't like her to ignore his instructions, in fact, she usually followed them to the letter. Rene' thought he had heard a male's voice echoing down the hallway, however, the thick carpeting muffled most of the sound. He couldn't be sure if he had actually heard someone, or if Vicki had turned the radio up. Again, that was very uncharacteristic as well.

Rene' felt a cold wave of panic wash over him once he realized that he was indeed hearing voices coming from the lobby. And as far as he could tell, they were now heading down the hall toward his office. He couldn't believe that the police had found them so quickly. Part of him was relieved, yet, he was saturated with cold sweat caused by the anticipation of the unknown.

Suddenly, the noises in the hallway stopped. At first Rene' thought the voices might have been those of one of the other doctors who shared the building talking to a patient on their way to the lobby. But then Rene' remembered there weren't any other doctors in the building at the present time. The building consisted of four suites and one of those was vacant. Of the two remaining suites, Walter French, another psychologist was on vacation. And James Prescott was reaping the benefits of a fellowship in Paris. The building should have been completely empty except for him, Vicki and Tim. Now, after hearing several male voices, Rene' was certain there was someone else in the building with them. He glanced across the room at the deadbolt knob. His heart skipped when he realized that he had inadvertently left the door to his office unlocked.

Rene' cautiously moved across the room. He wasn't sure what good it would do, but he had an undeniable urge to lock the door to his office. Maybe it would buy Tim a little time, time for what Rene' was unsure of. Maybe it would keep the police from shooting his friend down in cold blood before he was able to give himself up peacefully. There was one thing he was sure of, he was quite confident that the cops weren't going to be in a good mood.

Rene' had only made it halfway across the room before the door burst open and his world was thrown into utter chaos. The three masked intruders had surprised him to the point that he was paralyzed with fear. Within seconds he was face down on the carpet.

"What the hell is going on?" He asked, his mind trying to assimilate the information his body was receiving. Rene' had seen as few as three men wearing ski masks flood into his office. Cops sometimes wore masks, but usually only in drug raids. And, he recalled, not one of them had identified themselves as the police.

"Shut the fuck up," the first man through the door said, straddling Rene's back.

"You can't come in here without a warrant," he protested.

"Get this. This mutha fucker thinks we're Five-O, JC," Little Man gave a short chuckle and continued with his job of securing the prisoner. He ran a length of duct tape around Rene's wrists and ankles and then a strip to cover his eyes.

Rene's was thrust into total darkness. He could feel his heart beating against the hard floor of his office. He quickly came to the realization that these people weren't the police and that fact scared the hell out of him. In fact this latest revelation gripped him with an icy fear. The intruders had yet to demand anything from him and he couldn't begin to understand what they were doing in his office. What could they possibly want from him?

"I don't keep anything of value here, just the money me and my friend have on us," he probed.

"Shut up, bitch, we ain't here to rob you," Little Man viciously kneed Rene' in the rib cage.

"Save it, for him," another man's voice roared thunderously. Rene' couldn't see him, but he got the feeling the man meant Tim.

"So, you're the brave mutha fucker who likes to beat the ladies? Don't seem like much to me. Whatcha got to say for yourself," Luther taunted Tim with his calm, collected voice.

Tim just stared blankly across the room.

"Ain't got nothing to say, huh, bitch?" Little Man reared back to hit Tim.

"What the fuck is wrong with him?" JC commented.

"Mutha fucker looks all tranced and shit."

"He's under hypnosis. He's my patient," Rene' breathed laboriously.

"How the fuck do we wake him up?"

"Let me loose and I can do it, but it has to be done gently and it will take a little time," Rene' explained.

"Fuck that," Little Man said, striking Tim across the face with the pistol in his hand. Tim's eyes focused and darted wildly around the room. The man then kicked Tim squarely in the chest, knocking him and the chair backward onto the floor.

"Hey," Rene' screamed out in protest and tried to struggle back to his feet. One of the men kicked out, hitting him in the ribs and knocking him back to the floor.

"This ain't got nothing to do with you, doc, just shut your mouth and you'll live to see another day."

As many questions as Rene' had, he knew the best thing to do was to keep his mouth shut and hoped he could figure out what was going on just by listening to the men's conversation. He didn't have a clue about who these men were, but he could tell they meant business. And the bottom line was, in no way would he be able to help Tim if he were dead.

"Pick Billy Bad Ass off the floor and put him back in the chair," JC, the apparent leader of the group ordered.

Tim felt two sets of hands grasping at him and pulling him of the floor and slamming him back into the chair he had been sitting in. He was still dazed from both the effects of having been under hypnosis and having just been pistol whipped. He was trying to shake the cobwebs from his head and listen to the men at the same time.

"I'm going to put this as straight as I can, we ain't got no beef with you, personally, but there is someone who does. And they pay pretty good."

"I got a personal beef with this candy ass mutha fucker. He fucked that sister up for nothing, man. Crazy mutha fuckers like this don't deserve to walk the earth with the rest of us," Little Man jammed his pistol into Tim's eye socket.

The blood vessels in Tim's eye broke under the pressure of the gun barrel. He could feel his eye already beginning to swell shut.

"Like I said, I ain't got nothing personal against you, but I still have to kill you. And it's going to hurt, a lot. You see, my instructions are to make you pay for what you done to that girl. You should have stayed in your white bread world fucking with them bitches, they ain't got nobody caring about them enough for paybacks."

"You can't be serious. He didn't do anything. He had nothing to do with that girl," Rene' struggled.

"Shut him the fuck up," JC ordered.

Immediately one of the men crossed the room and stripped off a piece of duct tape, wrapping it around Rene's head.

"Listen, doc, like I said, we're going to do what we have to do and there's nothing you can do or say to change that. Ain't a one of us got a problem with putting a cap between your ears, but someone I wouldn't want to cross does have a problem with it. Don't make me have to go against our orders," the man put his gun barrel against Rene's temple. He felt the coldness of the steel and immediately understood the meaning. He could feel pockets of his tears welling up inside the duct tape blindfold he was wearing.

Tim sat in the chair, cold and unresponsive. His guilt had been eating away at him and he truly felt he might deserve whatever was coming his way. What goes around comes around was about as true a proverb as they come.

"Get his wallet out," JC ordered.

"What do you need my wallet for," Tim finally spoke, a numbing fear spreading through him. Tim knew that there could only be one reason they wanted his wallet.

"See, that's all part of making you hurt," the man explained as he thumbed through Tim's wallet. He tossed aside the credit cards and useless business cards, the pictures were what he was after. "Looks like you don't have much of a family, just that pretty little bitch we saw earlier."

"Damn, she's fine, too. What's she doing with a low life like you," Little Man commented, grabbing his crotch and rubbing it suggestively to slam the point home.

"Please, no," Tim burst into tears.

"Rene tried to squirm on the floor, becoming acutely aware of the horrific gravity of the situation.

"We already got someone picking her up from your place and bringing her here."

"Yeah, man, we gonna all take turns with your bitch right in front of you, and then we're gonna do her just like you tried to do our client's granddaughter."

Tim started to get to his feet, "you can't be serious. She's got nothing to do with this."

Luther knocked him back into the chair.

"What do the women you like to cut up have to do with anything?" Little Man spoke with hatred flaring up in his eyes.

Tim remained silent. He could sense that the men were on the verge of violence and he didn't want to push them over the edge, at least not with Rene' in the room with him.

"Just what I thought. And the whole time we're doing your woman, we're going to tell her why we're doing her. Cause her man's a little pussy who likes to get his jollies off by hurting women."

"Please, I beg you, don't hurt my Elsa," Tim began to sob un-controllably.

"You should have thought of this earlier," JC said, feeling a twinge of pity trying to assert itself. Maybe, he thought, there wouldn't be a reason to torture the man by using his woman. Even for JC that seemed obsessive.

The hopelessness of Tim's situation began to sink in. It was one thing of they wanted to torture and kill him, but he just couldn't let them hurt Elsa.

"Not only are we gonna hurt your bitch, we're gonna let her live so she can suffer for the rest of her life. And every time she thinks of what we did to her, she will think of you and know it all happened to her because of you. She gonna hate even the memory of you after I'm through with the bitch. I'm gonna shove my big Johnson right up her tight white ass," Little Man hissed through his teeth, leaning right down into Tim's face when he said it.

Tim went wild. He exploded on the man like a demon pos-sessed. He sank his teeth into the man's cheek and began hitting and kicking him. Instantly he turned his attention to the next closest man to him. He tackled the man with the force of a football lineman, send-ing the man sprawling to the ground. He slammed his elbow to the man's throat, incapacitating him instantly.

"Stop," JC barked, pointing the muzzle of his gun to Rene's temple. "Do you like this man? Cause he sure as hell about to be dead."

"Okay, okay," Tim said, the fight taken out of him immediately.

"Mutha fucker bit me," Little Man screamed, leg sweeping Tim and knocking him to the floor. Tim head crashed against the carpet and immediately his vision went black.

"Get that prick back into the chair," Luther said, picking himself off the floor and rubbing his tender throat while grabbing the roll of duct tape off Rene's desk.

————————

"It looks like this place is locked up for the day, Blain."

"Damn, is everything a dead end in this case? Why don't we just take a little look around before we go back to the station? I mean, since we're already here," a devilish grin spread across his face.

"I don't know, little things like warrants and probable cause pop into mind."

Inside the office, Tim was dragged back into the chair and his ankles were quickly bound to the legs of the chair with duct tape. He was still woozy from hitting his head on the carpet and offered little, if no resistance.

"This will keep you from trying that shit again," Little Man said, placing the barrel of his pistol to Tim's foot and pulling the trigger. Instantly, Tim's foot was on fire. He screamed out in pain and began writhing in his chair.

"Tape his fuckin' mouth," JC ordered.

Out on the street in front of the building, both detectives tried to decipher the sound they had just heard.

"What the fuck was that?" Premoe asked, instinctively dropping to one knee and drawing his revolver.

"Sounded like a gun shot to me," Freeman responded.

"Sounds like probable cause to me," Premoe said as he immediately wheeled around and headed back for their car.

"Unit Fourteen Hotel to dispatch, we have shots fired at 1215 King Street, send additional units to our location.

Premoe popped the trunk of their car and pulled out a tire iron.

"Watch your eyes," he said, smashing the tire iron into the plate glass window, shattering it enough for the two of them to walk through.

"So much for the element of surprise," Freeman shook his head.

"Look," Premoe pointed at the secretary's feet sticking out from behind the desk.

Quickly the detectives moved to Vicki's prone form. Premoe checked on her vitals and found that she had a pulse and was breathing.

"Are you injured?" He whispered close to her face.

Vicki shook her head. Premoe began to carefully unwrap the duct tape from around her wrists and head. He rolled her enough so that she could see him and put a finger to his lips. She understood what he wanted and nodded slowly.

"What the fuck was that?" Little Man asked, hearing the glass door shatter out front.

"Go check on that bitch out front. Make sure she ain't called the cops," JC ordered.

Tim was trying to fight the pain in his leg, trying to get his head clear enough to think. Things were moving fast and he was certain they were about to move even faster. He tried to come up with a plan to get himself and Rene' out of there alive.

Rene' had heard the crash out front as well. He hoped that Vicki had somehow gotten herself free and was running as far and fast away from the place as she could.

Jesus Christ, Doc! What have you gotten yourself into? Tim's head echoed with Cracker's deranged laughter.

"Leave me alone, you son of a bitch!"

Now, Doc, is that anyway to talk to the man who's going to get you out of all this?"

"Just stay away from me. I don't need your help."

"Who the fuck is he talking to?"

"Ain't got a clue. The boy's touched. No telling who he could be talking to."

Premoe and Freeman were still leaning down checking on Vicki's condition when Little Man rounded the corner, giving the detectives the element of surprise. Premoe saw the man's shoes from under the desk and tapped his partner's arm.

"You causing trouble out here, bitch?" The man called out loudly.

The detective looked at each other with a confused look. This wasn't one of the players they were expecting. Immediately Blain trained his weapon in the direction of the voice.

"Police Department," Freeman announced, raising up from behind the desk. Immediately he saw the man's arm starting to raise up from his side, he saw the pistol in the man's hand and instinctively dropped back down behind the cover of the desk. Blain fired from under the desk, hitting the man in the shin. He and Freeman had been partners for long enough that Premoe was able to read his body language. And what Freeman was telling him was that the man had a gun.

The man fired before being hit, but the shot went wide and struck a picture on the wall. He screamed in agony as Premoe's bullet ripped through his leg. He fell to the carpet clutching his shattered shin bone.

"Fourteen Hotel to dispatch, we're going to need that back up, now! Send a wagon to 1215 King Street, we have a man down," Freeman screamed into his radio. Premoe pushed the panic button in his radio to alert dispatch of officers needing assistance. At this point, the more the merrier.

"Damn, JC, Little Man shot the bitch! What the fuck you bring that crazy son of a bitch into this for?"

"What the fuck? I told that little prick not to hurt her," the leader of the trio said, stepping out of Rene's office and into the hallway. He listened for a few seconds before calling out, "Little Man. Little Man." The passageway was silent.

Premoe and Freeman crouched behind the desk waiting for the other intruder to make his way into the lobby. These unknown aggressors confused both detectives, but neither one of them wanted to rush finding out who they were or why they were there. Premoe drug the wounded man over to them and shoved his hand over the man's mouth. Little Man tried to struggle but soon realized it was useless and opted for the less painful avenue of lying still.

Tim could feel the entity taking over his mind once more. He tried to fight Cracker's intrusion, but the man was quickly gaining a stranglehold on his psyche. For the first time since his ordeal began, Tim actually felt the tangible presence of another dancing within his mind. It felt as if someone were toying with the physical aspects of his very persona. Something told him that this was no schizophrenic delusion. Tim fought between the idea of him being mentally ill or demonically possessed, the later seeming more logical at the moment. Slowly, a fog began to envelop his conscious thought, leaving him at the mercy of the interloper.

Cracker took several moments to glance around the room and assess the situation. He could feel extreme pain radiating from his foot and shooting up his host's shinbone. The room was becoming clearer, he finally had total control over his host. Glancing down he saw the bullet hole in his shoe and a puddle of blood on the carpet beneath his foot. He tried to lift his leg, but quickly realized he was restrained.

Cracker looked at the man who was obviously his captor, there was fear and apprehension radiating from the man's eyes. He knew it was going to be easy taking him out. Cracker knew the man would hesitate when the time came. He began twisting and wiggling his ankles while the man was distracted. He wanted to loosen up the bindings as much as possible before bending over to undo the tape the rest of the way. The man might not notice him moving his ankles, but he would certainly see him bend over so he would only have seconds once he acted.

"Little Man," JC called out once more, easing down the corridor toward the lobby.

Premoe tried to get a bead on the man as he moved down the passageway. Freeman had moved from behind the desk and was standing beside a half wall partition in the foyer of the building. Both detectives waited patiently for the target to come into view.

"Shit, Five-O," JC screamed out and fired at the desk. He continued to fire as he ran back the way he had come.

The detectives dove for cover as the hallway erupted with the man's muzzle flash. Premoe was only able to get off one round before the man darted back inside the office and slammed the door shut.

"Are you all right? How the hell did he see you?" Freeman

asked.

"I'm fine. Shit, he saw you. He saw your reflection in that picture," Premoe pointed to a large frame hanging on the wall.

"I wonder if he's alone?"

"I doubt it. It sounded like he was warning someone else to me. No telling how many of them there are."

"What in the hell have we stepped into, Blain?"

"I don't have a clue. Where in the hell is our back up?" He growled, trying to catch a glimpse down the corridor. A shot rang out, forcing him to dart back behind the desk like a snail retracting into its shell when touched.

"What the fuck was all that, JC?" Luther cried out as soon as the big man was safely back in the office.

"There's cops out there."

"What about Little Man?"

"Didn't see him. They probably pinched his ass already. That bitch must have made it to the phone somehow."

Cracker knew it wasn't the secretary who called the cops. They were there because of him, or his host anyway. He had half a mind just to let the good doctor be arrested right then, but he needed the release that a good fight would give him. He was going to have to be a good boy from now on, at least until the doctor was safely on death row and he learned more about his newly found powers. Besides, he had one more job for his host, one that would certainly seal his fate forever.

Rene' cringed with each and every shot that rang out. He prayed that Vicki was all right. His stomach felt queasy at the thought of these men having done something to her.

Cracker carefully eyed the two men. He wiggled his ankles one more time, even though it hurt like hell. He wished he had spent more time reading the book trying to find out more about its mysterious powers. He wondered if there was a way of getting inside someone's head without feeling their pain.

Feeling that the tape had loosened quite a bit, Cracker bent over and pulled the tape off from one of his ankles. Quickly he rose back up, seeing the leader of the two men turn toward him.

"Mutha fucker, sit still," the man pointed his gun at their prisoner.

There was suddenly a lot of commotion coming from the lobby.

"What was that, JC?"

"Sounds like more five-o got here," he said with deep concern in his voice.

"What are we gonna do?"

"Quiet, let me think."

"This is the police," Premoe yelled, standing beside the closed door of the doctor's office. "There's only two ways out of there, I'd prefer you do it walking."

"JC, they gonna bust in here any minute," Luther cried out nervously.

"I know, now shut the fuck up and let me think," the leader said nervously. In one quick motion Cracker leaned all his weight into the chair and toppled to the floor. As soon as he connected with the carpet he ripped the tape from his other leg and scooted behind the desk beside Rene'.

"Shit," Luther cried out and made a move for their hostage.

"Forget them, we gotta get out of here."

Cracker fought furiously to get the tape off from around Rene's arms and legs. He was certain that he could play the good doctor convincingly enough that Rene' would never notice that Tim's alter ego had unexpectedly joined the fracas.

"We have to get out of here, Tim," Rene' said the minute his gag was off.

"How?"

"The emergency exit."

"They'll be covering the door."

"Maybe it's time for you to just give up and we'll see where things go from there."

"You heard the gunshots. They aren't playing around. I think they want me dead," Cracker pleaded, not wanting to give up just yet.

He knew he could play on this sucker's emotions. Part of the transference process allowed him access to the good doctor's personal filing cabinet in his brain. He was privy to all sorts of sickening sentimentalities and emotional baggage. He had hated that aspect of it at first, but grew to enjoy being able to prey off the man's weaknesses.

"The remodeled office might throw them off," Rene' offered.

"What?" Cracker asked, actually thrown by the man's comments. He might be able to draw from Tim's mental library, but not if the book wasn't in there.

"Just like the bathroom. When they remodeled, I had them add a small sleeping compartment. It's hidden behind another panel."

"Won't they find it if they search?"

"Maybe, but I doubt it. It is almost seamless and it locks from the inside. If they don't know to look for it they might not find it. We can just hide out there until things clear up."

"Sounds like a plan. Where is it?"

"Hell," Rene' laughed nervously. "I'll have to get my bearings straight or I won't find it."

"Hurry, I don't think we have much time before the gunfight starts," he nodded his head toward the panicked kidnappers.

Both men were standing in the center of the office turning their heads from side to side, looking for a way out. There were no windows in the place and the emergency exit was slightly hidden behind rubber tree plant in a small alcove.

"Okay, I got it. It's over on the wall with the thermostat, exactly twelve panel boards from the thermostat. We just push on the wall and the door will open."

"This is the police, there's no way out," a voice boomed from the hallway.

"Good, that's shielded from the emergency exit, the trick is to get those bastards to go for that way out. We've got no shot if the cops come in through the front door. Hang on, you make a move for the panel as soon as I get them to take the bait," Cracker explained.

Quickly he leapt to his feet and made a move toward the emergency exit.

"What are you doing mutha fucker," Luther screamed at him the moment he spied his movement.

"Police! You've got one minute."

Cracker gave the alcove a scrutinizing glance and then looked away.

"JC, look there's, a door."

JC moved around the room and saw the emergency exit. "Where does that lead?" He asked, jabbing his gun into the face of his captive.

"Police!" A voice cried out followed by muffled conversation.

"JC, they're gonna use the ram."

"A storage room and the basement," he lied.

"Any way out from the basement?"

"There's a service entrance that leads to the back alley," Cracker found it hard not to smile.

"You're one lucky son of a bitch. Don't think this means we're through with you. You just bought yourself some time is all. If I were you, I'd make myself disappear," JC said, moving quickly for the emergency exit.

He considered shooting the man right where he stood but he knew that would draw return fire from the cops and JC was in no mood to be dodging a hail of bullets.

"I plan to," Cracker whispered. Once the men were past him he hit the floor, not wanting to be in the line of fire.

Rene' took the movement as his cue and half ran, half dove across the room. He came to rest at the edge of the door and pushed the panel. He heard the telltale click of the latch giving way and waited for Tim to make the next move.

Luther was the first one to the door. In a near panic he undid the deadbolt and jerked the door open. Suddenly, he was standing face to face with more than a dozen of Jacksonville's finest. He raised his gun, without giving a single thought to the consequences. His body was flung backward from the hail of bullets pummeling him. The gun was dislodged from his hand as his body crashed to the ground. Cracker picked up the Glock and rolled toward where Rene' was holding the paneled door open for him.

"You mutha fucker," JC screamed out, turning to fire at the doctor.

"Get in there," Cracker screamed at Rene' and fired, hitting JC and spinning him around to meet a second volley of gunshots head on.

The office door burst open and a concussion grenade was tossed into the room. Cracker heard the dull thud of the grenade and knew to take cover. He fired a volley of shots at the front door hoping to keep the police at bay for one more second. He then turned to the bleeding man on the floor and put several shots into his back. In his last burst of energy he dove for the cover of the paneled room. The concussion grenade exploded, but the secret room shielded them from the brunt of the blast's force. Rene' quickly set the latch on the door and locked it from the inside. The pair of fugitives sat and listened quietly as the police rushed the office. Cracker fought hard against the urge to laugh out loud. He had always thought the police were idiots, now he was certain of the fact.

———————

"Christ," Premoe cried out. "Put a rush on that meat wagon, we've got an officer down."

Freeman's felt his body slowly losing internal temperature and wondered if he was dying.

"Hang in there buddy," Premoe said, tearing off his clothes and using his T-shirt as a bandage.

"Pretty bad, isn't it?" Freeman mouthed.

"Nothing you can't handle," he replied, pressing even harder on the wound in his partner's neck.

"Awe, shit," Frank said, walking up on the scene. "I want that ambulance here, now!" He screamed at the crowd of gawking uniformed officers.

Each and every one of the dozen men in the cramped corridor

felt helpless. There was nothing they could do but watch their brother in arms slowly bleed to death. Some of the men felt anger welling up inside of them like a torrential storm. Others fought to hold back the tears brought on by the brutal realization of their own mortality. It was nothing more than dumb luck that Freeman had been hit during the barrage of gunfire. It was a bullet that could have easily killed any one of them.

"I'm getting weaker, Blain," Todd said, feeling panic spread through his body along with the creeping chill of death.

Premoe fought hard to hold back his tears as his partner's blood pumped between his fingers. He could feel the man starting to shiver beneath his grasp and knew that meant death wasn't too far off.

"I'm starting to get cold. Blain. I don't think I'm going get the chance . . ." he said weakly while staring into his partner's tear stained eyes.

"I know, buddy. I'll call her. Don't worry, I'll take care of everything, you just worry about hanging on. Get me some kind of blanket," Premoe yelled. "You hang in there, buddy. I can hear the ambulance coming down the street now. You'll be on your way to the hospital in no time," Premoe tried to comfort his partner.

He witnessed the glazed look spreading across the man's eyes and knew it wouldn't be much longer and he would bleed out or die of shock. The force of the blood squirting out of the wound had diminished drastically, indicating the man's blood pressure was dropping. Tears began fighting their way to the surface, but Premoe knew he couldn't cry, not yet anyway.

"They're here," Frank cried out.

Premoe slid over to make room for the paramedics. One of the men took over for him and continued to apply pressure to the wound while the other man started an I.V. The small corridor instantly exploded into a flurry of activity as the paramedics began trying to save the man's life. Premoe saw that he was just going to be in the way and moved down the corridor toward his boss.

"What the fuck happened, Blain?"

"I'm not sure really. I guess the perps tried to go out the back door and the shooting started. Todd was the first one through this door and must have gotten caught in the crossfire."

"Why would the perps be shooting at this door if they were going out the back?"

"Maybe we surprised one of them when we used the ram on the door."

"Who the hell were these guys and why were they here?"

"I don't have a clue, Frank. We just came down here to talk with the doctor. He's Duggan's best friend."

"Do these guys have anything to do with the case against Duggan?" Frank Walker asked, pointed to two bodies on the floor.

"I'm not sure. It could all be just a dumb coincidence. Maybe they were robbing the place and we just surprised them. The confusing thing is that neither Duggan or the Doctor Meade were even here."

"Rob a psychiatrist's office? Where's the money in that?" Frank questioned.

"Maybe they thought there were drugs on the premises."

"We're ready to roll," one of the paramedics called out to the crowd.

"Frank, I'm going to ride with Todd to the hospital. Do me a favor, have someone box up everything in the doctor's desk, files and all. There might be something in there that will give us a clue to this freaking mess."

"Sure thing, Blain. I'll have the stuff sent back to the squad room along with anything else that the investigation team might find. Make sure you give me a call as soon as you know something and I'll try to make it up to the hospital as soon as I get the ball rolling here," Frank called after Premoe.

"Yeah," he responded half-heartedly, his attention now focused on his partner. He felt a small ripple of relief when he saw Freeman on the gurney in the back of the ambulance. The color had started to return to his lips and he no longer looked like one of the many unfortunate stiffs that they had dealt with during their days together.

The wail of the siren was drowned out by Premoe's thoughts. He prayed to a God he barely believed in, hoping that if He did truly exist, He would extend his merciful hand down from the heavens and save his best friend's life. Looking down, he caught Freeman's eyes and smiled just before the man faded out. At first, sheer terror tugged at his heart, but then he realized that the monitors hooked up to his partner seemed to be working and neither of the paramedics had seemed to notice anything unusual. He was just asleep. Premoe returned his thoughts to prayer.

CHAPTER SIXTEEN

"T he little prick really did it, didn't he?" Carl Lettimore said.

"Who? Did what?" True asked, coming back to reality.

"Cracker, he got himself out of here," he looked over at the empty cell.

"Sort of looks that way doesn't it. You know what they say, good things happen to bad people."

"Kind of strange not having to listen to the crazy bastard."

"I know the feeling. I think I can still hear him at times though."

"I heard that. Hey man, how are you holding up," concern flowed out with the inmate's words.

"I'm okay."

"I missed you while you were away. I heard you got time in the box."

"Yeah, but it was all good. It gave me a chance to grieve on my own. The warden knew what was up and he made sure they took it easy on me."

"How's your granddaughter?"

"She's recovering well. But the baby may not make it," tears glistened his eyes.

"I'm sorry to hear that. I'll say a prayer for them both."

"Thank you," True said, lost in somber thought.

The row fell into an uncanny silence. Carl Lettimore studied the look that had washed over the old inmate. The lines in his face had deepened over the past couple of weeks, making him look much older than he really was. His skin looked like old leather that had been left outside to bear the cruelty of the elements. His eyes no longer held that little glimmer of hope the old man always seemed to convey, even in the bowels of their personal hell. Carl Lettimore learned a lot about life in that one single, precious moment. He understood what pain could do to a person. Pain that he himself had caused others during his lifetime. For the first time in the convict's miserable life did he truly feel remorse. Not just sorry for sorry's sake. Not just empty regrets hoping to earn the sympathies of those who might grant him a reprieve from his punishment. No, this was true, deep-rooted remorse. Carl Lettimore began to cry.

True stood in front of the man's cell trying to fight back his own tears. "What's wrong, Carl?" He asked sympathetically

"With Cracker gone, I'm next." He paused long enough to choke back his tears. "True, tell me something, and no bullshit."

"What, Carl?"

"Am I ever going to be forgiven for all the bad I've caused?"

True thought for a minute before answering, "Yes, I believe you will. There's no need to be scared, Carl," the man replied without hesitation.

"I am scared, True, more scared than I have ever been in my life."

"Why are you so scared, Carl?"

"Because, as long as I'm alive, the devil can't get at me. But the minute they kill me . . ." his voice trailed off into tears.

True patted his arm and said, "there's no need to worry about that, Carl, God has a place for you, as long as you're ready to accept it."

"Will I make it to heaven?" He looked up into True's face with red, puffy eyes.

True caught the man's gaze and read the pure penitence in the man's eyes. "Yes, Carl, you will make it into heaven one day."

"Then I guess this makes it all worth it," he glanced around his cell. Death wouldn't be such a penalty to pay to the living if it bought him a ticket for the big dance.

Are you still with me, Doc?"

Tim's head echoed with the intruder's voice. He watched Rene' standing poised at the cleverly concealed door straining to hear what was going on in the other room. He felt weak, too weak to keep fighting the beast living within his own mind.

"I think they're packing up their stuff and getting ready to leave for the night. God, I hope so, it seems like they've been here forever," Rene' whispered.

I've got one last surprise for you, Doc!

Tim struggled for control of his own mind. He could feel his sanity slipping away with each tick of the clock. He wanted nothing more than to tell Rene' about the voice he was hearing, but it had grown too late for that. He no longer had enough control to think or speak for himself. The accursed entity had gained complete and utter control of him, only allowing his consciousness to come along for the ride.

"I think they're gone now. I haven't heard anything for quite a while."

He truly is your friend, isn't he? It's going to be a pity when you have to kill him.

Tim fought hard to regain control of his mind. He fought with everything he had. Nevertheless, for every step of progress he made, it seemed that Cracker took him two backwards.

"What wrong, Tim?" Rene' asked and turned around. He thought he had heard his friend whimpering.

Tim didn't say a word, he just sat on the edge of a small cot in the room and stared back at his friend. Tears streamed down his face. He understood what he was about to do, and he knew there was nothing he could do to stop himself.

"What is it, buddy?" Rene' asked, making his move to cross the short distance between the two of them.

Nothing personal, Buddy, but this is going to hurt a bit.

Tim stood up from the cot against his will. He moved much too quickly for Rene' to be able to react. Before he knew it, Tim had raised his arm and put the muzzle of the pistol against his Adam's apple. Rene' noticed something wrong with Tim's eyes; they were no longer his blue eyes. They were the same eyes he had seen hours earlier. Green, laced with red tints.

"Tim?" Rene' breathed his final word.

"Sorry," was all the sound that Tim was able mouth before pulling the trigger.

Rene's body was thrown violently backward onto the carpet. Immediately he clutched and clawed at his throat. Blood sprayed from the open wound and a sickening pink foam began to form around the gaping hole as he struggled for breath. Merciless laughter echoed through Tim's mind as Cracker decided it was time to leave the good doctor to his designed fate. Wordlessly Tim watched as his best friend struggled for the last minutes of life. Rene' stared back at him with wild-eyed confusion. Then he stared back with nothing at all.

Wracked with violent sobs, Tim placed the muzzle of the pistol in his mouth. He prayed a short prayer and pulled the trigger. He pulled the trigger again. And again. Then he dropped to his knees and laid his head on the idle chest of his best friend. The gun was empty. He had been cheated once more.

Tim sat on the floor for what seemed like hours. Finally, after having made the only decision he thought feasible given the situation, he opened the hidden panel door and went into Rene's office. The place still looked like a battle zone. There was blood sprayed all over everything.

Tim stepped over a puddle of blood that was outlined in the shape of a human form. He realized it had been where the leader of the three men died. He felt surreal, as if he were moving about on another plane of existence. Like all of this was just a nightmare and he was about to wake up and be lying next to his lovely wife. He glanced back into the private office and saw Rene's corpse sprawled across the carpet and knew that was just wishful thinking. This was a nightmare all right, but one he was never going to awaken from.

He picked the telephone up off from the floor. There was a bullet hole going straight through it. He placed the received back on the cradle and waited several minutes before picking it back up and placing it to his ear. There was a dial tone. He dialed 911 and hung up. The phone rang back, he didn't answer. It rang back again.

Tim picked up the receiver and exhaled his entire life. "Help," was all he could manage to get out before letting the phone drop to the floor. He laid down on the carpet in the fetal position and began to cry.

Cracker was still feeling the rush of his transcendental murder when the phone interrupted his daydreaming. He was reluctant to pick it up. It was probably just the bastards from the Police Department keeping tabs on him. What they called "passive surveillance" was nothing more than legalized harassment.

"Yeah, what is it," he answered on the fifth ring.

"Mr. Graham?" A familiarly annoying voice chimed through the receiver.

"What is it, Patterson?"

"I just thought you might like to know, an officer from the Jacksonville Police Department will be stopping by there sometime today. They wouldn't tell me exactly when."

"What the fuck do they want?"

"They are going to remove the tether. You are a free man, Mr. Graham. The real killer turned himself in to the police tonight. He has confessed to everything. The district attorney has been forced to drop all charges against you."

"I could kiss you, Simon," Cracker said, knowing that his attorney hadn't done shit. He had done everything.

"I don't think that's necessary, Mr. Graham. I still need to see you at the office to sign some papers and discuss the next course of action you may want to pursue."

"Next course of action?"

"Lawsuits Mr. Graham. You were wrongfully imprisoned."

"Oh, this just keep getting better," he laughed and hung up the phone.

He felt so revitalized, like he had been given a second chance at life. In fact, that's exactly what he had been given. A chance to put things right. A chance to be a better person. A chance to kill again and never get caught.

CHAPTER SEVENTEEN

"Frank, don't you find it a little strange that this Duggan character gave himself up so easily?" Freeman asked, his throat still quite tender from the gunshot wound.

"He knew it was hopeless. You know for a fact that most of these vicious serial killer types are really cowards when it comes to them getting hurt themselves. More often than not they can't even find the nerve to kill themselves."

"I don't buy his confession either."

"What is your problem with this, Todd?" Frank asked.

"My problem is that it all seems to be in a nice neat little package hand delivered to us."

"He's right, Frank, it does seem a bit too tidy for my tastes as well," Premoe butted in.

"What do you guys want from me? The mountain of evidence we have against this guy is indisputable. Gun shot residue, fingerprints, DNA and only God knows what else, how can I ignore that?" Frank argued, even though he didn't believe Duggan was guilty himself. He had been a homicide detective for a long time before earning the Chief's job and had the instincts needed to be a detective. And his instincts were screaming that this was wrong, no matter what the evidence suggested.

"Just don't close out this case yet. I'll be out of here tomorrow and Blain and I can start going over the files together one last time."

"And then you'll give it a rest?"

"Yes, if we sift through all of the evidence one more time and don't turn up anything new, I'll concede that Duggan must be the killer and admit we owe Graham an apology."

"I wouldn't go that far partner," Premoe said.

"He's suing the city, you know?" Frank blurted.

"Does he have a leg to stand on?"

"The way things are going right now, I'd have to say not only does Graham have a leg to stand on, he'll probably end up a millionaire at the city's expense," Frank explained.

"Damn it," Premoe grunted.

"Unless," Frank thought out loud.

"Unless what, Frank?"

"Unless you two are right and can come up with some compelling evidence that will either exonerate Duggan and implicate Graham once again, or if you can prove that they were accomplices."

"How long do we have?" Freeman asked in a fragmented sentence, beginning to struggle with conversation due to his injury. His throat was becoming dry and raw from talking.

"I don't think you have very much time at all. Word is that Duggan is planning to plead guilty at arraignment. I also have it on good authority that he plans to ask for the death penalty and also plans on waiving his appeal rights."

"Christ, Frank, does that sit right with you?"

"Actually, no, it doesn't. I spoke with the FBI profiler again and he claims Duggan's behavior doesn't fit the profile of the killer. In fact, he spoke with Duggan himself and he said he would stake his reputation on the fact that Duggan has never killed anyone or anything in his life. You can read the report for yourself once you get back to the station house."

"So, is Duggan covering for Graham?"

"I don't know. There seems to be a lot about this case that I don't know."

"I get released from here this afternoon. Blain and I can get started first thing in the morning."

Premoe chuckled out loud.

"What does the doctor say about returning to duty?" Frank asked.

"Limited duty. I'm supposed to take it easy for the first couple of weeks. He doesn't think I should be out on the street, but he said desk duty would be fine. I'll make Blain do all the leg work."

"You're damn lucky, you know that?"

"Yes, Frank, I do. The doctor said that the bullet narrowly missed destroying my larynx by a fraction of an inch. They claim that Blain saved my life by getting pressure on the wound so quickly. And just what in the hell are you grinning at?" Freeman turned to his partner who was wearing a shit-eating grin.

"You sound like that kid from the old Little Rascals television show, you know Froggy," he could no longer contain his laughter. Frank was quiet for a few seconds but then joined Premoe in laughter.

"Funny. Blain, you're such an asshole," he chuckled.

"Yeah, but I saved your life, now you owe me one," he winked at his partner. An overwhelming glow rushed though his body and he almost began to cry. Premoe really would have been lost had his partner died. Although neither of them, would admit it in public, they were best of friends.

Cracker spent the first few days of his freedom locked away in his mother's house. He wanted nothing more than a little peace and quiet. The old bitch had welcomed him home with open arms, well at least with open arm. He had only been home for two meals and had already started craving prison food. Tasteless boiled chicken and boxed macaroni and cheese was not his idea of home cooking. Nevertheless, it was good to be free again.

When Cracker finally saw his mother for this first time in years he had to step back and admire his work. He had beaten and maimed her long ago but she still seemed to love him dearly. Maybe it was her way of trying to repay him for her whoring ways during his youth. He was actually quite impressed with the way she had adapted to the loss of her hand and most of her mind. She was incoherent and babbled for a good portion of the day, yet, could still answer most of the questions on Jeopardy in the evening.

Edna Graham moved around the house with as much grace as a one armed idiot could muster. She took good care of her son. He was such a fine boy.

By the end of the first week, Cracker was ready to kill again. The old bitch was driving him crazy. Late one evening he had almost lost his self control during Letterman. The old bat just wouldn't shut up and when he yelled at her she began to cry. And not regular tears like a normal person, but the incessant wailing of an idiot. He had watched her rocking back and forth on the couch with her knees pulled up to her chest for half an hour before he'd finally had enough of her pathetic display. He had gone as far as to have gone to the kitchen and rifled through the knife drawer looking for the perfect tool. He pulled the honing rod from the knife block on the kitchen counter and began honing a razor fine edge onto his favorite knife. Finally this diversion helped to abate his anger and he settled for two of his mother's powder blue Halcion tablets, three bottles of beer and a long, restful sleep.

Over the course of his first week of freedom, Cracker had tried his transference magic several times hoping to be able to gain the release he needed. However, the only success he had were brief periods of floating in and out of the doctor's mind and that would do him no good now that the man was incarcerated.

The bastards at the prison had found the book tucked away in his personal belongings and refused to let him take it home with him. The damn thing had been stamped front and back with Property of Starke Prison. True was getting more and more difficult to visit with each passing day and Cracker was certain that his days of haunting the old man were drawing to a close. Nevertheless, he was still mildly comforted by the fact that he was still able to move in and out of the doctor's mind with ease. He thought that talent might come handy someday if for nothing more than a way to relieve his boredom. Maybe he would haunt the good doctor with visions of his wife. Cracker was suddenly itchy for some action. And against his better judgment, he relented to his urges.

The night air was cold against skin, but it was a good kind of cold. A vibrant kind of cold that only a free man gets to experience. Several dogs barked in the distance, but none in the upscale neighborhood he was walking through. He admired the subtle differences in architecture as he passed from home to home. He felt so good he almost began to whistle, but then, he might accidentally disturb one of the slumbering, unsuspecting denizens of the quiet little hamlet.

He stood outside of a blue-gray Cape Cod, staring at a solitary light burning through a downstairs window. The window was open and he could hear the sounds of running water echoing off the tiled walls of the room. He closed his eyes and breathed in deeply, partaking of the sweet scent of lily of the valley drifting through the night air. He felt a familiar stirring in his loins and this time it was his own organ rising to the occasion, not the good doctor's. Cracker silently crept closer to the blonde's house, making certain that he remained hidden within the comforting darkness of the shadows. Tall pampas grasses grew up along the back wall of the house. He slid between the wall of the house and the grasses so that their large white plumes conveniently obscured him from view of the other houses in the neighborhood. Standing beneath the bathroom window, Cracker listened to the sounds of life emanating from within the house. He found that he actually adored the sweet smelling blonde with nice tits and decided that he had to have her. He had to taste her innermost beauties for himself.

Cracker lost himself in his passion. He unzipped his trousers and began to fondle himself. A snicker escaped his lips as he thought of the good doctor. He wondered if the man's pecker had healed yet. The excruciating pain of that moment had scared Cracker immensely. He worried that his pain might have been something that lasted as long as the man's injuries did. It made him wonder what would happen to him if the man were to get his dumb ass killed while he was still in his mind. But within a few days the pain had passed, easing Cracker's worries of any kind of permanent damage. He could deal with a little bit of discomfort for the price of admission into the man's mind.

Cracker let out a pleasurable moan as his erotic adventure reached its apex.

"Hello," a woman's voice called out from inside the house.

Cracker melded himself into the shadows against the side of the house.

"Is there someone out there?" Elsa called to the darkness. Her skin tingled with the pinpricks of goose bumps.

Cracker held his breath.

Elsa quickly finished up with her nightly routine and shut the window. Panic nearly swept her away as she rushed through the house checking the rest of the windows. As she made her rounds she stopped in the foyer and checked the alarm system. All of the security zones bore a solid green light, indicating that all areas of the house were secure. She reset the alarm just to be certain. The little gray panel went through the motions of its self diagnosis and flashed back to solid green in all zones. Elsa breathed a little easier. She sat on the couch clutching her robe tightly to her body and thought about Tim.

Elsa found it nearly impossible to accept the fact that she had been living with such a monster for so long without ever suspecting anything. She couldn't begin to fathom the fact that she had been sleeping next to a cold-blooded serial killer. At first she didn't believe the evidence, even after the police told her that Tim had killed Rene'. But when Tim confessed to everything her whole world collapsed. She was both hurt and angry and had been seriously contemplating filing for divorce for several months. In fact, Elsa wasn't sure why she hadn't filed yet.

Cracker waited until the object of his desire had stopped walking around the house before darting out of the shadows and making his escape. He was definitely going to have to talk to the doctor about what a sweet piece of meat she was.

———

Tim was still quite numb. Even though several months had passed since his nightmare had culminated in the death of his best friend, his alienation from his wife and his new cell on death row, it all seemed as though it had happened just yesterday. And although his life seemed to be passing by at an accelerated rate, the events of his past seemed forever trapped in time; never changing.

Prison psychiatrists had poked and prodded him during his quarantine period to see whether he was sane or not. He found them to be quite peculiar. Half of them wanted to prove that he was sane so he could fry, while the other half expected him to act completely wacko in order to save his own life. One doctor had even coached him to do exactly that, even if it was an only act. The man just couldn't seem to understand the weight of Tim's guilt. For now at least, he felt dying would be the easiest way out.

One of the hardest things for Tim to get used to was that the hollow chamber reverberated even the smallest of sounds. A mouse scurrying across the floor sounded like a herd of elephants to him. All he wanted was peace and quiet before they came to take him to the chair.

A stab of pain shot through him as Elsa's voice came to him on a whisper of a memory. She never forgave him for Rene's death, in fact it had cemented her belief that she had somehow married a monster. She vehemently despised him for that betrayal. Nothing would ever seem quite right to her ever again. She would never trust another soul or her own judgment ever again.

Tim had been on the row for more than a week. He watched the old black man pushing his cart down the long corridor every day at the same time. He watched the old man stop in front of a vacant cell a few cells down as if to say something to someone that was no longer there. The sadness of the place had already begun eating away at what was left of Tim's soul.

"Excuse me," Tim said softly as the man neared his cell.

The old man just continued to push his cart, never once so much as even glancing at Tim.

"Excuse me, sir," Tim said a little louder.

Still, there was no response from the man. Tim began to think the man was deaf, or maybe just hard of hearing. His heart felt heavier when he noticed a trail of tears slowly escaping from the corner of the man's eye.

"All I want is a book," Tim pleaded.

True finally turned and looked toward Tim with a look that could have melted the polar ice caps. Yet, he still made certain not to make eye contact. The last thing True wanted was to see the truth about his little girl's pain.

"And all I want is to kill your sorry ass," he seethed.

Tim recoiled from the venomous assault.

"Judging by the look on your face you don't even have the decency to know who I am."

"But, how could I possibly know who you are? Why are you so angry with me?" Tim asked, sensing the hatred the man felt for him oozing out of his every pore.

"You've really got some nerve, boy," True hissed and continued on his way.

He couldn't take facing the man who had stolen the life from his granddaughter. Granted, she lived through the ordeal, but she didn't survive. With her husband and unborn child gone she was nothing more than a mere shell of what she had been. He hadn't received as much as a note from her since it had happened. The old man had no way of knowing that his granddaughter was so shameful of what had happened to her that she couldn't find the words to express her emotions to her grandfather. Regina had written to True almost every day, but he never knew that because she never quite found the courage to mail any of the letters. True found it nearly impossible to even breathe the same air as a man who could destroy such vitality.

Tim watched the old man until he disappeared through the large steel door at the end of the tier. He returned to his melancholy state of mind once more. He felt so drained of energy he found it difficult just to remain awake. At least he had one thing to be thankful for, he no longer heard the voice in his head. It had mysteriously vanished after he had killed Rene'. But even that solace came at a price. It had convinced him that he was truly insane.

"Man, you are either one stupid son of a bitch or you got no feelings at all," a faceless voice called from one of the cells on the row. It was hard to tell what direction sounds came from in the echo chamber.

After a brief patch of silence Tim spoke out. "Are you talking to me?" He asked after no one else claimed the conversation.

"Yeah, man. I'm talking to you."

"What are you talking about?"

"You really don't know, do you?"

"Know what?"

"That girl you cut up, that was his granddaughter. It was his great grand baby that was inside her."

"Oh my God," Tim gasped. After several moments of silence he asked, "How is she?" he suddenly felt extremely nauseous.

"Man, you sure you don't belong down in the loony unit? You killed the baby, and the woman's a basket case. I couldn't have done better myself," the inmate burst into a round of maniacal laughter.
Tim took the news like a sledgehammer against his chest. Just when he thought his emotional turmoil couldn't possibly get any worse, he

was spoon fed another bowl of guilt.

CHAPTER EIGHTEEN

"Hard to believe it's been more than six months isn't it?" Freeman stated, his voice no longer resembling that of a cigar smoking reptilian boy.

"Six months of nothing."

"Ever think we might be wrong?"

"Sometimes I stop and think about the fact that there hasn't been any activity since Duggan has been in prison, and yeah, I wonder if we're full of shit."

"Makes me wonder too, especially when we come up empty handed after spending another day down here in this pit," Freeman commented, tossing a box marked evidence up onto a table.

"How much longer do you think Frank's going to put up with this?"

"Not much longer I suspect," he replied.

"Do you think he knows we're dragging our feet?" Premoe laughed.

"If he doesn't he's an idiot, and we both know the answer to that one."

"I've got to admit, he's giving us a lot more leeway that I ever expected."

"I've also got my suspicions that he's been feeding us clearable cases too," Freeman said.

"I kind of figured the same thing. It's a good thing that the other detectives believe in our cause, otherwise this would have been over a long, long time ago. But I'm afraid we need a break in this case soon or it's finished."

"Very soon," Freeman responded, not looking up from the files he was poring over.

Both of the men sat at the table in a room adjacent to the evidence locker, each with his own box of goodies he was combing through. They had been over the files, shell casings, affidavits, confessions and testimonies more times than they cared to count over the past few months.

Sounds from a radio in the evidence room echoed through the dank basement. It wasn't loud enough to be able to discern any certain song or news tidbit, just loud enough to be annoying.

"I wish he would either turn that damned thing up or off," Premoe bellowed.

"Go tell him. I'm tired of hearing you bitch about it day after day."

"I don't feel like dealing with him today."

"You chicken shit," Freeman laughed.

"Hey, that guy is spooky. The way one eye always follows you around while the other one just stares at you."

"Damn, Blain, the man ate his windshield during a felony pursuit, what do you expect. He's as normal as you or I. Well, at least he's as normal as I am. You, on the other hand are a different story. You are such a chicken shit."

"What did you call me?"

"Read my lips, chicken shit," Freeman pursed his lips at his partner and spoke slowly.

"Yeah, well if you're wanting to have a face to face conversation with me, you'd better bend over."

"Up your ass," he laughed.

"I'm putting in a transfer, I can't this shit anymore," Premoe laughed as well.

Both men returned silently to their work. The radio continued to annoy Premoe, and he continued to annoy his partner. It had become their daily routine, when they didn't catch the occasional case, which wasn't very often lately. Frank understood their need to figure the Duggan case out and finally put this thing to rest once and for all, especially with Duggan's death date drawing ever closer.

"Hey, look at this, I never noticed it before," Freeman said, pushing a file folder at Premoe.

He read over the file and looked up at his partner with a doe in the headlights kind of stare.

"It says Duggan was adopted. That means maybe his real parents are still alive. Maybe he didn't really have such a nice, storybook childhood after all."

"Yeah, maybe we are wrong," Premoe sighed. "Where did that file come from?"

"It came from the box we gathered from his friend's office. The damned thing was marked "Financial Records" so I never even bothered to open it up before. What a rookie mistake," Freeman beat himself up over his oversight.

"It's forgivable, you're a putz."

"It doesn't look as though this Meade guy was actually Duggan's doctor, but it does look like he had referred him to another doctor. The referral form has some information about the adoption."

"Are you saying even Duggan's best friend thought he was nuts?"

"Hard to tell from this. According to Meade's notes, Duggan himself thought he was going insane. Also, this other doctor, Hughes, suggested that Duggan may be suffering from multiple personality disorder."

"Oh great, he is a whack job."

"I don't know about all that. Let's not jump the gun here. I think our best bet would be to talk to his parents, find out what he was like as a child. Find out why he was given up for adoption. We need those adoption records."

"They'll be sealed. We better call Frank and see about getting a judge to sign a warrant."

Both men stood up from the table and headed for the stairs leading out of the catacombs. Premoe positioned himself on the outside, against the peeling whitewashed wall, away from the wandering eye of the evidence clerk. He tried to stay in the shadows of the dimly lit corridor. Freeman laughed and shook his head.

"Excuse me, detectives," Connolly called out from behind his locked cage.   Premoe cringed.

"What it is, Connolly?" Freeman turned to face the man. Instantly he realized just how on the mark his partner was. He had never taken the time to study the man's face before. It was truly quite unsettling.

"I was going over the quarterly inventory yesterday and I found this box of stuff. I thought you guys might be interested in it."

"Hey, thanks," Freeman said, looking at the label and seeing that it was from the Duggan case. "Can you put it on the table in there for us, please."

"No, you guys are supposed to log that stuff back in when you're finished with it. It's not supposed to be left sitting out. That's why I have to keep doing these damned inventories, because you detectives keep losing things," he began a familiar tirade.

"Thanks a bunch," Premoe said, tugging at his partner's arm as he headed up the stairs.

They spent the next few hours kowtowing to everyone from Frank, several judicial types, to the adoption agency, trying to obtain the elusive background of Timothy Duggan. Their leg work finally paid off and they had the paperwork they needed to get the records from the agency.

After getting the documentation they desired from the agency, the detectives were too anxious to bother with driving back to the station to go over the new information. Instead, they sat in the parking lot of the adoption agency, poring over their latest discovery. They huddled so closely that to the uninformed passerby, they would have looked as though they were a couple sharing an intimate moment.

"Are you seeing what I see?" Premoe asked, pointing to a specific spot in the file.

"Two names at birth? What does that mean?"

"Damn, Dick Tracy, it means, Duggan is a twin."

"You're right. How did I miss that?"

"Look here. It says they weren't adopted together. Baby Timothy went with the Duggans, but for some reason they chose not to take the other baby, Rueben. Damn, we're going to need another court order to get at those records."

"We won't be able to get that until morning, by the earliest," Freeman said.

"Looks like we're back to the hurry up and wait game."

"Shit," Freeman said, throwing the car in gear and driving back to the station.

They drove for miles without saying a word to one another.

"We can try to look up Duggan's birth mother tomorrow, while we're waiting on the court to sign the papers we need."

"Sounds like a good plan, Blain."

"Don't let it get you down, at least we're on the right path."

"It's just that we're so damned close to the truth, I can taste it. I just don't want to see an innocent man fry."

"Me neither, besides, I still know in my gut that Graham is still guilty."

Another mile went by without a word from either of them.

"Son of a bitch!" Freeman blurted out, slamming his fist against the steering wheel.

"What's your problem," his partner responded, his tongue already swelling up from where he had bitten it. "You damned near made me bite off my tongue."

"Sorry," he said shortly. "Maybe I'm way off base here, but what is Graham's first name?"

"Rueben," he replied cautiously.

"And the twin's name?"

"They're one in the same. What are you trying to get at?"

"Think about it, the DNA matched. They're twins. Charlie said it could be possible that the other killer was related."

"They both might be guilty?"

"It's quite possible, but we're never going to find out without that other adoption record."

"Sounds a little crazy, I sure hope you can sell it to Frank."

"You mean you sure hope *we* can sell it to Frank," Freeman said, pressing down the accelerator with a new found sense of urgency.

———————

True spent the last few months doing battle with his inner demons. On one hand, he could rip Duggan apart with his bare hands, and on the other, he wanted to embrace the man and tell him the truth. He knew that Duggan was struggling with his guilt and would have committed suicide had it been possible. And even though the man had destroyed his Regina, True knew he had had no control over his actions. He knew because Cracker had been haunting him day in and day out with the images of the attack. And although it was Duggan's face that flickered in True's nightmares, it was Cracker's pure, unadulterated hatred that was the driving force. True had finally made a decision to let their healing begin.

"I hear you asked to die," True said, not sure why he had decided to confront the inmate, other than to rid himself of his nightmares. He hoped that the truth really would set him free.

"Yes, I did," Tim replied somberly from the shadows of his cell.

He had started getting used to the solace it afforded. Without the voice to bother him anymore he almost felt normal. But just about the time normalcy began to set in his memories returned with a vengeance to haunt him. He would never be able to forget the last sounds that Rene' made as he struggled for his last breath. Nor would he forget the look in the man's eyes. They painted Tim's soul with guilt.

"That only means one of two things."

"What are those?" Tim asked, not really wanting to have the conversation, but needing some human interaction regardless of the topic.

"Either you are sorry for what you done, or you're a pussy and don't want to face the consequences of your actions."

The row fell into a contemplative silence for a few minutes.

"So which is it?" True asked.

"I'm sorry."

"That's a start. Now, get up off your ass and come over here and tell me that to my face. I want to put all this hatred out of my heart,

THE SANDMAN

and I will never be able to do that without knowing that you are truly sorry for what you've done."

"I'd rather not get into this right now," Tim said.

"Why not? Only man enough to hurt women and babies?" True hissed. He could feel his anger rising within him. He knew his failing heart and high blood pressure wouldn't take much anymore, but he figured it was now or never. He wasn't sure about a heart attack, but he was damned certain about the anger that was eating him up alive.

"No, nothing like that," Tim said, emotionally drained.

"Listen, I know a thing or two about guilt and how it has a way of eating a man up inside. I know it's eating at you, just like it's eating at me. Would it help if I said I was sorry first?"

"Sorry? What have you got to apologize to me for?"

"For trying to have you killed. For believing that you are someone you're not."

"What are you talking about?" Tim asked, getting off his bunk and walking over to the bars to face the old man.

"I wanted you dead when I heard about my little girl. I hired some men, and for that I am sorry. And I'm sorry about your friend, he wasn't supposed to get hurt."

"How do you know about Rene'?

"Word travel fast around here."

"Doesn't matter, I'm the one who killed him, not your hired thugs."

"No, you didn't. And neither did they."

"What are you saying."

"Look me in the eye, and tell me that you are sorry about all that has happened."

Tim wasn't sure why he trusted the old man, nor could he figure out why he had the sudden urge to do exactly as the man said. He caught the old man's gaze and let him stare directly into his soul. "I'm truly sorry. I never meant to hurt anyone," Tim said, tears beginning to form in his eyes.

"I believe you. And again, I apologize for being such a fool. I let my anger cloud my judgment. I guess I knew all along it wasn't you, but it was much easier blaming something I could understand."

"I still don't understand."

"A man who calls himself Cracker did those things, not you. Granted, he may have used your body, but your mind was his."

"Ding, ding, ding. Give the man a prize," Cracker's words flowed venomously out of Tim's mouth. Tim could hear the man's voice in his head. It sounded as if he were eavesdropping on a conversation from across the room. The fringes of his consciousness began fading to black and within seconds, Cracker had full control of the man's mind.

True jumped back away from the cell. He had seen the man's eyes change from a delicate blue to a color of pure evil. Red threads of color were interwoven into the man's greenish eyes. True could feel the heat emanating from the man's hatred.

"Cracker?"

"You bet your ass old man. I'm getting pretty good at this ain't I?"

"Not doing you no good, is it?."

"Oh, but it is. And I'm still just practicing. I could do a whole lot better with the book."

"Too bad you don't have it."

"But you're going to get it for me, aren't you?"

"No."

"Been having nightmares lately, True?"

"No."

"LIAR!" He screamed.

"Cracker, leave me alone," True turned away from the cell.

"I thought that you would have learned by now that you pay dearly for your disrespect. Remember one thing, I'm on the outside now. I can come and go as I choose. How many granddaughters do you have, True?"

"How the fuck am I supposed to get you the book?" He used anger to try to hide the fact that he was scared as hell.

"You don't have to get it to me. Get it to him. I can read it through his eyes."

"Leave this poor man alone, Cracker. You got what you wanted."

"Ah, ah, ah, True. Watch that tone with me. Would it scare you to know that I haven't raped or killed since getting out? Can you even begin to comprehend the rage that has built up inside of me? Do you have a clue the amount of pain I can bring to you and your family?"

"All right. Anything you say. I'll bring him the damned book just as soon as I can find it."

"You can find it, True, it's why you're having nightmares. It's in your cell, right next to that box of letters you keep," he laughed insanely and loosed his grip on Tim's mind.

Tim scampered back across his cell like a wounded animal. True felt pity for the man welling up inside so badly that it hurt. He choked back his tears and left the row with his cart of books without another word. He knew he couldn't let Cracker have that book. But then again, he couldn't not let him have it either.

———————

Tim sat in the warden's office, admiring the man's taste in decorating. He must have been a seaman at some point in his life, or at least dreamed of it. A cloud of sorrow draped over Tim as he recalled how closely the paneling in the warden's office resembled that in Rene's renovated office. Although, he was certain it would be a completely different color now, no longer streaked with dried crimson and pock marked with bullet holes. And he was certain that the carpeting was no longer the same tranquil beige with unnatural, unsightly burgundy mottling.

Tim studied the trio of brass helm shaped instruments affixed to a plaque on the wall. The temperature was balmy. The barometer was holding steady and the humidity was all relative, as it always was in Florida. Pretty nice day, for some.

A picture of a salty old man fighting back against an angry, tumultuous sea, hung crookedly behind the warden's desk. It could have been either an artist's rendition of Captain Ahab or maybe just some Neolithic symbolism of man's timeless struggle against himself. Tim just thought it looked an awful lot like Charleton Heston with white hair. Perhaps it was his great escape from the Planet of the Apes.

"Mr. Duggan, I guess you're probably wondering why I called you here," the warden said, sitting down across from the prisoner.

"Yes, sir," Tim replied, giving the man a once over glance.

The warden was a tall man, yet he seemed smaller in stature once he sat down due to his terrible posture. His thin shoulders rolled forward and his back slumped in his chair. Tim thought he looked like a man who could no longer bear the weight of the world on his shoulders. He appeared to be in his fifties, extremely thin and undernourished, Tim supposed. His face was lined with years of constant concern and worry. Tim deduced that the man was far too compassionate a human being to be in the line of work that he was in and it was eating him alive.

"I am going to dispense with all the niceties, if that's all right with you."

"Yes, sir," Tim replied, barely hearing the man speak at all. His mind was a thousand miles away. He was replaying his conversation with True, over and over in his mind. The man knew something. But for the life of him, he couldn't recall how their conversation had ended.

"You have waived all your appeals, is that correct?"

"Yes, sir."

"And you do this of your own volition, I mean, your own free will," he adjusted his vocabulary out of habit.

"I'm an intelligent man, warden, no need for that on my account. I understand what you are getting at."

"Okay, I just want you to be aware of the fact that things will move rather rapidly now. Do you know what that means?"

"Yes, sir."

"In case you don't, it means you will be executed very shortly. I trust you have your affairs in order?" He asked stoically. His voice was smooth and calming. Tim noticed that his face seemed to sink with the question. It was obvious the warden was struggling with the interview.

"Yes, sir."

"I see here that you don't have much in the way of a goodbye list. People that you'd like to see one last time."

"No, sir."

"But it says here that you are married," he shot an inquisitive glance at Tim. His pale blue eyes seemed to fade to a shade slightly paler than when the interview started.

"Yes, sir, I am. But we haven't spoken much since, well, you know," Tim responded, his face betraying the fact that he was fighting back his tears.

"I understand. I felt compelled to speak with you about the gravity of your decision. I just wanted to make damn certain you understood what you were asking for," the warden explained.

"Sir, quite frankly, I can't live with the guilt. I can only hope God can forgive me where men cannot."

"All right then. If you're certain about this, I will push the paperwork through as soon as possible. I want you to understand that you are not going to have much time left on this earth. If you're going to make peace with yourself or anyone else, you need to think about doing that. I can see about getting your wife to come and visit if you'd like."

"I doubt you'll be able to."

"I'll try anyway. If for no other reason than for my own peace of mind."

Tim just nodded his head.

"If there's anything I can do, you just let me know," the warden offered.

There was something different about the convict sitting across from of him. Sean McIntyre had been around the worst kind of criminals for most of his life and he prided himself on being a fairly good judge of character. This one nagged at him. He would have bet his life that the man sitting across from him was no killer.

CHAPTER NINETEEN

The two detectives just stared blankly at each other. They had been replaying the tape from Rene's office over and over again during the past few hours, always coming to the same conclusion that there were two distinctly different people on that tape. Both men had kicked themselves in the ass for not remembering the box of evidence Connolly had told them about sooner.

"Play that part again," Premoe said.

Freeman rewound the tape and pushed play. The tape hissed with dead air for several minutes before a man's calm, soothing voice could be heard.

"Tim, can you tell me how you felt last night?"

"I was tired. Very tired."

"That was from the medicine you took. Tell me what you were feeling, emotionally."

"Elsa was still mad at me. I was sad. I just wanted to sleep."

"Did you sleep?"

"Yes. I think so. But I remember waking up."

"What did you do when you woke up?"

"I can't remember. I think I went outside. I felt cold."

Freeman pushed stop. "So, he can't seem to remember leaving his house the night he attacked Regina Chamberlain."

"Don't you find that a little odd?"

"Not if another personality took over his mental state."

"But then that would make him insane. I mean, enough to keep him out of the chair," Premoe said.

"In most cases yes. I think the politicians got their hands too far into this one. No one is coming forth on his behalf."

"Maybe we need to."

"That's not our job, Blain."

"I know, but if the man is really crazy then sending him for a visit with Old Sparky seems like cruel and unusual punishment to me. Play the rest of the tape."

"There's only a few more lines and we've heard it a dozen times already. There's nothing on the tape that's worthwhile."

"I know. Just humor me."

Freeman shrugged his shoulders and pushed play on the recorder.

"Tim, do you remember where you went?"

"No," he paused. "Yes, I think I went across the river."

"Don't you remember how you got there?"

"No. I only remember waking up there," he began to get agitated.

"Do you remember going to someone's house?"

The speakers echoed sounds of someone moving around in the office.

"Tim, do you remember anything about what happened in that house?"

The speakers echoed with a deep sigh from Tim then the tape played nothing but dead air.

Premoe looked at his watch and realized it was getting late. Wordlessly he began packing the evidence back into its container. Freeman took his cue and began helping to stow away their gear.

"Yes, I remember what happened in that house," a voice hissed over the speakers. Although it held a lot of the characteristics of Duggan's voice, it was also serrated with evil undertones.

Both detectives stopped what they were doing and sat back down.

"Yes, I remember. Are you sure you want to know?" The voice seemed to be taunting the doctor.

"Tim?" Rene' asked, sensing there was something quite different about his friend's new demeanor.

"Are you going to shut the fuck up and let me tell the story?" The voice mocked.

"Tim, is that you? Are you still with me?"

"No, you ignorant bastard, the good doctor is no longer with you. You wanted to find out about me, now you have. Now, you're never going to be able to forget me," Cracker seethed.

"Who are you?"

"I'm the one who slipped in through that window. And I'm the one who slit that poor bastard's throat. And I'm the one who should have killed that bitch. I should have added her fucking whore hand to my collection."

The tape was quiet.

"What's the matter, cat got your tongue?"

Still more silence.

"Is this beyond the scope of your medical expertise, doc?"

"If this isn't Tim, who is this?"

"I told you, there's no need for you to know that."

"Are you saying you don't have a name?"

"Yes, I have a name. And let me clue you in on something, the doc here is not suffering from an identity crisis or multiple personality disorder like you seem to believe. He's suffering because I need him to."

"Why do you need him to?"

"Still trying to be clinical about this?"

"Damn, I've got to get someone with more expertise in on this," Rene' said aloud to himself. The tape echoed the sounds of Rene' opening a drawer and pulling out a file folder.

"This is where I tell you that you have learned too much for your own good."

"What do you mean?"

"It looks like I'm going to have to shut you up, and seal the doc's fate at the same time."

The faint murmur or other voices appeared as background noise on the tape.

"What was that?" Premoe asked.

"Don't know," Freeman responded, turning up the volume.

The tape was silent for several minutes, save for the background voices. Then suddenly, the speakers resounded with utter chaos. No discernible sounds presented themselves through the turmoil. The sounds emanating from the tape were nothing more than clamorous noise. Then the tape recorder clicked off. It had run out of tape.

"Shit," Premoe leaned back in his chair and gasped.

"What do you make of that?"

"Must have been when those punks broke in to rob the place."

"I meant the conversation between Meade and Duggan."

"I think it proves we were wrong, Duggan really did do it, he's just too damned crazy to know it," Premoe responded.

"Didn't that sound a lot like Graham to you? Not the voice so much as the attitude, vocal inflections and the things he said."

Premoe thought long and hard before answering. "Now that you mention it, yeah, I guess so. What are you trying to get at?"

"I don't know. I guess I'm just thinking foolishly. I want Graham to be guilty so badly that my mind is open to just about anything."

"Me too, partner, but it doesn't look that way."

"Come on, let's put this shit away and go get a beer," Freeman sighed.

The two detectives packed away the evidence and logged it back in with Connolly, before heading back out of the pit.

"Premoe," a voice called across the squad room. "Mail room just called, they've got a package downstairs for you."

"That must be what we're waiting for," he said eagerly to his partner.

Their investigation had all but come to a complete stand still while they waited for the legal eagles to determine who's interests were better served, the public's or the adoption agency's solemn oath of secrecy. The detectives had breathed a sigh of relief when the courts finally ruled in their favor. Although, it came with a warning that the evidence may be suppressed by the time it was needed in court. The detectives, along with their boss, had reassured the judge that they had enough evidence without the documents. Of course they had lied.

———————

"Duggan, I need to talk to you," True called out in front of the man's cell.

He had fought against Cracker's nightly intrusions but he was also quite aware of the fact that he was quickly losing the mental battle with the psychopath. He figured that Cracker had never quite be able to honed his transference skills to their sharpest. And for some reason the man wasn't yet able to get into True's head and remain there for very long. However, the images that Cracker had been able to implant in True's mind haunted the old man's every waking minute. Cracker subliminally suggested all the bad things he was going to do to True's remaining family. And True believed him. He needed help fighting the madman and Duggan was his only option.

"I don't feel much like talking," Tim replied ruefully, having fallen further and further into the grips of his depression. His mood was a blight of melancholia. Without Rene' or Elsa to help him he felt like a lost soul. He no longer possessed the strength to save himself.

"I said, I need to talk to you."

"What?" Tim questioned gruffly, reluctantly dragging himself out of the shadows.

"Closer. Let me see those eyes, I need to know who I am dealing with."

"What are you talking about?"

"I need to know if you are yourself, or if you are him."

"If I am him? Who?"

"Cracker."

"Who is Cracker?"

"Never mind that for right now, just let me see your eyes," True insisted, trying to coax the man further out of the shadows.

"You're even crazier than I am old man," Tim turned around and receded back into the sanctuary of darkness.

"I just might be, but humor an old man. Besides, together, we might be able to stop these bad dreams we've both been having," True said, hoping that Cracker had been visiting the man in his sleep as well, so then Duggan would understand what True was talking about.

"How do you know about my bad dreams?" Tim asked, turning back around to face the old man.

"Before I say another word, I need to see your eyes. I need to know if it's safe to talk to you."

"I'm not quite sure I follow you, but here," he said, moving out of the shadows to face True in the dirty wash of the overhead lighting.

True almost gasped at the sight of the man. All the men on death row took on an ashen pigment to their skin from the lack of sun and most lost weight and began looking gaunt, but Timothy Duggan was wasting away. His lack of sleep was as obvious as his loss of appetite. His eyes were ringed in bright red from crying and the sockets had begun to sink in giving the man's face a hollow, near-death appearance. True gazed into Tim's paling blue eyes, looking for anything that might give away Cracker's presence.

"You're okay," he said after determining that Cracker must be off haunting some other poor soul.

"I guess you've got the floor," Tim said, his curiosity piqued by the man's knowledge of his nightmares. "How did you know I have been suffering from bad dreams?"

"If you thought I was crazy before, you're definitely going to think I'm crazy after I tell how I know."

"Can't be any crazier than I feel."

"Let me just say it. I know you're innocent. You didn't kill them women, and you sure as hell didn't kill your best friend. It was Cracker," True started to explain.

"Who is this Cracker you keep rambling on about?"

"He used to have your cell. That was before he put you there in his place."

"You're starting to lose me again," Tim started back for his cot.

"You've heard him in your head haven't you? You've felt him inside your brain," True called after him.

"Yes, I have heard voices in my head, but that's because I have something terribly wrong with me. Now, I know I can't apologize to you enough, but please, quit tormenting me. You'll just have to figure some other way to reap your vengeance," tears began to trickle from the corner of Tim's eyes.

"The only voice in your head is Cracker's. Do you believe in voodoo?"

"Are you serious?"

"Dead serious. Here, read this," True shoved the book through the bars at Tim. He wanted to rid himself of the evil manifestation as if it were a pit bull chewing on his fingers..

"What is this?"

"That is what Cracker uses to get into our minds."

"You've got to be kidding?"

"I wish I was. He's been using it on me lately. Only, for some reason it doesn't work too well on me, like it does you. Maybe I'm too old or too stupid," he showed a half-hearted grin. "I have to tell you this now, because he is making me give you this book."

"Making you, how?"

"He threatened my granddaughter. He says that now that he is a free man, he can do whatever to whoever he wants. He got to her once through you and I'm sure he can get to her even easier now."

"When did he tell you this?"

"He visits me every night in my sleep. He can only stay with me for a few minutes or so but it's still enough to scare the ever loving shit out of me."

"You don't expect me to buy any of this do you?"

"Do you have another explanation? One that makes sense. Even I know you're not crazy. I've been watching you. Think about it. The only time you do crazy things is when Cracker wants you to. Had you ever killed anyone before? I mean before all this."

"No, I don't think so."

"Not even a year ago?"

"No."

"Two years ago?"

"No. What are you trying to get at?"

"You didn't do anything even remotely crazy, that is, until I gave this book to Cracker last year. And in that time you've murdered at least four women and your best friend and yet have no memory of doing any of those things? Am I right?"

"Yes," Tim replied weakly.

"I don't know all the secrets hidden in that book. I'm afraid to read it myself. I have enough sense to know you don't play with fire without getting burned. You, on the other hand, you don't have much of a choice."

"What are you trying to say?"

"Damn, man, are you dense? You need to find a spell to counteract the one that Cracker uses. You need to find some way to turn the tables on him."

"How do you suggest I do that?" Tim responded, his voice betraying his disbelief of the old fool's story. He stared into the man's milky gray eyes and a shiver ran through him. The old man was serious, deadly serious.

"Damn it, Duggan. You have to believe me, Cracker is planning on reading that thing through your eyes. I'd be prepared for a few visits if I were you. You have to somehow keep your mind together long enough to lead him where you want him to go," True explained. "Listen, I know how hard this is to believe, trust me, I don't believe it myself half the time. But it's true. And you of all people should know that it's true."

"It sounds mighty far fetched, don't you think?"

"Maybe you did kill those girls. Maybe I was wrong about you and you are one crazy son of a bitch," he spun angrily away from the cell.

"Maybe."

"But your eyes don't lie," he softened his tone and reverted back to his fatherly demeanor.

"What?"

"I've had this, let's call it a gift, of being able to read people's eyes. Not your run of the mill police or psycho-analyst's tricks, but really read them. I can see into your soul and know even your darkest secrets. The eyes can never lie."

"Really? And what do my eyes tell you?" Tim scoffed.

"Boy, you really are one tough customer. With all that has happened to you, you'd think you might be open to anything that might help you."

"Sorry, I've become quite the cynic as of late. Please, go on."

"Truth is, I don't see much of anything in your eyes. Nothing bad that is. You don't have what it takes to kill, never have had."

"And you see this in my eyes?"

"It's not so much what I see, as what I don't. You're an honest man. There's nothing hidden. It's time for you to believe your own heart."

"So tell me, why is this Cracker making you give me this book?"

"I don't know really, but I would bet he needs something from it."

"And I suppose I become part of that equation as well."

"I'm afraid so. He still needs you, just like he needed you to get out of prison."

"What do you mean by that?"

"I guess I haven't been completely straight with you. When I said you never killed anyone I was lying. You did kill those people, even your friend."

A completely bewildered look washed over Tim's face.

"But you didn't mean to kill them. You didn't even know you were going to do it, let alone remember it."

"But, I did remember it," he revealed.

"Yes," True thought for a minute back to his dealings with Cracker. "Yes, I believe you do remember. But Cracker made you do those things, and he made certain that you remembered doing them as well. He has controlled your mind to the point that you were no longer acting as yourself, you were actually him."

"I'm really starting to get tired of all this nonsense."

"After seeing you in here that first day, I hated you even though I knew the truth. I wanted to hate you because it was much easier than trying to believe the truth. The truth is, well, far-fetched as you have already said. But after I saw you I had to face the truth. And the truth is that Cracker killed those people and there wasn't a damn thing you could do to stop him."

"But why?"

"At first I thought it was just a way for him to be getting his rocks off. But then I used my privileges of the library and read up about the man. He had you killing those women just like he did years ago. My guess is that he set you up to take the fall, which bought him a get out of jail free card."

Tim thought hard for a minute. "I hate to drudge up bad memories, but why your granddaughter?"

"To get back at me. He was punishing me. You see, I owe you an apology, I am more to blame for what he did to Gina than you are."

"Can you get me those news reports you read?"

"I think so."

"I need to learn as much about this guy as I can."

"Make sure you understand one thing, he's crazy. And he'll stop at nothing to get what he wants. What about your wife? I read you were married?"

"She filed for divorce," Tim's head sagged with the weight of his depression and gnawing guilt.

"Is there any way you can get her to listen to you or get a message to her?"

"Why?" Tim perked up, not liking the direction the conversation was taking.

"He'll go after her. If he has the slightest idea you, or I, am doing anything to mess up his plans he'll try to get even. You need to warn her somehow."

"I don't know how."

"You just write her a letter, I'll make sure she gets it. I got to get going now. I'll get you that stuff you want as soon as I can. And read that book with an open mind. Believe what you read, we both know it's true," the old man walked away from the cell and headed for the end of the corridor and the end of the tier.

"Thanks," Tim called after the old man. "I think."

———————

Cracker sat on a bench in the food court area in the center of the Orange Park Mall. The sunken oasis was surrounded by such irresistible teen attractions as Taco Bell, Dairy Queen and the always popular McDonald's. This semi-private paradise afforded him a perfect vantage point for watching adolescent activities. He stared around and through the resplendent plume of spewing water jetting toward the ceiling. Smaller fountains danced in rhythm around the larger fountainhead. Circular discs of silver and copper glimmered from the bottom of the pool that surrounded the fountain. Wishes that would never come true.

The top edge of the oasis was a large planter filled with an eclectic array of broad-leafed plants. Fern fronds swooped toward the ceiling until overcome by gravity and bent with gentle curves and flowed back toward the floor. The plants were meticulously cared for and their healthy sheen was a testament to the groundskeeper's diligence. It appeared as though someone had stolen a chunk out of the rain forest and planted it right in the heart of the mall. Cracker had been a good boy for far too long.

The sanctuary was large enough for approximately a dozen or so people to escape the throngs of teens parading around the arcade. It was just large enough that no one would notice him. Just a simple ordinary man, doing simple ordinary things.

He peered through the vibrantly colored water as the women and girls walked by.

Blue. Fifteen, maybe. She wore lots of make-up, so she might possibly be even younger. Blonde, with her hair pulled tightly back into a pony tail. More than likely she was a cheerleader with her cute, bubbly personality. She played with her gum, wrapping the pink strands seductively around her finger as she talked with her friends about last night's game, boys, and the latest cosmetic tips. He breathed deeply and let out a sigh.

Purple. Definitely not much over thirteen. Shoulder length brown hair. Straight. Clean but not carefully groomed. She was pretty but not gorgeous. Well developed. Probably a farm girl. Good broad shoulders. A good fighter. He licked his lips with fiery passion.

Red. Definitely legal. Perfect makeup. Perfectly straight teeth. Talking with her friends and smiling only when she speaks, distant and uninterested when someone else's lips move. Too snooty. Knows her shit don't stink. She truly deserves his brand of attention.

Orange. Instantly she made him almost forgot where he was. She was a knockout. Jet black hair, long and straight past her waist. It teased him as it swayed back and forth across her tight buttocks as she walked away from him. Her eyes were dark and mysterious. Alluring. She was more than amply endowed for his tastes. He would have to keep his eye on her. Cracker sighed as he lost sight of the love of his life when she disappeared through the archway of a lingerie store.

He smiled with the thought of so many women careening through their own little worlds, never once giving thought to him or the fact that they were all so dangerously close to colliding with his world. Which one would it be? Who would be the lucky girl today? Who would get to hear his heartfelt proposal up close and personal?

He glanced down at his crotch without dropping his head. The copy of the Florida Times-Union was performing rather nicely. The cold newsprint rubbing against his skin felt luxurious. Only the warm sticky fluids of a lover willing to give her life to him could best it. But that had to wait.

Yellow caught his attention. She was the best of them all. Old enough to know how to please him, but still flourishing in her youthful beauty. She stood in line at the Dairy Queen waiting for a banana split. Or maybe a hot fudge sundae, with a cherry. A snicker escaped his lips. Gently, slowly, he slid the newspaper back and forth across his lap never averting his eyes from the girl painted with splashes of yellow. She bounced as she laughed. He tried not to bounce as he rubbed. Her smile was a pure light from heaven.

Cracker looked down and saw a dark stain spreading over the front page. Some grinning councilman was now wearing the remnants of Cracker's pleasure as a perverse beard. It wasn't the best release in the world, but it would have to do. For now.

He made sure that none of the sheep wandering around mindlessly gawking through the store windows were watching him before quickly putting himself away and zipping up his pants. He laid the soiled newspaper on the seat next to him and got up from his seat a refreshed man. Cracker got an exhilarating rush of excitement as he fantasized about who might find his sticky little gift. Maybe little Miss Yellow might pick it up and wonder what it was. He would gladly show her.

As he was exiting the mall he caught a glimpse of Orange's hair shimmering in the sunlight. Her pants pulled tightly across her buttocks as she slipped into her car. He felt himself swelling again. Making a mental note of her license plate number, he fled to the sanctity of his car where he could get his release in semi-private. He knew it wouldn't squelch the flames of desire burning through his loins. Only one thing gave him that kind of release.

Cracker started his car and drove out of the lot. His nerves were already screaming out in frustration from the lack of a suitable release. A small tremor of guilt, or pity, coursed through his veins. His mother would have to bear the brunt of his frustrations, at least for now.

CHAPTER TWENTY

"Mrs. Kilbourne, I'm Detective Freeman, this is Detective Premoe. We'd like to talk to you for a few minutes if we may," he gave the woman a quick once over while offering her a friendly hand which she summarily refused.

Freeman's best guess was that she was in her late forties or early fifties, yet she looked as though she tried to pass for someone in her late thirties. She wore a low cut top, which showed off her salon bronzed, surgically enhanced cleavage. Her make up had been impeccably applied and it helped to soften her aging features. Freeman hoped his partner wasn't staring. Premoe was looking, studiously, and he was certain that her breasts weren't the only part of her body that had seen a plastic surgeon's knife.

"Is this about Timothy Duggan?" She returned.

"Yes, Ma'am," Freeman replied, taken aback by her intuitiveness.

"I watch the news, detective. I've been expecting you," she said, aware of the fact that she had surprised the men with her insight into their line of questioning. "I still love my son, I always will. But that was a long time ago. In a whole different life."

"We just need to ask you a few simple questions, ma'am. I'm truly sorry for the intrusion."

"Listen, I'm married to a wonderful man, but he's a man who wouldn't understand some of the mistakes I made in my youth. He doesn't know anything about the twins, and I'd like to keep it that way."

"We understand, Mrs. Kilbourne," Premoe broke in gruffly. "We're only asking for a few minutes of your time."

"You've got five, and the clock is running," she replied, standing half in and half out of her doorway. She glanced behind her and stepped out onto the porch, closing the door behind her.

"Can you tell us why you put them up for adoption?"

"I was young, too young to raise a child by myself, let alone twins. I did what I thought was best at the time. I still think it was the best thing for them."

"Did you know the adoptive parents?"

"Yes, I met them once, before the adoption and a couple of times after things were final. Meeting them beforehand was a condition I set on the adoption. Our meetings afterward weren't such joyous occasions. Please don't get me wrong, detectives, I truly loved my sons. But I was fifteen, it was the sixties, and things weren't very easy for single moms back then. Not easy at all."

"I understand completely, ma'am," Freeman said.

"We're not here to judge you by any means," Premoe added.

"Damn good thing, because I wouldn't let you," her blue eyes seemed to light up as she shot them both a fiery glance.

Freeman almost shot his partner for his lack of tact. "I only have a couple more questions for you and then we'll be on our way. Why were they separated? Why didn't the Duggans take both babies?"

Betty Kilbourne's face glazed over as the question rolled off Freeman's tongue.

"That's none of your business," she replied weakly, turning her face to the ground.

"Mrs. Kilbourne, please," Premoe changed his demeanor.

"He was evil and they didn't want him, okay?" Her voice broke.

"Didn't want who?"

"Rueben. They did take him, at first, but they brought him back several weeks later like a puppy they couldn't potty train. They said there was something wrong with him. I knew they were right. I had known the minute he was born and I looked into his eyes. He was punishment for my sins," she began to cry and put her face in the palms of her hands. Her loosely curled brown hair fell over her hands, the golden highlights spilling through her fingers like errant rays of sunshine. She abruptly lifted hear head back up to face them and defiantly wiped her tears with the palms of her hands. Both men had been detectives long enough to be able to detect her venomous feelings towards the Duggans even after all these years.

"They were just babies, how could either one of them be evil?" Freeman asked, his face contorting with confusion.

"By the time the adoption went through, the boys were over a year old. The Duggans claimed that every time they put Tim to bed, Rueben would try to suffocate him. They also claimed to have found bruises on Tim from his brother. Rather than argue with them, I reluctantly split the boys up and agreed to take Rueben back in order to save him from becoming a ward of the state."

"One thing you have to understand about the Duggans, they

weren't outwardly pompous, yet they still had a certain air of sophis-
tication about them. It was an attitude that could intimidate a young
girl like myself. Also, please believe me, I never believed them when
they said my son was evil. I thought to myself, just as you are thinking right now, there was no way that a little baby could be evil. But I
was wrong. Rueben lived with me for another six months and during
that time I came to understand what the Duggans were talking about."

"You saw the child as being evil as well?" Premoe asked, his
voice betraying his disbelief.

"Listen, detective, there was never anything tangible. Nothing in
the way of evidence that you could put your finger on. It was in his
eyes. It was the way he looked at me. With pure hatred. Like he knew
I had tried to give him away. I have to admit, I was relieved when his
adoption finally went through," tears streamed down her face as she
recounted her story.

"I'm sorry to have to put you through this, Mrs. Kilbourne. I
only have one more question for you. Do you know the name of the
family that finally ended up with Rueben?" Freeman asked.

"Yes. Her name was Graham, Edna Graham," she revealed,
rocking the detectives back on their heels. Although they strongly
suspected this, hearing their suspicions confirmed caught them by
surprise.

"Do you know where we can find her?" Premoe's voice
cracked.

"You don't know the connection, do you?"

"Enlighten us, please," Freeman said, certain he already knew
what the connection must be, but wanting to hear it from her to see if
it still sounded as crazy.

"The man you people just let back out on the streets, Rueben
Graham, is my other son, Timothy Duggan's twin brother. And he's
evil. You do know what he did to Edna don't you?" Her voice
showed her surprise at their obvious lack of details.

"No, I guess we haven't gotten that far."

"Well, you're in for a surprise when you meet her. I'm through
with this, detectives. I do want you to know one thing though," she
paused, her hand on the doorknob.

"Yes, Ma'am," Freeman said, truly feeling sympathetic towards
her.

"Timothy was, is, a good boy. He didn't do any of the things he
has been accused of. And for the life of me, I can't understand why
he pled guilty. Please, straighten this out, before it's too late," she
turned and went into the house without another word.

Both men stared blankly at each other for a few moments while standing on the woman's porch. As they turned to leave, the door opened and Mrs. Kilbourne reappeared.

"Here, this is Edna Graham's address, if she still lives there," she said, stuffing a tattered piece of yellowed scrap paper into Freeman's hand and quickly disappearing back into her current life, leaving the past behind forever.

"This is getting just too weird," Premoe said, shutting the door and putting on his seat belt.

"Where to now," Freeman asked, starting the car.

"Edna Graham's, of course."

Freeman put the car in gear and pulled away from the upscale neighborhood en route to Edna Graham's. They would be going from one end of the social spectrum to the other. From the pristine streets lined with oleander and magnolia to backwoods lots of gnarled cypress laced with Spanish moss.

After nearly an hour of gator country driving, they pulled up in front of a run down shack of a house. The paint was peeling off the sides of the house in long strips the color of stale, flat beer. It looked like long, thin slices falling away from a brick of moldy cheddar. The windows were dark and the grimy shades were pulled tight. The wooden clapboard porch sagged terribly in the middle. There were several places where the detectives tested with their toes before putting their full weight down. A porch swing hung by one chain at one end of the porch. Little white flecks of dandruff were the only evidence that the decrepit swing had ever held a coat of paint in its life. The wooden screen door was twisted in its frame and wouldn't shut all the way. When Freeman knocked on it a dust cloud of rusted screen particles rose in protest. He waved his hand in front of his face to clear the air and knocked again.

"Christ, what is that smell?" Premoe snorted and pinched his nostrils together with his fingers.

"I don't know, but I'd be willing to bet it's coming from that," Freeman pointed to a cluster of black plastic bags piled in a corner of the porch. The bags were alive with the buzzing of unseen insects. The bags had obviously been there for quite some time, they were no longer black, but the light purple of an eggplant's skin. Freeman doubted they were as thick.

"Do I have to look?"

"Not unless you really want to," a sarcastic grin spread across his face.

"Up your..."

The door opened with a nerve fraying screech, sending Premoe's words scampering in retreat into the back of his mind. A cloud of stench wafted out onto the porch. It was no worse than the smells secreted by the garbage bags, but different. So different that it nearly doubled both men over.

"Mrs. Graham?" Freeman choked.

"Yes," the disheveled woman replied.

She wore a blue gingham dress that had long since faded to gray. The white collared neckline looked sooty in some places, yellowed in others. She reeked of sweat. Her round face was a road map of long healed scars. The jaundiced skin under her eyes and on her cheeks had been permanently discolored from years of bruising. The detectives knew the look all too well. They had seen it more than they'd care to admit over the span of their careers, every time they responded to a domestic assault call or sent a battered wife to the morgue.

Premoe glanced down at her right arm and shuddered. Her handless right arm. "It was an accident," she smiled, catching the men ogling her mangled limb.

"We'd like to ask you a few questions about Rueben," Freeman said, fighting back his disgusted anger.

"He's a good boy. The accident wasn't his fault. He's not in trouble is he?"

"No, ma'am," Freeman decided he'd better play along with her game if he wanted a chance at getting some answers.

"Are you friends of his?" She stepped further out onto the porch.

A torch flared up inside Premoe when he caught sight of a viciously ugly bruise under her eye that had been previously hidden by the shadows. Her upper lip was split at the seam and blood had crusted into an hideous scab. The detectives knew they were fresh wounds; a day old beating at best.

"Yes, ma'am," Freeman responded, nodding at Premoe.

"He should be back from the mall soon. Would you like to come in and wait?"

"If it's no trouble, ma'am."

"No, no trouble. There's never any trouble. You seem like nice boys, just like my Rueben. You said you were friends of his right? Would you like some lemonade? It's fresh squeezed."

"Yes, ma'am, we're friends of Rueben's. And yes, some lemonade would be nice," Freeman responded, drawing an admonishing glance from his partner.

"You said he'd be right back. Does he live here with you?" Premoe asked, trying to conceal the shudder rippling through him caused by his imagining anything in that house touching his lips.

"Of course. He has always lived with me, I'm his mother after all," she looked at them as if the question were preposterous. "Except for that time when the bad policemen put him in jail for something he didn't even do," her syrupy sweet demeanor took on a scowl.

"Mrs. Graham, where does Rueben sleep? He said he left something in his room for me," Premoe asked, earning a look of indignation from Freeman.

"Back there, last door on the right. Does he know you're going back there?" She called after Premoe with agitated concern.

"Yes, ma'am, he said it was okay just to pick it up," Blain's voice trailed off as he walked down the hallway.

"Why did they do that, Mrs. Graham?" Freeman asked, trying to avert her attention away from his snooping partner.

"Excuse me? What were we talking about?" She asked blankly.

"Why did the bad policemen put Rueben in jail?"

Again, her face creased into a deep scowl. "Because they wouldn't believe him about the accidents. That's all they were, accidents."

"What accidents were those?"

"Those girls were so clumsy. I don't know why on earth he would bring them here," she was interrupted by the sound of the screen door opening. Freeman tensed and placed his hand on his weapon.

"Ma, who's here ma," Cracker's voice conveyed a sense of urgency.

"Your friends, Rueben. They stopped by to see you. I said they could wait for you," she smiled at Freeman. "He's such a good boy."

"You stupid bitch!" He bellowed once he caught sight of the detective.

"Watch your mouth," Freeman said without thinking.

"Fuck you. Where's your fat ass partner?"

"Your other friend, dear? He's getting something out of your room like you told him to."

"You stupid fucking bitch!" He reared back to hit his mother but Freeman grabbed his wrist before he could deliver the blow.

Todd's heart ached. He realized that the woman hadn't even as much as flinched in anticipation of the coming blow.

"Let me go," Cracker glared at Freeman and jerked his wrist free. "And I'll deal with you later," he glared at his mother.

"Do I have to remind you of our domestic violence laws here in the state of Florida?" Freeman asked, blocking Graham's path.

"Move out of my fucking way, now!" Cracker demanded confrontationally. Although he had only been out of prison a short time, he had already started gaining weight and his new size only added to his over-inflated ego.

Freeman didn't budge.

"Do I need to call my lawyer?" He quickly changed course, knowing that any threat of a lawyer would get more results than brute force with this maggot.

Freeman stepped aside slowly, hoping he had bought Premoe enough time to get out of whatever he had gotten into.

As soon as he burst through the door to his room, Cracker was thrown against the wall by a steely hand gripping his throat. He tried to speak, but his airway was cut off and the only sound he was able to manage was a guttural moan. He clawed frantically at the man's enormous hands, trying to pry them away from his collapsing wind-pipe.

"Listen here you little fuck, it's just you and me right now. There's no one around to save your sorry little ass."

He struggled, but Premoe only pressed and gripped harder. A whimper of submission was all he could muster.

"You touch that woman out there one more time and I'll pay you a midnight visit that you'll never forget. I am going to come back here and check on her from time to time, maybe even once a day. If I see as much as a zit on her forehead, your ass is mine. You got that?"

Graham tried to protest, but the bear of a man only clamped down that much harder. He began to feel lightheaded and knew that death was only a few measures away.

"Consider yourself duly warned," Premoe let go of his death grip and dropped the man to his knees.

Graham tried to curse him as he walked down the hall, but he choked on his own blood.

"Let's go," was all Premoe said as he entered the living room. Freeman could tell that something was amiss. He prayed his partner hadn't killed the little bastard, but then again, a little part of him wished that he had.

As they turned off the dirt road, which lead away from the di-lapidated shack, and onto the pavement, Freeman finally spoke. "So?"

"I didn't hurt him, much," he grinned.

"You're a brute."

"Yeah, well , ya gotta love me," he said, pulling a notebook out of his back pocket.

"What's that?" Freeman nodded in his direction.

"Something I swiped from his room."

"Damn, it, Blain. You know that will be inadmissible now."

"Yeah, maybe, but at least we have it. We needed a break. I had to make one."

Freeman eased the car onto interstate ten and headed back to the precinct.

Cracker peeled an orange carefully, tossing the aromatic rinds onto the passenger floorboard next to him. The peelings joined a one-foot section of coil wire he had surreptitiously removed from the little red Nissan an hour earlier after watching its owner, the raven haired Miss Orange, bouncing into the theater with her friend. His car was filled with the fruity aroma. Soon, it would be full of love's special bouquet.

A matter of public record. He loved that term. It was nothing for him to stop by the Department of Motor Vehicles and get little Miss Orange's address. All he needed was her license plate number, and a complacent, easily manipulated clerk. He poured on the charm, she poured out more information than she should have. Little did she know, he would never have anything to do with a shriveled hag like her. But vanity is a strange thing. Stroke a person the right way, they would believe anything that was spoon-fed to them.

Cracker had watched Miss Orange's house for several hours. He watched as she walked out of her house and got into the little red Nissan. The girl of his dreams was wearing an overly large silver, black and blue letterman's jacket with a large letter's FCH on the right breast and an embroidered caricature of a buccaneer on the back. Little Miss Orange was dating a football star. This fact thrilled Cracker. Her gladiator might slip her the salami every Friday after the game. He might even bring her to orgasm before leaving her alone so he could go out drinking with the rest of the guys, although Cracker doubted that fact. He was sure she was some cock teasing little virgin. And even though her superstar jock might be her knight in shining armor, the bastard would never even get the chance to save her from Cracker's unbridled lust tonight? He would give her the ultimate orgasm of her life. He was going to bust her soul's cherry.

Cracker's plans had almost been spoiled after his run-in with that idiot Premoe in his house that afternoon. In his fucking room! He swallowed painfully and vividly recalled their barbarous encounter. His mother would still pay for her faux pas dearly, but not while that maniac cop was still on the prowl.

Nevertheless, he ignored the possibility that the detectives might be tailing him and followed through with his original plans. He fol-

lowed Miss Orange to her friend's house where she picked up a licen-
tious looking brunette. His first instinct when he saw the other girl
was to abandon his plans, there were just too many risk factors involved and he had no desire to revisit Starke anytime soon. But then
he figured that girls together might feel safer than one and might not
be as cautious, making things even easier for him. And the second
girl didn't look like she'd be too much effort to handle.

Cracker followed them to a Cineplex that was butted up to the
Orange Park Mall. An ironic chuckle escaped his lips. Everything in
this world makes a full circle. This is where they met for the first time
and it would also be the last.

He drove around the perimeter of the parking lot several times
making certain that the girls had both gone into the theater, and then
he circled some more. He waited for the perfect parking spot where
he could see the girls and their car without any chance that they
would be able to see him before he wanted them to. He turned off his
headlights and waited. Once the movies had started and the parking
lot was void of activity, he used his well practiced methods to disable
Miss Orange's car.

For the next one hundred and seven minutes, Cracker entertained his thoughts of retribution. He had whiled away his time waiting for Miss Orange by thinking of ways he was going to dispense his
brand of justice on detective's Premoe and Freeman. And while he
was at, he might as well visit Frank Walker's family as well. And
then Simon Patterson's. Then he would be free to take care of his
bungling mother once and for all, leaving the rest of the world at his
mercy. And all the while savoring a juicy orange.

His anticipation almost overwhelmed him. He turned his attention back to his requital, but that only aroused him more. Within
forty-five minutes he had released himself under the dashboard of his
car more times than he could remember.

He eagerly watched the horde of moviegoers flooding out of
the theater en masse. Each of the theaters staggered the end times of
their movies so that there was never a complete deluge of traffic trying to leave the theater or parking lot at any one given time. This fact
couldn't have pleased him more. The fewer people in the parking lot,
the better. Cracker had been lucky. Miss Orange and her present
company had chosen the latest playing picture, which incidentally
had the latest exit time. It was also, as luck would have it, the last
picture of the evening. Soon, most of the Cineplex's parking lot was
barren. There were but a few cars, Miss Orange's little red Nissan,
about a half a dozen cars which must have belonged to the pimple
faced teens working the concessions and Cracker's car.

He listened to the Nissan's motor struggling to start. The little car had no way of reporting the missing coil wire to Miss Orange and she wasn't learned enough about automobiles to recognize the car's ailment. Nor would anything be able to warn her about the danger lurking in the shadows.

"Excuse me, miss, do you need a hand?" Cracker called from the shadows a good distance behind the girl. He had given her a wide comfort zone, yet, she still jumped at the voice coming from out of the darkness.

"No, I think we can get it," she stammered.

Her friend tried the key in the ignition one more time. The Nissan was beginning to show signs of weakening. Its battery was quickly draining and Cracker knew that soon the girls would be hearing nothing but a series of dead clicks coming from the car's ignition. And then they would welcome their savior with open arms.

"Okay," he replied without a beat and moved toward his car.

He fumbled with his keys for a few minutes, appearing to be looking for the right one in the darkened parking lot. The Nissan rolled over a few more times. Then, click, click, click. He saw the interior dome light dimming to a sickly glow of attrition.

"Mister," he heard Miss Orange's voice calling out to him.

He wanted to spin around and come dashing to her rescue, but opted to revel in the moment by playing the fish a little longer.

"Sir," she called out to him again.

He felt himself swelling at the intonation of her sweet, innocent, unsuspecting voice. The consummate victim.

"Excuse me, sir," she raised her voice a couple of decibels and inserted just a touch of panic.

"Yes," he spun quickly around on his heels as if he had only just heard her for the first time. His every nerve tingled with electric excitement.

"I'm sorry, but I guess I was wrong. We really do need some help."

"I'm not much of a mechanic, but I'll see what I can do," he said, smiling broad and friendly.

He reached onto the passenger floorboard of his car and retrieved the Nissan's coil wire. He slipped the culprit into his pocket before walking over to their disabled car.

Cracker fiddled around with things under the hood for a while. Twisting this and pulling that. He even banged his knuckled a couple of times for good measure.

"Go tell your friend to turn off everything electrical. The radio, the lights, stuff like that. And if there's a cell phone, make sure she unplugs it, we'll need as much juice as the battery has left in it."

As soon as Miss Orange walked out of sight he slipped the coil wire out of his pocket and slipped it back into place.

"Okay, everything is turned off," she sang.

The anticipation was killing Cracker. His sense of excitement was heightened by the fact that he had never formulated a concise plan. He was playing an improvised game with the girls, taking advantage of each new opportunity as it arose. At first, he had never planned to hurt them, only get close enough to have done the deed if he so chose. But now, his erection was directing his every move. His perverted passions were taking over his self-control and better judgment.

"You don't have enough juice, in your battery," he grappled with the irresistible urge to stare at her crotch. "I'll pull my car up. I have a set of jumper cables in the back."

Miss Orange watched him walk away with a smile of innocence. Her fears and apprehension ebbed with the waves of the stranger's kindness. She had really not been in the mood to listen to one of her father's lectures about taking care of the car. Her night in shining armor had saved her about three hours worth of haranguing, besides, he was sort of cute for an older guy. In fact, he'd be down right handsome, if it weren't for his eyes. She couldn't quite place it, but even in the darkness she could tell that there was something peculiar about his eyes.

Cracker could barely contain himself during the brief walk back to his car. Her beauty was intoxicating. Even through the darkness of night he could see her hauntingly dark eyes teasing him with their brilliance. They caught even the tiniest sliver of light and turned it into a sparkle that sprinkled him with desire. He took a deep breath of her innocence as it wafted through the air and went back about his business of ensnaring her completely in his trap.

Cracker eased his car forward until it was face to face with the little Nissan. He made certain that their bumpers were almost touching. He vaulted out of his car and walked briskly around to the trunk to get the jumper cables. His titillation was growing out of control. He glanced down at his crotch the moment he was shielded from Miss Orange's view. He hoped she wouldn't notice the throbbing bulge in his jeans. But then again, he sort of hoped she would. He wondered if the sight of his desire would elicit a gasp of virgin surprise, or a moan of slutty anticipation from her.

"Normally I wouldn't pull so close, but I have short cables," he huffed a little air of disgust, wiggling in between the two bumpers. "Here, let me show you how to do this, just in case you ever need to know," he offered with a warm, inviting smile.

"Okay," the young girl replied, scooting in along side him between the two car bumpers.

The fit wasn't quite as tight for her as it was for Cracker. She smiled and slid so close to him that their thighs touched. He could feel her warmth radiating through him and he almost pounced on her right then.

"Be right back," he called, quickly sliding out from between the two cars. He hoped she hadn't detected the ripples of delicious anticipation that rocked him the moment the two of them touched. "I have to tell your friend what to listen for before turning the ignition over."

Miss Orange nodded in agreement, not quite being able to hear him over the din of his motor. She saw the direction he was walking and figured he was going to talk to her friend about something.

"Hello, miss," he tapped on the driver's window. He waited for the electric motor to roll the window down. It moved quite slowly, not getting enough juice through the car's dead battery. His car hadn't charged up the little Nissan quite enough for it to be able to power itself. The brunette inside smiled up at him.

"Hi," she bubbled.

"I'm going to go rev my engine a little. . ." he never finished the conversation. In one swift motion he chopped her across the throat with his stoma and clamped his other hand tightly over her mouth. He finished her off by punching her several times in the temple. She was out cold within thirty seconds of him appearing at her window. He hoped she would stay out.

As he passed Miss Orange he gave a friendly wave and bright smile. He slid across the passenger seat into the driver's seat of his car. Everything was flowing smoothly. He still hadn't figured out how he was going to subdue Miss Orange, but that was all part of the thrill of the hunt. Then, he heard a muffled cry. The brunette had awakened too early. Much too early. He heard the car door slowly open up, followed by a dull thud. The brunette had made it out of the front seat and was crawling toward the front of her car.

He felt his anger rising up within him. How dare she spoil his plans. Just like mother. Always spoiling his plans.

He caught a sliver of motion from gap between the hood and the car. Miss Orange was on the move. The hunt was on.

Quickly Cracker slammed his car into gear and floored the accelerator. The car lurched violently forward, crunching into the little red Nissan. Intermingled with the sounds of the two cars uniting were the sickening wet crunch of Miss Orange's thigh and her subsequent screams of pain. Cracker was thrown forward into the steering wheel by the force of the crash, but quickly regained his composure and threw his car into park. He jumped from the driver's seat and ran to where Miss Orange was trying to awaken the neighborhood. He savagely chopped her across the front of her throat, instantly quieting her. Without missing a step he continued on to where the brunette was struggling to get to her feet. He kicked as hard as he could, catching the poor girl square in the middle of her face. Blood sprayed from where his steel toe boot had connected with her tender flesh. The girl's blood splattered up the front of his pants legs. Cracker admired the legs of his denim jeans as they shimmered gorgeously in the wash of light from the parking lot lights.

He dropped his knees viciously into the small of her back. The force of his weight crashing down on her forced the air out of her lungs with a sickening wet gurgle. Cracker began bashing the girl's head against the cold, black asphalt. A pool of blood spread out across the parking lot like a disease. He experienced a rush of excitement as he felt the last of her life tremor throughout her body. She gave one last, long heaving sigh and was of this world no longer.

Miss Orange was thrashing wildly, trying to free herself from between the two cars. Her pain had been negated by her sheer terror, having just witnessed the kind, helpful stranger transmute into a brutal killer. Her parents' droning words of warning played in her head like a bad recording. She wanted to tell them she would listen this time. Little Miss Orange stared wide-eyed at her friend lying motionless on the ground, a pool of crimson painting a gruesome halo.

Cracker was pleased to see that Miss Orange wasn't as badly damaged as he had first thought. Only one of her legs was pinned between the two bumpers. It was obviously broken and quite badly judging by the dark stain on her right thigh. He had thought he wasn't going to be able to have as much fun with Miss Orange as he had originally desired. But with only one leg pinned, he had perfect access to her.

Cracker got behind the squirming young girl and yanked her jeans down as far as he could, pulling the leg of her pants away from her free ankle. Miss Orange was still unable to scream, though she tried, over and over again. The only sounds the poor girl was able to manage were gurgled tears and incoherent pleas for mercy. Cracker entered her from behind and exploded almost immediately the moment he slipped into her luxurious warmth. She used the remnants of her waning energy to fight him, which only excited him more. He reached around and gripped her throat as tightly as he could, trying to time his thrusts with her screams.

He gushed with pride, they had both reached an apex together. Him with his release, and her with her dying breath.

In a final act, Cracker used a jutting piece of steel from the Nissan to sever the young girl's hand at the wrist. He sawed her arm back and forth across the recently bared metal until he was able to twist it around in circles, breaking the bones and tearing the cartilage and tendons. The appendage let loose from her body with a sinuous pop. Dirty little Miss Orange couldn't be dirty anymore. Except of course, for the generous handful of sand that Cracker couldn't resist pouring into her eternally restful eyes.

Cracker watched her lifeless body slide off the hood of his car and crash to the ground with a hollow thump as he backed his car away from the carnage. The letterman's jacket glistened as his car lights reflected off the blood coated silver leather sleeves. Cracker held the sack with her hand in it between his legs as he drove home. He felt his excitement begin to rise as the sensation of her drying blood against his skin washed over him. He felt a sharp poke of pity for the fact he would not be able to share this intimate moment with her ever again. He smiled and patted the sack between his legs. But he would always have her tender touch.

———————

Tim began getting a morbid sense of his own mortality. As each day faded with the sun, a new dawn brought more paperwork for him to fill out. He filled out insurance papers, medical forms and even an organ donor card. He had to laugh at that one. Who would want a fried liver transplant, at least not without sautéed onions.

He looked down at his last meal request form. Having a medical background, Tim knew he would expunge his bowels upon death and thoughtfully considered which meal might produce the least offensive aroma. He wished the form would allow for a dinner partner, but then again, Elsa had never even written the warden back let alone him.

He put down the depressing paperwork and picked up the peculiar book that the eccentric trustee had given him. To say that Tim had his doubts about the book and about True would be a gross understatement. He held the mysterious book on his lap for quite some time before opening it. He traced his finger along the ornately designed leather cover. Although he was never one to believe in magic, voodoo or the many other things that went bump in the night, the book made him feel uneasy. The leather had a strange texture to it, and an even stranger smell. It smelled of rancorous death. This odor combined with the book's unnaturally cold aura brought back memories of his medical school days spent in the morgue.

Although he wasn't ready or willing to believe the old man's story, part of his brain screamed warnings at him. The more time he spent in contact with the book, the more he questioned his own rationale. And as hard as it was to fathom, somehow, he began to think that there may be a shred of truth to the old man's story. He had to wonder how the book had ever ended up in this place, in the hands of a maniacal serial killer. But then again, evil was an unknown entity with seemingly limitless powers.

Tim warily opened the cover of the tome. He was instantly taken aback by the nauseating fetid breath the pages exhaled. He couldn't have expressed his feelings with words if he had tried. He felt a cold tingle begin in his lower back and spread throughout his entire body. He touched his fingertips to his face. They were icy cold. He felt a sudden urge to urinate. Tim threw the book down onto his cot. The two of them just stared coldly at each other. He sensed that the book was somehow alive. That it was seeing him, just as he was seeing it. He shuddered against the icy blood in his veins.

His prison cell suddenly began to feel like a tomb. He was filled with an overwhelming sense of dread. He no longer wanted to die. He no longer felt the deep-rooted guilt that had been eating him alive. He understood now. As farfetched as the old man's story was, it was true.

"My God, Elsa, what have I done?" He asked the darkness.

An overwhelming sense of grief and self pity invaded his soul. The realization of that everything in his life was now finite came rushing at him. Suddenly, the aromas of the prison became welcomed in their vulgarity. Even his Mother-in-law's fruit cake would be gladly received and gratefully devoured.

CHAPTER TWENTY-ONE

"Hey, you two," Frank called, his voice sullen and subdued.
"Yeah, Frank, what is it?" Freeman replied, looking up from his desk.

"In my office, please."

The two detectives followed their boss into his office and chuckled at the sight. Frank's office was in its usual disarray. One of the characteristics of a good detective was his ability to catalog and maintain impeccable records of evidence, interrogations and discoveries. This structure was a requirement once a case finally went to court. And Frank Walker was a damned good detective. In fact, Frank was such an organized, anal-retentive person that he drove most people crazy, not the least of which were his family and friends. But his office was where it all fell apart. Nevertheless, Frank could still extract even the smallest tidbit of information from the chaos on a moments notice.

"Have a seat," he directed them to two open chairs that had seen many better days.

"This doesn't sound good," Premoe blurted.

"It's not."

"What's up, Frank?"

"I just got a call from Charlie. He responded to a call with Baker and Revall."

"And?"

"And, it wasn't pretty. Two young girls, one seventeen, the other we haven't been able to ID yet."

"You need our help on this one?" Freeman tested the water.

"No, not exactly," he paused. "This one is already yours."

Both men's faces took on a sour look.

"Both girls were beaten and mutilated. One of the girls was raped, and she was missing her right hand."

"Fuck me!" Premoe exploded. He rose quickly to his feet, flinging his chair across the room.

"Damn it, Frank," Freeman exploded.

"From what I gather from Charlie, there's no possible way that this was the work of a copy cat. Too many variables are right on the money, including sand in both of the girl's eyes. It was Graham, he's certain of that. I'm also certain of the fact that he is taunting us," Frank said.

"Where are they?"

"In the Cineplex parking lot at the Orange Park Mall. The uniforms should have it pretty well contained by now. A patrol unit found them, so we were able to seal off the area before any civilians wandered through, thank God."

"We're on our way," Freeman said, glancing over to his partner who was still fuming. Premoe was so angry he was at a loss for words. And he was so angry because the guilt had already begun to gnaw away at his soul.

"Before you two leave, I have something else to discuss," Frank said, not looking forward to the upcoming exchange of words and emotions.

Both men stopped at the door and turned to face their boss.

"Here, read this," he said and handed them a restraining order. "I got a call from Simon Patterson, Graham's attorney, this morning. And when I hung up from talking with him, I got a call from Judge Corvina and then another one from the mayor. What the fuck did you two do yesterday?"

"We went out to speak with Graham's mother," Freeman revealed.

"Is that it?"

"I talked to Graham," Premoe added, not wanting his partner to take the heat for him if the axe was going to fall.

"Blain, I thought you understood the situation," Frank sighed, more like a disappointed father than an irritated supervisor.

"I know, Frank, and I'm sorry. For getting you into hot water, not for having a little chit chat with Graham, and now, for not killing the little bastard when I had the chance," he added as an afterthought.

"Frank, the son of a bitch had already kicked the shit out of his mother. Blain just took it to heart a little too much."

"I know about the mother. At my request, the locals have already gone out to her place and taken her statement. She swears, in a signed affidavit I might add, that her injuries were the result of an unfortunate accident."

"That's fucking bullshit!" Premoe blurted.

"God damn it, don't you think I know that? Don't you think I would love to be able to go to the bastard's house and kick his ass

203

myself? Listen, I am going to stick my neck out and cover your asses on this one, but stay the fuck away from him, at least for now," the veins in his neck and temples throbbed viciously.

"Yes, sir," Freeman responded.

"You two don't do anything stupid out there,"

Premoe just shot a fiery glance at his boss.

"You heard me, Blain. Don't go after Graham, at least not just yet," Frank ordered, speaking to the men's backs as they strode down the corridor.

The drive was wordless, except for the occasional outburst of explicates followed by a fist into the dash from Premoe. Both men's stomachs were a pit of roiling emotions. Guilt stirred by fury and mixed with a generous helping of exasperation, not to mention homicidal inclinations.

As they came upon the parking lot they were immediately greeted by yards of somber yellow tape strung from lamppost to lamppost around the crime scene which made the reality of the situation immediately apparent. It no longer entertained an air of the surreal. It was true, they had indeed turned a madman loose on the public.

Although the brunette's corpse had been moved already, much of her life's essence still stained the asphalt. There were fragments of scalp, bone and gray matter ground into the blacktop. Freeman felt his guts spinning as if he had just spent the last hour on a Tilt-a-Whirl. He glanced over at his partner and saw that he too was having to swallow extra hard to keep the ingredients of his breakfast a secret.

"Charlie," Freeman nodded at the man as he walked up. He still wasn't quite ready to hear the explicit details of the crime.

"Sorry about being the bearer of bad news," Charlie said.

"Where are Baker and Revall?"

"They've already headed back to the station, Frank's orders. He called and told them that this one was yours. I asked them to drop a few samples off at the lab for me, sand, blood, semen stains. I thought you guys might like to get on jump on this one," Charlie replied. His eyes reflected the burden this case would eternally leave him carrying.

"Thanks, Charlie," Premoe grunted.

"So, walk us through," Freeman sighed.

"You see where the first girl was lying," he pointed to a blood smear on the pavement.

"Uh huh."

"The meat wagon already hauled her down to county, that was before you caught the case. Baker and Revall have all the info. I've already sent a few rolls of film to the lab."

"How?" Freeman asked, still not ready for lengthy conversation.

"He caved in her skull. Bashed her head against the concrete until he crushed her skull, and then he bashed her some more. I'll know more when I run some tests at the lab, but I think there was semen on her shirt."

"Are you sure?"

"Let's just say, I have a pretty good hunch."

"What about her?" Premoe choked, pointing to a mangled heap of flesh that was once a vibrant teen.

"Looks like she was in front of this car when it was hit," Freeman observed.

"Between the two bumpers is more accurate. But she wasn't struck with a whole lot of force, in fact, the only reason her leg was even broken was because of the difference in the heights of the bumpers. The leverage worked against her. But that's not the worst of it."

The detectives just looked at the forensic team leader with acknowledgment. Charlie knew to proceed.

"As best as I can figure it looks as though the perp," he paused to think. "Graham, left her pinned between the two cars. Hell, he might have pinned her there on purpose for all I know. After dealing with her friend he came back for this girl here."

"So, she watched her friend's head being bashed into the ground?" Premoe asked.

"Yes, it appears that way."

"Why didn't she scream?"

"From what I have seen so far I believe that the perp chopped her across the throat. The force of the blow was hard enough to severely damage her larynx and keep her from screaming, yet not quite hard enough to kill her."

"I see. Go on," Freeman said.

"The short version is, after he raped her, he hacked her hand off by grinding it back and forth across the fender well, here," he pointed to a bloody piece of sheet metal. Scraps of tattered flesh and strands of jet black hair dangled from the twisted steel. Freeman quickly averted his eyes.

"Is it gone?"

"Yeah, it's gone. He took it with him."

"No chance this was a copy cat?"

"There's always an outside chance, but I'd have to say that would be way outside. Listen, I've worked all the evidence associated with this case for more than five years now, since the beginning, and this gives me the same feeling. I've looked at all of this before, only then it was a different face and a different time," his face reflected the pain of a haunted man.

"Even if the killer was in prison at the time of the murders?" Freeman asked, using Charlie for a sounding board more than anything else.

"I don't know how you guys feel, but I'd have to say that the wrong man is in prison."

"Me too," Premoe said. "Now, let's go get that little bastard, Graham."

Charlie's face took on an expression the two men had never seen before.

"She was just a fucking kid. She was wearing a letterman's jacket from First Coast High. That's where my daughter goes to school," a tear sat in the pocket beneath his twitching eye.

Both detectives sighed and collected their thoughts. As bad as it was, and as angry as it made them, they still needed to think with a clear head. They would mourn the teen when the time came. They always did. She would prove to be another lost soul that ate away at them during long sleepless nights.

"Let's call Frank first. See how he wants us to proceed."

"I'd rather not," Premoe argued, Freeman dialed his cell phone regardless.

"Frank, this is Todd."

"What did you find out?"

"According to Charlie, not to mention everything we saw at the scene, I'd have to say the evidence all points toward Graham. We were given a key piece of evidence by the mall security people as well. A surveillance video tape. It seems our Mr. Graham was stalking the victim. He even felt the need to pleasure himself for their cameras. But as for enough evidence for court, we can't be absolutely certain of a conviction without some more time to go over the evidence more thoroughly."

"You don't have any more time."

"What do you mean, Frank?" They both stared at the phone.

"Duggan's date, it's midnight tonight," his voice sounded sour and morose.

"Well, they will just have to hold off until we can sort this out."

"It doesn't look possible, the Governor is the only one with the authority to make that decision."

"So call the Governor," Freeman's voice became frantic. Premoe took the phone from his partner.

"He's out of town," Frank said.

"That's bullshit, Frank," Premoe yelled. "There has got to be someone who is taking his place."

"I'll do whatever I can on this end, you two just have to give me as much ammunition as possible. We've lost a lot of credibility with the Governor's office, not to mention the Mayor and every other God damned politician in the state."

"I don't care what it takes, Frank. Duggan does not fry tonight," Premoe said while pushing the off button on the cell phone.

Freeman looked at him with his patented "what the fuck did you do that for" look.

"I didn't want to have him tell us how to run the investigation. We go after Graham and we go after him right now."

"Are you hurt, Rueben?" The woman's voice grated on his nerves.

"No, ma," he replied, trying to remember the combination to the lock as her voice incessantly pecked away at his brain.

"Did someone have another accident?"

"Yes, ma."

"Boy, the girls you date are so clumsy."

Every fiber of his being wanted to scream out, "you stupid bitch," but he held his temper.

"Go back to the house and make me some breakfast, please, I'm famished," he cooed.

"Okay," she replied with an adolescent smile and bounded down the wooded path like a carefree little schoolgirl.

She wore the same gingham dress she had worn the previous day, as well as the day before that. It had little to do with Edna's concern for her personal hygiene, rather, she just didn't remember when one day turned into another, nor could she recall what she had worn the day before. Years of abuse had scrambled her cohesive thought process to the point that her memory was nothing more than a crap shoot. Today was a good day for her, her memory seemed much better now that her son was back home.

Cracker shook his head, heaved a sigh and went back to work on the rusty lock. His bloody clothes were clinging to his skin like scabs. His psyche was screaming out its rejuvenation. It had been long time since he had been able to feel a last breath passing over lips he was kissing. The padlock hasp popped open with a resounding click and Cracker yanked open the heavy oaken door. He stood at the doorway for several seconds before walking down a short set of steps carved out of the earth itself. The strong, pungent odor of tannin gusted forth from the depths of the cellar. The stinging in his nostril was delightful. He truly missed the nuances of his work.

The coolness of the air was refreshing. It blanketed his skin with familiarity. He was finally home.

Lighting a lantern, Cracker took quick inventory of his private hideaway. All of his beauties still hung obediently in a symmetrical row against the far wall. White, spongy roots had grown out of the walls of his hand made cavern and had rudely wrapped themselves around the decaying fingers. When he originally processed the hands he had formed them in a shape that allowed him to use them for his perverse pleasures. Now he was tickled, and aroused, to find them awaiting his return and eager to satisfy his needs.

He could hardly believe he had been away for more than five years. It seemed like only yesterday that he had hung the last of his treasures up for display. Cracker peeled away the roots that were intertwined on a vacant meat hook once used to hang cows at an old slaughterhouse. The hooks worked perfectly for his purpose. Little Miss Orange took her place amongst his other lovers. The first appendage in the row was completely black and shriveled. The fingernails were chipped and gray. It was his first. It always looked so out of place amongst the others. They were so perfectly shaped and sized.

But hers, hers was nothing more than a mangled piece of bitch flesh. It stood out from the others like a hooker at a convent. Cracker was tempted to throw it away. Burn it. Bury it. Anything to get rid of it. Amusingly, he wondered if his mother would appreciate it if he were to try and sew it back on for her now. His laughter died against the dirt walls of the hand dug cavern.

Cracker disrobed and shoved his bloody clothing into a black plastic garbage bag. He would take the time later to properly dispose of them by burning them. He was lost in his musing when the first sound reached his ears. Although he was underground, sounds from the above world echoed their warning to his subterranean realm. Tires on gravel.

Quickly Cracker put on a clean change clothes that had been stashed in his secret hideaway for more than five years. He was pleased the find that they still fit him quite well and as an added bonus, they were impregnated with the stench of tanning chemicals and decayed flesh. He then opened a footlocker that sat against the far wall and pulled out a Browning 30.06 rifle. He worked the bolt several times and then lifted the rifle to his eye, it had been more than five years but he was sure that he still had the touch. It was just like riding a bicycle or stalking a victim, one never quite seemed to forget how to do it right. He laughed to himself as he wiped off the lenses of the scope before blowing out the rusted lantern and creeping out of his underground chamber. He closed the doors and hurriedly scattered leaves and debris across the entrance to his dungeon in an effort to hide it from the prying eyes of his uninvited guests.

Cracker sat on his knees, peering through the thick underbrush. Instantly he recognized the car as the two men he hated the most in the world; Freeman and Premoe. He checked the clip in his rifle. A full magazine, exactly as he had left it. He chambered a round and scampered through the underbrush until he was on top of a small hill. He smirked. How fitting, a grassy knoll.

He was poised perfectly for an ambush. Not only did his grassy knoll afford him a clear shot at anyone coming up the trail, it also furnished him with perfect cover. Cracker had practiced this routine many times before, like all of his planned escapes. In fact, the bastards would have never caught him the first time had he not gotten drunk and passed out.

They were in the house talking to his mother. Patiently he waited. Soon they would both be moving up the path toward their destiny.

"Mrs. Graham," Freeman called through the decrepit screen door.

There was no reply. Both men strained at the door, listening for any sound.

"She's in the kitchen, singing," Premoe said, yanking open the screen door.

"There goes admissibility."

"Probable cause," he fumed.

"Probable cause?"

"You hear that singing? Sounds like someone's dying to me," he smiled.

"Oh, you boys startled me," she spun around with a large butcher's knife in her hand. Premoe jumped back. His heart was instantly aflame with anger, there was a fresh cherry under her left eye and a dried over split in her lower lip.

"Easy partner," Freeman said, seeing the man tense up.

"Did you come to see Rueben?"

"Yes, ma'am we did."

"He's such a good boy."

"Can you tell us where he is, please."

"He helped out another young girl last night. They always seem to have accidents when he's around. I wish he would date someone less clumsy," she said, a look of ignorant innocence oozing from her every pore.

The detectives stared back at one another with harried expressions.

"Would you like some lunch? I'm making some lunch for Rueben. It's no trouble at all."

"No, ma'am, but we really would like to speak with," he paused. "We'd like to speak with Rueben."

"Is it time for Jeopardy yet? Rueben says I'm really good at Jeopardy."

"Ma'am, where is Rueben?" Premoe asked, his voice starting to take on the edge of his impatience.

"There's no need to get upset, he's out back. He'll be up for lunch in a few minutes. Now you boys just sit down and wait for him," her offer was overpowered by the sounds of the screen door squeaking open, then slamming shut.

Although the trail leading behind the house was overgrown from five years of non use the detectives could still make out the narrow footpath. There were light footprints in the dry sand leading back into a tangle of thick underbrush and trees. Freeman bent down and grabbed a handful of earth and let the tiny granules sift through his fingers.

"Is it the same?"

"Could be, it feels the same," he replied, taking a small paper envelope from his pocket. He brushed the leaves and debris away from the path and slid the envelope along the upper layer of dirt, gathering a sample of the sand as evidence for the crime lab to analyze. It was a bittersweet victory.

Premoe stepped a couple of feet into the thicket to the left of the trail and Freeman did just the same on the right side. Both detectives had their weapons drawn and began cautiously creeping along side the overgrown path. The woods were uncannily quiet, as if the furry denizens were aware of the humanoid dangers abounding in their domain. It was almost high noon.

Cracker watched the two cops sneaking down the lane. They thought they were slick. They thought they were well concealed within the thicket. However, from his crag along the hilltop he had a perfect line of sight. In fact, Premoe was a dead man within a matter of minutes, just as soon as he cleared the thickest of the underbrush. Cracker slowly turned a knob on the rifle scope and changed the power from four to eight times magnification.

Premoe's ugly face grew at an alarming rate until he was larger than life. Impossible to miss. Right between the eyes. Cracker felt a ripple of pleasure career through him as he pulled up tension on the trigger, one more micron of pressure and the showdown would be under way. He had a few empty meat hooks left in his hideaway, no reason they couldn't join his circle of friends.

The path began to jog to the right. Freeman waved his hand at his partner, directing him further back into the woods. Premoe didn't like the clearing that lay before him. He would be vulnerable for several moments, bare to the world like a fat, naked baby. He paused for a moment at the edge of the tree line.

"Come on, come on, you bastard," Cracker whispered.

Sweat beaded up on the back of his neck and began trickling down his back in tiny rivers. The sensation was fabulous. He loved the rush of adrenaline as he waited for the moment of truth. Unexpectedly, Cracker began to feel bizarre. His eyes began clouding over with a hazy darkness. He lowered the rifle's scope from his eye and stared into the blue sky, blinking repeatedly in an attempt to clear his vision. The burst of daylight only seemed to make things worse. He began feeling slightly nauseous. Then, he heard a whisper of a voice. A faint murmur of intrusion.

Cracker's heart began to race faster. Was this what it was like for the doc? He shook his head back and forth to try and free the cobwebs. He could feel the intruder forcing their way past his cerebral cortex and into the deepest sections of his mind. He was being invaded. A glimmer of movement caught his attention. Premoe was moving. Cracker raised the rifle and tried to focus on his target once more.

Premoe made his move into the clearing in one swift motion. He moved quickly, but not so much as to make too much noise trampling over the dried leaf carpeting of the forest. He stayed low, almost duck walking. His calves burned and screamed at the unfamiliar exertion.

Regardless of Premoe's efforts, Cracker saw his target easily. Then suddenly, his eyes began to fade in and out once again as he trained the crosshairs on the detective's forehead. He applied constant pressure on the trigger. "Squeeze, don't pull," he chanted over and over in his mind, trying to push the intruder out.

Hello Cracker! A vaguely familiar voice rang out in his head.

Cracker fought against the interloper and tried to maintain a steady aim on his target. His head began to pound as every fiber of his gray matter tried to remain in control.

Freeman caught a diminutive flash of light out of the corner of his eye. Glass. Rifle scope. It only took a matter of seconds for him to process the information. "Down!" Was all he was able to scream before the shot rang out.

Premoe lurched forward, then rocked back on his heels. His

overly large body was thrown backward onto the verdant carpet like a rag doll. Immediately Freeman began emptying his pistol into the tree line where he thought the shot had come from and ran toward his partner. He ejected the empty clip and popped in another while on the run and continued to fire.

His heart raced with fear the moment he saw a blood stain already beginning to spread across his partner's white shirt. Freeman fumbled for his radio while dropping to his knees, pushing the panic button and screaming at the same time.

"Officer down, officer down."

Cracker almost laughed out loud at the exhilaration he felt from walking so close to death's doorstep. Bullets were ripping bark away from the surrounding trees and he could hear the whistle of Freeman's slugs flying passed him. As soon as Freeman started to reload, Cracker bolted from his prone position and ran deeper into the forest.

Freeman ripped open Premoe's shirt and heaved a sigh of relief. The cobalt colored vest had done it's job, almost perfectly. The bullet had struck Premoe at an angle and had fragmented, throwing a piece of jagged lead into his armpit. Freeman quickly assessed the wound as non-lethal and trained his attention back to the tree line. He heard the faint sounds of someone running through the thick trees. He tried to get a bead on the man's location, but the sounds echoed throughout the forest betraying any sense of true position.

"Shit, that hurts," Premoe moaned, trying to get up but still too dizzy to manage.

"Lie still."

"Where is the son of a bitch? Did you get him?"

"He's gone, now lie back and take it easy."

"What do you mean he's gone?"

"He ran off into the woods."

"Why didn't you go after him?"

"Maybe a little thing like you being shot changed my priorities," Freeman scowled.

"Yeah, well, maybe you shouldn't worry about me so much," he winked and then quickly grimaced.

"I got a wagon on the way."

"Cancel it."

"Are you nuts?"

"No, but we have to go after that maniac, there's no telling what he might do."

"Not a chance. At least not until we get you looked at."

"I'm fine," he said, forcing himself to his feet with a grunt. The blood had all but stopped flowing from the wound under his arm.

However, the thumping in his chest wasn't quite ready to quit. He stripped off his clothes and body armor and looked at the glowing red mark already turning to crimson, rapidly headed for purple.

"Ouch!" Freeman grimaced.

"That's gonna leave a mark," Premoe tried to laugh, but caught himself after a bolt of searing pain shot through him.

"Glad you chose to wear your armor today."

"I have, ever since you took that one to the neck. Kind of figured I'd been playing the odds way too long. Guess I was right."

"Time to head to Vegas," they both laughed. "Think you can walk?"

"Yeah, just not too fast or too far," he started to concede to the fact that he was truly injured.

Body armor might stop a bullet from penetrating the body, but it doesn't do much for the blunt trauma. He could tell by his labored breathing that he had probably bruised a lung and was certain he would be coughing up blood sooner or later.

Cracker leaned against a wide oak, struggling to catch his breath. His years in a cage had taken a toll on his body. He wasn't used to this kind of physical activity. He turned an ear to the wind and listened. Nothing. The chicken shit bastards hadn't followed him into the woods. The blanket of silence began lifting as the forest creatures began scurrying about, resuming their daily chores.

He wondered what had happened. Why had he blacked out? He could tell something was wrong, indefinably wrong.

Tim rocked back and forth on his bunk, his brain aflame with lancinating pain. He threw the book onto the floor out of frustrated anger. He had tried to stop Cracker from shooting the man, but the psychopath's will proved too strong. Tim had seen the man go down.

Although his transference felt like a failure to him, Tim realized what a triumph it had actually been. He had proved to himself once and for all that True was right. The magic did work. He was, in fact, innocent. And yet, blackness descended upon his heart. He was still condemned to die. Tears began to trickle out of the corners of his eyes.

Tim picked up a small box of stationery the warden had forced upon him and began the last letter he would ever write. *My Dearest Elsa,* it began. Tears blurred his vision as they flooded out of his eyes. He was inundated with so many things to say that his pen scribbled furiously across the page. He wanted to say everything to her that he had neglected to say. He wanted to say everything he had remembered to say, but not quite often enough. Yet, with all the words he scrawled across the parchment, he couldn't find any that would, or could, profess the depth of his love for her. His newfound lust for life was an agonizing emotion to deal with, especially with his fate sealed, and looming just around the corner. He glanced at the clock in the corridor.

Tim felt it was the most venomous act he had seen since arriving at the prison. A clock on the wall for men who had nothing but time to count their limited time. The second hand continued its sweeping motion around the black and white face, oblivious to the significance of each tiny little black pip it devoured.

The squeaky tires of the library cart yanked Tim out of his rumination. Impatiently he waited as the man made his way down the row. He wanted to scream out at him to hurry up. But the others living, existing, on the row were also on borrowed time. So, patiently, he waited.

"You don't look so good today, Duggan."

"I kind of figured as much," he slowly exhaled his sadness.

"Not much time, is there?"

"None. I'm a bit surprised that they let you come up here today."

"Let's just say that the warden has a soft spot for you. He thought you could use someone to talk to."

Tim just nodded.

"You talk to the preacher man yet?"

Tim shook his head.

"You want to? I can get that arranged," True asked.

Again, Tim nodded.

Both men stared silently at the floor for a few minutes. *A moment of silence for the damned.*

"True, you have to do me a favor."

He looked into the man's eyes and tried not to break out into tears.

"Get this to my wife Elsa," he handed the letter to True. "Any way you can."

"I'm not supposed to do this. They frown upon mail going out or coming in that hasn't had its privacy breached. But this will be my pleasure."

"Thanks, I'll owe you my life, even if it isn't worth much right now."

"It's worth more than most up here," he glanced down the row of cages.

Again, both men fell into silent contemplation.

"What about the book?" True asked.

"I don't think I found anything that can help me now, there's just not enough time. But, at least I'll go to my grave knowing the truth."

"So then, you were able to get into that monster's head?" True asked with a glimmer of hope and a sliver of satisfaction gleaming through.

"Yes, I was able to get into his mind. And yes, I believe you. I believe it," Tim said, looking down and setting an open hand on the mysterious book. "I never thought I'd hear myself say it, but I know the book's magic is real. Promise me you'll get rid of the damned thing once this is all over."

"That's a deal I can live with."

"There is a bright side to legitimizing Satan's existence."

"What's that?"

"If there's a devil, there must be a God. I've been in hell, and now I'm standing in line for heaven."

True took the man's hand in his and smiled. His eyes were watery and his nose was beginning to run.

"I'll get this to your woman, even if it kills me," he promised, hiding the envelope between the pages of a worn book.

True was sure the big man wouldn't mind getting a few more tapioca puddings for doing a dead man a favor. He turned away from the doomed man before he could no longer contain his emotions. As he passed the one empty cell on the row he reached over and touched the cold steel bars. If he thought hard enough, he could still hear Carl Lettimore's voice. He was certain that Duggan's would haunt him even longer.

CHAPTER TWENTY-TWO

"Slow down," Premoe half grunted, half laughed.

"Sorry, I didn't think you were hurt that badly," Freeman's grin was wide enough to block out the sun.

"Don't even say it," he laughed.

The men were walking back and forth across the overgrown trail following the canine unit in front of them.

"Sorry, detectives, he's lost the scent," the handling officer commented.

The border collie paced mercilessly, it was obvious that the dog was disturbed by the waning scent.

"There's just too much water and too many places where his scent was lost."

"That's okay, I didn't expect to be able to track him too far in all of this anyway. We'll head back to the car and call in an APB. We'll get you looked at too," he looked over at Premoe who was struggling for breath with every step. "The meat wagon should be here by now."

The three men and a dog walked casually down the now familiar trail. Freeman had to laugh at his tousled partner. Usually Blain's hefty midsection was well hidden beneath his suit, however, with his shirt unbuttoned for comfort's sake, everything was hanging loose in all its glory. Vanity was no longer an issue for Premoe. He hurt bad and he didn't care if he looked that way.

"Just shut up, I know what you're thinking," he stopped the barrage of insults before they had a chance to start. Freeman just chuckled.

Unexpectedly, the dog began barking behind them. The unanticipated baying had both detectives checking themselves for unsightly stains.

"What the hell did he do that for?" Premoe groaned and recoiled in pain from the combination of jumping at the dog's yelps and yelling at the handler.

Laughing, the handler explained. "He got a hit on something."

"On what?" Freeman asked.

"I'm not sure, but he picked up something with the perp's scent on it."

The trio once again followed the instincts of their smarter colleague. The perky border collie raced back and forth over the path, frantically searching for new life for the semi-cold trail. All at once the dog stopped and began barking and pawing wildly at the ground.

"Whatcha got, Prince," the handler called in the soothing voice of a man who spent far too much time with his animal.

The three men finally caught up to the dog and saw the hastily concealed entrance to Cracker's cave.

"Good boy," the handler rewarded the panting dog with gentle, loving strokes.

"It's unlocked," Premoe said, pointing to the open combination lock hanging from the hasp.

Freeman drew his gun and waited while his injured partner struggled to yank the door open. A foul odor rose from the pit the moment the door sprung open. The dog turned its nose up and began to whine a high pitched plea for mercy.

Cautiously the three men and the dog entered the underground chamber, at the forceful protest of the canine unit. The room was quite small and they were immediately aware of the fact that Graham wasn't in the hole. The handler quickly backed himself and the dog gratefully back out of the reeking pit.

Premoe fumbled around on the makeshift workbench and found some matches to light the lantern with. The room exploded with light as soon as he struck a match. He touched the flame to the lantern wick and the room was soon awash with a warm, albeit, eerie glow.

"Look," Freeman pointed to the row of hands hanging against the back wall.

"That one is fresh," Premoe jerked his hand away from the oozing appendage as if he had just stuck his arm into a nest of hornets.

"What's in the bag?"

"I guess I have to look in this one?" He shot a glance at his partner hoping for some leniency.

"You're closer," Freeman took a step backward.

Premoe reluctantly nodded acceptance and apprehensively started untwisting the top of the black plastic bag. As the thin material peeled away, the bag opened to reveal a wad of clothing. Premoe, relieved there were no vile odors involved, slowly pulled the clothing out of the bag. He laid the blood stained garments on the makeshift bench.

"We better quit right now, at least until we get a forensic team and some warrants down here," Freeman said.

"We better put a call in to Frank too. We've got all the evidence we need to pull the plug on that execution."

Both men were more than willing to take a brief respite from the horrific abyss. Completely spent, Premoe rested against his partner as they walked back to their car. He felt a flicker of relief when he spied the obtrusive orange and white van parked in the driveway. He knew he was getting just too damned old for all this macho shit.

"Frank, it's Todd," he announced over the cell phone. He shot a smile over to his wincing partner who was trying to be tough for the pretty paramedic compassionately attending to the ruffian's bruised physique. If one would dare to call his body a physique.

"I heard the radio call, how is he?" Freeman had forgotten all about his frantic call. Frank's voice carried the tone of a worried mother.

"Nothing too serious, more his ego than anything else. Dumb ass was actually wearing his armor for once."

"What a prince," they both laughed and then sighed in relief.

"We got him, Frank. We've got Graham dead to rights. I think we recovered the hand from last night's attack. We've got his clothes, everything. I wish we could place him as the person who shot Premoe, but no such luck. We never even got a chance to see the shooter. We did recover the gun though. I'm sure we'll get lucky and get something off it from forensics. Although, ballistics won't be able to do much with what was left of the bullet. It fragmented when it struck the body armor. Blain's damned lucky he wasn't killed. Graham used a thirty aught six. Got a thirty two power scope on the damn thing too. It's a damned good thing Graham didn't aim for the head."

"Todd, I still can't get through to the Governor, he's on a boat off the coast, somewhere near the Keys," Frank solemnly broke the news.

"Can't the coast guard get him on the radio?"

"If he were still on his boat, yes. He took the skiff and went off to one of the islands."

"Damn it, Frank. I don't care how you do it, but get someone to authorize a stay of execution, even if only for the damned weekend."

"It's not that easy."

"It's a hell of a lot easier than it will be for us to bring Duggan back from the dead, or for us to try and live with killing an innocent man."

"I'll see what I can do," Frank mumbled as if he were already defeated.

"That's not good enough, Frank."

"God damn it, I know it's not, but what else can I do?"

"I've got to go, Frank, I'll call you back in a little while," Freeman said, trying to decipher his partner's frenzied gestures. "What?" He screamed across the gravel driveway.

"They've spotted him."

"Spotted who?"

"Graham."

"Where?"

"Heading east on interstate 295."

"East on 295? You'd think he'd want to head west, away from Florida."

"Unless he's got something else on his mind."

"What is going on in that pretty little head of yours?" Freeman asked.

"Duggan's place is across the Buchman Bridge," Premoe said.

"What in the hell is Graham up to?"

"Can't be too sure, but my best guess is that he's going after Duggan's wife. Don't ask me why, but it's the only thing that makes any sense right now."

"What time is it?" Freeman asked, glancing up at the bruised horizon which was darkening by the second.

"A little after ten, why?"

"That gives us less than two hours."

"Two hours? You mean Frank hasn't gotten the Governor to grant a stay of execution?"

"You got it. Says the Governor had a press conference earlier today announcing that there would be no last minute stays and then he promptly left for the Keys."

Premoe shook his head in defeat. "What do we do now? Go after Graham or head for the prison?"

"Both. You head for the prison, I'll go after Graham," Freeman suggested.

"I don't like it, but I guess it's all we got. Do me a favor," he called after his partner who was already trotting off to his car.

"What's that? Kill him for you?" He smiled.

"Okay, two favors. Don't go charging in there without back up. Get some units rolling right now."

"Will do. I've been shot once, I don't intend on letting that ever happen again," they both smiled weakly at each other.

Freeman was gone twenty seconds later and Premoe was already regretting letting him go alone.

Cracker was livid. He had held that fat bastard Premoe right in his sights. The bastard should have been his. It had taken him several minutes to clear his head and concentrate on what had happened. Once he regained his composure it didn't take him very long to figure out that somehow the doc had gotten into his head. The danger of the man having the book had never dawned on him. Cracker never figured the man would ever open the book, let alone read it unless prodded into the act by Cracker himself through a transference. Or that wrinkled old bastard, True.

Cracker's anger swelled inside him like the guts of a raging volcano. Scalding magma of rage pushed its way up his throat. His body shook as a result of his inability to cope with his indigence. The doctor would have to pay for his insolence, just as True had paid for his. And his mother before them.

Cracker cursed himself for his lack of self-control. He should have never allowed himself the pleasures of release with those girls. Never. Now, he had ruined everything. He might have still had a chance to make everything work out if the doc wouldn't have made him miss his opportunity to get those detectives off his back.

Cracker made his way into the city, hoping to blend in with the multitudes of people, at least for a while. All he needed was a little time to figure out his next move. This time, the exhilaration of the hunt wasn't a pleasant sensation. This time, he was the hunted. He saw a familiar face looking at him. It was a face painted with a look of despondency, yet it was painfully obvious the expression was suppressing a once jovial man. His anger began to fester once more.

Cracker put in two quarters and pulled out the evening edition of the Times-Union. Doctor Timothy Duggan's face was plastered all over the front cover along with controversial articles both opposing and defending the death penalty. There was a side bar item with an itinerary of Duggan's last day on earth as if it were some major sporting event.

Some of the articles proclaimed the man's innocence, despite the fact that he was a confessed killer. They questioned the condemned man's sanity and argued that his confession should have been rendered useless. Other articles defended the state's stance on capital punishment. The crimes attributed to the good doctor were all outlined in chronological order and explained the gruesome murders with horrific detail with blatant disregard to the victim's families.

But not even once had they even mention Rueben Graham's innocence. At least not on page one. Buried in the back was a one paragraph blurb about his lawsuit against the state for wrongful imprisonment. And even then, the item had mentioned Simon Patterson more than it had Cracker.

"You want to play, doc? Then let's play," Cracker spat at the picture on the front cover.

He was no longer without a plan. In that exact moment he admitted to himself that his game was over. He knew that at best he was headed back for the row, but more than likely there was a cold spot of earth with his name on it waiting for him. But none of it would happen without a fight. Nor would it be before the state had fried an innocent man. Cracker was bound and determined to take some company to the grave with him.

Cracker threw the newspaper into the trash and focused his attentions to the posh neighborhood where the sweet, lily of the valley scented blonde lived.

———————

Timothy Duggan felt an icy chill spreading over his entire body. The sound of the row door clanging open resounded throughout the dungeon. Even the other inmates felt the chill enveloping the room, abducting their very essence like curious aliens. The chill was the indifferent disease of death creeping down the corridor. Stoic men with apathetic faces came to do the angel of death's bidding.

Even the priest, a man of God, had traveled this path far too often to care. Too often to even realize that he no longer cared. His façade had become a genuine mask to hide his pain.

Unbelievable panic began to ebb over Tim. He wasn't ready. He truly was not ready to give up his life. Not now. Not after learning the truth. He wondered if Elsa had ever gotten his letter. And if she had, had she even bothered to read it? Or had he done such irreparable damage to their relationship that she would never forgive him? The thought of Elsa hating him so vehemently churned in his stomach like an intestinal virus on a rampage.

Tim began wondering if she would be in the gallery. He didn't want see her in the gallery. It would rip his heart out to have her watch him die. He tried to choke back his tears to no avail. His throat tightened to the point that he could barely even swallow. The coldness of fear gripped his skin. He felt the hair raising on his arms, then spreading to tiny tingles across his scalp as if he had consumed too much caffeine.

Boot laden footsteps resonated down the dank corridor, each one resembling the "bong" of a grandfather clock announcing the grave importance of the passing time. Their shadows spread out fifteen feet in front of them, appearing as though a horde of giants were coming to take him away. Tim's bladder began to argue.

Tim glanced down at the remnants of his last meal scattered across the stark white plate. In the end, he had opted to savor Elsa's favorite meal of blackened swordfish, lightly peppered Alfredo and blanched asparagus tips. When Tim had filled out the form he thought it would serve no other purpose than to be a little sliver of remembrance of his life. At best he thought the kitchen staff would get a nice laugh out of it. He had prepared himself for eating a tuna sandwich with mushy green stuff and mushy white stuff on his plate to complement it. However, the dinner had been superb. There was even a nice helping of fresh tapioca pudding which he had never asked for. He regretted the fact that he would never be able to offer his compliments to the chef. Even True had found him several sprigs of lily of the valley to use as a centerpiece. The old man had talked one of the guards into finding a nice vase to put them in. Everyone in the prison had been infected with the gnawing disease of guilt. They knew an innocent man was being executed and not one of them was brave enough, smart enough, or resourceful enough to do anything about it.

The shadows were almost to his cell. Now, that same luxurious dinner threatened to come back for seconds. Tim saw the shadows had stopped moving and looked up to face the pernicious entourage.

"Dr. Duggan, I'm sorry, but it's time to move down the tier to the isolation cell," the warden's voice flowed like honey laced with cayenne.

CHAPTER TWENTY-THREE

C racker spied a familiar hedgerow of lavender framing the perimeter of a house several blocks in the distance. He cut to his left and walked down the block adjacent to his objective. Moving stealthily, he crept between the ample rows of forsythia and azalea bushes that adorned the neighboring houses. With movements as delicate as a surgeon's touch, he slithered up to the back of the blonde's house, once again concealing himself behind the tall, white plumed pampas grass. The small rectangular bathroom window was open just a sliver, allowing a soft ray of light to wash over his feet.

Gathering his composure, Cracker leaned against the wall of the house. He sniffed at the air and was disappointed by the lack of her sweet scent. Then he began to panic. Maybe she wasn't home. Maybe he would never get his chance. He was just about to slide the window open and pull himself up inside when a telephone inside the house rang, immediately followed by the sound of the toilet flushing. He pinned himself tightly against the wall.

He listened to her footsteps fading away from the bathroom. And then her voice, echoing, sweet as caramel from deeper inside the interior of the house. "Hello," she said.

Cracker judged her distance away from the bathroom by her voice and immediately sprung into action once he was certain she was far enough away. He quickly disassembled the window's closing mechanism and slipped silently into the house. He crouched in an alcove created by a small linen closet just inside the door of the posh facilities. Cracker smiled at the irony of such a small portal leading into such opulence. He admired his golden reflection beaming back at him from the mirror frame. The mirror was surrounded with ornamental lights, eight on the top and bottom and four on each of the sides. The white frosted globes cast soft light like that of the full moon on a snowy field. He admired his reflection for several minutes, grateful to finally have his own body back together with his mind. No more creeping around as some pseudo freak. Now he was free to enjoy the fruits of his labor for himself.

The water faucet was patterned after a long necked swan, sweeping elegantly up from the base, curving perfectly at its apex, then flowing back down into an open-beaked mouth. A pair of opal eyes stared at Cracker from the swan's head. He grasped the swan by the top of the neck and bent down as hard as he could until he felt the metal give. It folded up at the base. He bent the faucet back and forth until it broke free in his hands. He hefted it a few times, letting it smash into the palm of his hand. It stung. It would work just fine.

He measured the crook of the faucet's neck. It fit perfectly around his throat. He laughed gently as an image of an old vaudevillian getting the hook and being yanked off stage flashed through his mind. The only difference was that in his mental portrayal the vaudevillian was a naked, voluptuous blonde.

The fastest hour in Tim's life concluded with the door to his cell standing open like the gates of hell welcoming him for all eternity. The devil's minions stood around him dressed in their ceremonial garb, waiting to lead him to the sacrificial altar. His hands were shackled along with his ankles with an added measure of safety linking his wrists to his feet. As if he were going to run. As if he had someplace to run to. Tim was certain it was a custom carried over from earlier times when escape was still a slight possibility. But now, it only served to pacify the condemned, in turn placating the ravenous guilt of the executioners.

Two apathetic correction's officers positioned themselves on either side of him and took an elbow in their firm, yet gentle grasp. The preacher man took a place next to the guard on the right. The warden took the point. And lastly, the supervisor of the tier picked up the rear. Finally, the funeral procession was set to march.

As they stepped through the portal of steel, an image flashed through Tim's mind. It was but a brief millisecond in time. But it was clear. For one blink of an eye he was at home, in his bathroom. But why was he holding a broken pipe?

The march had begun. With each footfall the chrome plated chains danced across the hard tile floor. They tinkled across the glassy surface with the sounds of coins being thrown in a jar. Tim's feet would not let him move. He was frozen in place by a hint of lily of the valley. Memories flooded his mind and he almost passed out.

The entourage paused briefly allowing him time to regain his composure. However, the very moment he was able, they resumed the

224

foreboding trek. You can't cheat death out of what's due.

Tim could barely make out the words the priest was mumbling. He hoped they were prayers of absolution and not pleas of mercy for a guilty man. He sniffed at the stale air and smelled the pungent aroma of his own nervous sweat. If the others smelled him, they surely didn't show it. But then again, they had a hell of a lot more practice at this than he did.

Although he never looked up into the faces of the men in the other cages lining the row, he could feel their sympathetic glances. He knew that their remorseful feelings were more for themselves than for him, but it still made him feel a touch less alone. His walk down the row brought to life the reality of their own fading mortality. But it was somewhat comforting nonetheless. At least someone would be thinking about him when the lights dimmed.

Tim had to pause once more as a tremor of fear rippled though him, brought on by the sound of the row door shutting behind him. That and another mental image of his house. Of his wife's drawer full of unmentionables. The one with the red teddy with black lace trimming. His muscles tensed, but the correction's officer's only pushed him on.

At last they came knocking at fate's door. The steel door swung open smoothly on its greased hinges, exposing the death chamber to Tim for the first time. He stared at the back of the portentous piece of furniture and shuddered.

Timothy Duggan, meet Old Sparky, Old Sparky, Timothy Duggan!

Cracker impressed himself with his own self-control. He wanted the woman so badly he could taste it, but he wasn't ready to do her, not just yet anyway. The man had to suffer. Cracker wanted the doctor to experience every precious second of his cherished wife's agony. He was only feeding the doc little fragments of the unfolding drama at a time, certain the idiot doctor hadn't even put two and two together yet. There was no sense riling him up completely, at least not until he was safely shackled into Old Sparky. He chuckled softly and took a deep breath, breathing in the essence that was Elsa, the newest love of his life. He put her red teddy back into the drawer and pulled out a skimpy black outfit that lavishly revealed much more than it covered. He felt himself stirring but fought hard against the arousal.

As he watched and listened he was able to discern that she was morose and melancholy from the way she sighed against the silence.

She was quite aware of what day it was. Her soft sobbing came and went in spurts of torn emotion. Her tears played at his heartstrings and it was a song he longed to dance to.

Cracker almost felt pity for the woman once he caught sight of her. Elsa was sitting in the breakfast nook with two cups of coffee sitting on the cozy, decorative table. Both mugs had stopped steaming long ago. Curious, he struggled to capture a glimpse of the photo in the frame she was holding. He slithered with his back against the wall until he was a mere dozen feet away from her. The butterflies dancing in his stomach were exhilarating. This was the kind of situation he lived for, and was willing to die for.

The blonde convulsed into another round of gut-wrenching sobs. Elsa reared back and flung the picture frame across the room, forcing Cracker to hug the wall as tightly as he possibly could. Through the shattered shards of glass he could see that the picture was of the blonde, the good doctor and his fat, red-headed friend. Undoubtedly it was taken during a much happier time in their lives.

Cracker averted his attention away from the unsuspecting blonde and wormed his way back into the doctor's mind. He walked along with Tim on a journey that had been previously reserved for him. He briefly glanced around at all of the familiar surrounds and felt a wave of warm satisfaction ebb over him.

———————

The air inside the execution chamber was quite chilly. The yarmulke shaped disk of bald scalp atop Timothy Duggan's head flamed with fresh razor burn. His bare, tender skin still stung from the antiseptic solution they had applied due to its high alcohol content. He laughed ironically to himself. It was absurd that the prison's doctors and lawyers wanted to prevent him from developing an infection before they fried him to death. What was he going to do, sue them from the afterlife? *Timothy Duggan vs. The State of Florida, Department of Corrections for Malicious Execution. Co-Defendant; Mr. Executioner for Negligence and Dereliction of Duty; specifically for allowing the Plaintiff to become infected before he could be properly executed.* The first time that this sort of lawsuit was successful there would be even more lawyers dying to go to hell. Timothy chuckled out loud, drawing an array of inquisitive glances from Death's entourage.

The guards gently seated him into Old Sparky and began fastening the various straps and buckles. First, a pair of four-inch wide leather straps were cinched tightly across his chest. The buckles dug uncomfortably into his skin.

He was trying desperately to concentrate on nothing at all. He focused on a little black spot in his mind. But it wouldn't stay a little black spot. It spread across his vision like a dollop of pancake batter spreading across the bottom of a hot griddle. The edges of the black spot began to spit and sputter. Then, he saw her. The black spot had morphed into a vision. A lovely vision. His eyes traced up the backs of her silky, smooth legs, up to the hem of her yellow and orange sun dress.

Tim could sense someone strapping his arms and legs into the chair, yet his mind was completely centered on the supple shape of the woman's buttocks. Her perfect shape smoothed out into the small of her back where two cute dimples winked back at him. He studied her further. She had her arms crossed, cradling the left elbow into her right hand. Her flowing blonde hair parted strangely on one side, exposing the cream colored phone pressed against her ear. Tim thought his vision oddly descriptive and familiar, but still, he let his mind wander away from the reality of his death. They would prepare him for the chair regardless if his mind were with them or not.

Then, Tim breathed deeply out of panic. The blonde turned around. It was Elsa. She was standing in their living room talking on the cordless phone. Her face was lined with worry and her eyes streaked with tears.

Tim fought off the images and for a second, even though it was merely a brief wrinkle in time, he was back in the chamber with Death's retinue. He wiggled his wrists, trying to gain some semblance of comfort. The gentle hum of the generator was almost soothing. Almost.

Tim's moment in reality was shattered by the haunting image of his wife. In his mind he was closer to her now. In fact, it seemed as though she was just mere fingertips beyond his reach. He watched her walking around the room, stopping in the foyer and peering out the small ornamental windows that bordered the front door. Then, she turned and glanced down at a small end table. Although Tim couldn't get a clear mental picture of what she was looking he, he knew it was his letter. Unopened; unread.

Tears flowed from his eyes as the image left him. His allowed his eyes to scan over the sober faces in the gallery. He spied a few sympathetic faces amongst the growing crowd, yet not a one of them belonged to a drop dead gorgeous blonde with blue eyes and his last name. Elsa didn't show. Tim's chest caved with the knowledge that he'd never see the love of his life again.

Cracker left the condemned man alone to enjoy his moment of intimacy with the executioner. The good doctor had yet to figure out that his flashbacks and memories were not what they seemed. Cracker had to fight hard to keep from letting his little secret out of the bag. He wanted to scream at the idiot, make him understand what was going to happen and let him know that he was absolutely powerless to stop him from exacting his revenge. Like a shadow at sunrise, he slowly crept further into the living room. He slithered behind the couch unseen. Huddled against the berber, he observed the long legged blonde as she went about her daily routine, oblivious to the vermin sweating in concealment. Once again the telephone rang.

"Hello. Yes, this is Mrs. Duggan. May I ask who's speaking?"

"Mrs. Duggan, I'm sorry to bother you. My name is Todd Freeman, Detective Todd Freeman," he repeated, trying to talk over the static on his cellular phone. The steel structure spanning the St. Johns River was playing havoc with his reception.

"What can I do for you detective?" Her voice became suddenly terse.

"Listen, and listen carefully. I have reason to believe that you are in grave danger. I need for you to get out of the house."

"What are you talking about?"

"I don't have time to explain right now, just listen to me and get out of the house right now."

"Is this some kind of sick joke?"

"No, this is no joke. I have reason to believe there is someone coming to hurt you."

"Goodbye, detective, or whoever you are," she let the title roll sarcastically off her tongue before pressing the off button on her cordless phone.

She had been inundated with phone calls all morning. Calls from people who had never even met her husband, but swore he didn't deserve the chair and that their sympathies were with her. Others wanted to taunt her with her husband's impending doom, claiming the bastard was getting exactly what he deserved. There were even a few marriage proposals from men who had seen her picture in the paper during all the publicity, and they knew she was going to be a single woman in just a few short hours. She would have quit answering the phone altogether had it not been for her yearning desire to answer it and have it be the governor or the warden calling to say it was all one big misunderstanding and her husband would be home in no time at all. "Just a few formalities, ma'am," she could almost hear the warden explaining. She reached over and picked up the sealed letter from the stand.

Cracker tensed in the shadows. "Detective?" That bastard Premoe must be coming after him. Now he was certain the good doctor had made him miss. And just for that reason alone, it was time for him to pay.

The phone rang again.

"Look, I don't know who you are but," she never finished her sentence, instead she let out a blood curdling scream.

"Mrs. Duggan?" Freeman screamed into the phone. He heard her scream, but he also heard a dull thud followed by the phone careening across the floor. He pressed his foot down on the accelerator and prayed he could reach Elsa Duggan in time. He also prayed that Blain was doing a hell of a lot better than he was.

Blain Premoe fought his way through the congregating crowd picketing the perimeter of the prison. There were signs of all shapes, sizes, colors and political stances bobbing around on sticks and poles of one fashion or another. One read: KILL THE BASTARD. Another read: THEY DIED - YOU FRIED! And yet another; EXTINGUISH MCINTYRE'S PYRE. Blain thought it looked more like the entrance to a wrestling match than a prison. He thought better against using his gold shield to help part the crowd, certain it would do more harm than good. Best to let the crazies think he was just another one of them until he was too close for them to mob him once they realized differently. Premoe had to worm his way through several check points before finally gaining entrance into the prison proper.

"Listen, you don't understand, I have to talk to the warden, immediately," Premoe barked at the nervous young correction's officer sitting behind a large Plexiglas window that made him look like an exhibit at a zoo rather than someone with any authority. The young man continuously moved his eyes from the big man standing in front of him and the seething mob outside.

"Sir, do you have an appointment?"

"No, I don't have an appointment."

"The warden is extremely busy, if you haven't noticed," the correction's officer squawked sarcastically. "You'll need to make an appointment if you want to see the warden. His office hours are," the officer said tersely and looked up at a piece of paper taped to the inside of the Plexiglas barrier.

"I know what his office hours are," Premoe interrupted. "Listen carefully, my name is Detective Blain Premoe. I'm a homicide detective for the Jacksonville Police Department and I have pertinent information concerning," he paused for a moment to rethink his plan of attack. "I have information concerning a member of his family. It is of grave importance," Premoe let the misdirection flow over his lips, knowing that it would quite possibly have dire consequences.

"One moment please," the correction's officer echoed a sincere sense of uneasiness. If this person were lying it would be his ass, if they weren't it would be his ass as well. The Corrections Officer quickly relayed the consequential message as discreetly as his two-way radio would allow.

Premoe fidgeted in the sterile lobby of the prison. It was hard to believe that just beyond the one door at the end of the room were housed some of the state's most dangerous criminals.

He desperately wanted a cigarette, but the last time he tried to smoke one he nearly died. The paramedic had advised him that he needed to see a doctor right away. She was certain that his lung had been bruised. He put an unlit Marlboro in his mouth and sucked at the smokeless tobacco, it wasn't nearly the comfort he needed, but it would do. He exhaled a transparent plume of spurious smoke and tried to let his tensions erode away.

"Sir," the mousy correction's officer squeaked. "The warden is on his way. He said it would only be a few minutes. Uhm, and you're not supposed to smoke in here."

"Ungh huh," he turned away from the glass and began reading an information board screwed to the lobby wall.

The backs of his calves ached from overexertion. In fact, the more he thought about it, the more he realized that more of him hurt than didn't. He wanted to sit down, but was afraid that his muscles would seize the opportunity to go on strike.

"Hello, I'm Warden John McIntyre," a tall, thin man burst into the lobby and extended his hand to Premoe. The handshake was firm and a look of trepidation coated his face.

"Sir," he paused to clear his throat. "Let me start by apologizing for the means which I used to get you to come here to talk to me. There is no family emergency."

"I don't quite follow you, detective," he replied through a veil of glowing anger.

"I needed to talk to you about Timothy Duggan."

"For that, you chose to tell such a reprehensible lie?" His eyes flickered with a growing hatred for the man standing close enough to strangle.

"Listen, I understand your anger, but once you hear what I have to say I think you'll understand my motivation."

"I don't have time for this," McIntyre growled, turning away from the detective and nodding to the lobby officer, an indication to open the door to the prison.

The officer's bowels loosened slightly, completely comprehending the look on his boss's face. He became acutely aware of the fact that he was going to be pulling shit duty for the next few years of his career, if it even lasted that long.

Blain reached out and grabbed the man forcefully by the arm. "Listen, you need to hear me out."

In a surprisingly quick move, the man spun around, dislodging Premoe's grasp and forced the big man into the wall. Premoe was caught off guard and completely stunned by the slender man's speed and strength. A jolt of unexpected pain shot through him, reminding him that he was an injured man. The warden jammed his forearm against the detective's throat with enough force to bring tears to the man's eyes.

"Don't fuck with me, and never, never put your hands on me. Do you even have a clue as to the thoughts that were running through my head as I rushed down here?"

Premoe tried to struggle for a second but the combination of his battered body and the man's superhuman strength told him it was futile. He nodded acceptance of the terms, hoping the man would release his grip before too much more damage was done.

"Obviously you think you have something important to say, so say it," the warden said, feeling some relief from his anger. "You have one minute."

"Duggan is innocent, you have to stop the execution."

"Is that what this is about?"

Premoe nodded, gingerly rubbing his throat.

"Well, I'm sorry you wasted your and my time by driving all the way down here to tell me this."

"Listen, I have evidence that will exonerate the man."

"NO! You listen. Even if I believed you, even if I wanted to, I don't have the authority to stop the execution. Only the Governor can make that call now. Maybe you should be talking to him."

"He's unavailable at the moment," Premoe strained.

"And so am I," the warden turned around once more. Premoe nearly grabbed the man again, but thought better of it at the last second.

"Have you spoken to Duggan? Have you even bothered to read his file?" He blurted angrily.

"Yes," the man's voice softened.

"Then you should know, he's not the type."

"I do know, detective, but it's out of my hands."

"Wrong. Just make the call. Stop this thing before it's too late. We can sort out the details later."

"I wish I could," the warden said, sinking down into a visitor chair in the lobby. "Tell me about your evidence," he conceded.

Premoe sat in a chair next to the man. He glanced up at the large wall clock hanging above the reception desk. Eleven forty-five. He had fifteen minutes to save an innocent man's life.

"Well hello Mrs. Duggan. It is truly an honor to meet you," Cracker taunted the woman whom he had just recently duct taped to a chair. *Remember this Doc?* He taunted Tim through his thoughts.

Tim saw Elsa's form quite vividly even though a thick leather skullcap masked his vision. He saw the gray tape circling her body, like it had bound Regina Chamberlain to her rocker. Tim suddenly realized the significance of his memories. They weren't memories at all. He was being visited by ghosts of the present, not ghosts of things that would never be.

"I'm glad you're awake Mrs. Duggan, this just wouldn't be any fun without you," he laughed, the chortle echoed through Tim's mind as well as Elsa's ears.

Elsa struggled fruitlessly against her bonds. Although the moment felt dreamlike and surreal, she knew that this horror was authentic. She gazed upon her captor's face in confusion. Even though the man standing over her looked nothing like Tim, she felt her husband's warm, sympathetic eyes fixed on her nonetheless.

Tim watched helplessly as the twisted, live action movie played on in his head. He saw Cracker's hands reaching for Elsa's breasts. A Linoleum knife gleamed against the iridescent lamplight from the street beaming in through the window. The knife was an ominous looking instrument. Even though the blade was only four inches long it was wide and swept upward into a curved hook at the business end. Cracker had honed the blade to razor sharpness and was more than eager to put his favorite tool to work.

Cracker started a small incision in the bottom hem of Elsa's shirt. Slowly and methodically the monster sliced upward until the fabric fell away, exposing the woman's lacy black bra underneath. Tim could sense the man's exhilaration mixed with his own helpless panic rushing through him.

Nice doc! Very nice!

"God damn you, leave her alone," Tim screamed against the

leather bindings covering his mouth. A muffled scream was the only audible sound in the execution chamber. Some of the gallery members jumped, startled by the doomed man's sudden outburst.

"It's okay, son," the priest put his hand on Tim's shoulder.

"Not it's not okay!" Tim mumbled.

Come on, Doc. You should be thanking me for this. This will be the last tender moment you'll ever be able to share with this lovely woman.

Elsa's stomach muscles clenched uncontrollably as Cracker lightly ran the razor sharp blade up the length of her abdomen, stopping only to slice through the flimsy strand of material holding her bra together at the center. The elastic snapped as he cut through it, sending a shudder of reality through her body. Her breasts fell out of the cups of her bra, causing a bolt of excitement to rampage through Cracker's body. His arousal was almost at its apex.

Tim struggled against his bindings. There was no clock within sight of him, perhaps a humane gesture, or maybe an oversight, or even a budget cut. Either way it didn't matter much, he knew they were painfully close to killing him.

The uniformed custodians were still going through their motions. He felt a chill race through him as a wetted sponge was applied to his fresh bald spot. Water trickled down his head through his hair. Little rivulets of anxiety tickled the back of his neck.

Cracker cupped one of Elsa's breasts in his hand and bent to suckle her nipple. She arched violently against his touch. He looked up into her eyes with pure content and hatred. How dare she think she could refuse him?

"Please," she mumbled against her duct tape gag.

Cracker softly caressed her breasts and nipples, watching them harden despite her protests. Then he pinched them between his thumb and forefinger as hard as he could. She began to thrash and fight against her bindings and his brutal touch. Her struggles only fueled his passions. He let go of her breasts and undid his trousers, letting them fall around his ankles. He picked his pants up off the floor and meticulously folded them. He carefully laid them on the couch with his shoes arranged symmetrically on the floor in front of them and each of his socks rolled neatly and tucked into the toe of each shoe. His erection stabbed at the helpless woman like a sharpened lance.

He turned his attention back to Elsa and smiled an inhuman, sadistic grin.

You're going to love this part, doc!

"So that's it in a nutshell," Premoe finished.

"And you expect me to stop this execution without the proper authorization with based on that flimsy story?"

"I know it all seems too far-fetched to believe, but we don't have any other choice in this matter. The bottom line is this, we can always continue our investigation of Duggan, but not if he's dead. If we prove he is innocent in the morning then that will be too late. And let me put it bluntly, this is an election year, people will remember if you execute an innocent man. They won't remember it if you just reschedule an execution. If I am right, and I truly believe that I am, everyone from the district attorney's office on up to the Governor will be kissing your ass for saving their careers."

"I hate to say this, but I have to agree with you. You do under-stand, that if you're wrong, this will not only be both our asses, but our careers as well?"

"I know, but I'm willing to take that risk. I'd rather have that hanging over my head than the killing an innocent man."

"Likewise," the warden agreed. "Johnston, get me an open line to the chamber," he barked at the trembling correction's officer be-hind the reception desk.

"Yes, sir," he said, picking up a telephone that was sans a dial pad. It was a direct line to the execution chamber.

Unexpectedly the lights dimmed.

"Damn it! But it's not midnight yet," Premoe yelled, glancing at the clock on the wall reading 11:50.

"Relax," the warden said, hiding his own burst of anxiety. "That was just the test, they don't have the electrodes hooked up yet. We've still got time, but not much. Johnston?" He turned and yelled.

"Sir, no one is picking up the phone," he replied timidly.

"Shit, Foster, the man in charge of the phone is my alternate. He's not in the room with the phone. He's probably standing too close to the generators to hear it ringing and he wouldn't be able to see the light from where he is standing."

"What now?"

"Let's go. Johnston," the warden yelled, taking off on a mad dash toward the entry door to the prison. He and Premoe hit the bank of double doors just as the buzzer sounded. Officer Johnston breathed a sigh of relief, not certain if he was going to be fast enough or not. He sat and wondered if his paycheck was worth this kind of stress.

———

"This is Freeman, how close is the nearest unit to Lynnhaven Terrace?"

"I'm three minutes away, sir," an unfamiliar voice crackled over the car's radio.

"Ten four. I'm hitting the driveway right now," Freeman said, pulling into the Duggan's driveway.

"It's show time darlin'," Cracker smiled, hearing Freeman's car outside. He ripped the tape off her mouth and planted an unexpected kiss on her lips. He was careful not to let it linger long enough for her teeth to strike out at him. He had learned that painful lesson already. Using the knife seductively, he sliced open the nylon pair of shorts she was wearing. There were no panties underneath which sent an unexpected rush of excitement rippling through him. He let his gaze fall to her crotch. Excitedly he thrust her legs apart for a better look.

She's nicely trimmed for me, isn't she doc?

Tim struggled against his bindings.

With a flick of his wrist, Cracker laid open the flesh of her abdomen with the point of the curved blade. Blood spewed from the fresh wound. Elsa screamed.

"This is Freeman, I can't wait, I'm going in. Just follow me in when you get here," he ordered into the hand mic and flung it to the floor of the car. Hurriedly he exited his car and ran to the front door.

"God damn it, Todd, wait for back up!" Frank's voice crackled over the airwaves and was duly ignored. He turned the radio up on his desk and began rummaging through his drawers for some aspirin.

Cracker took another swipe at his captive. Blood spurted from yet another wound. Elsa screamed hysterically.

Freeman kicked in the front door and crossed the threshold with his gun drawn.

"Look out," Elsa screamed in a sobbing voice, but it was a fraction of a second too late.

Cracker's arm came slashing through the air, connecting with Freeman's forearm. The detective's arm exploded into a fiery flash of pain as the hook of the Linoleum knife formed itself around his wrist and sliced through the fabric of his jacket sleeve and into his flesh. He felt the warm flow of his own blood spreading across the inside of his jacket sleeve. The attack was so sudden and brutal that it knocked the gun from his grip. Freeman caught sight of Cracker leaping across the small gap between them and tried to brace himself for the impact, but he wasn't fast enough and both of them were knocked to the floor. Freeman struggled to get to his feet in a hurry. One up, he was able to jump backwards, narrowly escaping Cracker's next slice, one that would have easily laid open the detective's jugular.

Tim fought and squirmed in the chair. His mind had been given back to him. The images were gone. Although the respite from the imagery was comforting to a degree, now he had no idea of what was going on at his house; to his wife. Tim fought hard against his own fears and tried to get into the Cracker's head. He had practiced the incantations over and over until he had committed them to memory. He was never sure why he had done that, except that True had told him to. Now he had his answer.

Cracker lunged at Freeman once more, catching the wounded man completely off guard. His shoulder crashed into Freeman's mid-section and knocked him backward into the kitchen. The detective was dazed and surprised by Cracker's relentless attack. He scampered to his feet and tried to find a corner to box himself into and brace for the next blow and hoping that his back-up would get there soon.

Cracker quickly scanned the kitchen counters, looking for a weapon more devastating than the short knife. Smiling, he pulled a foot long butcher knife from a maple block and began to advance on the backpedaling detective.

"What's the matter, not so tough without your fat assed partner, are you?"

"Fuck you, Graham Cracker," Freeman gasped through bruised lungs and broken ribs. He hoped he could antagonize the beast into forgetting about the woman in the other room, at least long enough for the cavalry to show up. If they showed up.

The air made a hissing sound as Cracker slashed the knife in front of himself several times for practice. Suddenly, the maniac's head exploded with darkness. He felt cramped; claustrophobic. He felt as if he were being restrained.

You little bastard! The doctor's voice echoed through his brain.

"Not now," he spat and continued with his advance on Freeman who was now poised to sacrifice his arm to Cracker's blade.

Tim could see the retreating detective through Cracker's eyes. As the blade reached its apex above the madman's head, Tim took over his motor controls and forced the blade to be swung wide of its intended target. The butcher knife was buried into the drywall a good six inches. Cracker struggled against Tim's intrusion while trying frantically to wrench the blade free.

Freeman seized the opportunity and kicked out as hard as he could, catching Cracker in the armpit. Cracker staggered backward and slammed into the counter. He grappled to reach the maple block full of knives. Quickly he withdrew the ten inch carver from its slot and brandished it in front of him. He slashed at the air, keeping the struggling detective at bay. Freeman was tiring quickly from losing so much blood. As he backpedaled, Freeman slipped in a pool of his own blood and crashed backward onto the cold, hard Linoleum. He was tired; very tired. Elsa's soft sobs from the other room gave him the strength he needed to stay awake. If he gave up the fight, she was a corpse.

Tim entered Cracker's head once more.

"Leave me alone," Cracker screamed.

How does it feel you pathetic little fuck! Tim taunted.

He almost felt pleasure from making the man squirm and gyrate against his intrusion. But the man's will was strong and Tim wasn't as practiced in the magic. He could feel Cracker fighting desperately to regain control of his own mind. He could see Cracker gaining enough control to force himself forward, the knife slashing wildly in front of him.

Freeman concentrated on the advancing lunatic, but his mind was fading in and out. He glanced down at his arm and realized he was loosing a lot more blood than he had first thought. The slash had made it around to the underside of his wrist and must have cut through an artery. Freeman tried to focus but found it increasingly harder.

Tim struggled against the man's mind, trying to overpower him long enough for the detective to escape the crazed onslaught.

Cracker continued to advance in spite of Tim's intrusions, screaming incoherently at the top of his lungs with each labored step. He was within seconds of reaching his nearly spent opponent.

Tim gained control once more, stopping Cracker in his tracks.

"Get out of my head," Cracker seethed.

Suddenly both men's brains were aflame. White-hot sparks of light danced around in Cracker's head. He could see them, but from behind his eyes, inside of his brain. It was suddenly so God awful hot. He dropped the knife and clutched his head at both temples.

Freeman watched as the man began thrashing wildly, clawing desperately at his head.

Tim was no longer in Cracker's head. He was barely even in his own. His brain was nothing more than a conglomeration of pain and bewilderment. His body flayed around in the chair as much as the straps would allow. Steam began to rise from the hot metal buckles and wet leather straps.

Freeman struggled for consciousness, maintaining his vigil on the man wracked with seizures.

"No," was the only sound Cracker was able to muster. His jaws clenched until blood spewed from his lips. He jerked horrendously and then crashed backwards against the counter, sending the maple block of knifes spilling across the countertop. Cracker grappled with the wooden handles until he felt the familiar feel of a knife's hilt in his palm. He labored against the tremors of pain careening through his body. He opened his eyes, against his better judgment, and located a blurry image of the detective. Desperately he lunged for Freeman's limp body propped against the wall.

The searing flames in his brain were joined with the jolting force of a bullet striking him in the chest. Cracker's body was flung across the kitchen, coming to rest against the cabinets along the floor's edge. Freeman's arm dangled limply at his side, the barrel of his back up piece still smoking. He remained awake long enough to realize Cracker had finally stopped moving. Then all was black.

———

"Get him out of that chair right now," the warden ordered.

Immediately the room exploded into a flurry of activity. For as long as it took to strap the condemned man into the chair, it was only a matter of seconds and he was out and onto a gurney.

"How is he?" Premoe asked one of the half dozen medical personnel frantically attending to Timothy Duggan

"Hard to tell. He didn't take a lot of electricity, but then again, sometimes it doesn't take too much. He's breathing, if that helps," the man replied, quickly rolling the gurney out of the chamber and down the corridor. Premoe watched them load Tim's unconscious form into the service elevator and said a short prayer as the doors closed.

"Warden McIntyre," the radio on his side squawked.

"What is it, Johnston?" He answered, still flustered from the evening's events.

"Uhm, sir, I have an urgent message for the detective."

Premoe nodded at the warden.

"Frank Walker said to tell Detective Premoe that Todd Freeman has been rushed to St. Luke's in Jacksonville."

Premoe shook his head and started for the door.

"Mr. Walker also said for him not to be too worried, it was nothing too serious. But he also said for him to get back as soon as he could. Sir, he said to drive safe," Johnston replayed the message.

"Thanks, John, I'll be in touch," Premoe called out as he dashed for the front door.

"You better be," he laughed. "If this things explodes, I want you right here with me. Now go see your people in Jacksonville. Carter, see that Detective Premoe finds his way out," the warden said, returning his attention to matters at hand.

Premoe left the prison and felt a chill in the air, even though it was quite warm. Absent-mindedly he calculated how long it was before he could retire.

EPILOGUE

"Y ou are such an asshole," Premoe announced, bursting into
Freeman's room at St. Luke's.

"And you're not," Frank laughed.

"Good to see you too, Blain."

"How are you?"

"I'll be fine. I lost a lot of blood and got a hundred or so
stitches. I'll need years of physical therapy, not to mention countless
hours with a good shrink, but all in all, it was a pretty good day," he
groaned.

"I got some news from Starke," Frank said.

Premoe gave his attention to his boss.

"Duggan is going to be fine. They sent him to County General
where they will hold him for observation for a few days, but it looks
as though he'll survive this."

"And his wife?"

"I didn't quite get to her as soon as I would have liked, but
she'll be fine too. I think she'll have more emotional damage than
physical. Though, I'm only getting that through her doctor. I never
got a chance to talk to her," Freeman explained.

"And Graham?"

"I'm sorry to say, he'll survive as well. They're digging Todd's
slug out of him as we speak," Frank explained.

"Ain't that a bitch," Premoe offered his usual take on things.

"However, the doctor also said that Graham's brain short-
circuited somehow. He said they weren't sure if he would ever recover mentally," Frank added.

"Way to go, partner," Premoe laughed.

"Wasn't anything I did. Strange shit happened, Blain," Freeman's face did a complete one eighty from cheerful to perplexed.

"How so?"

"I can't explain it, and I'm not even going to try. I'm afraid that
if I understand what happened it will scare me into retirement," Todd

said.

"I've already been that scared," Premoe confessed.

"You two just shut up with talk like that. If I'm staying around, you're staying around," all three men chuckled weakly. All three of them would have loved to have been able to call it quits but just didn't have the heart, they didn't know anything else.

———————

"Damn it, Preston, I leave here for a minute," Doctor Williams bellowed.

"Sorry, Doctor Williams," the orderly said, fumbling for the right key to open the cell door.

Both men peered through the glass portal. Rueben Graham sat in the corner of his room stabbing himself in the head with a cleverly stolen pen. He was chanting gibberish and rocking back and forth with his arm swinging up to meet his forehead with each completed motion. Blood had already begun to stain the front of his light blue coveralls.

"Where did he get that pen?" The doctor asked.

"I have no idea. I searched him right after you left."

Both men entered the cell and easily subdued the heavily medicated patient, taking the pen away from him. He waved his hands at them and scampered away into the corner of the room.

"Get someone up here to take care of those wounds. Crazy bastard," Doctor Williams commented as he walked out of the cell and headed for his office.

Once in his office, the doctor jotted down a few notes on a medical chart in a manila folder marked; GRAHAM, RUEBEN.

Patient continues to display paranoid/schizophrenic delusions. He is still quite harmful to himself and others. Up his medication across the board. Patient still maintains there is a man named True living in his head. He complains of taunts and torments from this other personality. At this time I am prescribing full restraint until he shows signs that his aggression is abating.

———————

True closed the book and slid it between his mattress and the steel frame bunk. He hoped he wouldn't be looked dimly on in heaven for doing what he was doing. Regina was getting better by the day. Maybe he would give up his daily torments of Cracker once she was fully recovered. Maybe.

Printed in the United States
17991LVS00001B/58-114

9 781589 393479